The Shadows of Owls

THE SHADOWS OF OWLS

A Novel

JOHN KEEBLE

UNIVERSITY OF WASHINGTON PRESS   *Seattle and London*

© 2013 by John Keeble
Printed and bound in the United States of America
Design by Thomas Eykemans
Composed in Sorts Mill Goudy, typeface designed by Barry Schwartz
Display type set in Univers, designed by Adrian Frutiger
17 16 15 14 13   5 4 3 2

UNIVERSITY OF WASHINGTON PRESS
PO Box 50096, Seattle, WA 98145, USA
www.washington.edu/uwpress

LIBRARY OF CONGRESS CATALOGING-IN-PUBLICATION DATA
Keeble, John.
The shadows of owls : a novel / John Keeble.
     pages. cm
ISBN 978-0-295-99315-7 (cloth : acid-free paper)
1. Women scientists—Fiction.
1. Title.
PS3561.E3853 2013   813'.54—dc23   2013006160

A version of Chapter One appeared in Black Warrior Review 22, no. 2
(1996) under the title, "Hostiles," and a version of Chapter Three
appeared as "Outlaws" in the *Idaho Review* 1, no. 1 (1998). An excerpt
titled "From Guide to Insurrection" appeared in *Northwest Review* 45,
no. 3 (2007).

FOR CLAIRE

For early reading and encouragement in various forms, grateful acknowledgment is made to Elizabeth Cook-Lynn, Christopher Howell, Derrick Jensen, Michelle Huneven, Marianne Keddington-Lang, Natalie Kusz, Clyde Lynn, Barry Lopez, Julie Mayeda, Denise Shannon, and Mitch Wieland; also to my longtime friend Fred Newberry, and to my late, revered editor, Ted Solotaroff.

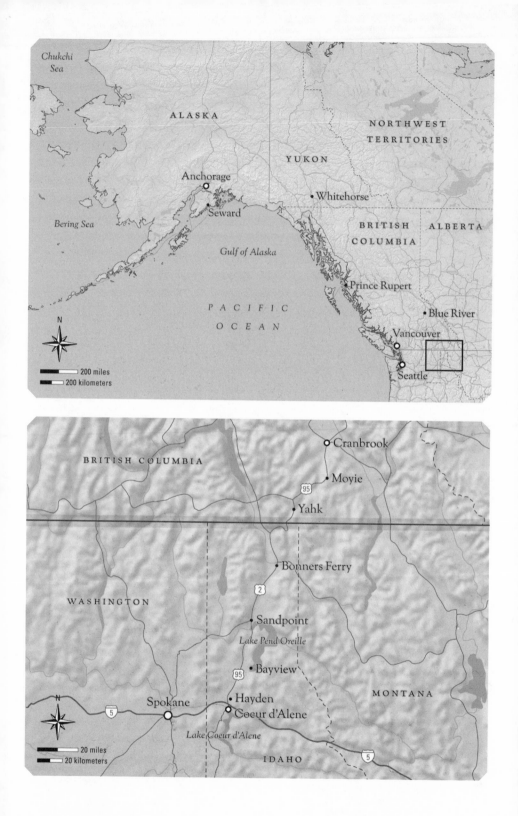

The Shadows of Owls

1

Secrets

UNDER THE WASH OF HEADLIGHTS, snow formed a webwork among the trees across the ditch. The tree trunks were black and they stuttered in the periphery of Kate's vision as she passed, while the snow that bedecked the limbs was a dancing white cloud above the black stems. Along the edges of the road ran ditches gorged with the snow that had been plowed into them. The black shine of pavement rolled under her car. The centerline was obscured by a sheen of snow dust ground into ice pale as surgical latex. The Subaru's studded tires moaned. Snow had been falling not an hour ago. Soon, according to reports, it would snow again, but just now if she leaned forward and looked up through the top of the windshield, she could see a clear patch of sky. She did that, peered at an opening in the cloud cover polished in the cold to shining black flecked with phosphorous stars, then pushed herself back into the seat and concentrated on the far reach of her headlights, the ever-forward-riding apogee of illumination beyond which her road lay waiting.

Once, when the strip of black didn't rise into the light and she could see only the white of the bank before her and the white under the trees, she panicked, gripping the wheel and poising her foot above the brake. Then she picked out the way the road had been laid, swinging to the left, and the reflectors that marked it glittered in a long arc like teeth. She allowed the car to decelerate and gradually sped up again on the straightaway, recalling that there would be a stretch of this now, as the road steadied to its northward course through the woods to the foothills of the Rockies. She had passed by Coeur d'Alene and Hayden,

Idaho, that crunch of city light flaking back into the dark. After a time, her head listed to one side and the whole world seemed to tip and slide her off its edge into velvet. Her body jerked to right itself. She blinked and stared straight ahead into the white and black, surprised that the car was just where it should have been, going along in the grooves of its lane.

"Jesus," she murmured.

She cracked open the window at her side to create a stream of chill air.

She had closed up the lab for the winter down at Dworshak Dam, where for the last few months she'd been doing a habitat survey for the state of Idaho. Now, exhausted from the last two-week shift on her contract, she was going home to her husband and son in the house on the hill. There would be a fire in the wood burner to welcome her, food, tea, and a shot of Scotch, her son asleep, most likely, his filling out body straight under the covers; then to her familiar bed upstairs, her husband's legs entwined with hers and his hand on her thigh as they bridged their way toward the next day with love and talk.

Just today . . . or yesterday! . . . She turned on the radio dial and pushed the button to show the time—11:40. Today was almost yesterday . . . Friday. Tomorrow would be Saturday, November 11, 2000. White noise from the dead station issued from the speakers into the blackness of the car, and, suddenly wondering if the nation had its president-elect yet, she scanned the call numbers of stations . . . soft rock, hard rock, country and western, more country and western. She switched it off. She'd find out tomorrow. Earlier in the day, she'd been distracted by a man waiting for her when she and her intern, Max Tanaka, had come out of the water onto the deck. The man claimed he was from DDM, her former employer—Dodge, Drainier, and Massey—a Seattle-based research firm. "Doctor Katherine McDuff?" the man had asked, using what had become her formal appellation, her maiden name. She still used it to sign off on articles she'd authored, offprints, and grant applications. She paused while Max went on, lugging his gear through the lab to the dive shed. The man explained that he'd been hoping to catch her. She set down her fins, popped the hoses off her vest, slung down the tank, and pulled off her mask and diving hood.

The man was tall, young, and handsome in the way such young men had of appearing exactly like each other, like filled-out digits. He

4

had milk-colored skin, gray eyes, a square jaw, a purple birthmark that passed from his neck under his shirt, and in his movement the self-important air of too much muscle gained by "working out." He hadn't been out of school long, maybe . . . Richard. In her fatigue, her near-inchoacy in the car, she groped for his name . . . Troop.

"Richard Troop," he'd said. He passed a leather briefcase from his right hand to his left and leaned forward and held out his hand, a gesture she didn't acknowledge. Just then, she had her weight belt slung over her shoulder and was bending to detach her tank from the vest. Besides, something about his manner made her prefer not to accept his hand.

"Troop?" She stood straight and gazed out at the gorge, the dark, wooded slope, the Clearwater River, the dam with its chutes and made-over fish ladders at its edge. In the twilight, what she could see of the dam looked like a gray strip pulled tight across the opening in the landform to create the reservoir that stretched beyond, beneath the sky that had begun to elucidate itself with slivers of ice.

"Right." Still smiling, he added, "There's just one of me, though."

She glanced at him, then down at the parking lot and saw a new, freshly splattered SUV parked next to her and Max's cars. She turned and headed inside. Troop trailed her and set his briefcase down on a workbench. She could hear Max out on the back deck, hosing off his gear. Troop said he'd been sent to talk about her work on Long Beach Harbor and Puget Sound.

"I left DDM six months ago," she said.

His voice deepened. "I understand."

Her severance agreement with DDM put her on retainer as a senior advisor and allowed her to keep her files and continue working up the data as long as she submitted her findings to the company for review prior to their release. The agreement mainly protected DDM's proprietary rights, and Kate well knew that the company would sue in an instant if it felt she or anyone had a chance of gaining from what it claimed as property—its information, research methodologies, anything emanating from the use of its facilities and equipment. Intellectual property, this was called in the parlance of the age, which, even as accustomed as she was to having her work driven by the pragmatic, had always seemed a little preposterous to her—that ideas, inventive meanderings of the mind, and the effectuation of dreams might be so claimed.

For her part, the wish to keep access to the files had to do with scientific passion, a long-standing interest she'd held in reserve through the years of mothering her children while also working for institutions. She and Abby Leonard, a physical oceanographer, an old friend from graduate school and now her research partner, had fashioned what Kate's husband called their "big brain" scheme: an interface of their data with data from hundreds of other researchers that was in the public domain and more yet they were seeking permission to use. The whole would give them an information base on the patterns of migratory fish, sea mammals, and birds that extended from San Diego, Long Beach, Puget Sound, Glacier Bay, Prince William Sound, and Bristol Bay into the open waters off California, Oregon, Washington, British Columbia, Japan, the Kuriles, and up the Pacific reach through the Gulf of Alaska to the *Bering* and Chukchi Seas. It ran inland to the mid-continental flyway through Alberta clear up to Hudson Bay and the Beaufort Sea. Finally everything converged and turned on its gyre in the Arctic Ocean.

They had received a three-year grant, awarded mainly for their research design, the capacious computer program from which they were already seeing results. They had published two articles in hopes of securing funding, but the bulk of what she and Abby had—the raw data just beginning to be directed through a carefully crafted set of matrices—was far from ready for review. And then there was the growing heap of material Kate had first stumbled upon several years ago in her computer files at DDM, which kept nosing into her machine and had the dank smell of deep secret. Since she had determined that it belonged neither to her nor DDM but was government information, she'd kept copying it and—her audacity mounting to insurgency—had spirited it away home: the agreements and findings beginning with a thirty-year-old, détente-era scientific exchange between the United States and the Soviets of which she had been a part, and now extending into new agreements between American petroleum companies and Russia's Schtok Oil. She had fully believed she'd been right to take the material, since technically it was in the public domain, but now she wondered if someone at DDM had realized what she had . . . secrets.

All DDM wanted, Troop told her, was some help interpreting a couple of the reports she'd filed before leaving. "There are a few loose threads they want glossed. It's the sources, I think."

—Sources? she thought. A pro forma question that could lead to a tangle. "Is that so?"

Troop bought two Cokes from the machine in the corner, popped up the tops with his thumbnail, and passed a can to her, then moved back near his briefcase at the work bench against the opposite wall. There was a bench behind her, too, and she set the can on it, having no intention of encouraging him.

This was the cause of her unease:

First, she'd broken loose and resigned her position at DDM, though many would have felt it was the best possible job she could have hoped for in these parts. It paid well, much of the time she could work out of the Spokane office, and her mentor in the company, Otis Drainier, had developed early onset Alzheimer's disease and announced his retirement. Some believed she had a chance to move up, but she found Drainier's illness sobering. It convinced her that time was short all around.

Second, she'd taken on the habitat survey at Dworshak—grunt work—in order to reduce the strain on her domestic finances while she made the transition. As of today, she was finished with that.

Third, she and Abby had received the grant they'd been hoping for, and Kate was filled with anticipation about going to work on the project, which, whenever she thought of it, created a compelling radiance in her mind.

And now, the appearance of this man, raising the possibility at best of having somebody mucking in her files, or at worst of claims and legal complications. It felt like an ambush, the long arm reaching out of DDM's world of maddening bureaucratic impediments to pluck her up.

"I'm an independent now," she said.

"You're on retainer. They want your expertise," he said. "They'll pay."

"DDM has my address. They know how to reach me."

"I was in the area," he said. "I called. I was told you were in the water." He paused. "DDM has just transferred me from Seattle to the sonar center on Pend Oreille. They thought I could easily find you."

That put his base about ten miles from her house. There was something odd in it, and something about the man that struck her as disquieting. She scrutinized him, marking the faint glaze in his eyes, what looked like a residual drug effect . . . a part of his buffed-out regimen, perhaps . . . amphetamines, cortesoids, EPO. . . . "Not now. In a few weeks, maybe." And then, using civility as a fortification, she added, "Please ask to have the questions sent to me."

By then, she'd skinned out of her dry suit and dropped it into her duffel bag along with the rest of her gear. She heard the compressor start up out back as Max prepared to recharge the tanks. She walked out front to get her tank and specimen net and toted them inside. It had begun to snow in earnest. She set the tank in a rack and stood in her burgundy Lycra, facing the man. He had finished his Coke and was leaning against the bench, above which hung coils of hosing and a line of weight belts. He positioned his can between his palms and suddenly crushed it. His face kept its deferential expression, as if it and his hands occupied different worlds, and now in the dark of her car and as she began once again to slide toward a drowse, the image of the hands— clean, white, and disembodied—snapped her alert.

She remembered Max, dressed in his bright yellow sweats, coming to retrieve the rack of tanks. A graduate student in fisheries from the University of Washington, Max couldn't have been more than four or five years younger than Troop. She had felt relieved by his presence. Also, a distrustful expression had flickered across Max's face when he looked at Troop, which triangulated and confirmed her disquiet. Max rolled the rack away, bumping through the swinging door. She'd marked the difference between the two young men. Max was lithe and light, alive with his love of science and with everything he did to further his fascination, even recharging scuba tanks, while Troop seemed weighted with debris. She remembered the decorous words that crumbled from his mouth like filigreed bits of shell squeezed through a vise: stray, gloss, admirable, and finally charming.

She told him she needed to change and head for home, and moved to the locker at the wall, taking out her corduroy trousers and the wool shirt she'd brought in expectation of snow and cold. The trousers were deep brown. The brushed-wool shirt was the color of doeskin and had buttons made of bone. It was a gift from her husband and she would wear it home for him. Hooking her clothes hanger over the locker door so that Troop could see she was ready to leave, she carried the specimen bag through the doorway at her back into the lab. Again, Troop came behind her. She slid a tray to the edge of a counter and gently poured the contents of the bag into it—mollusks, a small pile of them like delicately colored pebbles. They were to be identified and given a tissue analysis. She saw Troop taking in the layout of the lab . . . the stainless steel counters and trays, specimen canisters, two computers, a microscope, a spectrometer, white sinks, white refrigerator, the shelves loaded with field manuals, offprints, anatomies, and boxes of disks. The floor and ceiling were white and the walls were pale blue. Everything was cool and antiseptic and bright under the ranks of fluorescent lights. "This is Spartan," he said. "But your work here is admirable, too, I'm sure."

"It's a state lab."

"Your work-ups come from here?"

The answer to that was a given: contract work for the state, yes; independent work, no.

When he stepped toward her, holding out his card, his running shoes squeaked against the polished vinyl floor. "My card," he said.

She glanced at it just long enough to see the company logo and his title—DDM, Systems Analyst, and then off to the side, Watchcap Security and Information Group. He must have been one of the growing numbers of subcontractors DDM was employing, not of her world. She set the card next to the specimen tray, then reached out and smoothed the mollusks into a plane. Freshwater snails and limpets, they felt cool to her touch and slippery from their desperate secretions. The moisture was evaporating quickly from her Lycra bodysuit, and she was chilled. She positioned herself under the heating blower in the ceiling. She heard the compressor motor throttling up again and guessed that Max had come to the last of the tanks.

Troop swung nearer, rising on the balls of his feet and smiling down at her. "The best thing would be for us to get together and run through your files. I've got queries in my computer . . . not many. It should take less than an hour."

"There's no chance we'll do it that way," she said. "Who sent you?"

"I'm reporting to Bill Massey."

One of the founding triumvirate, Massey was known to Kate mainly for his habit of micro-managing, or meddling, and for his thousand dollar suits and his Porsche.

Emanating from Troop's mouth was a faint smell of mint, and from his body, still hovering too close, a chemical-smelling cologne. She resisted the urge to poke him in the chest to back him off.

"We're closing up. Please ask to have the questions sent to me," she said, standing her ground.

At last, Troop took a step back. "They said you'd be cagey. It's charming."

A jolt of anger passed through her. She remained unsure whether the man had unusually bad manners, the brutishness of a very large boy freewheeling his way along the path of whatever directive he'd been given, or if in his role as a lackey he conveyed an actual mischief that needed to be rooted out, but without doubt he was what she'd learned in her childhood to call common. She disliked him intensely.

"Now," she said. "I'm asking you to leave. Next time, make an appointment."

2

Her Traveler

THE CAR'S CONSOLE LIGHTS WERE OUT. The darkness put her out of touch with the gauges. The car needed a fuse . . . a fifty-cent repair, her husband had said. It would take him two minutes. He knew machinery. It functioned as his domestic.

She knew science.

His income came from trading in material items—at the moment, trees, that is, timber—but in college he'd studied philosophy.

His name was Jack DeShazer, and her name of record was Katherine M. DeShazer. So it was written on her driver's license, Social Security card, voter registration card, and marriage license and on the bank accounts and deeds. Her maiden name, McDuff, was affixed to her scientific work when it appeared in print, as it had been before she was married, but even at DDM she'd come to be known as Kate DeShazer. It seemed a little strange to her that the man Troop had used the other name.

Jack's prime medium was the earth while hers was water.

He should have his logging equipment off the mountain and be home by now. She expected he'd taken Travis, their son, to help drive the equipment, which brought on a new wave of uneasiness . . . too young. . . . Travis was too young yet to be driving in a mountain storm. She made herself stop thinking that way, for Jack was nothing if not competent and cautious. He would have the fuses for her, too, because of the sense of chivalric duty to one another that they shared. This was a mode of conduct laced to the ways in which their work and natures at times put them at cross-purposes with each other . . . bullheaded . . . each of them could be bullheaded. Beneath that, though, nestled snugly and surely, lay their passion for each other.

It had begun to snow again. Driving carefully, she had mused her way from the curse against fatigue to Richard Troop, whose gift of a Coke she hadn't touched, whose business card she'd dropped into the trash on her way out, and who himself had departed compliantly enough when she'd told him to, and then to Jack and Travis. Soon, she and Jack would be in the kitchen or stoking the living room stove, and then in bed while Travis slept in the room below. She would tell Jack about Richard Troop and ask what he thought, and he, his hand leathery from work and driven by the long lope of his desire, sliding under her nightgown to her hip and poising upon her belly, would say that Troop's appearance meant nothing to her and less to him.

Her car was white, but Kate felt held within its darkness as if inside a glove that probed the night for the highway that passed along the valley at the foot of the Bitterroot Range. It was nearly midnight and she still had thirty miles to go, most of them on the back road to her place on the hill above the southern toe of Lake Pend Oreille. The nearness of home sharpened her wakefulness. She had passed one snowplow and now, judging from the thinning snow cover on the road, she was coming near another.

An ichthyologist, her specialty was anadromous fish, those whose name meant literally running upward and whose life cycle passed through salt and fresh water . . . shad, whitefish, lamprey, sturgeon, and salmon. In the compartment she had her instruments and crates loaded with gear, which clinked softly when the car's weight shifted. A mossy odor suffused the car. On the seat next to her lay a four-inch stack of papers, the printouts and flowcharts, findings from the habitat survey at Dworshak that she had to go through once as a check, to add the last bits and then to ship off to Idaho Fish and Game. The survey was actually a sidebar to the main action of that moment in this region— the extinct and endangered species of salmon on the Columbia and the Snake, and the smoldering furor over the dams that had helped to make them so. On top of her stack was a case of CDs, the raw data. All of it was to be kept confidential according to her contract, which meant that the work would be inserted into the tangle of politics and litigation as if into a snakeball, and that once there, the meticulously gathered findings would be ravaged before being released. Government money came that way, bubbling up out of the boondoggles. Her portion had been merely spooned out of the slime that oozed over the lip of the holding tank. That and now her and Abby's project were forever set against the work on the fish for which she felt not affection, exactly, but certainly love, the love in her blood and brain for fish, rock, underwater litters, even the deranged hulks of submerged cars and machinery, loops of wire and cable, for shadow and the dark, the spin of the eddies out of the chaotic bottoms and turns, and the savage promiscuity of currents.

She'd had a staff of four at Dworshak. Since leaving DDM, she'd alternated between two weeks down there and one at home. Several hours ago, before Richard Troop had appeared, she and Max had been picking their way along the river bottom to the reflectors that marked her transepts, taking samples and doing a last count of fish, an activity at once mundane and completely preposterous. A school of fingerling white sturgeon—hatchery-raised and stocked in the Clearwater—had darted into the lantern beams as she and Max sought holdfasts among the stones with their gloved hands and feet. The current had throbbed against her. The fingerlings, which, if given their liberty of the dams, might have grown into fifteen-foot behemoths weighing hundreds of pounds, arose by the thousands out of a deep hole, a storm of tiny, moon-colored chips coming out of the lair where an ancient progenitor could once have lurked.

The vision made her feel buoyant. The white ditches streamed past her temples, the tree trunks stuttered, and up ahead the tape of road kept unrolling. She came upon a curve, slowed, and in the middle of it as the car skittered over ice scabs, she saw something else glimmering, a white, out-of-place thing suspended in the air above the ditch, and behind it a massy blot of tipped-up dark. By instinct, her foot lifted off the accelerator pedal, but it took a moment for the images to assemble themselves out of their incongruity.

It was a face. And in the ditch, a car.

The back country code absolutely forbade leaving anyone stranded in such weather. She pulled to the edge of the road at the far end of the curve and made a U-turn. Returning, she picked out nothing in the dark on the other side. She made another U and coming slowly along the way she had at first, she saw it, the ghostly hanging shape catching light . . . a figure, a waving hand. Angling onto the shoulder, she saw the car plunged into the ditch behind the figure. She switched on her flashers, got out, and called, her voice thin in the cold: "Are you all right?" Hearing no response, she moved around to the edge of the shoulder and said it again, "Are you all right?"

Still nothing, only the figure, a woman, Kate saw, leaning against the rear fender of the car. Kate scooted down the bank into the ditch, sliding near the woman, who was wearing a thin dress and open jacket and standing knee deep in the snow. Her face, lit by the white of the headlamps and the pulsing orange flashers, was absolutely immobile. "Are you hurt?" Kate asked. She moved to peer through the windows of the car, looking for someone else, but saw no one. "You're alone?"

The woman said nothing. Kate clambered back and touched the woman's arm, feeling the wetness, the cold. Kate unlooped the cord of a duffel bag the woman had around her wrist, heaved the bag up the bank and reached to help the woman climb up, but the woman abruptly surged on her own, almost pulling Kate upward. At the top, as if she'd tapped a last reserve of strength, the woman crumpled into Kate's arms. Kate held her steady with one hand and twisted to open her car door. She tossed the papers and disks into the back, and half-lifted the woman into the passenger seat. The woman sank back, her head lolling sideways. Seen under the dome light, the face—pallid and drawn, the eyes glazed—all but confirmed what Kate had suspected from the first—hypothermia.

She lifted the woman's feet, pulled off the soaked-through sneakers and the socks, and set the feet, which were chill, on the floorboard. "We've got to get your clothes off," Kate said. She moved to the rear of the car to retrieve the blanket she kept there, returned, reached across to switch the heating fan to high, and setting the blanket down on the floor, worked off the woman's jacket, straightened her and shimmied the dress up to her waist, bent her forward again and tried to pull the dress over her head, but found it tangled with the strap of a purse the woman had been carrying under the jacket. Kate untangled the purse, dropped it to the floor, and pulled off the dress. Under it, the woman wore a long-sleeved polo shirt, also wet. Kate drew it off, eased the woman back against the seat, and felt her panties at the waist. They were cotton, soaked through, and Kate bent, murmuring, "These, too. My God, how did you get so wet?" as she pulled them free of the clammy legs and off over the feet. Then the woman was there, naked with her long legs, heavy breasts, and delicate, shivering shoulders pale against the dark seat.

Kate knew very well that once a margin was passed, the stages of hypothermia heaped rapidly one upon another. She wrapped the woman in the blanket, closed the door, threw the duffel bag in the back with her gear, climbed into the driver's seat, and paused for a moment, thinking: The hospital was fifty miles behind . . . more than an hour in this weather. Home was not far ahead, twenty minutes away. Her impulse was to go home where the woman could be warmed the soonest, but if something went wrong, there they would be, sixty miles from the hospital. Thinking through these things, she felt a twinge of exasperation at the inconvenience of it all, but then she went straight back to the need of the moment: Get this person warm. Jack and Travis would be home. The prospect of having help with whatever decision came next confirmed this one.

"Okay," she murmured.

The woman moved, tilting tremulously toward Kate. Her mouth opened as if to speak, but nothing came out. Against her white face, her mouth was like a pit.

Gently, Kate eased the woman back into the seat, readjusted the blanket, and said, "I'm taking you home."

She started out, her hands light on the wheel. In time, she came upon the line of businesses set along the road—the Texaco station, an appliance repair shop, Edna's Flea Market, and the Victory Wrecking Yard. She saw a curl of recent tracks in the snow in front of the wrecking yard and the sign—24 HOUR TOWING—and slowed because of a connective flickering of thought: towing, Bud Willy, the proprietor with whom Jack had occasional dealings, and the car behind her in the ditch. The snow sifted steadily down, heaping upon the ranks of parked cars and trucks. The wrecking yard's windows were dark.

—Worry about that tomorrow, she thought.

Accelerating, she asked the woman, "What's your name?" The woman stared back at her, her eyes wide and terrorized. When Kate reached out and grasped her arm beneath the blanket, the woman let out a stream of air. "Okay," Kate said softly. "I'm Kate. It's okay. You'll be all right."

She turned off the highway, downshifting for the unplowed road. The snow deepened after the next turn northward onto the access road, the white extending from the roadside to the ditches and into the woods, where lay nestled the occasional house lit from the outside by peach-colored storm lights. The road dropped toward the canyon and rose again as it climbed the side of the hill. Briefly Kate saw the aura through the snow from the lights of the town of Bayview down at the lake. The woman was hunched forward now, rocking with the motion.

The road twisted along the edge of the slope, cut back, went out and returned, always rising. The nearness of the lake was registered in the densening of the white in the air, the snowflakes fattened by moisture. In a few minutes, the big cedar leaning out toward the road, its limbs heavy with snow, reared out of the obscurity, and just beyond it glittered the blue reflector on their mailbox. Kate turned into her drive, and as she fishtailed up the steep climb to the house, their dog appeared, darting out of the trees and dancing in front of the car. She pulled up to the head of the walkway. Their van was before her, parked close to the bushes with a tall pile of snow on its roof, but next to it in the space where Jack's truck should have been lay only the undisturbed snow. She was looking at a maw, a visible, ill-boding emptiness. To herself she whispered, "Shit."

The kitchen light was on, but the storm light was not. The dog, Berg, a black shepherd, stood on her hind legs to peer in the car window. Kate left the headlights on and the engine running and eased out, bending to touch the dog's head. She walked to the door and entered, flicking on the stormlight. The house had the raw smell of freshly split tamarack and pine that had been packed into the box near the stove, but the feel of the place, the creak of the floor under her feet in the cool, told her that Travis wasn't here, either. She switched on a floor lamp, moved to the kitchen and cut her eyes to the blinking light on the message machine, then turned up the baseboard heater. Jack had called from the warehouse, she guessed, but still worried and a little confused, Kate made herself keep moving. She walked back into the living room, loaded up the woodburning stove, and lit a fire. Berg sat next to her, watching with ears up. Kate dragged the sofa near the stove, then moved into the hallway and found more blankets and a sleeping bag in the closet opposite the bathroom. At the end of the hall, she pushed open the door to Travis's room. The room was absolutely still, the made-up bedcovers flat. Above Travis's dresser, the shadowy, glaring figure of Roger Clemens in his poster lunged to hurl a baseball straight at her.

She gathered the covers at the sofa, walked outside to fetch the woman and, half carrying her, guided her in and made her lie down on the sofa, dried her feet, covered her, and looked closely at the angular, pallid face. The pale blue of the eyes was swallowed into the dilated pupils. The woman's blonde hair was oily and disheveled, and above her right cheekbone was what Kate hadn't seen before—a bruise. Kate leaned near, again asking, "Are you hurt?"

The woman stared blankly upward. Her chin quivered.

Kate parted the blankets. What she saw made her blood jump— dark bruises on one thigh, and up the same side to the shoulder, a welt. The body was long, white, pale as a corpse decorated with brown and yellow bruises. It emanated a fungal odor like mushrooms. One askew leg hung toward the floor. Kate bent and gently ran her hands over the woman's ribs, pressing to see if the woman recoiled, which she did not. She did not respond at all. Kate straightened and looked away at the opposite, shadowy wall, thinking . . . more trouble here, nastiness, the primordial evil, for God's sake, in the lot of certain women.

She pulled the mouth of the sleeping bag over the woman's feet and legs, worked the bag over the hips, and bending the body up and holding the bag, slid the rest of the woman in, laid her down, spread the blankets over the sleeping bag, and positioned the woman's head on the pillow. At her back, Kate felt the first warmth radiating from the wood stove. The woman's face and stony eyes were unchanged.

Kate returned to the kitchen and following the next remedy for hypothermia—the administration of fluids—rummaged in the cupboard for a can of consommé. Berg sat in the middle of the floor. "You're hungry," Kate said. She started the soup, opened a can of dog food, found the dog's dish, filled it with biscuits and canned meat, and returned to the porch where she set the dish down. Berg, who wouldn't eat in the presence of another, stood waiting. Kate scratched behind the dog's ears, allowing herself a moment's distraction in the animal who always observed her own strict standards of propriety and otherwise knitted together the world of the woods and house with her missions. Berg would turn up with things from who knew where—antlers, bones, once a coyote head, and the desiccated, frozen remains of birds and porcupines that she dropped on the lintel. The Subaru's engine hummed. The air streamed with snowflakes, and as Kate gazed into the slot where Jack's truck should have been, anxiety twisted in her.

Back in the kitchen, she poked on the message machine while stirring the consommé. The voice that came out was not Jack's, but her own, the message the one she'd left for him yesterday . . . eons ago. She poked off the message and looked through the window toward the empty parking slot, her confusion deepening. She walked outside again, moved her car next to the van, and sank into yet another momentary stillness as she sat touching the steering wheel. Snow flooded across the beams, heaped on the ground and around the side of the house. Penetrating into the woods, it collected like a white archipelago with the rocks in it for islands. It sheeted the back lane that passed between the corrals and shed to the hayfield up above. The boughs of the trees sagged, and saplings bent double under the heaviness. If it was snowing this hard here, it could be bad for Jack running equipment off the mountain . . . and Travis . . . and Gene Scratcher, too, Jack's helper. Up there, this would be big snow, which could abruptly consolidate into menace.

—He needs a cell phone, she thought, which she had advocated, but Jack in his Luddite-like ways had resisted. She didn't have one, either. —But soon he'll call. Something has happened, a delay, that's all.

She switched off the car and got out, holding the woman's purse and pulling the duffel bag from the back, hugging it awkwardly as she moved, hurrying with it. When she turned onto the walk, one foot flew out from under her on the slick ground and she felt herself pitching in mid-air as if in slow motion. One foot came down and planted itself in a patch of gravel. She caught herself in a crouch, clutching the bag, astonished by her carelessness and her luck. Here she was, desperately tired, worried, inside the house was a hypothermic stranger, and now she'd nearly knocked herself out cold.

She went in, depositing the bag in the hallway, came back with the purse, and thinking to learn the woman's name . . . or something . . . zipped it open. Its contents made her eyes skip to the woman who lay with her eyes closed. Kate spread the purse's mouth and stirred the stuff . . . money, dog-eared twenties and fifties bundled with a rubber band, what looked to be several hundred dollars. She glanced back at the woman who now slitted open her eyes like a lizard. Warily, Kate closed the purse and stepped to the shelves at the far end of the room.

"I'm putting it here," she said, placing the purse next to a computer monitor. The purse sat there, squat between the screen and a crystal decanter. "Right up here where it'll be safe. It's all right."

The woman didn't speak. Kate went into the kitchen and lifted the telephone receiver from its cradle, and then the woman's breathy voice trailed from the other room: "Not the hospital." As she dialed the number to the warehouse, Kate heard the woman's voice again, a plaintive whine: "No police."

Kate hung up and walked back into the living room. The woman was sitting up with the sleeping bag and blankets heaped around her waist . . . naked, thin white body, pendulous breasts, bruises, stringy blonde hair, hands slowly twisting in each other, and deranged eyes. "I'm calling my husband," Kate said. "Please lie down." Obediently, the woman lay back. Her lips moved stiffly as she tried to form a word. "What?" Kate said, leaning near.

"Messengers," the woman whispered. "He has his messengers. The Brotherhood." The words came out in an almost inaudible hiss. "Don't let them find me."

"All right," Kate said, feeling her own eyes narrow. She pulled up the covers, smoothing them under the woman's chin. "It's okay. I'm calling my husband."

She returned to the kitchen and punched in the number. On the other end of the line, the machine came on. After the beep, Kate said, "Jack, where are you?" She paused, and started again: "I've got somebody who wrecked her car down on ninety-five. She doesn't want to go to the hospital. I've got to get her warm." She didn't tell Jack about the bruises, but even just talking to the feasibility of his hearing her, she discovered that she was shaking. Her emotion, her sense of being scattered over urgencies, had made the words shudder in her throat.

Her silence, then, seeped through the whir of the tape on the machine way out there in Jack's warehouse at the bottom of the mountain to the north. As her imagination chased the trails that might explain why she'd found the woman as she had—some brutishness, no doubt, a bank account, maybe lunacy, a desperate escape—the forming thing made her feel as she'd felt flying wildly through the air with the duffel bag but then setting one foot down to grab the ground. The movement in her mind felt as physical as her body finding its balance: She had to attend to the woman.

"She's got to be on the run. Stop at the car and check for the registration. Anything. She can hardly talk. She's hypothermic." Kate tucked the receiver against her shoulder, sat on the floor, unlaced her boots, pulled the boots off along with her socks, and unbuttoned her shirt as she went on describing where the car was located. Standing, she stared at her reflection in the window—short, dark hair, triangular-looking face, and her shirt open over her thermals . . . it was herself here. She took a deep breath, touching ground again in that way. "Okay," she said. She could see Jack's speckled, examining eyes and the crow's feet deepening toward his temples as he listened. "You have Travis, right?"

The smell of warming consommé cut through the air. "The car's buried in the ditch," she said. She looked at the clock above the counter. "It's almost two. I'm all right, do you hear? Jack, where are you?" She hung up, poured consommé into a mug, and headed for the living room, pausing at the door to let the dog in. She knelt at the sofa, lifted the woman's head from the pillow, grasped her gently by the back of the neck, and kept the mug poised at her lips. The woman drank it all down.

"Good," Kate said. The woman's eyes flickered. Kate turned and loaded the wood stove as high as she could, rolled in the damper, then pulled off her pants and shirt, and her thermal underwear. She switched off the floor lamp, went to the sofa, and shimmied in next to the woman.

The woman looked at her. Determined to get her warm, Kate pulled the woman's body tight. They were belly-to-belly, thigh-to-thigh, the woman's coldness chilling Kate. She closed her eyes and saw fingerling sturgeon, thousands of them spilling out of the hole and whirling into the black rush of the current. She felt a hand touch her neck. Opening her eyes, she saw the woman's face as white as porcelain, whiter than the dim, snow-whitened light that came through the windows, and on her face a fixed smile. The woman brought her lips close to Kate's ear and whispered, "My Elijah. The Lord loves you." Kate smelled the woman's milky breath and Berg at her back, the pleasing scent of melting snow on dog hair, and heard Berg circling the rug next to the stove, then moaning with pleasure as she settled down. The woman pressed her brow into the hollow of Kate's neck.

Astonished by the intimacy of her position, yet abdicating everything to her task, she also wondered if she'd heard the woman right. It seemed a curious exactitude, the reference to the Old Testament prophet who returned the dead to life by calling forth their spirits with his corporeality. Kate inhaled deeply and once again closed her eyes.

Her brain reeled with the images of what she wasn't thinking about: Richard Troop's hands crushing the can, the woman's pale face as if suspended above the ditch, and the sturgeon like white, whirling seeds in the black.

3

Outlaws

EARLIER, JACK HAD EASED HIS PICKUP down to the nose of the runout
and switched off the engine. Snowflakes landed on the windshield,
dilated, and ran in rivulets down to the molding. He switched on his
hazard lights so that the pickup would act as a marker for the others,
swung open his door, and slid off the seat to the ground. As he came
around at the back of the pickup, his boots struck straight through the
softly heaping snow to the gravel . . . a good sign. It meant that the tires
could still bite through. He stopped for a moment and peered up the
road, listening. On this side, the road was flanked by woods. On the
other side from the edge of the shoulder lay the drop into what some
called Weaver's Gulch. The red from the blinking taillights washed
off and on against the bank and across the narrow roadway. A quarter-
mile up, the road disappeared around a bend. Against the backdrop of
silence, he heard the soft ticking of his engine as it cooled, and then
faintly from the distance the skidder engine. It was Gene, coming off
the dirt spur onto the gravel and heading down first.

Behind him would be Bliss, and Travis in the flatbed, but Jack, distracted by the snowfall and telling Travis to be careful in it, had forgotten to tell him to be sure to let Bliss get out ahead. He hoped to God
Travis was behind Bliss, so that the log truck wouldn't be hounding
him all the way down. He had an uncomfortable knotting in the stomach born of a father's anxiety over the contrary inclinations to free his
sixteen-year-old son to the wildness of the world and also to protect
him from it. Turning and lifting the hatch to the pickup cap, he leaned
against the tailgate and used his penlight to check off the articles in the

bed: toolbox, bar oil drum, mixing oil, the four five-gallon fuel cans, hauling chain, the cooler into which he'd put the elk heart and liver and a heap of snow, a spare battery, pry bars, peavey, shovel, maul, ax, sledge, a leftover bundle of stakes, spare cutting chains and used-up ones hanging from hooks, the three Stihl saws, and two sets of tire chains in burlap sacks. Surveying the tools made him feel positioned in the world. The truck bed had the pleasing, sweet smell of petroleum and its additives.

The forecast said that the snow would increase steadily through the night and into the next day . . . a big November snow, the first of the season. All day he'd been filled with the prospect of parking the rigs in the warehouse and leaving them until he felt like going back to work them over, and taking the pickup home and unloading the tools into his tool shed, and hanging the elk he'd shot yesterday, building a fire in the living room, and being with Kate while the snow heaped softly outside, pressing against the house. Winter. They'd travel out to Travis's basketball games and fly south to visit Kate's father in Alabama between Christmas and New Year's, and his folks on the way home, and then come back to the quiet snow. Winter was the best time.

He bent into the bed and dragged the two burlap sacks toward him and draped them over the edge of the tailgate. He and Travis should mount the chains for the rest of the haul off the mountain. He aimed the beam back into the far corner of the bed . . . canoe bag. He'd wanted to make one more run down the Clark Fork but hadn't been able to work it in. He took a step back. Everything was there, and so was the elk, gutted and wrapped in a tarp up on the rack next to the canoe. Its head poked out of the tarp, its rack stuck up next to the canoe, and the snout inclined downwards. In the silvery light, its eyes, also as silvery as two quarters, looked back at him from the other world.

He walked across to the drop-off and gazed up the roadway. The waxing moon filtered through the cloud cover and reflected off the snow, giving the air a radiant quality. He could hear that Gene had the skidder out onto the gravel and was working around the mountainside. He heard the log truck, too, the low-decibel rumble in the distance, and the echo ricocheting against the mountain walls as the truck followed the snaking road, but he had no idea where the flatbed was. If Kate were here and knew her son was driving the flatbed down the mountain in this weather and pulling the Lowboy with the dozer on it, she'd have questioned it.

Jack pictured her face, the strong cheekbones, her quick green eyes, and her hair flicking at her jaw. "Are you kidding me?" she'd have said. Finally, she'd have deferred to letting Travis drive, but if she learned he'd forgotten to tell Travis to stay clear of the log truck, she'd have come right at him. "You did what? And how many pills did Bliss pop tonight?" Suddenly, Jack had the sense of Kate's whole bristling person inside him, but certainly if he tried to drive back up to change things now, everything would get worse ... the others already headed down and him going back up the opposite direction into the blind switchbacks and forcing them out onto the crumbly shoulders, in the snow and the dark. He saw that as if it were actually happening ... himself wedged against the wall, Bliss in the loaded log truck, like a train, huge and unstoppable, barreling down from above, and Travis squeezed between in the flatbed, pulling the trailer, veering toward the edge ... his son! What he'd forgotten to do was irrevocable. He wished they'd at least mounted the chains up top. "Fuck," he said.

An hour ago, he'd driven from the loading deck to the spur where Jim Bliss was setting his load, and he'd found that Travis and Gene had staked down the last of the hay bales ... these, set in the cuts to act as bars against the spring runoff. They'd loaded two cords of tamarack on the flatbed. Travis had backed the Lowboy up to a bank and Gene was about to drive the dozer onto it. Jack stood next to the flatbed's window and by Travis's demeanor, the composure of his face, the bill of his cap sticking straight out from his forehead and his hands touching the wheel, Jack could see that Travis alertly awaited what his father would tell him next. Travis was at the age when the flickering motion back and forth between boyhood and manhood was visible and daily. Jack did not want to breach his son's pride. "Double-check the hitch and tie-downs for yourself before starting out," he'd said. "Then come down slow enough for it to bore you, but stay awake. That's where you want to be in your head coming off the mountain in this thing. Just slow enough to be bored by it all, except don't get bored."

"Okay," Travis had said, the word spoken absolutely evenly.

"And keep it geared down," Jack said. "Don't get in a pickle where you have to brake on the bends. It's snow, for God's sake. Be careful."

"Okay."

He'd forgotten to tell him to let Bliss go by first. That was all. And now, either way, behind or in front of the log truck, and rattled though he was, he had to wait for Travis to manage it. He kept looking up the road toward the dark abutment around which the road vanished into the pale, then took a deep breath and let it out in a fog.

The air swirled with puffy flakes, blown around by the draft that rose from the ravine. The snow piled softly on the ground and dripped from his stocking cap. His fingertips felt numb inside the wool gloves. He looked into the ravine and then a couple hundred feet up along it, and thought that in the blur he could still pick out the roof of the ply-wood cabin he knew lay down there. He imagined the other roofs of the outbuildings, too, laid out within a cleared space like ramshackle bunkers inside a defoliation ring—a homestead turned into an armed camp. Where he stood, others had been, stake-outs and snipers scoping the bottom for movement. Some, carting their guns and radios, had slid down the rocky slope to the cover of the trees near the bottom. The runout he'd parked in had been cut by army reserves to be used as a staging ground back in 1992 when the place had crawled with ATF and FBI agents, and sheriff's deputies. The Highway Patrol directed traffic down at the entry to the road. Driving by it, since he'd been cutting on this side of the mountain for the last month and a half, made it a commonplace oddity to Jack. In ninety-two, onlookers had arrived from miles away, and the media had mounted its circus on the killing ground. Food wrappers, pop cans, film canisters, and discarded cartridge boxes still turned up along the roadway. Jack had heard that Vi Owens, who ran a little motel and restaurant down at the corner of the highway, had long given up trying to collect her bills from the networks, and she was permanently pissed.

Light swiped the air above the ravine as the skidder came up to the bend. Jack heard the engine clearly, now, throttling down. The light arched around the abutment, and headed directly toward him, jiggling in the air as the skidder bounced in the ruts. Gene had the flashers on alongside the headlights. The shape of the machine became apparent, the big mud tires, and carriage like an open Hummer with a cable feeder rising from the back like a scorpion tail. The skidder veered toward the runout, stopped behind the pickup, and then Gene's form bent to cut the engine and headlamps. He left the flashers on and climbed out of the seat, clinging to the crash cage as he stepped to the ground. His body, bulked out with clothing on the top and with its skinny, gimpy legs on the bottom, had an antic, sideways hitch as he limped across the road toward Jack. It was the pain he had sustained from old injuries, logging injuries built upon his war injuries. It stiffened him up in the cold. "Shit," Gene said. He stopped and shook himself wildly like a dog. "I got snow down my neck and up my sleeves. My balls are so cold they're up to my armpits."

Jack looked past Gene up along the mountainside. In the distance a faint light stuttered in and out of view. He could hear the log truck engine, too, closer now. He heard just the one engine, but if the log truck and flatbed were anywhere near each other, the diesel would drown out the flatbed's gas engine, anyway. "According to the weather report, we're going to get hammered," he said. Once more, he saw a flicker of lights, and then they disappeared, and for a moment he watched the spot, hoping to see a second flicker some distance behind. He did not. He wouldn't see lights again until the trucks were almost upon them. "Did Travis let Bliss get out first?" he said. Gene's face turned toward him, the teeth and the whites of his eyes glimmering. "You don't know?"

"No," Gene said. "I pulled out in front of the both of them. Hey," he said. He reached out to poke Jack in the ribs, then bent to light a cigarette. The flare of the match lit up his face for an instant, his wispy beard, prominent nose, the scar on his cheek, and the tangle of thick hair coming out from under his cap. The sweet smell of tobacco drifted past Jack. Gene flicked the match over the edge and said, "The kid'll do fine."

Jack grunted and looked back into the ravine. The dark deepened as the cloud cover hardened against the moonlight. He thought he could hear the trickling sound of Ruby Creek down there, but he couldn't see the buildings, now. He imagined the layout and felt filled with phantasms. Gene turned and looked down. There had been Congressional hearings in Washington, D.C., over the incident, a reexamination against what then had evolved as contrarily drawn backdrops of the government siege in Waco, Texas, and the Oklahoma City bombing, of FBI field practices and the rules for the use of deadly force. They led to a demotion, a reassignment, a couple of early retirements, a rules revision and a ritual meal of crow. Here in the Idaho Panhandle, where the talk about the incident still juiced the backwoods kitchens and the taverns in the towns, the hearings were considered to have led to nothing at all. No matter what the political persuasion of the talkers, there prevailed a common anger over the years of having agents stake out houses, helicopters buzzing overhead with their infrared sensors, and the strangers materializing out of nowhere, decked out in waxed boots and new flannel shirts, trying to "pass." Jack had his own opinion: The attack on the homestead below was a stage in the long and sure-to-continue sweep that included rousting out the marijuana farms and meth labs, selling the national forests, and scaring off the radical environmentalists and also the white supremacists—both the violent cells that kept cropping up and the Aryan's ideological stronghold, the church and compound operated by the Lord's Weapon, which was, as it happened, staging a conference this weekend. The sweep was an extended brush-clearing operation in preparation for turning the entire Panhandle into a refuge for the polite society of tourists. All manner of hazards had to be erased to make the place comfortable for the helpless.

Jack himself was belligerently moderate in this immoderate, mountainous, reactionary place. He was steady, reliable, and resourceful, but with a few wild erratics in him like nuggets. He earned his living as a contract logger, a kind of high-grade, environmentally conscious gyppo. Up to a few years ago he'd operated a small shake mill out of his place, but he'd closed it down because the only reasonably priced cedar he could get was the bandit variety, stolen out from under the Forest Service's nose.

As to Gene, he was a decorated Vietnam veteran, and for a time had been a "tripwire vet" after coming back from the war, keeping his own little marijuana plantation hidden away on public land and holing up in a tightly built cabin with its perimeter laced with bells strung on fishing line. He was ferociously independent. A "natural man," he called himself. Since the government had nabbed him and turned its back on him once already, he was making sure he wasn't there when it turned around to nab him again. He lived strictly on a cash-and-barter economy and registered for nothing. He'd bought a house down near the town of Rathdrum, which he paid for in cash and put in Marlene's name—Marlene, whom Gene called his "anchor." He'd arranged to have his V.A. disability benefits deposited in an account for his son, Chris, who'd come up to live with Gene two years ago. Gene worked for Jack on the condition that Jack not claim him as an employee. He'd told

Jack to subtract whatever he lost by not reporting the expense from the wage, which Jack had never done. Jack just doled out Gene's cut in cash and so he himself was drawn inescapably into Gene's hinterland. "I'm flesh and blood, all right," Gene would say, "but otherwise, I'm damn near legally extinct and proud of it."

Sometimes, the difference between Gene's and Jack's own politics seemed to have thinned to a line drawn by Jack's stronger inclination to be circumspect, to pause and lift his feet up out of the mud, to worry. Jack's ruminations over the raid on the homestead down in the ravine inclined toward the lugubrious. He felt that the episode was a parable for the precarious balance on which the world hung—the demons making tracks from out of all the dark crevices to light up the complete deviltry up above. Gene might have felt that, or something like it, and he would listen with pleasure if Jack talked about it, but what he said and did came out in cunning thrusts. He liked mucking in the mud.

Gene's cigarette flared when he inhaled on it. "Look at that," he said. Jack guessed he meant the ravine they were both staring into and in which neither of them, because of the increasing obscurity, the snow, the fog, the twilight, could see a thing. "Weaver was a Green Beret, but all he probably did was pack the chutes for the rest of them. He must've never been asked to think about anything. Look at it."

"Hard to see," Jack said.

"The canyon, the road, the woods," Gene said. "They sent a couple agents to get him in ninety-one. That didn't work, so they spun off a few more from the surveillance of the Lord's Weapon boys. Then it was a dozen, then twenty. The position he took up was indefensible. He put his wife and kids at risk so he could make his point. He's a jackass."

Jack glanced up toward the bend in the roadway again, his anxiety tweaked by the thought of having put his own kid at risk. He heard the diesel engine. Since the snowfall's intensity had increased, he couldn't even see the outline of the abutment at the turn.

"They got him to be exactly what they wanted him to be. That's what he didn't figure on." Gene flicked his cigarette over the edge, the point of fire arching out and vanishing. "Weaver," Gene said. "Good name for him. Spider. Caught in his own web."

—Scratcher, Jack thought. Gene's last name. Also a good name. Jack kept looking. What he saw was the dark with a sheen of white and faintly the rhythmic wash of orange from blinking hazard lights at their backs.

Gene crouched and peered into the murk. "Degan and the other two were scouting right down there," he said. "Right below us."

Jack imagined the three FBI agents, seeking position in the trees near the bottom for a vantage point on the homestead. They'd been planning to take Weaver down.

"The dog comes out after them."

Jack imagined the dog, a German shepherd mix, routing the agents out of hiding. That part of it had always seemed ludicrous to him, the highly trained, heavily armed agents flushed out by a surly dog.

"The kid's out there. Harris and Weaver come out. The agents don't know what the fuck to do or where anybody else is and they panic. They're not supposed to panic. It's their job not to panic, but it ends up with Harris killing Degan and the fourteen-year-old kid dead, shot in the back."

Jack imagined Randy Weaver seeing his son, Sam, lying face-down on the ground, the blood oozing out of a hole. He imagined the shock of it. He imagined Weaver bending to touch the boy, and the shock suddenly electrified into rage and shunted over to his friend, Harris. From that moment on the die was cast. They had killed his son, for God's sake.

"Now he's got two hundred agents on him and the next day Lon Horiuchi nails the wife in the breezeway. Weaver didn't have a clue what he was going to do when they surrounded his place. He thought he could just go on thumbing his nose forever at the federales, the fucking coward and his death wish. The first rule of combat," Gene said, "is leave a route to get your ass out unless you mean to die. For him, that had to mean a way out to Canada. He'd have needed a chopper to get out. But guys without running water or electricity don't usually have choppers."

Jack slipped his hands into his coat pockets to warm his fingers and flexed his cold toes up and down inside his boots. He could hear the diesel engine throttling down and then coming up again. It wouldn't be long, now. He wished he'd given Travis the pickup to drive and brought down the flatbed and Lowboy himself. He looked up the roadway, but saw nothing, only the dark and the luminous white on the dark like a thin glaze. He moved a little nearer to the edge of the shoulder where he could feel the earth give way. If he rocked forward on his toes, the earth sagged beneath him. If he rocked back, the earth was solid. He rocked back and forth, making a slow rhythm against the twitching of the hazard lights behind him, and gazed down into the darkness. He could see the breezeway in his mind, the line of windows at the corner of the cabin. Vicki had passed by them, carrying her infant daughter, and a sniper picked her off. She was found clutching the baby, who was unharmed, bathed in her mother's blood. "It's an idea, though. No electricity and a chopper." Jack said.

"Yeah," Gene said. "The other guys had the choppers. Outlaw, my ass."

"Right," Jack said. It was what was taken to be the outlaw in Weaver that caused the excitement: Weaver's defiance of authority, his refusal to bend, and his success for years at evading arrest on a weapon's charge. But Jack knew Gene was working something out for himself. Last week, he'd seen Gene standing right where he was now, staring down into the bottom. Besides being a "trip-wire vet," who'd consorted with some others who had later joined the Lord's Weapon, Gene was also a Jew, or what he sardonically called a "Jack-Jew," an inveterate nonpractitioner. Few besides Jack knew this, and he had mused over Gene's demons, both the cantankerous ones loose for display and the more dangerous ones hidden deep inside his sense of betrayal.

Gene stood up, moaning. He bent over and lifted one leg up with his hands and tottered near the edge. Jack stepped back onto solid ground and grabbed Gene's arm. "Easy."

"Shit." Gene placed the leg back onto the ground. "I should know better than to hunker." He eased back and lit another cigarette. The match flared, and then he had the orange dot poised in front of his face. The dot danced as he spoke: "You can't be an outlaw without charity."

"He had some of that," Jack said. "Otherwise he'd have never lasted as long out here as he did."

"I don't mean what he got," Gene said. He inhaled on the cigarette and in the brightening orange Jack saw his brow crabbed inward toward his eyes. The light from the blinkers washed faintly off and on across his face. He took the cigarette out of his mouth. "I mean what he gave. He didn't have any charity in him. Anybody who'd screw up the tactics of his position like he did and put his wife and kids at risk like that doesn't have a piss ant's worth of charity in him."

Jack heard the trucks clearly, now, both of them. He heard the diesel engine and a resonant clanking that he knew was the noise of the pulling chains swinging from where they'd been hung against the steel rails of the flatbed. The trucks were proceeding along the straightaway toward the last bend and in the air above the ravine he could see the aura from the headlights. The noise receded. The light disappeared for a moment as the trucks turned in close to the mountainside. Jack knew exactly where they were. The road followed a cut between slopes and broadened before turning against itself to run down the straightaway. It was a safe place. The straightaway led to a dangerous place.

"Travis is in front," Gene said.

But Jack had known that by the sound echoing off the opposite side of the canyon, by the way the clanking of the chain was snuggled into the sound of the diesel.

Gene poked him again. "Hey," he said. He bent around and looked at Jack. Jack could hear the grin on Gene's face, brimming up to fill the words: "The kid's got it. He's got a head on him. He's casing that thing out every inch of the way."

"Maybe," Jack said, believing it more likely that Travis was simply hanging on.

"Vicki was an asshole, too," Gene said. "More rabid than Weaver himself, they say. Weaver's an asshole and he's got his head stuck way up in it. He sues the government and all of a sudden he's inside the law. So, he's collecting his damages and paying off his lawyers, and maybe he has enough left to sit around and drink beer for the rest of his life. Maybe he can get his chopper, but his wife and son are dead."

Jack's eyes were fixed on the widening light in the air past the corner. "Bliss is an asshole," he said. "I bet the son-of-a-bitch is coked up."

Gene grunted, the sound of the diesel rose, and Jack thought he heard the whir of the flatbed's gas engine. The chains slapped against the rails. The light grew bright and extended out into the air above the canyon, defining itself into shafts. From the sky and curling upward in the draft, snowflakes swirled like hordes of minnows trapped in the beams. There came a pause, an instant in which everything hung. Nothing moved. Nothing changed in the sound. It was himself, Jack realized, holding his breath until his ears started to hammer. He let the breath out. A pair of headlights appeared, emerging from the bend and starting down the center of the road. On the inside, Jack glimpsed the flatbed's running lights, and then the Lowboy's yellow running lights jumping behind the truck. The truck and trailer veered a little. He saw the trailer swing, as if cut loose from the truck for a split second, and then the truck canted slightly rightwards to counter the trailer's skid . . . just as he'd taught Travis to do, as Travis in that situation was absolutely required to do. The whole of the rig sidled nearer to the drop-off.

Jack watched all that, holding his breath again, even as he saw the log truck coming around right on Travis's tail, the Kenworth tractor first and then the log trailer, the headlights from the tractor washing over himself and Gene, and as the log trailer's left hand wheels bounced through the shallow ditch on the inside, up close against the mountain while Bliss cut the corner as thinly as he could, the load of logs shifted. The log trailer's steel rails crashed, and the log truck kept coming, pulling itself out of the corner into a line. Its headlights flooded right over the top of the dozer on the Lowboy and through the window into the flatbed cab. He glimpsed Travis's silhouette in there as the flatbed came along, his head poised. Jack's body filled with panic, but that was happening to him after everything else had already happened: the rightwards slide of the Lowboy, corrected by Travis's countersteer, and then the log truck jamming around, and now the flatbed already easing toward the inside of the road. The flatbed and its Lowboy trailer began to slow down and Bliss let the log truck ride up even nearer on the Lowboy trailer. The flatbed's left signal went on, the brake lights blinked off and on as Travis turned his rig closer to the mountain and dipped into the ditch.

Jack found that he'd inched back toward the soft edge of the road. He and Gene stood right next to each other, touching elbows. Along with everything else, they'd left themselves in a bad spot. The flatbed nosed into the top of the runout and he heard it downshift to slow up behind the skidder. The brake lights stayed on. The chains clanked. The log truck hovered behind the right-hand corner of the Lowboy, and then the Lowboy and flatbed vanished from sight as the log truck roared by, already accelerating on the straightaway. Bliss leaned on the air horn as he passed. The blast of it made Jack jump violently and grab Gene's arm. Gene yelped and jerked forward. The log truck clanked ponderously under its load. A long sheet of snow kicked up by its tires slapped against the two of them, and then the truck passed, suddenly gone as if sucked into a tube. For a moment the air was filled with snow, the pale, icy dust ballooning up around them. Jack peered through the snow at the obscure lights across the road. The flatbed was there, safe, and behind it the Lowboy trailer, and in front, illuminated by the flatbed's headlights, the prehistoric-looking skidder with its blinking hazard lights and the pickup with its blinking lights and the outline of the canoe on top, and as the veil of snow slowly cleared he saw peering out from behind the canoe the two silvery eyes of the elk, and then out of the trees up on the bank above the pickup a white bird appeared. Big, it flapped its wings once.

Gene was bent over, slapping the snow off his pant legs.

The bird sailed over his head and vanished. Jack took another deep breath. "So far as I'm concerned, Bliss's ass is in a sling."

Down the road, the log truck's taillights were tiny and paled to pink behind the plume of snow. Growing ever fainter, the taillights then disappeared as if they'd clicked off. The noise of the engine receded to a low snarl. Jack had a furious vision of Jim Bliss up in the tractor cab: big rings on his fingers, big belly hanging out of the Gypsy Joker vest, big speckled beard, curled lips, and the dimples under his black, dazed-looking eyes. Before him, Travis's form was absolutely still.

"Some kid," Gene said as he and Jack walked toward the line of machines and into the wash of lights. Gene's teeth glimmered behind his grin. "Looks like you want to chain up here, huh?"

"I should have done it up top," Jack said. "Along with making sure Travis came last."

Gene peeled off toward the pickup. When Jack pulled open the passenger door, Travis turned to him. Under the dome light and catching the green of the four-wheel-drive indicator, Travis's skin was stretched tight in bands under his eyes. He had his foot still jammed down on the brake pedal. "Should I leave it running?" he asked.

"Yeah," Jack said. He scrutinized his son's face, which was set to conceal the extent of his relief. "Safety brake."

"Oh, yeah." Travis shoved in the lever with his foot, then took his other foot off the brake and stretched out his leg. "I probably should have let Jim come out ahead of me."

For a moment, Jack felt something akin to felicity as his pride welled into his relief. He chuckled and touched Travis's arm. "Right."

"He was a little close."

"Damn close. I should have told you. Let's put the chains on and get out of here."

He walked down to the pickup where Gene had pulled the burlap sacks off the tailgate and dumped the chains onto the roadway. "That's one hell of a kid," Gene said.

Jack grunted. If all went well, if he and Travis and Gene got down to the warehouse and parked the skidder and flatbed and dozer without a hang-up, he and Travis would still be home ahead of Kit. He'd stop at the grocery in Sandpoint on the way down and get ice cream and a bottle of wine and something for Travis, for God's sake . . . whatever damn thing Travis wanted. He'd feed the dog, get Travis to help him hang the elk in the tool shed, maybe finish dressing it out, and cut off a few steaks to cook. He'd make soup, put some potatoes in, cook up a steak for Travis and get him into bed. Travis had a basketball game tomorrow. Jack would have the other steaks, green beans, and a salad ready. He'd have the fire lit, warming the house. He'd plow the lane, take a shower, and by then Kate would be home. Afterwards, they'd go to bed, and even here in the cold and deepening snow, thinking of the smoothness of her legs and of having her muscle up against him caused a pleasure to rise in his loins.

"I'll help Travis," Gene said.

Jack fished a set of chains out of the snow, dragged them to the front of the pickup, and crouched to fan one out in front of the right wheel. He glanced up at Travis and Gene, who stood in front of the flatbed's headlights, separating the chains. Far in the distance, faintly, he heard a crash. He revolved on his toes to see down the road, listening as the noise echoed off the mountains. Soft and muffled, it had a quality to it, a big cracking sound followed by a rumble like a train coupling a long line of cars.

He revolved back toward Gene and Travis, both of whom were looking past him toward the noise, and called to them. "Was that Bliss?"

4
Hostiles

WHEN THE TELEPHONE RANG, Kate pulled out of the sleeping bag and stumbled into the kitchen, groping around the cooking island in the dark toward the machine's red light. The worried way Jack said her name—"Kate?"—conjured his face, the brow furrowed, and his eyes digging into her.

"God, where are you?" she asked. "What about Travis?"

"We're at the warehouse. Dog-tired. He's here. What's going on?"

She told the story again in its succinct version: "The woman wrecked her car. She was standing beside the highway. I brought her home to get her warm." Remembering the warmth of the body she'd just left, she said she believed the woman was all right. She straightened to stretch out her legs, then switched on a light and bent to see the numbers on the machine—3:50. "Jack, it's really late. Why didn't you call?"

"We're coming. We're ready. I'm sorry. Everybody's fine, do you hear? Bliss dumped a load all over the road in front of us."

"Oh," she said, picturing the road glutted with scattered logs heaped and rearing up, a big truck jammed into the midst of it, snow everywhere, and the tiny figures of men picking their way through the jumble.

"Yeah," he said. "We had no phone. Bliss has one, but we couldn't find it. He flipped his tractor sideways."

"God, I'm glad to hear your voice," she said.

"Me, too."

"What about Jim?"

"He's okay."

Through the line, she heard an engine fire up, the noise of it sailing to a roar in the cavernous metal shed, then dropping to an idle, and Gene Scratcher's voice calling over it. She felt chilled, standing naked in the kitchen with the floor cool against her feet.

"In a half hour, we'll be out of here," Jack said. "Home by dawn. Gene asks if you can call Marlene and tell her."

"Now?"

She heard Gene's voice again, a rooster squawk cutting through.

"Wake her, he says."

After hanging up, Kate returned to the living room where she put on her thermals. She leaned close to the woman, peering in the dim light to see her face, which was still. The covers slowly rose and fell with her breath. She was deep in sleep.

—Good, Kate thought. She'll be famished when she awakens.

Softly, Kate knelt in front of the wood stove, opening it to stir the coals with the poker. Berg nuzzled her hip. Kate added wood to the fire and stared for a moment as the flames curled around the wood. She closed the stove, fetched a robe she kept in the back bathroom, put it on, and whispered to Berg to come to the front door. Let out, the dog stopped at the end of the walkway and sniffed the air, then went off to be absorbed into the woods. Although the snowfall had ceased for the time, Kate could see in the light coming through the kitchen windows that the ruts from her Subaru were nearly filled. Tiny bits swirled out of the fog and landed like needle pricks on her face. Kate felt calm in the doorway, and filled with relief.

She returned to the kitchen to call Marlene, who picked up the receiver immediately. "It's Kate," she said.

"Yes?" Marlene said, the foreboding clear in her voice.

"Jack just called. They're coming."

"Oh, thank goodness."

"Gene wanted me to call you." Thus, Kate slipped into the role of mediator in the relationship between two people who made her uneasy. Marlene was a talkative, self-absorbed young woman, a college dropout who came, she'd pointed out in Kate's presence, from a family of PhDs. She was the latest and most durable of the women willing to bite into what Gene called the "prime social order." Gene had family in southern California, and a wife, or ex-wife. Kate was never sure which.

It would be like him not to affirm by law what he in his own mind had decided was dissolved, and Marlene, Kate guessed, had gone through her own string of bad relationships. She had the telltale combination of bluster and vulnerability.

"Thank you," Marlene said. "I was afraid I'd get you up if I called you."

That, too. Marlene took great care not to offend Kate, and for her own part, she'd not even considered Marlene's worrying until now. "They're all fine," she said, and then remembered what she should have thought of last night: Besides managing a restaurant, Marlene volunteered at the Battered Women's Center. Kate told her about the woman, how she'd found her and believed she'd been beaten and was on the run.

"You did right." In Marlene's tone, Kate heard the gears abruptly shifting. "Including not taking her to the hospital. It's better to keep her out of that system." Marlene asked what the woman's name was, which Kate didn't know. "I have to leave early to open the restaurant. But please call me if you need to. I'll come. I have to work to four, and I'll come up anyway then. Get her name. Find out if she has children."

"And if she does?"

"It's much more complicated. The first thing is to keep her safe."

"She's carrying money."

"That's good. It could mean she's made up her mind."

Afterwards, Kate walked back through the living room, glancing at the still sleeping woman as she passed, and then drifted into her study and switched on a floor lamp near her desk. She'd landed like a goose moving about before the dawn, edging quietly into the cover of the rushes, now pleasuring in the room, which during her stints at home from Dworshak, she'd been reorganizing in preparation for serious work. The filing cabinets along the wall opposite the doorway were loaded with carefully ordered documents, and the shelves along the wall to the left, shadowy in the lamplight, were filled with manuals, stacks of offprints and binders of data, cases of floppy disks and newer CDs, books, taxonomies, field guides, natural histories, and at one end a smattering of literary works—O'Connor, Faulkner, Hurston, a signed copy of *To Kill a Mockingbird* her mother had given her.

She moved to her desk where rested two computers—a brand new IBM purchased with grant money, and her old Gateway. Above them

was a tack board where she put directives to herself along with familiarities, constituting a mélange of her life: fish charts, photographs of
her three children, including the grown ones, Pamela and Ron, one
of Jack, and one of herself as an eight-year-old decked out in an Easter dress, posing with her parents in front of the First Presbyterian
Church in Demopolis, Alabama. Her father's pale red hair tufted up
in a breeze and her mother looked austere in a navy blue dress. There
were postcards of Arctic landscapes and another photograph she'd
discovered a month ago while reorganizing her files—a group picture
of the détente-inspired National Science Foundation crew on board a
research ship in the Bering Sea.

Kate leaned toward that one, drawn to look at it by the appearance
yesterday of Richard Troop and the provocation of her doubts over what
she'd done with the errant files from DDM. There were two rows of
smiling people in the photo, most of whom had dropped out of her life.
Certainly, the five Soviet scientists standing in the back row had. One
person, Clinton U, she'd almost forgotten about. Even while carrying on
an affair with the crew's chief scientist, Sophia Kopat, he'd had a crush
on Kate, or so she'd eventually realized. Not a scientist, but a corporate
attorney, and likely an armature of the driving force behind the whole
undertaking, he stood at the far left-hand corner of the group, looking
on from the margin. He wore thick glasses which the sun caught, making two flashing wafers where his eyes should have been.

Kate herself, her bobbed hair blowing, fresh-faced in her innocence,
stood in the front next to Sophia, who, having made a small industry out of her fame as a "deep diver," still flickered by Kate's attention
with regularity. She'd come to loath Sophia. In the way of rediscovered
mementos, the picture conjured up a tangle of stories: the adventure,
the intrigue, the secret of the cruise's true purpose—oil exploration—
conducted under the sham of scientific exchange, and Otis Drainier,
her mentor-to-be at DDM, who had flown in by float plane for a few
days on the ship and whose arrival occasioned the photograph, the
Canadian woman Kate remembered for her frightening account of the
child she'd lost in a fire, and then Sophia, who was laughing. She had
her arm around Kate's shoulders, clutching at her. A week after the
photograph was taken, by an act of negligence, Sophia had left Kate to
nearly die at sea . . .

. . . the net! . . .

To this day, Kate's teeth ground at the thought of the abandoned seine net curling over her head and coming down to surround her.

She straightened. The research cruise marked a passage in her life. Her love for the far north had been awakened, and yet afterwards she'd come back to marry Jack. In her story, and thanks in part to Otis Drainier's offer of a position in his firm, she took a very different course from what might have been, what was in a way the causative of who she'd become.

Beside the computers lay documents she needed to sort through. There was a FedEx package from Abby Leonard and mail Jack had left for her. Kate switched on the IBM and typed the entry codes for her project files. As the computer beeped the commands, she fanned out the mail—what she knew at a glance to be requests for information and forms to be completed. She also had the Dworshak files to bring in from the car. She poked at the keyboard again, calling up the columns of numbers that showed the mortality rate in her model salmon runs. If she had been ready to work, she'd have begun by checking the links between the graphs that assigned mortality to probable causes and projected them into the future: weak plankton blooms, other negative and positive trophic cascades, the rise and fall of contiguous species, shifts in the predator regime, changes in water temperature or in the currents, and the effects of defilement: DDT and PCBs transported to the Pacific by wind from China and the Koreas, toxins entrained in currents from off Mexico, radiation, oil from everywhere, land-based runoff and spills at sea, benzene and xylene implanted in the tissue of fish.

Elaborate in the extreme, the research system held the data from the several thousand field studies and historical material from ships' logs, fur harvest counts, fish cannery records. . . . The challenge had been to devise nexus strings that would allow the data stores to communicate with each other and then to mount matrices in which the results could find sensible form. Because of the discreteness of the data clusters and the gaps between them, Abby and Kate sometimes had to guess at how those stories might work out . . . if that has happened, then this must happen next. Such surmises, if wrong, could warp the results. Plus, it was always possible that the power of the model they'd devised would outstrip the data and that everything would twist away into false conclusions. And finally, the reverse effect and devilmost of pitfalls: Because of the effects of the six billion humans, the whole of the earth was changing faster than could possibly be monitored, even by a system as advanced as theirs.

. . . big brain . . . Jack called the undertaking.

Whenever Kate tried to hold the whole design in her mind, it took the shape of countless luminous grids, pliant as nets . . .

. . . these nets, now, of the speculating mind . . .

. . . made out of the light of the Cenozoic mind, a presumptive god flirting with a shifty horror of its own device as it tried to track the shifty horror out there . . .

. . . these nets wild as the world itself, made to snare the proof of ruin and poison and mutation and extinction, charged with information and yet ever-bending, passing through each other like ghosts, roped together in their ephemerality by the patterns of plants and animals . . . her salmon, the several species and new generations of them swimming out of their freshwater homes as fry to the estuaries, the unknown numbers of them preyed upon by osprey, say, or eagles before commencing their huge sea-going loops.

The columns of numbers on the screen blurred into each other as Kate felt herself becoming drowsy. Idly, she typed in the code for a mock-up she and Travis had annexed to the research program a few weeks ago—a game called Zamiatin Aquarium that Abby had sent up for Travis. It depicted the sea and had animated creatures tagged to represent matrices in her program. It allowed for time to pass, imitating the predictive elements of her schemati. The rate of time could be set, which she did, tapping in a command for the program to chase her system in real time. Travis had wired in the monitor in the living room, also for the fun of it, so the mock-up could be viewed from there. She could do that, go back, watch it for a while, then sleep, and get up in time to start breakfast. Jack and Travis might be three hours yet. Before her, the monitor lit up in an aquamarine. In it appeared silvery things small as motes—tiny, caricature fish.

She collected another blanket from the hall closet and returned to the living room, pausing to look at the sleeping woman whose face was now stained blue by the glowing monitor on the shelf above. A mystery composed itself, made out of the woman's plight and her strangeness, informed by the certainty of Marlene's instruction—"Make sure she's safe"—and by Kate's having spent time with her in complete bodily familiarity. During the night, as Kate had lain awake worrying, the woman had slept with one hand affectionately resting on Kate's side and a foot between Kate's ankles. The woman's breath on Kate's lips—steady and light and long, and curiously aromatic, like the breath of a nursing child, the brushing of air from the life within—had been as intimate as the touch of her flesh.

Kate moved the easy chair and footrest near the stove, wrapped herself in the blanket, and snuggled in . . . here now, the goose come up out of the rushes settles into its nest on the bank. The swimming fish in the monitor grew larger. An off-white dot, what she and Travis had tagged to represent toxic quantities in the system, a cartoon monster that Travis had dubbed Boo, bobbed into view and sank. She fell asleep.

*   *   *

When she awoke, she gazed up at the monitor where Boo had grown into an undulating thing that crept along the bottom. The cutting edge of a huge school approached from the distance—humpies. The mock-up humpies, or pink salmon, the Oncorbynchus gorbuscha, as she, suddenly quite awake, named it to herself, had turned from their gyre off the coast of Japan into a mid-Pacific sector. The fish made a line that spanned the top of the screen.

At her side, the woodstove ticked as it cooled. Before her, the gray of the sofa had been tuned to the color of steel by the light from the windows. The covers still moved with the woman's breath. Her cheek and pale blond hair were lit by the dawn. She thought that when the woman awoke, they would talk, and maybe call Marlene for advice. From outside, the quiet was broken by the musical chimera that had awakened Kate, a faint rumbling and muffled ringing. It was Jack coming along the road.

The engine dropped to idle, then revved as the wheels took purchase on the lane, and the snarl of the engine and the ringing sound of revolving slack in snow chains came nearer. Kate rocked out of the chair, discarded the robe, pulled on her trousers and shirt, and bent to feed more wood into the stove. The engine rumbled noisily. Through the window, the truck's nose thrust into view, and she moved for the alcove, slipped into her rubber boots, and walked out into the cold.

Snow banged against the wheel wells as Jack jerked the truck through a bank. Behind the windshield, his form twisted as he backed the rig in next to the van. It was snowing again, lightly. Pine fragrance wafted from the chimney. The house was surrounded by trees—pine, tamarack, cedar, and fir. Limbs sagged under snow and from behind them rose a pale, lime-colored light. Jack's body bent inside the cab, then came out behind the creaking door to the running board, and he peered at her from beneath the bow of the red canoe mounted on the rack. Next to the canoe lay a bulk wrapped in a blue tarp and a pair of hooves stuck out over the truck's gutter. He'd got his elk.

She smiled, meaning for him to understand that everything here was all right, and said, "Where's Travis?"

He plunged back into the cab. The lights and engine went off. Reappearing, he said, "What?"

"Travis?"

"He's coming." Jack jumped to the ground. The door creaked shut. The brown Dodge sported a steel canopy over the bed, and on top of it stretched the canoe that had patches of silver putty all along its bottom, a forever enlarging set of badges gained from his love for what he called "bony rivers." He liked hauling it, too, along with the rest of his equipment. Icicles hung from the boat's gunwales, and it looked like a large, hoary ornament. Jack kept a full toolbox in the truck at all times, jumper cables, at least one chain saw, sleeping bags, and, up in the cab, a rifle. He'd mounted the snowplow at the warehouse, she guessed, and along its top edge were pasted two bumper stickers: Free the Snake and Support Your Local Sheriff. He traveled that way in a state of full but seemingly contradictory preparedness, and thus turned whatever he drove into a compact parade. Whenever she drove the truck, Kate felt she'd eased inside his interior world. Jack, resplendent in his grit-filled clothes, came toward her, kicking through the snow, and not strange in the least. Berg had appeared from her nesting place in the hay barn to dance around him. He grabbed her and vigorously scratched her ears. When he stopped, she crouched, wired for play. "Gene'll drop him off. He's got a game."

"Game," Kate said, ticking it in. "Basketball," she said. "That's right." She began thinking of how to organize her day, and how the woman would figure into it, then stopped herself. "Wait, it's light. Gene's driving in the light?"

Jack stood before her. "I know. We put him in Gene's cab to rest, and he went to sleep, so we left him there. I had to drop Bliss off, too."

"Jack!" Kate said.

Normally, Gene was taxied around by Marlene during the daytime, since he had out-of-date tabs and no license. This condition was a function, as Gene described it, of his "field of honor," but Kate believed that it was as much the result of the string of drinking and driving arrests he'd had after his logging accident four years ago. He'd rolled a skidder on a slope and said he counted eleven full revolutions before the skidder hit bottom. He'd managed to hang onto the cage, but came out with both legs, an arm, and his collarbone broken, and a vertebra cracked. Jack had found him, gurneyed him out of the gulley, and driven him to the hospital, and Gene came to believe he owed Jack his life. All things attached to Jack, he would defend, including Jack's wife and children, which was too complicated in its obligations for Kate's taste. She did not like Travis riding with him in the daylight. He might be pulled over. Gene hated the police and there was no telling what he might do.

Jack touched her cheek. "They're coming the back way. They'll be fine."

She clutched the cloth of his shirt under his wool coat, pulled close, and drank in his dank aroma of wood sap, engine oil, and sweat. He smelled like a savage thing that had just crawled out of the woods. Berg wormed between them, forcing their legs apart. Kate pushed back and gazed at Jack. He had dark skin, a beard cropped close, and curly hair that snapped out from under his stocking cap.

He reached down and scratched Berg's ears again, then straightened up. "We got an elk," he said, cocking his head back at the pickup. "You sure didn't sound good in that message."

She hooked her arm in his as they moved for their basalt house. The rock had turned dark in the moist air and was iced with snow. She loved the house they had built, its solidity. The main portion was built in the round, as a tower with an attached rectangle. Visitors said it was monumental. If so, to Kate's mind it was a monument to the satisfaction of having accomplished it, which included not only intense pleasure, but also the long strain of the work, and on occasion the sheer terror of the rocks in a sling dangling from the makeshift derrick and, once, of a tie log that had dropped and almost landed on her and Travis, then a baby. To this day, her mind sheared away from thinking about that.

"We had a time," he said. "Bliss is one lucky son-of-a-bitch. He was going too damn fast. So, we had the truck across the road, and the snow, and logs everywhere. He ripped out his hitch and smashed up the tractor cab pretty well. We had to unload the dozer and use it and the skidder to clear the logs and push the trailer out of the way, and then load everything up so we could get to the warehouse to unload it all again."

They went in. She stepped out of her boots. Jack knelt to unlace his Snowpacs and said, "There's another eight loads in the woods, still, that Bliss should have hauled out before the storm. So, there's eight up there and another one scattered. It all ends up several days' worth of work. I can't leave that green wood decked out up there."

"Was he stewed?" Kate said.

Jack shrugged and looked up. A darkness flitted across his face. "Coked, maybe. Beetles. There'll be beetles in the green wood. Boy, am I glad to be home." Then his eyes glimmered. They were blue and green with flecks the color of chalk. He smiled, displaying the hole left by his missing lateral incisor. He had a small dent of a scar, too, just above the lip, that and the missing tooth both caused by the whipping end of a choke chain. He had a partial for it that he never wore except to weddings, funerals, and school ceremonies.

"There's no car back there in the ditch," he said.

"Oh?" She leaned out and peered into the living room. She could see the top of the woman's head, poking out of the far end of the sleeping bag.

"It's nasty out," Jack said. He pulled off his boots, then came up behind her to look. "Sleeping."

Kate murmured.

"Slick as snot," he whispered. "Coming down, I passed half a half-dozen cars abandoned in snowbanks, but not where you said, though I think there'd been one there."

Kate moved back to the front doorway. Steam rose from the truck's hood. Even while the air swirled with snowflakes, the cloud cover had begun to break up. Across the way a shaft of sunlight illuminated a stand of trees. "It's beautiful," she said, closing the door.

"Nasty." He set his boots next to hers, hung up his coat, and whispered, "The world's getting excitable." He grinned again. The gold tooth deep in his mouth glimmered.

He followed her into the kitchen where she filled the kettle with water and set it on the stovetop in the cooking island. She turned and opened an overhead cupboard, took out the coffee beans, filled the electric grinder, and switched it on, making a racket. Kate turned the grinder off and looked toward the living room. It was quiet. She poured the grounds into the plunger pot and backed up against the counter to wait on the water.

Jack bent into the refrigerator. He came out with a white package and snapped it open, took out four sausages, dropped them into a pan and switched on the burner. "I've had nothing since yesterday except a bag of corn nuts and a doughnut." He raised his eyebrows at her. "I had visions of late night elk steak and a bottle of wine."

Through the rank of low windows to her left, more light broke through an opening in the clouds at the horizon, passed in a broad shaft into the kitchen and rose on the wall opposite her until it touched the ceiling. For that moment the kitchen was bright. Jack had on his black-and-yellow-checked work shirt, the sleeves rolled up over his arms, black jeans, and red suspenders. As he moved in the light, particles of dust floated from him. He looked fine, grizzled and hardy.

"We're cooking for our guest, too, I presume." He glanced at his watch. "Travis and Gene'll be here. What the hell." He dumped the remaining sausage into the pan, bent back into the refrigerator, brought out the egg carton, and set it on the counter next to the sink. He filled a pot with water, took potatoes out of a basket and began cutting them in thirds. "Carbs," he said. "Protein. Animal fat. Cholesterol. Yum. Are we sure the lady is alive in there?"

She paused, feeling crosswinds arising out of the mystery of the woman's predicament. The sausage began to hiss and water in the kettle spat onto the burner. She moved for it and poured the water over the grounds in the coffee pot. She found their blue mugs and set them on the counter, then a red bowl. "Scrambled?"

"Sure."

She cracked the eggs into the bowl. Strands from the whites clung to her fingertips. Jack filled the pot with potatoes. Outside, clouds passed before the sun again and the bright light vanished from the kitchen.

"There was a gouge in the ditch where you told me to look," he said. "Also oil. Maybe she cracked the pan. Could be somebody pulled it out. I passed Bud Willy down the road, parked with a car in tow."

Kate crouched to put the eggshells in the compost bucket under the sink. Jack leaned back, reaching to touch her shoulder. She came up, hooked her thumbs in his belt loops, and pulled close. He put one arm around her and slid the other one up her ribs. Her blood crashed in her ears, but then she pushed away, still hooked to his loops. This was ritual, as was their disagreement over Gene bringing Travis. Contention was a way of clearing out the junk when they came together after being apart. "It's about time," she said.

Jack smiled impishly and held her by the skin at her waist. "And our guest?"

"It's not quite time."

"What'll we do with her?"

"Make sure she's okay." Kate paused. "And get her where she'll be safe. Go to the game, I guess. Come home. Sleep."

"Fuck."

"Shh. Come home. Sleep, for God's sake. Aren't you tired?"

"Fuck. Go to the game. Come home. Sleep. I'm tired, all right, but I'm looking at all winter to rest up. Ski. Rest some more."

"Except for the trip." She didn't want him forgetting they were traveling to visit her father for Christmas and his folks on the way home.

"Go fishing in the Gulf," he said. "Catch grouper. Eat oysters. Shoot pool with the old man. Check in on my folks in Arizona. Fuck. Fly home and rest. Ski."

"And work," she said, resting her head on his shoulder. "I have to get this thing off the ground. I'll have to go down to Berkeley to see Abby."

"Right."

She felt something alien like an omen crawl through her, a weasel. It caused her passion to flake away and left her chastened into almost a bodiless cool. It felt like the pose she took on in the labs, not here in her kitchen with Jack who had merely affirmed what she felt. But in the labs, she'd learned to stay armed against the low trajectories of those—usually, but not always, men—who were jockeying for power. She'd learned to stiffen her barricade and place extra members into it so that it came to resemble a Mexican fence made out of post, stone, cactus, and willow wand thick as a child's wrist.

She knew such fences from her traveling girlhood and had even lived within one for a year when she was eight and her father was working in the town of Saltillo. For a child, the fence was a wonder in endless variety, its seeming disorganization, the way it absolutely forbade entry to creatures above a certain size and yet was loaded with lairs and laced with openings to the light outside. She'd spent hours probing it or merely being near it, sitting in the packed dirt and smelling the tart scent of the sweat that crystallized on her arms in the dry desert heat, awaiting a parade of ants or the flicker of a lizard that might give up its tail to her hand if she were quick enough to catch it. She remembered how safe it had felt to be within such a fence that was still open to the world. She remembered the sense of calm it gave her, the radiant, full alertness that flowed out of her being. There, she believed, she had learned to form the question of science she would build her life around:

—What is this?

The fence held within it an edge of benign aggression . . . the cactus spikes. It was at once forbidding and permeable. It allowed passage to any creature smaller than an armadillo. Wrens, roadrunners, pocket chipmunks, flies, dung beetles, tarantulas, and household cats passed through it with ease, as did the lizards and snakes, which even made their lairs in it, and the spiders that joined cactus spines to stone and grass with webs to snare the bits of airborne meat, and so became also its proprietors. Big things, like dogs, had to go around to the gate.

"What's wrong?" Jack murmured.

"It's the woman, I guess," Kate said, catching herself adrift. "She's in need."

She eased away, reached out, and depressed the plunger into the coffee pot. Jack moved to the oven, turned it on, and put in a loaf of bread to warm. He leaned forward, checking the oven's elements, maybe. It was his way. Her memory of the Mexican fence, as she kept reimagining it, had long ago created a layer in her nature that applied to conduct. It was at once a protection, a net within her being, and by its openings also a way to avoid becoming doctrinaire.

She poured cream into the two cups, then coffee. She took a sip. The heavy cream coated her teeth and the acid in the coffee assaulted the flesh of her mouth. It was pleasing to satisfy this addiction. Jack came and took his coffee.

"I didn't call Dan."

Jack smiled. Dan Painter was the bespectacled, always distracted-looking county sheriff Jack had known since his school days. "Maybe just as well. You'd have been up the rest of the night listening to his theories." He rolled the sausages to their uncooked sides, causing their hiss to accelerate into a sizzle. "What about the money?"

"She has money."

He stuck a fork into a potato, testing it. "How much?"

Kate glanced back through the passageway into the living room. There was not a sound. "A few hundred, anyway. Maybe more. I was looking in her purse to find out who she was when I came on it." She dropped her voice to a whisper. "Jack, she's been beaten." When she saw his fork stop above the pot, the empiricist in her kicked in and she backed off: "I mean it looks like she's been. She's got bruises."

Jack lifted the pot, turned, and drained the water into the sink. White steam lifted into the air. "Do you know where she's from?"

"I don't think I've ever seen her before."

He poured the potatoes out onto a cutting board and began peeling them, but gingerly because they were hot. "Maybe we should call Dan."

She moved next to him, allowing his elbow to jostle hers as he peeled. "If she's on the run, she's afraid her husband will find her, maybe. She's got to be scared. I talked to Marlene."

"Good."

"Yes," she said, feeling the shifting currents in herself, which she recognized as her sense of obligation to the woman and, at the same time, a countering wish to deliver the woman into the proper hands and be done with it. Jack would want the latter and to not be messing in someone else's affairs.

Before them was the sink and the window that looked out toward the garden, where last year's cornstalks drooped, pale and engulfed in snow. A shovel they'd neglected to bring in stood plunged into the soil. Beyond the garden the spikes of fruit trees were etched against the snow and the far woods. Between the fruit trees and the woods lay a ten-acre field, a cultivated indentation in the rise. A spring ran out a corner of the field, expanding to a pond that overflowed every year and passed through a culvert in the county road, then dropped over the cliff toward Lake Pend Oreille. Deer bedded down in the bush near the spring. Early every fall an elk herd passed through, traveling to lower ground. Occasionally, moose and black bear appeared. The site had woods, field, water, bitterroots around the rocks, saskatoons, and huckleberries and chokecherries at the margins of the clearing.

A part of Kate believed that the ghosts of the people who had preceded them were up there, too, an emanation of a place alive with such extinctions.

Jack had cut a farm lane alongside the garden and fruit trees to the field. On the low side of the lane stood his tool shed, another shed he'd used to house the shake mill he'd operated for a few years, a barn stacked with hay from the field, and a corral and horse shed for a pair of Percherons he'd used to experiment with horse-logging. The two enterprises, the first one given up entirely and the second put in abeyance, expressed his struggle to bring himself into a respectable alignment with economy and nature.

"And?" he said. "Marlene says?"

"She says, make sure she's safe and keep her clear of the system for now. If she's on the run, it's a good thing she has some money."

Jack took the last potato out of the pot, peeled its skin onto the heap in the sink, and set the knife down on the counter. They both stood still, touching arms, looking out the kitchen window. She had the sensation that they were like a pair of orangutans in a zoo, gazing out of their cage while behind them a spook was piecing itself together.

"But you don't know she's on the run," he said.

"No."

"We need to find out a little more."

"Yes."

"It could be any kind of trouble."

"Marlene said to ask if she has children."

Jack grunted softly.

"But still, I don't even know her name."

"Winona," a voice said. They turned as one. The woman stood just inside the kitchen, barely covered by the beige blanket she'd draped over her shoulders. "It's Winona. I'd like some coffee, too." Her harsh voice sounded like a bray: "I'm hungry. I need to pee."

Kate glanced at Jack, whose face had grown sharp, and she moved quickly, taking in the woman as she approached her—the lightly built ankles beneath the blanket, the long, delicate neck and collarbone and chiseled face, the disheveled hair, and then a gesture of body that was clearly addressed to Jack. The woman inclined toward him, allowing the blanket to fall further away. Kate moved to the woman, grasped the blanket's hems, and drew it close around her, saying, "I'll show you."

She guided the woman through the living room to the back bathroom where the woman plunked herself on the toilet.

"Do you want your duffel bag? For the clothes?" Kate asked.

The woman . . . Winona . . . sat hunched and staring at the floor. "Everything's dirty. I was in a hurry. I want my purse."

"I'll get it for you," Kate said. "You can wear something of mine for now."

She went out, climbed the stairs to the bedroom in the loft, and found a dark blue sweater, underwear, a black body suit, and stood looking at them for a moment, thinking that she and the woman were nearly the same size, only strung together quite differently. Something flashed through the window and she heard a string of barks from the distance, and then through a screen of leafless aspen trees she saw the shape of a wrecker with a car in tow out on the county road. The barking started in again and two large figures appeared from around the bend in the lane. Berg circled them, keeping her distance but barking wildly. Two men in gray coveralls and caps with bills scrunched low on their brows marched forward in unison, lifting their feet out of the snow and swinging their long arms mechanically, absolutely oblivious to the dog. Kate recognized Bud Willy, who ran the wrecking yard down the road, and his brother, Zack. Not fathoming it at first . . . but feeling an obscure menace . . . she scooped up a pair of shoes and a blue skirt and went down the stairs.

From the hall, she heard Jack's voice at the front door, calling off the dog. Back in the bathroom, Winona stared at herself in the mirror. Kate shut the door behind her. "Here." She placed the clothes on the counter. "You should take a shower. And there's a glass," she said, pointing at the glass next to the clothes. "You should drink water."

"I'm all right," Winona said, touching her chest. She turned to Kate. Her lips quivered and her pale blue eyes seemed vacuous.

"You mean you're not hurt?"

"I'm always hurt," Winona said. "Like Jesus. I'm a sacrament."

"I see." The words came out of Kate's mouth just so . . . guarded and yet amazed.

Winona loosed a rush of words in a twanging voice that made Kate step back. "A shower would help, if you don't mind. I would feel better if I took a shower. Or I can wait. It doesn't matter. I don't need a shower." She paused and took a breath. "You've been so kind to me."

"It's fine," Kate said. She pushed the shower curtain clear. "There's shampoo and soap in there, and towels here." She opened the closet, took out a towel, and set it down.

"I'm glad they all match," Winona said. "Thank you."

It was true, the towel, skirt, and sweater were all the same shade of blue, which seemed lunatic. Kate bent to turn on the shower, then pointed. "The hot and the cold. Listen," she said. "Stay here until I come get you."

Winona stepped gingerly into the tub, and then turned to face Kate. "Why?"

—Why?

Kate wasn't sure why, but what she hadn't fathomed now turned into a glimmering . . . by rumor a reclusive woman at the wrecking yard. "Don't come out. Somebody's here."

"All right," Winona said. "You betcha. But I want my purse."

"I'll get your purse." She drew the curtain over Winona's pale form and moved into the hall, shutting the door on her.

She heard voices from the kitchen, Jack's baritone then a rumbling voice. As she angled out of the living room and past the foyer, she found them, two men leaning against the counter just inside the doorway into the kitchen, and Jack back behind the island. She entered and took a step away from the two, to her left.

The brothers were big, bigger than she remembered them. Their bodies shifted toward her and their heads followed, swinging heavily like the heads of bulls. The bodies stood poised, rhino-like, huge and raw under the loose-fitting gray coveralls. They each wore black baseball caps with Red Man patches. Their faces were broad, but Bud's had definition in it, an address of the skin to the glint of rapacity in the black eyes and to the mouth, which was fixed in a curl at one corner like a scar. Zack's face had the placid, eager-to-please expression common to what once had been referred to as idiots. His eyes, nose, cheekbones, and mouth were simply there, floating like disconnected bits of debris in a pond of flesh. Each of the two stood in his own puddle, the thaw from the ice crusted to their boots and cuffs.

Jack said, "You know Bud and Zack?"

She nodded at the pair without speaking, but she thought—barely.

Bud took off his hat and said, "Ma'am." He had black hair, cropped close to the head in a butch. His brother took off his hat, too. He had brown hair, cut the same way. They held their hats at their bellies, but while Zack held his delicately, as if it were an elusive bit of fluff, Bud's became crumpled in his huge, grease-stained hands.

"We got this car," Bud said. "We're wondering if it's the same you saw."

Her mind skipped—How does he know?

She said, "It could be."

"We were wondering if you'd look."

"I saw it from upstairs," she said. "It could be. But it was dark when I saw it last night." She'd been about to lie and say she'd only glimpsed it, driving by, but unsure of what was transpiring here, she stopped herself. She glanced over at Jack, who looked back at her evenly.

"A Nova?" Bud said.

"I wouldn't know," she said. Jack turned the heat down under the sausage and covered the pan. For a moment, the din of grease pinging against the lid filled the kitchen. Jack leaned back against the edge of the sink again, watching. She moved toward him, passing around the island to the refrigerator. "The car was nosed into the ditch," she said.

"Right. This has nose damage. Ran into a rock. What we was wondering . . ." He paused, and Kate thought it odd that he kept saying "we" when his brother didn't appear to have a thought in his head that would lead him to wonder about anything in particular, but rather about everything all the time, the great, blank, obscure, chaotic mystery of life that swirled around him. ". . . is if you saw the driver."

"I saw a car," Kate said. "There didn't appear to be anyone in it."

"She might be hurt, you understand."

"She?"

The brother spoke. His brow screwed with worry and his voice came out a high-pitched tenor: "Not hurt! No!"

"Shush," Bud said, lurching his head at Zack, but speaking softly so that he seemed at once filled with menace and gentleness. Zack's face drained. Bud glanced at Jack. Jack cocked his head and smiled faintly. It was the expression Kate knew well, the animal-like alertness. He could be like an owl in the night, listening for prey. "There's woman's things in it," Bud said to Kate. "A hairbrush and the like."

"I see," she said. She wanted to say: We have a phone. The number's in the book. Why didn't you call? Get the hell out of my kitchen. An engine snarled from outside, and between the two men and through the window, she saw Gene's dilapidated black pickup slide by.

Jack slipped behind her to check the bread in the oven, then returned and set another pan on the stovetop. The hiss of the sausage had softened. He began grating potatoes to make hash browns. The white ribbons heaped up on the counter next to the stovetop. Kate picked up the red bowl and a fork, and stirred the eggs with great deliberation. She was glad to hear Travis and Gene's voices from outside in the cold, bright air. She said, "I hope she's all right."

"Got a ride, most likely."

"One would hope so." She heard the door suck open and then the sounds of Travis and Gene pulling off their boots in the alcove.

"We saw Jack looking where it'd been and thought he'd know whose it was." In Bud's way of speaking, the words sounded like chips off hunks of rock, and his voice was almost deep enough to set silverware to rattling. He pulled away from the counter to stand square and look straight at her. The glitter in his eyes made Kate feel she was being assayed. "There's no registration in the car. It's our business peeling wrecks off the road. We want to know who's going to pay is all." His eyes bored back into Kate. "Somebody's always got to pay."

Travis and Gene came in and moved along the wall to Kate's right. Travis said, "Ma," the single syllable uttered as if it were all of several declarative sentences that also said: Here I am. I'm fine. Nothing's wrong.

Dressed in his jeans and a red sweatshirt with the hood pulled halfway up the back of his head, he held himself straight next to Gene, who next to Travis seemed filled with latent electricity. Travis's was a measured composure like his father's, but there was a droop in his eyelids. He was exhausted. As Kate examined him, the skin of his face visibly knitted together in resistance to her scrutiny and he looked over at Bud and Zack, nodding faintly at them.

When Kate glanced at Gene, his face bunched toward his nose like a coyote's. He flashed a smile that she took to mean—Hey, the kid's here. Lighten up. The smile grew mischievous as it skipped to Jack, and then over to Bud and Zack. "Bud," he said.

Bud said, "Gene."

"Zack," Gene said.

"It's Gene, Bud," Zack said.

Bud grunted.

"Gene Bud," Zack said. He lifted himself up on his toes and said, "Gene," then dropped to his heels and his face collected itself into something like an expression. "Bud," he said.

"It's biology," Gene said to Kate.

"Gene Bud," Zack said.

"Shush you." Bud said. Zack froze. Again, Bud had spoken with what seemed an impossible equal measure of gentleness and menace, and Kate wondered if these were two parts of his nature warring against each other, or if he actually had a sense of propriety that had been called out by the act of standing unwelcome in somebody else's kitchen and that kept him from slamming Zack across the side of the head.

Gene's chin was grizzled. One cheek was scarred with two long slits. Lightly built and wiry, he wore a stained, leather, fleece-lined vest. He had a weathered complexion and dark hair that hung in a ponytail from under his greasy stocking cap. He leaned in Bud's direction, grinning over one shoulder as if to make his body into a blade . . . a provocateur. "Burned any crosses lately?"

Thus, Gene summoned up the neo-Fascist enclave near Hayden Lake, what called itself the Lord's Weapon Universal Christian. As Kate positioned that next to the woman's circumstance . . . on the run . . . the suspicion that had been shape-shifting through her thoughts and that she'd been trying to hold off out of fear, abruptly formed into a conclusion. She named it, speaking the sentences clearly in her mind: —He is one of them. He is her husband. I see. It's him she's running from, for God's sake. She watched Bud in the pause now with an almost morbid fascination for what his response would be, but to her surprise a smile eased into his fixed sneer like a snake sliding back into its discarded skin.

"Them assholes don't know when to quit," he said.

"I hear they're having a to-do this weekend," Gene said.

"It ain't my affair," Bud said. "They got cobs up their butts, every one of them. They got . . ." Bud stopped himself and turned his eyes to Kate. "Begging your pardon, ma'am." He glanced warily at Jack, as if he expected a price to be exacted for the use of profanity in the presence of Jack's woman . . . that ancient compact. Jack turned and took down the long, iron griddle from the hooks on one side of the sink. He turned back and held it before him in two hands, then set it over two burners and switched on the heat. All the burners were covered now . . . by the griddle and the pan with the sausage in it and the big pan warming for the eggs. She still held the red bowl and fork, but had stopped stirring. On the side of Jack's face, she could see a hint of amusement. He edged back and leaned toward her, and the expression turned into a quick, searching exchange between them.

—*Easy*, she believed he was saying.

—*Now*, she was saying. Let's get them out of here, now.

—*Okay. Easy*, he was saying inside her.

Gene said, "They just had to light up another one?"

"I read the papers like anybody else," Bud said.

They were talking about a cross-burning a month ago on the lawn of an interracial couple over in Post Falls. Jack picked up a bottle of oil and dribbled some onto the griddle and pan.

Bud added, "You'd think that pair'd have some protection after the first time. The surveillance was probably eating doughnuts at Zip's."

Jack looked up and cocked his head.

"Or that they'd get the hell out themselves," Bud said, sneering again. "They're as dumb as the FBI. Every week I'm pulling one of them FBIs out of a ditch back in the woods where they figure they've got to be to keep track of everybody. Them and the media, who brought in the Feds in the first place."

He ran his eyes toward Jack, and back to Kate, who'd glanced at Gene and back again at Bud, and as he stared at her, his eyes seemed to withdraw into his head and then come out again, shiny as the tips of two small tongues. Kate grew acutely conscious of her kitchen being filled with men—brooding, potent, playing cat-and-mouse from behind their masks. She resumed stirring the eggs, finding a calmative in the tick of the spoon against the sides of the bowl. Her subliminal sense of the Mexican fence rose to make a ring around her, her permeable armor, and she looked from one to another: Jack, Travis, and Gene. By the way they stood, even Gene, poised and well-enough prepared to give way, the chinks in their armor through which air could pass was revealed. She granted them that. Zack stared wide-eyed straight up into the light fixture in the center of the ceiling. He might have had his own copious measure of such openness, were he allowed the freedom for it. He might have had a floodgate, which if unhasped could have let the world rush in, but Bud . . . that was a different matter. Intelligent as she'd begun to suspect he was, his mind was of the snap-down sort. Nothing entered unchecked.

She listened through the hissing sausage for a sound from the bathroom. She heard nothing. She worried about what the woman . . . Winona . . . was doing in there. Before Bud had arrived, her sympathy for Winona had spun off the unknown version of whoever "he" would turn out to be. Then he'd walked straight into the unknown, jamming it full of himself. The spoon ticked against the bowl. The kitchen smelled of meat and of the onion and garlic that had gone into it, and of the sweetness of heating bread. She didn't think Winona would come out of the bathroom, but she wanted Gene to stop baiting Bud. She wanted Bud out of her house. She wanted Jack to do something to get him out, and she had a flash of anxiety then, thinking that Travis or Gene might want to use the bathroom, but checking them, she thought not, not yet. They had the front one to use, anyway, and in the manner of men, they'd probably taken care of it somewhere along the road. Jack ladled the grated potato onto the griddle, and it spat and steamed as he spread it slowly and evenly over the surface.

Gene said, "I hear the bad press has Bender climbing the walls."

Kate saw the spatula stop in mid-air and Jack's head lift again to look at Bud. She set her bowl down, and placing the heels of her hands on the edge of the island, took a breath. Bender was Dalton Bender, a developer who'd bought up all the small town newspapers between Boise and the Canadian border, bankrolled county commission campaigns, positioned sympathizers on the planning boards, and built a huge hotel on Lake Coeur d'Alene. His vision of the Idaho Panhandle was as one huge resort destination, and he despised the infamous neo-Fascists for the no-man's-land aura they gave the Panhandle. Just a couple of weeks ago, Jack had amused himself by suggesting to Kate that as a scientist with an interest in preserving riparian habitat she might be better served by the neo-Fascists, the dog packs at the fringe, than by the impresarios of scenery. "Maybe they don't exactly get what the conflict is, or maybe they do, but they sure as hell define it," he'd said, and then he'd offered up a bowdlerized version of the second law of thermodynamics: "Any increase in the order of the system must be offset against a decrease in the order of the demons."

Bud said, "We don't touch FBI brake lines, but we damn sure jerk the cars out good and hard." Pleased with himself, he settled back against the counter and crossed his arms. "Bang up the running gear and stick 'em with a surcharge to make up for the cut rate Bender's charging for a wing in his fucking hotel. Some'd say it's Jew money. I'd say it's just money with a taint on it."

And again, Kate flicked a glance at Gene, whose eyes remained bright and intent. Next to her, the spatula moved again as Jack spread potato into an empty corner of the griddle, and then he said, "You'll have to excuse us. We need to have breakfast and get on with the day. I've still got logs up on the mountain." He nodded at Travis. "The boy's got a basketball game."

For an instant, Bud stayed absolutely still. His face came once again to be defined by the sneer. He rocked forward, put on his hat, and touched Zack on the hands. "Let's go."

Zack jerked out of his trance. "Time to go," he said.

"Hat," Bud said.

Zack said, "Hat on head." He put his on and meticulously positioned it, adjusting it here and there as if to make it perfectly even all around. He finished by running his fingertips along either side of the bill to the center, then softly clapped his hands together before dropping them to his sides. "Boots on feet," he said, bending to look. "Ready."

Just before they moved, Kate walked quickly around the island and out toward the alcove where she swung open the front door, then backed into the edge of the living room. She didn't hear the shower, or anything from the bathroom, nothing. The men came toward her, first Bud. He passed near, smelling sourly of sweat, and then lurched sideways to make way for Zack, who came, but didn't turn. Zack kept coming so that she had to take a step back. He was bigger than Bud and smelled not just of sweat but also of urine. He had an addled expression of anticipation. She put up her hands as if to stop him. "TV," he said, swinging right by her into the living room and going past the sofa that had the sleeping bag and blankets heaped on it. "Fire," he said, gesturing at the wood burning stove. "TV," he said. He went for the monitor . . . the bright aquamarine field. Stunned, Kate stood locked in place, thinking—The purse. I forgot the purse. Then—The duffle bag. She shifted to stand between the duffle bag and Bud.

"Zack," Bud said from the alcove.

Zack kept going. "Bud?" he said. He stopped in front of the screen and peered at it. Kate imagined what he might see . . . the line of salmon at the top, maybe a teeming phalanx of them coming nearer, tumbling upon themselves in their wild run to the mock seacoast, or maybe even Boo on the bottom. "Fish!" Zack said.

"Zack. Now," Bud said.

Obeying, Zack began to turn, but he hung for an instant, poised in the center of his act of turning away. By the position of his body, Kate had a flash of dread that he'd spotted the purse in the shadows between the wall and monitor. "A lot of fish," he said, completing his turn.

Kate looked at Bud, seeing only the abject ferocity in his face. Dishes clattered in the kitchen and she heard voices in there, then Jack appeared in the passageway. Kate saw his glance going to Zack, and his body poising itself.

"Fish," Zack repeated. "TV."

"Leave it," Bud said. "Zack. Now."

Zack turned and lumbered toward Bud. "Fire," he said, as he passed it. "Thank-you," he said to Kate as he passed her. He went toward his brother, who'd stepped to the side so that Zack could keep moving without pause, just go on, swing into the alcove, then pass through the doorway to the snow-covered walkway. Kate heard his singsong voice from outside: "Gene Bud. Thank-you. You're welcome. Gene Bud. Dance."

Bud touched the brim of his hat. "Sorry to trouble you, ma'am." He nodded at Jack. "Jack." He then fixed Kate once again with his small, bright eyes. "Whosever car it is, we got to find them, that's all, so they pay." He moved out and shut the door.

She stepped behind the sofa and looked into the hall at the bathroom door. It was closed. She went the other way after Jack into the kitchen. Gene had poured himself a cup of coffee. Travis was bent over the stovetop, picking out bits of potato from the edges of the griddle. She stood with Jack just back from the window and watched the two men go around the curve of the lane and behind the trees. Berg trailed them, her loose body like a whipping rag. If they had turned back, she would have barked.

She said, "He's her husband."

Jack grunted his assent.

"You knew that all along."

"I put it together after I let him in. I've seen her a time or two at his yard."

"How did he know?"

"That she was here? I don't think he does. Somehow, he saw me looking at that spot on the highway and he came up to find out why. I told him you'd seen the car last night. That you wondered if it belonged to somebody you knew."

They stared out into the swirling white. Truck doors slammed in the silence and the wrecker's engine started up. The shape of the truck and car in tow pulled forward and slowly jockeyed backward into their lane.

Jack said, "If he'd believed she was here, he'd not have let it rest."

"Her purse was there by the monitor. And the sleeping bag on the couch."

"I know. He didn't see them."

The wrecker pulled out of the lane and headed out in the direction it had come from, raising a cloud of snow dust.

"So, why didn't he just say he was looking for her?"

Jack reached back, pulled a revolver from his back pocket, and set it down softly. It was his old blued .38 with walnut grips . . . a pistol left for him by his grandfather. He squinted doubtfully "I don't know."

"What if they come back?"

"They won't get inside the house."

"Jack, that woman needs help."

He murmured, neither assenting nor disagreeing, and then said, "Breakfast?"

"Yes," she said. "I'll get her. Please put that thing up."

Pulling away, she glanced at Travis, who was listening intently from the other side of the island, and at Gene, whose face was wired into his scrutiny. She walked into the living room, retrieved the purse, and moved to the bathroom where she pushed open the door. Winona was there, dressed in the bodysuit, and she'd found Kate's cosmetics drawer and had the contents spread all over the counter. She leaned toward the mirror. She'd lined her eyebrows and was working on her eyes, highlighting them with blue. She had used the meager supplies in ways that Kate would never have imagined: the dark liner and blue beneath her eyes and silver under the eyebrows, the rouge she'd made circles out of on her cheeks. Her angular face looked other-worldly, planted on top of the spidery body dressed in black tights.

Kate set the purse down. "Breakfast is ready."

Winona picked up the purse, put it down again on her far side, and spoke in her little girl kazoo voice: "I didn't come out. I did what you said. I'm hungry."

"Bud Willy is your husband, right?"

"I heard him. I told you he has his ways. I didn't come out."

"He's gone, now."

"You didn't tell him?"

"No."

Winona leaned toward the mirror and feathered the edges of the rouge circles with her fingertips. Then she posed, smiling fixedly at herself in the mirror, and said, "God forbid that I should glory."

5

Cover

JACK AND TRAVIS set the kitchen table over in the corner just past where Zack had been standing moments before. They placed the platters of sausage, eggs, rolls, and potatoes, the yellow plates and cups, glasses, and utensils on the white oilcloth. They put down a pitcher of orange juice and the coffee pot, the salt and pepper, butter, jelly, and jam. "Please sit," Kate said, She touched Winona's elbow and gestured at the place at the end. Clutching her purse, Winona hovered, then sat. Everyone else took a place, Jack nearest the stove, since breakfast had come to be under his charge. When he sliced into the sourdough loaf, steam curled from it and played into the sunlight that angled across the table from the far windows.

The food circulated. Plates were heaped, and coffee cups and juice glasses filled. There was a pause, a naturally felt, momentary meditation, but at the end of it just as Travis lifted a bite of egg to his mouth, Winona said, "I'd like to give thanks." She set to it: "We thank you, Lord, for the food given to strengthen us. As you bless us, we bless you. Deliver us from the ungrateful." Then suddenly she plunged into an amalgam about government corruption, the scourge of the second coming, the purity of the "true commissioners," the promised land, and something about the "midst," "being in the midst," the "chosen who were in the center of the midst."

Besides Winona's, not one head was bowed: Travis stared at his fork as if it had just dropped into his hand from outer space. Gene had his head cocked toward Winona. Jack eyed her darkly. An inhalation spread at the table, collective, slow, and soft under Winona's voice, as everybody stocked up on air. Kate averted her eyes above Gene's head and saw the walnut handle of the .38 on top of the refrigerator where Jack had left it. Lightly, she touched her fingers to Jack's thigh under the table and stared at a pat of butter that slowly slid across her bread, stopping to pool at the crust. Winona jangled on: "Oh Lord, our strength, thank you for your protection, for interceding in the path of my persecutors, for bringing newfound friends to my aid. Deliver us from the horns of the devil." She stopped. There was a pause at the table, radiant and astonished. "Amen," she said, and then the air came out, a collective exhalation of relief.

They ate. The earthy potato and egg were set against the savory taste of the sausage, the tongue-brightening currant jelly, and the coffee. By the time Kate's plate was little more than half-empty, Travis was serving himself seconds. Winona had already taken seconds, another sausage, another heap of potato. She hunched close to her plate, ladling in the food and gulping it down as if she'd been starved for days.

Jack asked her where she planned to go.

She stopped eating, resting her hands on either side of her plate. "Far away," she said. "Maybe Skagway or Prince Rupert."

Kate knew the places, which were up in the corner of British Columbia not far south of the Alexander Archipelago.

"I went there, once, with my mother," Winona said, and then suddenly she spread her arms and cried out, "Tyee!" Her face fell into a pout, and she added, "Tyee would do. Very far away. How about White Horse?"

Kate considered that Winona had another life within her, a specimen of herself draped on the inside of the bright and glaring like a hide nailed to a barn wall and puckered around its pain, hanging heavily there, misshapen and dark. She leaned toward Winona, speaking as if to a child, "Plan. We're asking where you planned to go before you slid off the road."

"Paradise," Winona said. "Nadu. Hope. Dream."

"What about your car?" Jack asked.

"Ain't mine. I don't care if it's wrecked."

After a pause, Jack said, "We could put you on a bus." To Kate, he said, "I have to file my vouchers at the mill, anyway, and see what Bliss has in mind for those logs."

Winona sat poised as if she were about to rise. "They'll catch me," she said. "They're waiting. They'll fuck me."

Kate saw Travis avert his eyes toward the window at the far end of the kitchen. There was a moment of silence, and in it his eyes took on his father's expression—composed and steady beneath the thick shock of brown hair. Looking at him, Kate sought to measure what was impossible for her to measure—his ability to perceive the sexual fantastic in Winona, and the warp it could cause in such a person, and to weigh that against the metal Kate trusted was lodged at the bottom of his judgment. What she found instead was the strumming of her motherly chords by the uncharacteristic droop to his head. He was desperately tired. She wanted him fed and rested.

With her children, her habit of measuring and counting dissolved into excessive care, a skip of logic leading to an extreme vigilance that sometimes left her confused. Jack had gone right to her core a few weeks ago when she was worrying about Travis driving late. He'd said, "Your children are healthy and smart and we're damn lucky to have them. They are not endangered." And yet sometimes out of a deep anxiety and sense of impending loss she'd catch herself thinking—But the world! The world into which we've brought them out of our passion and love and then sent them into on their own! That world is in jeopardy!

At the far end of the table, Gene placed a hunk of sausage in his mouth and tongued it into his cheek.

Travis lifted his bread, took a bite, and chewed slowly.

"Over, I mean," Winona said. "I mean they'll fuck me over. They'll take my money." She reached down to touch the purse she'd hung from the rung of her chair. "I am on the run, you know. I need help. And no, I don't have children, cursed as I am."

There was a second moment in which air seemed collectively inhaled. "What if we take you to Spokane?" Jack finally said.

Winona turned her eyes to Kate, and answering Jack, pleaded with Kate, her words rattling shrilly: "Then you'll drive me south and west out into the open where they'll be looking. He'll find me and lock me up."

"Maybe we should call social services," Jack said. "Or what?" he asked, turning to Kate. "What is it?"

"No," Winona said. "Please no. Not the state." Her hands gripped the table edge and her breath grew panicky. "I'd rather walk. I'll go north. I have a brother. He'll help me."

"It's the Battered Women's Center," Gene said.

"Right," Kate said. "They have experience with situations like yours."

"Sure they do," Winona said. "I've been there. They report it and you end up getting jerked around by the state, anyway. Screw the do-gooders."

Travis rose from his chair and moved into the light at the counter with his dishes, clattering them as he placed them in the sink. When he came back after more, Jack said, "Go take your shower, son. Get some sleep. We'll wake you in time."

Travis went out. Jack began clearing their end of the table, but Gene stood and made him sit down, saying, "You'd better get this transaction straight. Besides, I like doing dishes."

Winona scraped out the last of the egg onto her plate and slid the platter into the center of the table. Kate passed it to Jack, who placed it beside him. Other things were moved the same direction, the bowls and cutlery, the rest of the plates, the juice pitcher, which Gene took away. "We never have food like this," Winona said in a quavering voice. "This is like a restaurant." She gulped down the last of her orange juice. "Bud'll think I'm running off to Seattle or to Missoula where my sister is. I did that once. The agency's head is up its ass. If I can go north I can get away from here and stay with my brother in Cranbrook."

"B.C.?" Jack said.

"You can leave me at Yahk. I got an old girlfriend there who'll take me to Cranbrook," Winona said. "It ain't hardly any further than Spokane. Bud'd never dream I'd do that, go back to start clean where my own people are."

Jack slid his chair back from the table. Kate took a sip of coffee. Silverware rattled as Gene placed it in the sink. The sunlight had moved so that its line bisected the refrigerator, placing the revolver on top in a shadow. From outside, the dog began barking wildly again. Kate's and Jack's heads went up. There came more roguish barking and from the distance the yelp of a coyote. Berg had her language—the bark for an approaching car, the bark for human intruders on foot, the one for porcupines, the one for other dogs, and this one that turned into a howl for coyotes. Kate stood and moved over next to Gene to look out the window. She heard the coyote calling from the woods, and Berg responding from the same direction. Gene let his hands rest in the dishwater. "Marlene could help with this," he said softly.

"I know. I talked to her," Kate said. She made a roundabout of the kitchen, passing by the other windows and looking down the lane toward the road, seeing nothing there—no vehicle, only trees and deep snow—then returned to sit, putting her hand on Jack's thigh. She understood that whatever Winona said was not to be taken at face value, that nothing was precisely named—not her fear, her intention, nor her gratitude—that in her state of siege she'd lost the ability to call things as they were. Yet the composite of her words gathered around her, like the language of grisly dreams, was convincing enough, as were her bruises, her dread of agencies, and the fact that she perceived nearly all the paths away from her crisis as having been already sealed against escape. Kate felt herself being drawn into this, the entrapment of brutishness. Something had to be done. She said, "It's true that Yahk isn't that long a trip."

Jack crossed his legs, bringing one foot close to her knee. "If you're serious about that, I'm coming with you."

"You need sleep."

"We all need sleep."

"I've slept. You haven't."

"You said she had no ID. She could have trouble at the border."

"Of course, I have an ID," Winona said. "But I'm still free."

"We could use the van," Jack said to Kate. "We could take turns sleeping and still be back for the game before halftime."

"Travis has to get to the high school, right?" Kate's concern for Jack was genuine, as was her concern for having someone here to watch over Travis, and she was going to continue proposing her solution, but the growing edginess between her and Jack made her pause.

Jack said, "She's got money. But if they search, she'll have God knows what else in her duffle bag."

"It's my laundry," Winona said. "My ID's in it, too."

"The money could be counterfeit," Gene said. One of his shoulders worked as he scrubbed the pot. "A couple of those guys are doing time for that."

"That's right," Jack said.

"It ain't," Winona said. "Bud won't consort with them. The money's mine. I saved it and otherwise it came out of a bank. It ain't his."

Jack ignored her. "If they search and find counterfeit money on her, it could be deep shit. They're on alert for the marijuana and meth and these days for illegals going back and forth."

"She probably hasn't got enough for a drug buy, if that's what you're getting at," Kate said.

"That's right," Winona said. "It's survival money. It ain't counterfeit. And I told you, Bud won't have nothing to do with them."

Gene said, "I could take Travis along with Chris. Or I bet Marlene could get off early and ride with you. Speaking of shit, this is the shit she knows."

Kate said, "Gene, please hush."

Gene stood straight with his back to them, staring out the window.

"They're not going to check us going into Canada," she said to Jack. "And if I have to, I'll say I gave her a ride, that's all. There's a research station near Yahk. Scientists travel for research. The car's got the gear in it."

"Research?" Jack said. Crossing his arms, he leaned away a little. His head was bathed in sunlight. The streaks of gray in his hair glimmered. His eyes were bright against his dark skin, his lips set, his expression telling her that he saw she had closed upon a resolution from which it would be hard to shake her. This mode of exchange, each of them measuring themselves by the reaction of the other, was a long-established custom they had of flushing out conclusions. "Rechercher," he said. He picked up his coffee mug, then set it back down, and looked at her directly. "To seek. You are seeking what, now?"

Also, she and Jack sometimes found points of triangulation for the divisions between them, which at this moment was Winona, yet Kate felt a momentary brightening at the question, flying at her from an unexpected quarter. "I picked her up last night. I have to see what I started to the end. I can't just walk away. Look," she said, softening. "The game's in Sandpoint. That's almost half way to Yahk. Travis has to be dropped off at the high school. You catch a nap, drop your vouchers off after you take Travis, then go on up to Sandpoint. It's the same direction, right? I'll meet you there. It's no big deal."

"Ordinarily, it wouldn't be," Jack said.

Turning to Winona, Kate said, "So, do you understand? If we're questioned at the border, I'm just somebody who picked you up. I don't know you from Adam."

"You're right, you don't," Winona said. Her eyes floated like pale blue balloons in the center of bright paint. "But Adam and the Lord and all the rest of them in the Holy Host know I ain't worth shit. I'm guilty as sin. Any time you want, just throw me out and run me down so I can keep on serving them the way I like."

Jack turned a pair of steely eyes on Winona. Gene, who was rattling the plates as he placed them in the cupboard, whistled through his teeth.

"Gene!" Kate said.

"Okay," Gene said.

"There's Bud," Jack said.

"That's the reason to get her out of here now."

Winona moved in her chair, lifting her hands, then dropping them to her lap.

Now Jack stared hard at Kate. "You're not going anywhere without our being damn sure he's nowhere out there to see you."

"Fine," she said.

What they arranged was for Gene to go first to check the road and wrecking yard, and wait for Kate, and once Kate was on her way, Jack would follow to the highway. Kate would deposit Winona in Yahk, and return and meet Jack at Travis's basketball game. She and Jack got up from the table, loaded Winona's duffle bag in the Subaru, and put in the sleeping bag and blankets. Since Winona had trailed behind them, Kate put her in the car, along with her purse. Gene set out in his pickup. Jack walked off down the lane toward the shed, and Kate got in the car to start the engine to keep Winona warm. Winona sat stock still, staring forward into the trees. When Jack returned, driving his ATV with its trailer, Kate got out of the car and watched as he backed in between the Subaru and his pickup. He stepped up on the truck's running board, loosed the tarp from the elk, and began working the elk sideways off the rack.

"Don't you need help with that?" Kate asked.

"I got it," he said, not looking at her. "Once I get the damn thing to the shed, I can winch it." He grunted as he tugged at the elk. "I got to skin it, too, and hang it."

Berg sat next to Kate, looking up at Jack and the elk attentively. The

ATV engine hummed. The elk slid. The body moved, and the head lolled over the side of the cab's roof, and just as the whole of it was about to topple off, Jack stepped down from the running board and pivoted, taking the weight on his shoulders, then eased the animal onto the trailer. Hanging off the front end of the trailer, the elk face seemed disconsolate in its death, the black snout grizzled with ice and the eyes glazed to white. Berg stood up, sniffing the air.

Jack turned to Kate. "I don't like this, what you're doing."

"I know."

He cut his eyes back at the Subaru where Winona sat, absolutely motionless. "There's no reason to believe a damn word that woman says."

"I know, Jack."

He leveled on Kate again. "She's crazy."

"Anybody'd be crazy living with him."

"You'd have to be crazy to start with. To be honest, Kate, you're pissing me off."

"Jack, for us this is nothing."

"Look," he said. "This is a mistake."

"Charity is never a mistake, Jack."

He squinted at her, then stepped over the ATV to straddle it and twisted the grip, making the engine burble. "Wait for me on the highway."

As he drove off, the elk's rear hooves, frozen close together, made a furrow behind the trailer. Berg followed, trotting with her nose up. They made a parade, the ATV, the man on it and the dog behind, and the dead thing in the trailer passing through the gateway under Travis's basketball hoop with its frosted net and plowing in the snow past the horse corral toward the shed. Through the trees, the sun gleamed against the snow on the tool shed's roof wherein the elk would be hung.

*　*　*

The Subaru emerged from the shadows into the light as the county road passed along a southeastern exposure of the mountainside. The town of Bayview lay below at the southern extreme of Lake Pend Oreille. Long pennants of fog floated above the town, fashioning a vague, cubist geometry of gray and black out of the industrial buildings, files of large Quonsets, and heavy equipment. Dozers, trucks, and cranes lined the docks, while barges and ships painted navy gray were anchored just off shore. A navy research center was based there, cordoned off by government-grade chain link and razor wire. In its turn-of-the-century days, the town had been a logging camp and lime processing center. The lime had been shipped out by steamboat to the Northern Pacific's railhead at the town of Hope. There were still vestiges of two towns way up to the north and over on the east side of the lake—Hope and East Hope. Near them was the site of Kullyspell House, the first white establishment, built by the Canadian David Thompson in 1809. Before that, the Kalispel and Kootenai people had maintained seasonal fish camps on the shores of the lake.

To the west of Bayview and on the edge of a vast flood plain, in what was now Farragut State Park, the barracks and command facilities had been installed for the navy in 1942, and FDR himself had visited it on one of his top-secret tours. According to lore, Eleanor Roosevelt, while flying back East from Seattle the year before and knowing that her husband sought a secure training base close to the Pacific, had spotted the big lake flashing in the mountain trench. It came to be yet another radical design born of a distant sighting and then a twitch back in Washington, D.C. The lake had been considered well enough out of range of Japanese bombers, hard to hone in on, and thus strategic, a place of heavy cover in which to keep big secrets. What was called the Acoustic Research Detachment remained in Bayview because of the size of the lake and its depth—143 miles long, as wide as 6 miles, and in one sink over 1200 feet deep. Scaled-down submarines were still deployed, testing camouflage systems, sonar detection, and underwater echoic triangulation—a methodology tricked out from the language of whales. The computerized models of sea-bottom topography generated by the angulation of echoic sound had been advanced here. Kate and Abby were employing such maps in their research and, often enough, Kate had thought it a peculiar irony to live so far out in the hinterland and yet right next to a source of the technology. The naval research was still secret, and extravagantly financed . . . support barges, scale-model submarines, launching docks, endless stores of diving equipment and hardware, cutting-edge communications equipment, elaborate Defense Department–grade computer systems, and high-priced consultants whose numbers now included, she remembered with a light jolt, Richard Troop. She'd forgotten to tell Jack about Troop.

She slowed for the corner that took her around the edge of a hill and glanced out her window at the silver ground fog. Through an opening, she glimpsed a patch of steel gray lake. Winona's face . . . attractive enough beneath the garish makeup, with its aquiline nose, sharply defined jaw and chin . . . was framed by it, and then by the black and gray buildings. In a moment, dark green trees and white snow took over again, rushing by the window. They passed a massive house under construction. Winona had her feet close together, knees drawn high, and her purse on her lap. She displayed not a flicker of interest in her surroundings. These days, the civilian Bayview was supported by summer people, who'd begun to appear in all the niches and to cavort on the edges of the research base. Increasingly, they joined forces with the California people who came and built million dollar homes on the lake to the south, Lake Coeur d'Alene and docked their pricey boats in Dalton Bender's slips. The Germans were coming, too. Soon, it would all be the same, the rich taking over the Panhandle, finding a place of refuge on one lake or another.

Kate had dived in Lake Pend Oreille. It was murky at depth, dark and cold. She had peered through the windows of a train that had derailed off a trestle back in the twenties and now lay on the lake bottom. Once, she'd discovered what she'd thought were human remains lodged in the slime against the roof of the upside-down locomotive. A school of bass flicked away from her lantern and went out the side window, and she saw the bones, two sets of ribs, dark, blunted, picked clean by scavengers, and filled with mystery. Yet her best thoughts of the lake remained luminous. She'd come over here with Jack; they, too, in their own way, seeking a refuge. They'd met in Seattle, where he was attending graduate school and working as a bank teller. She was a postdoctoral fellow at the University of Washington, conducting research in Puget Sound and southeast Alaska. They married, spent their first year together in Seattle, and then lived here through several hard years of building a house, having children, and making ends meet in the place that had seemed a wonder . . . radiant, wild, blue, cold. She'd traced a loop over the years . . . working up here on a fish count long ago, filled with hope, and now hiring herself out for another fish count down in Dworshak . . . the same work, but it had devolved into a casual exercise while she pursued a darker dream. The loop in her life was laced with the pathways of the intricate DNA as it tracked through the creatures:

Yellow perch.

Black crappie.

Bluegill.

Brown bullhead.

Large-mouth bass.

Brown, kamloops, bull trout, rainbow, brook, and also the hybrid, opportunistic trout.

Mountain whitefish.

Lake Superior whitefish, a marauding transplant.

Kokanee, the prized, secretive, landlocked salmon.

And what once had come to these parts, the several species of anadromous salmon.

The road descended the mountain and swung around a long curve. Chunks of ice slammed against the undercarriage. They passed behind a stand of trees and then broke into a clearing that overlooked the town. The lake was ringed by mountains. Kate glimpsed the clumps of woods and the blue glacier-scoured slopes dropping precipitously to the shimmering water. The vista always raised in Kate a strong melancholy, a longing to be ever and ever more exactly just where she was.

Winona still gazed ahead.

"You'd better scrunch down now," Kate said. "So it looks like there's only one of us."

Winona obeyed, slinking her body low so that the top of her head was even with the window sill.

They entered the woods on the mountain's south side and descended to the asphalt and into a diaphanous ground fog that floated just above the car. The road had been plowed since their drive the opposite way last night. They came out on the Rathdrum Prairie. Kate was checking all the turnouts and side roads, although for a reason she couldn't quite place—some sense of her advantage, maybe, gained from having Jack and Gene nearby—she didn't really feel afraid of Bud, not so long as they faced off here in the open. Ahead, she saw the stop sign, the intersection with Highway 95, and the black shape that as she approached formed itself into Gene's truck with its hood up.

She pulled over and switched off her engine. "Okay," she said, looking at Winona, who revolved her head and stared back blankly. "I'll be a minute. Stay down." She got out, taking her keys with her, and found Gene draped over the radiator with his feet dangling above the ground and his head stuck deep at the side of the engine. "Gene?"

"Fuel pump." His voice echoed resonantly in the compartment. He snaked back out and lowered the hood, then stretched up a Bungee strap from his bumper and slipped its end into the eyehook bolted onto the hood. "Bud's got the rig and the car parked out in front of his yard. I remembered that I'm due for a fuel pump in this heap, so I went in and asked. Those two are in there, sassy with their butts hanging over the stools." He balanced on one foot and scratched the back of his shin with the heel of his boot.

Kate looked back down the road.

Gene came next to her. "You could just do what she said, dump her here. Give her a coat and put her out with her bag of money. Somebody else'll pick her up. It's not that cold and it's not like she doesn't have anywhere to go. Her house is down the lane behind the wrecking yard."

It was cold enough, and damp. Kate judged that it was thirty-four or thirty-five degrees, just warm enough for the pungent scent of the ponderosas to penetrate the chill. The ice on the shoulder of the road had a skiff of thaw on its top. Just across the ditch a pine limb abruptly swung up as its load of snow slipped off. She could hear clumps of snow thudding softly as they fell from limbs all through the woods, a music shifting from the near to the inaudible. In the car, the pale, half-moon shape of Winona's forehead hovered above the dashboard. Now she was watching.

"That'd be cruel." Kate pulled the hood of her Gortex coat up over her head.

"But Jack could be right about this," Gene said.

Kate looked at him narrowly.

Gene snorted. "Okay."

They stood looking down the shining road. Kate put her hands in her coat pockets and with the fingers of her left hand turned the little scrimshawed salmon she kept in there. The dot of a vehicle appeared, coming their way.

"Look," Gene said. "If she tries to mess with you, unload the bitch on the spot."

The vehicle approached . . . blue truck, canopy, and rack. Jack had taken off the canoe after the elk. The hum of the tires on the pavement dropped to a hiss as he slowed, eased over to the shoulder, and pulled up behind the Subaru. Next to her, Gene reached through the open window of his pickup to unlatch the door, then slid inside and pulled the door shut. The pickup roared. He leaned out the window and said, "Be careful."

Kate started toward Jack, now out of his truck. At her back, Gene's pickup snarled to the stop sign. She watched Jack's eyes following the bend of noise as Gene turned onto the highway and headed south. Then his eyes angled back to her. He stood with one knee slightly cocked so that his plaid coat flared out from his hip. His blue wool cap was pulled low on his brow. Kate passed her car where Winona remained hunched down.

"Gene says they're at the wrecking yard," she said when she came up to Jack.

The speckle in his eyes darkened, and he said, "It's a fucking bad idea."

Turning the salmon in her fingertips, Kate felt with her thumb the arch at its belly, carved to make it appear as if the fish were leaping a rapid. "Don't do this, Jack."

Jack rolled back to his heels. "Don't express my opinion?"

Nuthatches scratched around for stored-away seeds in the bark of a nearby ponderosa. Another clump of snow fell, thudding softly. Kate lifted her face, drawn to look past Jack at a snowy owl. The bird's appearance was startling . . . far from unknown here, yet unusual. It glided magnificently, sailing above the margin between woods and road, presumably scouting for rodents. The pale of its underside flashed the reflected white of the snow beneath.

"It's a mistake. Everything about that woman looks like trouble," Jack said.

Kate squared her shoulders. Jack reached up to push back his cap. The shadow of the owl flitted past their feet, and when she looked again it cupped its huge wings against a draft, soared and scooted away over the far trees.

Normally, she'd have displayed her interest in the owl, and remarked upon it, but Jack was intent. "If Bud finds out, even a year from now, there's no telling what he'll do. He lives in a different world. Do you understand? He plays by a different set of rules. He has contempt for what we value. To us, his world is upside-down. To him, we've got it all backwards."

She clung to the specifics already named, the points like pieces of bone: the team bus Travis needed to be taken to, the basketball game they would attend, Jack's devotion to Travis's games, his fatigue greater than hers, the elk that needed to be skinned and hung, the vouchers he needed to deliver, the winter they were entering and the time it would soon give them together, and the woman she felt obliged to deliver to safety. Jack's objections, his manner of preeminence of which she knew he was hardly aware, and her resistance created a turmoil of feeling that belonged to their history together, to sexual positioning, the heat of the flesh they shared.

She brushed her hair from the side of her face, then reached under his coat and held his skin at the ribs. "But we've already lied to him and given her safe haven. What's the difference? I'll get her across the border and that's it. It's a short ride. It's nothing for us. For her, it could be everything. I'll call Dan Painter tonight and tell him what I've done. Or give me an hour's start and call him yourself, if it'll make you feel better."

"This pisses me off."

"I know."

"Why not wait for Marlene and get her help?"

"I'm taking her advice."

"You're awfully proud in what you call charity. What if I ask you plainly not to do this?"

"I'm doing it. You can help by allowing it."

The ice and gravel crunched under Jack's feet as he shifted his weight. He reached out and held her shirt where the top button was and turned his hand so that the backs of his knuckles lay against her throat. He then slid his hand around to the back of her neck to hold her. The exchange was far more complicated than when he'd first come home this morning, like an echo breaking up into its pieces—his smell, his force, his anger a little dangerous seeming, and her incipient, rising sexual force, which if she hadn't felt herself closing against him, she still wouldn't have minded letting loose. She leaned her bodily war into him, snuggling against his shoulder, this affection of their touch a ritual they practiced even when they were at loggerheads. Jack had the smell of the kitchen on him now, the sausage along with the trees and oil and sweat, the blood and hide of the elk, the wind.

"Why? What is it?"

She didn't answer, but just hugged him, wishing this wasn't happening. She thought that even at this moment if he'd stop crowding her and said, Okay, we'll call Marlene and get her to pick up Travis, and pull my truck onto a side road. The hell with it. I'll say nothing more, but just ride along with you. She'd probably have agreed to that now.

"Damn it, I fucking hope it's not a big deal," he said.

"It's going to be okay, Jack," she said. "I love you."

"Yeah. Me too. I love you."

She drew away, went to the Subaru, got in, drove to the stop sign, and looked in her rearview mirror. Jack stood rooted, looking far more formidable than he could have imagined in his flared coat and floppy hat. She waved to him. He raised his hand to waist level and flicked his index finger at her, pointing. It was his habit of understatement, the finger always seeming to indicate something in particular. She pulled onto the highway, going north. Far ahead, a line of black hung above the ridgeline, as distinct as if it were drawn in charcoal. Kate looked over at Winona.

Winona looked back with an off-kilter expression. "Can I sit up now?"

"Go ahead."

"Thank you," Winona said. "My brother won't believe it's me. I've been gone so long. Maybe he'll drive me to see my mother. She used to be a housekeeper at the Hotel Lake Louise in Banff. It's some place."

"Do you know your brother's phone number and your friend's?"

Winona leaned back against the headrest and stared straight ahead. The surrounding snow whitened her skin and made the rouge and eye markers look like garish smudges of decay. "Do you think I'm so stupid, to be going there and not know those?"

"I don't suppose you have a cell phone," Kate said.

"Are you kidding? One more way for the government to keep track of me?"

The highway had been plowed again and sanded and its dampness hissed against the car's undercarriage. The low-lying mist had burned away and Kate notched up her speed, thinking that if Winona had a cell phone she could have got her to call ahead . . . among other reasons, to test her truthfulness. She rued once again that she and Jack didn't have cell phones, either.

Winona grew talkative, chattering away in her piercing tone: "Bud has a sister who's part Nigger or Samoan. Different fathers. Lily's her name. Funny, for a gumbo, huh? But it's Bud who always took care of Zack. Even when his mama was alive, Zack was too much for her. Bud took him. When he came back out of the army, he took Zack and brought him here because he said his mama wasn't strong enough. Bud respected his mama in her weakness, but it was too hard for her to keep Zack in line. Zack has a purity of soul that his mama gave him, but it's Bud who let him keep it. Hard as he is, it's Bud's glory, what he done for his brother."

What Kate remembered was Zack's addled expression, his fascination with the monitor, his hugeness, his happiness, and his stench.

"I was raised Four Square Gospel," Winona said. "But for thirteen years I've been a member of the Lord's Weapon Universal Christian, which is nondenominational. Anybody is welcome so long as they accept the Lord Jesus as their savior and pledge themselves to protect the purity of the white race. People don't understand it ain't racist. It's separatist. There's a difference. They gave me pride and helped keep Zack burned clean. Bud's left them now because Pastor Sutter is too old and lost his edge and can't keep the young men in line, he says, but it's a division between us. I love Pastor and the people, and I take Zack to church there, but Bud won't go any more. God directed me to leave him. He told me to go north. Look at this. The Lord spun me around and left me in a ditch for you to find and get me there. God wanted me back north where I came from, home in the wilderness since I'm bereft."

They passed a road sign:

SANDPOINT 20 MILES
BONNER'S FERRY 52 MILES
CANADA 84 MILES

Kate turned her wrist to see her watch—10:15. North of Sandpoint, the road would slow the travel, but they should be in Yahk in two hours.

"Zack's like a lamb, the gentlest creature in the world," Winona said. "Even though he could break your neck just like that." She leaned in Kate's direction and dryly snapped her fingers, then dropped her hand back to her purse. "Bud beats us because he can't help it. That's his cross, the fury of the world that's resting on his shoulders. He that loveth chasteneth. A rod for the fool's back, and me and Zack are his fools, that's for sure." Winona pressed back into the seat and spoke with a kind of nasal jubilation. "But I'll be born again in the north!"

Kate was fascinated by Winona's face, by what she guessed a man would regard as beauty beneath the makeup. She thought she could understand how Winona's delicacy might provoke the desire to crush it, but for Kate the true fascination in Winona's beauty lay in the way her slightest gesture or utterance—coming out of her mouth like a kazoo, like a string of caws, all nose and roof of the mouth—ruined the effect. The very sound of the voice was like another wound. It was as if Winona were a living relic dedicated to the meaninglessness of her beauty.

"It's always hard to leave home."

"I'm going to miss the others and Zack most of all. I'm leaving just when they're having their congress with folks coming in from all over for sermons and potluck. It's being in their company that I'll miss. It hurts." Her voice broke. When Kate looked she saw Winona's eyes filling with tears.

"It's hard to leave people behind," Kate said.

Winona said, "But there'll always be somebody to put the hooks on a whore like me."

The road swung leftward, passing out of a clearing. They would stay in the woods now and ride the tailings of mountains until the road came out again at the head of the lake and they crossed over to Sandpoint. Long shadows of trees flicked across the roadway and stroboscopically over the car's windshield. "I'm sorry you feel that way," Kate said.

She had driven by the Lord's Weapon Compound a few times on the back road near Hayden. Rising from the dense stand of trees near the roadside was a bright, heraldic red-and-blue sign with crossed swords and a medieval helmet, and the words LORD'S WEAPON UNIVERSAL CHRISTIAN. The compound had razor wire, a steel gateway, and a guard station on the entry lane. At the top of the lane sat a scattering of buildings, including the sanctuary with a cross on its roof. Over everything rose an observation tower, spindly legged, its platform and roof visible from the road. Once, she'd seen a man in a black uniform there, holding a rifle. The look of the place was archaic, a play fortress that inspired the self-appointed pastor, Sutter, to spread his obscenities and the flock to act out its perversities. She had wondered which weapons were stored there, allowing the place to live up to its name, and which supplies—an underground fuel storage tank, maybe bunkers filled with dynamite, fertilizer, kerosene, nitroglycerine, anthrax, and all manner of contraband. Maybe they kept the heavy munitions hidden elsewhere. As a biologist, she certainly understood that the detail of behavior, guided first by the enigmatic kernel of genetic history within, was always capable of wayward twists. But what weird tracks the lives of the people in the compound chased, and within what margins such lives driven by outrage were contained, remained mysterious to her.

She chose her words carefully, "I'm sorry to see anyone brought to where you are?"

"I told you," Winona said. "God brought me here. He lays out the path. Wounded as I am, all I have to do is follow. He touched His hand to me."

At the bottom of a hill they crossed a creek and the metal surface of the bridge sang under the Subaru's wheels. As they ascended, the woods came close upon the roadway, broken sometimes by great fists of dark, thrusting rock, and the rock sometimes clutched by the massive root tangles of trees, ice-bedecked and exposed by the cut the road made. Kate's own religious upbringing had been strong enough to make Winona's need for inspired reasons understandable, and for Kate to know that Winona would not be easily shaken from that.

"Once, my sister hired a man and a woman to run an intercession on me," Winona said. "But Bud found out. They kidnapped me, but Bud tracked them down and took me back and told them next time he'd shoot them on sight. It's because then God wanted me to be where I was."

Unable to resist, Kate said, "God? God did?"

"Bud is the hardness of God's world, the metal in it. He left the Lord's Weapon because they'd turned soft, you see. He's got his own leaderless cell."

Kate felt a chill. One such group she'd heard about was called the Form, an offshoot of the Lord's Weapon suspected of robbing two Brink's cars and of murdering a Jewish newspaper editor. It was a secret organization, dispersed across the American Northwest and western Canada. One of its leaders had been cornered in a shack in the woods by over fifty FBI agents. He'd held them off for a week, but then the shack was besieged. His body was found riddled with bullets. Another group, the Phinehas Priesthood, had bombed an abortion clinic and newspaper office in Spokane. Two of its members had murdered a gun dealer in Arkansas and were believed to have associations with Timothy McVeigh, the Oklahoma City bomber. "You mean like the Form," Kate said. "Or the Phinehas Priesthood. Splinter groups."

"It ain't the Form. It ain't Phinehas. It ain't the Aryan Republican Army, neither."

—And that one, too, Kate remembered—held responsible for a string of bank robberies and train derailments.

"The Form don't exist no more and it weren't no splinter. It got cancelled out by the killing," Winona said. Once again, her voice took on a disembodied quality. "What I'm talking about is what you'd have left if you took the Lord's Weapon and boiled it down to stock. You'd have the pit of it, the consommé like you gave me last night. What is that word? Is it like consummation? Like in marriage? The consummation comes when you conceive the child. It's called the Harrow or the Brotherhood of Zealot. But that's Bud's. I got my own consummation awaiting the rapture, thank the Lord."

Kate didn't reply, feeling as if she'd just flipped over a big chinook on a bar and found it eaten out on its underside, teeming with maggots and creeping grubs.

At the crest of the hill, the road angled and dropped toward the lake. A vista of woods dropping low into the huge glacial trench and of distant ridges opened up before them. The road swung and ran alongside the lake for a time, and then across the two-mile bridge. Patches of ice and twining dark water stuttered between the guard rails. The car came up on a file of log trucks, and Kate slowed to keep her distance. Another truck appeared behind her, pressing near to her bumper. Some distance away, northward, ran the railway bridge, a newer incarnation of the old version from which the train had plummeted decades ago.

They entered Sandpoint and passed through the fringes of the residential area. Sidewalks were heaped with snow and people were out with their shovels. Snow was on everything, the hoods of parked cars, shrubs, posts, railings, roofs, the fancy gables and turrets of the Lakeside Inn, gussied-up for tourist trade. Snow encrusted the loads of log trucks that crawled along the street. She still had trucks in front of her, more to her side, and the one bearing down on her backside. As it was above freezing, water dripped and flowed everywhere. She pulled into a Chevron station, parked next to the pumps, and got out to refuel the car. Trucks roared and clanked as they passed.

From where she stood, she could see ahead to the intersection where the highway resumed its northward course. Across the highway, a vacant lot was filled with phalanxes of empty log trucks. Knots of men stood in front of the tractors, powwowing after hauling the last loads of the season out of the woods. Not far up the highway more trucks idled, waiting to dump their loads at the mill, and more yet bulled their way out of the highlands. The last of Jack's logs were up in the woods not far from here, scattered like pickup sticks around Jim Bliss's truck. There was a stripped-away look to the buildings where the drivers had gathered. She turned to look northward beyond the station. In the far distance a dark cloud bank seeped over the ridge line, then lowering her gaze, she spotted a phone booth at the far edge of the lot.

The nozzle clicked off. She walked up to Winona's door, opened it, and said, pointing, "There's a phone. Call your brother and your friend while I pay the bill." She watched as Winona minced to the phone booth and then went inside.

An attendant with a grease smudge on his cheek took her card. In a corner a TV was turned on while the picture showed a beefy man with a small crowd at his back beating upon a window. Within were worried looking counters and monitors. Here, the attendant snapped her card in his machine, took its impression, and grinned as he slid the receipt to her. "Chads," he said. "They're counting chads."

6

U

HE STOOD WATCHING SOOTY SHEARWATERS, three of them in tandem skimming low in a trough between swells. Their long, arched wings twitched to hold the draft that funneled within the banks of water as they prowled the glassy bottom for food, what he remembered to be small crustaceans and fish. The birds skidded along the trough away from the ship, the first, the second, and the third, and turned in the distance, each floating upwards and hovering for an instant. They then sailed back to the ship and, using the ship as a baffle, wheeled and dropped into another trough.

Considering that the season had passed deep into autumn and that the shearwaters should have flown south along their ancestral flyways weeks ago, he wondered what chance they had of becoming a migratory anomaly, and if they were somehow attuned to this weather which was so irregular—too warm. More likely, the birds would soon die in the concise light and ferocious cold and he felt a twinge of sadness for them. Their motion he found mesmerizing, the looping rhythm, the stitching sewn in the air against the heave of the dark sea. The birds ran their foraging oval over and over again, and he was grateful that the finest details of the motion—the play of the eddying wind, the shiftiness of the ship's hull, and of the glorious, mobile sea against the wing blades and bodies of the birds—were beyond his comprehension. It was enough to be soothed in watching at this moment, like staring into a fire.

A short, compactly built man of Chinese descent, he wore glasses thick as bottle-bottoms. His cropped black hair stuck straight out, pale freckles washed from his temples to his cheekbones, and his face was round and distracted-looking, but contrarily his jaw line ran heavily beneath the soft flesh, a bone and musculature made to lock down and never let go.

"Call me U," he would sometimes say to strangers. Even now after the years of it, he was still amused by the confusion it caused.

A prestidigitator of the world!

He stood at a side window high on the bridge of the drill ship, the Norsmar *Bering*. There was a faint, ceaseless hum that he felt more through his legs than he heard—the ship's engine and the motors driving the positioning system and the thousand-foot stem cutting its way into the earth beneath the sea bottom. It was just past one, full in the heart of the day, such as it was, abbreviated and lit by the angular, aluminum-colored sunlight that penetrated the November overcast. Outside, the air temperature hovered just above freezing. The ship lay in the Chukchi Sea a hundred miles north of the *Bering* Strait, and west by east slightly nearer to the Lisbourne Peninsula of Alaska than to Siberia's Chukotsk Peninsula: 177 N 19′, 168 W 00′ . . . very near one corner of the manic grid by which the wobbly planet was marked. A while ago, the captain had told U that a storm was approaching.

"Something dire may be sucked up inside it," the captain had said. A tall man with a Louisiana drawl, the captain then entered the crux of his conflict, turning his words softly in his mouth like lozenges as he informed U. "No matter what headquarters wants," he said, "we may have to pull the shaft and beat it out of here. Could be, we should be pulling it now."

To the east, the cloud cover appeared as a gray, luminous, upside-down dish that ran parallel to the sea. Along the length of the horizon lay a blue slit the color of a robin's egg. The sea was a darker gray than the clouds, the water broken in lines jagged as lightning bolts by the white froth that articulated the crests of the fifteen-foot swells. Out of the distance, another ship had appeared, first as an emanation like a nib rising into the northeastern corner of the surreal sky. Then it became a tiered thing like a white wedding cake rocking in the sea, the *Hermes*, a 150-foot research vessel, advancing upon its rendezvous. Years ago, U had been aboard the *Hermes* in the company of the woman now being brought to board the *Bering*. It seemed odd, the convergence at sea of strands from his past: she sent up from California to inventory the work on the *Hermes* and he helicoptered from Siberia to the drill ship.

He was a practitioner in international law, a division head in his corporation, ZAQ, but truly, money was his game. In the old days, he tracked it. Now, he herded it. What once was wild had become a domestic, and he its proprietor. The digits in the accounts were like farmed fish made out of egg and sperm stripped from their wild sisters and brothers, kept in incubating trays, transferred to pens, and as fry moved from those pens to larger pens cordoned off in the water, fed— their animus for long sea journeying kept muted—later withdrawn by mechanized nets, gutted, cleaned by machine, and dyed red, a monotonous meat loaded into crates to be trucked off. U regretted what the changed quality of money marked in his life, the inward flattening of his old fascinations, the loss of jeopardy and pleasure of the chase.

The *Hermes* loomed nearer, carving a turn that would bring its portside abeam of the *Bering*. Its superstructure bristled with antennae and satellite dishes and the ship pitched as it cut hard into the swells. U heard the captain murmur behind him, then glimpsed the first mate's arm rising to take the mike from its hook above the control panel. The mate spoke into the intercom, and U heard both the fullness of the voice here on the bridge and its ghost narrowed to a crackle in the speakers down below as the mate directed the deckhands to prepare the lines. The deckhands wore heavy, orange flotation jackets, gloves, and blue stocking caps whitened by spume turned to ice as it flew through the air. Two of them bent to coil the heavy rope leaders.

On the approaching ship, three deckhands had positioned themselves along the rail, while behind them appeared a fourth figure dressed in a bright yellow survival suit. U lifted the binoculars from the window sill to look. He recognized the way the woman balanced herself and the lantern-shape of her face within the yellow hood. Since learning of their appointment two days ago, he'd been thinking of the hazard of her person, her daring, brilliance, and mendacity. Seeing her caused these qualities of her nature to rise into an unsettling bone dance. In one hand, she held a case the color of the metal sky.

Doctor Sophia Kopat. Always the Doctor.

He set down the binoculars and ran his gaze along the *Bering*'s portside, seeking out the shearwaters whose feeding loop was about to be sundered.

Sophia Kopat was a world-class deep diver, a tenacious researcher, and ZAQ's head scientist. She'd been directed to pass to him the science crew's findings and her recommendations for their disposition. For his part, U had already secured the papers . . . actual, heavy papers, the originals of signed contracts, letters of intent, findings, lease agreements. Some were old ones from thirty years back that he'd hammered fresh boilerplates onto or inserted new conditions. It was a cache he had . . . government stamped, ornately watermarked, sometimes beribboned, irreplaceable documents. He had also made his own notes, as was required. Transmission of all these to his headquarters by any means short of hand-to-hand was considered unsafe, and so for the time being they were kept in his cabin in an attaché with a coded lock.

Included among them were blueprints for tying the Siberian oil fields to pipelines—one to China, one to the sea of Japan, another a seabed pipeline in the Chukchi and thence across northwestern Alaska to Prudhoe Bay. He also had options for service and transport in three recently emerged fields, two in the oil-rich Caspian states—Kazakhstan and Azerbaijan—and the third the vast tar sands in Alberta, Canada. During the past months, U had journeyed to Alberta and then shunted back and forth across the old U.S.S.R., down to Washington, D.C., and back again to Russia, where he'd met with ministers and struck the agreements to secure ZAQ's position in a political bedlam. He'd done this in the company of Carl Braun, the perpetually vigilant security agent who now awaited Sophia and him in the *Bering*'s officers' mess.

Even the thought of the machinations—new terminals in Siberia, another in the Aleutians, one in the Chinese city of Daqing, and in the port of Nakhodka, test drilling in the Chukchi Sea which the *Bering* was now doing, a proposed pipeline out of Alberta, in the Caspian Sea the ferocious battle being fought over the routing of yet another pipeline to feed the Atlantic and Mediterranean, and, here, the metal stitching proposed to be laid to Alaska, all the lines loading up with flow to be shipped to slake the ever-deepening thirst of the Japanese and the Koreans, to please the insatiable Americans and to placate the rising demands of the Chinese (his own people, after a fashion)—all merely deepened his ennui.

He was bored by the numbers, the dense clouds of detail, all the tiny twists and crevices in the law, the obscurities of international agreements to be tamped down, the Byzantine condition of unending siege, the personality cults, Mafia-like apparats, the oligarchs who following the Soviet collapse had survived to hazard and then to solidify their positions, and the tumultuous run of money like oil itself to the chutes. He had the sense that everything attached to petroleum was in an endgame, that the world of dwindling oil was like a lowering eyelid that would soon close just as certainly as would the blue slit in the sky before him, and thus that all this activity was nothing more than a terminal florescence, a spasm in the death-throe that merely aped in miniature the sensuous, long-loping pursuit of all of the past century after the black ooze. Perhaps it was being fifty-five years old, a stage of life that made him feel like an ancient soul for whom everything was in recorso.

Last night in the Siberian city of Steklyányigórod, when he was finally given his liberty by the security agent, he'd received a message from Sophia: "There is a breach. Arising from a person you will remember as Kate McDuff. Breaches must be eliminated."

The essential Sophia lay in the message's insubordination, terseness, and condescending use of imperatives—will and must. What was meant by breach? What had been breached? What did she mean—eliminated?

The full name of the woman he remembered from documents: Dr. Katherine Xaviera McDuff. And her married name: DeShazer.

He'd had a passing and, for him, momentous acquaintance with her on the same voyage long ago aboard the *Hermes*. He held her in his memory as a talisman at the portal to a world he'd never entered. He'd been infatuated by her independence and savvy, the way she courted chaos by standing on principle, and the way she provoked the wrath of her presumptive mentor—Sophia—when she stood her down in the presence of the crew over a diving incident. He might have loved Kate in the way a man could have of creating an unapproachable image out of a woman. Now, she, too, rose into the convergence out of the old years.

U remembered Kate's litheness of limb, the compact swimmer's body, the bob of auburn hair that flicked over her face, her quickness, spunk, and competence, her flashing green eyes, the courtly curl of her Alabama accent, and her devastating charm. At that time, she'd been engaged to DeShazer, and U had even relished the husband-to-be, about whom he knew nothing except that he must have been somebody who could contain the vigor of the woman.

He remembered being in Sophia's cabin and the wild pitch of the *Hermes*, its creak, the booming at its hull, the jiggling of specimen bottles in a crate. He remembered the berth, the coarse blankets, starched sheets, and the way the foot and sideboards offered shaky holdfasts against the ship's roll, and Sophia, a long-limbed, equine beauty. Her pale skin lay like a translucent laminate over a dust color, and her protuberant, dark eyes were glossy. He remembered her fury over being humiliated by her subordinate, the fight lodged in her muscles, and the burning hoop of her electricity.

7

The Ruin

"MAYBE I NEVER HAD A BROTHER IN CRANBROOK. That's what you're thinking, right?" Winona laughed giddily and threw her head back. "Well," she said, straightening herself. "But I used to. I talked to his machine. Her machine. His voice, but she picked it up. I mean he left his voice behind on the machine and I was talking to his voice and then her voice came on and said, 'Winona?' She knew my voice. It was her voice and she knew mine, like she was expecting me to call. How could she do that?"

Winona laughed again and went on. "'He's not here. Where is he?' she says. I say, 'What? I'm calling him there. How would I know?' 'Why are you calling here now after all these years,' she says. 'Exactly,' I say. 'So how would I know where he is. I'm looking for him.' 'Me, too,' she says. 'He owes me money. I got daycare to pay, the power bill, and bald tires on my car. We're estranged.' 'You mean you're divorced?' I say. 'Daycare? Kids? You've got kids? I'm an aunt?' 'Yes, we've got kids,' she says. 'Where have you been, huh? We're not divorced yet. Estranged,' she says. She said those things like it was nothing, the words just popping out of her. That means they're strangers? Estranged? Then she says, 'Winona? It's you? Well, fuck you.' Who the fuck does she think she is?"

There were aisles of slush alongside the highway and here and there chunks of packed-down snow in the lanes. The car swung to and fro according to the heaving in the roadbed from years of freeze and thaw.

"I am not a stranger to Bud." Winona took a handful of corn nuts from the bag Kate had bought at the gas station, pushed them into her mouth, crunched down noisily, and went on talking through the bits. "How could we be strangers when I've had his balls in my hands? Know what I mean?"

Few cars had appeared on the highway, but log trucks were passing the other way, emerging from the woods and heading south for the mills. One went by in a rush of clanking metal and slapped a sheet of slush across the Subaru's windshield. Momentarily blinded, Kate switched on the wipers and held fast to the wheel. The windshield cleared. A libidinous vision flashed through her mind: the feel of Jack's balls, the two oval glands hung loosely beneath his stalk, and the scent of his breath filling her mouth way back to the throat, his power in lovemaking at once passionate and circumspect. Everything in his being bore upon the act and yet at the same time he held himself back even as the act transpired, which was supremely erotic. "What are you trying to say?" she asked.

"She says he's not in Cranbrook. I think he's gone to Creston."

"He? Your brother?" Before them the ominous sky loaded up with black. "Yahk is where we're going. Did you call your friend?"

"Estranged, she said they were, the bitch. Wayne's wife," Winona said. "Me and Bud are not estranged. We're alienated. What it's like is a wall that drops, and you're left holding onto everything past and present. Balls, guns, junked cars, the smell of the grease on him, and tobacco juice, his fingers at you and his weight on top of you, and the weight of his dead Mama and his gumbo sister and his brother Zack on top of him, and all of them dead or alive are trying to fuck you. All I wanted was to be taken home safe to God and a family of believers. Is that asking too much? How long and hard do you have to look for that simple thing?"

—Forever, Kate thought. It's a life's worth of studying to find that.

She wondered where Winona had got that word, gumbo, a Southernism. "Where are your people from?"

"People!"

"Your family. Where'd they come from?"

"You don't have a future with a man like Bud," Winona said. "He's a mean sonofabitch, God forgive him. For the future you're behind the wall. But now I'm out there in the future I never imagined and I feel like less of a stranger to Bud because I can love him as somebody I don't have to fuck anymore. I honor my vows. Choice don't go that far."

Winona picked a few corn nuts out of the bag and crunched them decisively. "She's estranged from my brother, Ruth says. But she's a bigger whore than I ever was with her spray net and the seams in her nylons just so. She's a secretary. She made good money. My brother, Wayne, never was good enough for her. He's an electrician like our dad. He should reroute her wires, if you ask me. Ruth. Ruth, beloved of God, my ass. She was probably screwing her boss. She did this herself, I bet. Maybe she's got fat. I ain't estranged. All of life as it's touched by God's hand is sacred."

Winona poured corn nuts into her hand, shoved them into her mouth, and ground on them. Her pale and garish face, flecked around the mouth with bits of salt and corn dust, came near as she leaned toward Kate. "I don't talk like this to just anybody, you know," she said. She rocked back, lifted her purse with both hands, and thrust it toward Kate. "Know what this is? It's the skin off a buffalo ball." She burst into a raucous laugh. "It's a hand tooled buffalo ball Bud got me in Montana. It's got a buffalo on the side of it. See?"

Kate had already seen the incised figure bulged out by the purse's contents.

"Must've been a big sucker," Winona said. "Bud says you can get hats made out of them, too, at the Testicle Festival, and bull dicks made into boots. A nice place for a foot to be snuggled in, if you ask me." She settled back in her seat, cradled the purse in her lap, and stared straight through the windshield. "Gumbo means mixed, what we call niggers, mulattos, the pestilence upon the earth, but I was invented, if you really want to know. I've got no people now, only Jesus. I dwell in the midst of His thought where I was invented like a spark in the pure air so I could wait for the rapture."

Kate was struck once again by a realization she'd had before: Crazed as she might be, this woman like her husband was not stupid.

A truck passed. Kate cleared the windshield. Two more trucks appeared from behind a rise and went by in tandem. She clung to the wheel and strained to see through the white glaze, then found the road again arching leftward. Another truck appeared in her rearview mirror, slowly gaining on them. They went through Coburn, what looked to be mainly ghost town with its nibbled away core barely propped up by the old, declining industry. They passed a few houses. Up ahead lay the sawmill: towering heaps of sawdust, log stacks that dwarfed the processing plant, and loaded trucks parked in the lot. Snow. Snow over the stacks and stretching across the clearing into the trees. The sky had begun to spit more snow. Former business establishments were boarded up. One building had been burned and was sinking into the earth. A swathe of its rusted, corrugated tin roof draped downwards from a charred wall, outlining an image of collapse like what she'd seen so many times in her southern homeland. On the wall were an antique Coca Cola sign and a truncated file of pale red letters:

RGERS FRIES SHA

*   *   *

By her nature, as it had become, Kate felt drawn to wreckage—to the sunken train, to salmon at the far reach of their spawning run. Having consumed their stored-up fat in the upstream journey, then consuming their muscle, the fish lingered to haunt the redds they'd dug out in the gravel, and the depositions of roe and milt. Hunks of fin broke off the fish. Their jaws grew hooked and flesh fell away from their bellies. White fungus spread over them, cataracting their eyes. Their decaying bodies washed down the river, sometimes piling on the gravel bars and behind the snags. The smell of rot called in the carrion-eating birds, the big and the small dropping out of the sky to feast. The remainder of the meat and bone went in to feed the stream . . . eutrophication, it was called . . . the effect of sunlight hitting the dead.

When Jack had said—"*Rechercher*. To seek. You are seeking what now?"—he'd been knowingly probing the melancholy in her that seeped through her dispassion, her use of tools—dredge, cage, fish net, gaff, test tube and Petri dish, microscope, gas chromatograph, and the incisions of her computer into the numbers. Her melancholy was what was left to her of believing. It pulled her down to the chaotic heart of destruction where the demons shook loose from their order. Only there did the sense of a balancing mercy, filled with the breath of the dead, come alive to her.

The image of destruction had taken form in her dreams when she was a girl in Demopolis. It appeared as a man, slouched, lank, and tall. He wore a field coat, soiled trousers, mud-coated quarter-boots, and one spur. He had a ruddy face and bright black eyes. He was an incessant talker and his face would deepen in color and his eyes glitter the more feverishly as he spoke relentlessly of his tactics—the requirement that the cavalry be positioned here, the foot soldiers there, and the pincer action over there coming out of that foggy bottom, out of those woods across the tracks and into the plain—and of the rightness of the strategy—to burn, to carbonize, to keep the scrap of the South from breaking out of the whole loaf of the nation. He paced frenetically as he filled a room with his words, the solitary spur on his left boot ringing with every other step. A short time in his company left others exhausted. The venom with which his name was uttered by the men and women who came to church socials or fundraising teas was unforgettable.

The voices, soft and lilting, laced the air above the finger sandwiches and the wedges of pecan pie, and wound around the clicking teacups, then sharpened into daggers: He ripped out the tracks. He ordered the towns destroyed. He burned Atlanta to the ground. His soldiers dragged our women out of their parlors and raped them and then took their pleasure of the pantries. Under his command, our courthouse was burned, our foundry, our mansions. The anti-Christ, scorched earth, the horror! His soldiers billeted in our church and by day they went out to burn our cotton fields and gins.

Even Kate's father, as charitable as an Alabama Presbyterian could have been, regarded William Tecumseh Sherman as a devil. But after the Freedom Riders passed through the town of Demopolis in 1961, his politics moved several ticks leftward. Just when the entire South seemed to be swinging toward self-immolation, he delivered a sermon that rode the fine edge of what he believed his congregation would endure. His subject was the first principle of Calvinism—that, having sinned in the Garden, humankind is inherently corrupt.

His scriptures came from Mark: "For from within, out of the heart of man, proceed evil thoughts, adulteries, fornications, murders..."

And from II Timothy: "And that they may recover themselves out of the snare of the devil, who are taken captive by him at his will. This know also, that in the last days perilous times shall come..."

As always, Kate sat next to her mother several rows back from the front of the sanctuary. Just thirteen, yet knowing that something momentous was happening and that it had to do with beatings here and the killings that had been reported elsewhere, a fire-bombing in

Anniston, arrests in Mississippi, and with the hardening on people's faces, she listened as the church rang with her father's voice. From behind, the pews began to creak as the parishioners shifted uneasily. To one side, she saw an old man's bald head dip toward the man next to him. He whispered. She had heard her father speak guardedly of this man, Sam McKinney. His head came back and steadied, the eyes fixed on her father. Next to Kate, her mother was looking, too, and her body stiffened, and over on the other side, even her little brother stopped scribbling in the margins of the bulletin and looked up. Her father quoted Sherman's famous pronouncement: "War is cruelty. You cannot refine it. War is murder." And then, running straight into the face of his congregation's justifying Calvinism, and raising his arm and pointing over the people's heads southward and a little west downstream of the Black Warrior River where the black neighborhoods were, he said, "But either you give yourself to this cruelty and murdering and burning, or you do not. You can cleanse your life now. Understand that cruelty and hatred and heedless persecution and destruction by Christians are sins."

What a contingent in the congregation understood was that it had a vagrant in its midst, who himself seemed a little too much like General Sherman. Sam McKinney called the elders together for an "Election of Confidence," and Kate's father, seeing what was coming, resigned. The family moved to Birmingham where he came to be associated with the Quakers, Congregationalists, and the Fellowship of Reconciliation, and still, he received threats. Kate's mother received a letter denouncing him and, then, as much out of a loss of patience with her husband's willfulness as anything else, she took her children away for a year and a half to her parents in Arizona. It was 1963. From the distance, feeling that she'd been spirited away just when the eye of the storm touched down, Kate watched the newsclips and read about Bull Connor, the dogs turned on demonstrators, the fire hosings of children, church bombings, Martin Luther King in the Birmingham jail, and Bobby Kennedy's appearance as the second coming of the anti-Christ from the north. Years later, as a younger generation steadied the church's politics, the Demopolis congregation asked her father to return for an "interim," which turned into a three-year calling. Kate's mother, who had vowed never to return to Demopolis, died there while Kate was in graduate school. Her father retired and never left.

"Everything considered, the difference in this town," he said once, when Kate and Jack had come with their three children for a visit, "is that now the black folks come out to the edge of the shadows and the white folks allow them, and the black folks can stand up for themselves there." He'd learned by then to use the term "black," instead of Negro or colored. "There used to be an ordinance against a black man carrying a cane in Demopolis, as Katherine well knows," he said. "It was written out of the fear he'd use it in his defense if he needed to. Now, a black man can carry a cane. A black man will look a white man in the eye. They teach their children to do that, while up North they still won't do it. But Demopolis is a plantation hamlet and still the black folks here are allowed to come out only so far from the dark of their history. People want to feel they've done right in their lives. It's hard to get white folks to accept that they've been wrong and that some of their parents and grandparents were enablers of unspeakable atrocities. I managed to get a few black folks to come to church with us for a time, but now First Presbyterian is all white again, and the black folks still live downstream of the sewage plant. The South remains the stage upon which the nation plays out its obsession with race."

Kate drove past the charred building on the edge of Coburn, and then the town itself, which vanished as abruptly as it had appeared. The log truck behind her advanced close enough to fill the rearview mirror with its grill. Angry, Kate held her speed steady. When they came upon the mill, the truck dropped back and turned off. Kate envisioned her father in his Demopolis house where he now lived alone, two blocks up from the Black Warrior River and the Ecor Blanc, or White Chalk Cliffs, and by a route parallel to the river not a half mile away from the quarry, foundry, and black neighborhoods where abounded ruins just like Coburn—broken buildings, skewed old Coca Cola signs, rusted tin turning the color of the earth. Outside her father's parlor window stood a live oak, and the golden November light laid out the shadow of its limbs across the surface of his beloved snooker table. He played the game daily. Perhaps he was still positioning the passion of his middle age as he located the metaphysics of his old age in the complicated trajectory of balls.

Her girlhood image of Sherman came from a photograph of the general in his rumpled uniform, slouched, peering at the camera with eyes like two black dots. One shoulder touched the edge of a large, spoked wheel, and behind him rose the muzzle of a cannon. Yet Kate's true sense of the man's deviltry came from her mother. The matrons in her husband's parish, of course, knew Kate's mother's name, and therefore marked her black hair, the golden underlaminent to her skin, and the raptor-like flash of her eyes when she was provoked but compelled to keep silent. Up to the time of her husband's resignation, the matrons had held her in cautious respect, though once when Kate was little, she'd heard a querulous voice spin out from a cluster of women, using a word Kate then didn't yet understand, the slightly more veiled form of gumbo: "Is she Creole?"

When Kate was twelve, she went with her mother to a reception celebrating the reopening of an antebellum plantation house that had been partially burned in the Civil War, then left for almost a century, patched together to protect it from the weather, and finally restored. Afterwards, as she and her mother drove away from the pale yellow building, out the lane between files of pecan trees toward the highway, Kate asked about Sherman, whose name she'd heard when a woman, rustling in a blue hoop-skirted gown, rattled her saucer and teacup down on a sideboard and said bitterly, "First, Sherman wreaked his destruction in the South. Having finished with that, he looked to the West."

Her mother ventured even farther into a voluptuous Calvinism than her father was capable of. She told Kate, "What they don't see is that Sherman did not invent himself. General Sherman did not rise out of the dust. He was the evil who took his energy equally from the people he served and the people he destroyed. It took not only both the North and the South but even the far West for that Sherman to exist. What these people don't understand is that they love Sherman for what he did to them, as if he were the great avenging angel and they his chosen victims. The only part of it they understand is that they were chosen to suffer. Without the rest of it, the meaning is lost on them and they are paralyzed."

Kate had her caches of safekept memories, like haphazardly arranged files or the middens of otters, the shells and urchin husks piled up on the sea floor where they'd been dropped to be stirred by the currents. If sorted through, the shells could tell a story of how many otters had stayed there, for how long, and what they had eaten; and they could even, if measured against the creatures still living on the ledges—crab, clam, mussel, oyster, urchin, whelk—be extended to tell long, complicated tales of destruction and survival.

Thus she'd always harbored a fascination for ruins, and now her professional life had taken her into the study of desolation. Fatalistic, and still more than a little Calvinistic, she watched with despair. Given a choice between the extremes of the white Southerner's mindless sense of defeat, the blunted rage, or the white Yankee's lust-driven sense of never-ending victory, she would still take the former for the kinship it required with mercy.

As the road ahead bent toward Bonner's Ferry, she began to shape the answer to Jack's question. "You're awfully proud in your charity," he'd said, and then he'd asked: "What is it?"

She thought:

—First, the woman appeared on the roadside. I picked her up.

—Second, I learned she'd been beaten. Like Elijah, I warmed her with my own body.

—Third, it's the menace of certain men. The resistance to that must be shared.

—Fourth, it's deeper than that . . . something obscure in my own past. There's something almost foreordained in the invitation offered by Winona Willy's suffering. She is a ruin, too.

*   *   *

"Personally, I don't know what women see in sex, except for the few minutes of fun every once in a while when they need a nap." Winona picked up one of the cans of Squirt Kate had bought, popped its top, and drank. "I'm hungry." She took a breath and kept drinking, swallowing heavily, then rolled down her window and flipped the can outside.

In her mirror, Kate saw the bouncing glint behind the car. "I don't usually throw trash out my windows."

"Oh, I forgot," Winona said. "Yuppie environmentalism. I'm starved."

They passed a sign that said:

BONNER'S FERRY 24

CANADA 56

Kate gave Winona an arch, assessing look.

Winona was silent for a moment, and then started in again: "According to Ruth, Mama's at Lake Louise working at the hotel because her husband kicked her out. He ain't my father. Or maybe she's back in Banff, and Ruth thinks Wayne's hiding out in Creston, unless he went all the way over to Vancouver. He can't stay in Cranbrook because that's home for us where anybody'd look for him like maybe a PI that bitch would hire. 'He ain't listed in Cranbrook,' she says, 'but Lowell' . . . Lowell's Wayne's best friend from school . . . 'Lowell says he might be working out of Creston as a line rigger. Lowell's probably lying. If you find him, Wayne, I mean, let me know,' she says. 'I want his wages.' But I'm going to find him first. I need him. He'll help me. Ruth's always been a bitch and a liar herself. Yakity yak. I think we should go to Creston. I changed my mind. I got people over there, too, who know me. I'll be safer. It's no further and the road's better."

There was a fork in the highway north of Bonner's Ferry. One way led to Creston, the other to Cranbrook. Each way led to a border crossing. "It is farther," Kate said, keeping little of what Winona was saying straight, except the alternative she was proposing. "We're not changing plans. We're going to Yahk, unless you want me to drop you off in Bonner's Ferry. You could catch a bus from there."

"Oh, sure," Winona said. "Ride around with the Japs coming in for the skiing."

"Then it's Yahk." Kate turned her wrist to see her watch—11:10. Travis would be waking up soon, packing his game bag, and putting on his white shirt and tie. She hoped Jack had got some sleep. He'd have unloaded his gear into the shed. He might have the elk skinned and hung in the cold room.

"There's a pizza place in Bonner's ferry," Winona said. "I could've died, you know."

They drove through Naples, another town with a sawmill and trucks wheeling in from the high country. The road broke out of the woods into hay lands, and rode the flat of the opening between mountains, a broad U-shaped trench bounded by moraines. They were now well into the landform scoured by the last glacial advance and cut by the melt from which the rivers flowed. Here, the Kootenai River left its floodplain. People, their trails and roadways, followed the riverbeds. Winona sat still, her fingertips touching the bulging purse on her lap.

The hay land gave way to grain fields, where winter wheat seeds lay waiting beneath the snow. Ahead, as the road dropped and arched down the deep bank, a file of log trucks slowed. Billows of white mist churned up and Kate kept her distance. Another file of trucks edged up from behind. Kate could see specters of dark loads and tractor snouts through the boiling white, and at the side in the cut, ponderous-looking boulders from the glacial till protruding from the sediment. She followed the highway down and out around the edge of the moraine. The road widened, broke left, and tight-roped across the bridge that spanned the Kootenai.

They entered "new town," which was built up on the hummocks: small stores, grocery markets, fast food restaurants, motels, and used car dealers working out of mobile homes. A mill lay below the bridge to the east. To the northwest rose two grain silos. A freight train loaded with logs crawled along low on the far embankment. Log trucks and pickups were parked in the lots and along the edge of the road, while more trucks prowled up and down the road. A school bus from Sandpoint was parked in the McDonald's lot. Clusters of girls moved between the bus and restaurant. She'd been in that very McDonald's with Travis's teams when they came up to play the Badgers.

"It's down there," Winona said, pointing.

Kate checked her watch again, knowing that after what Winona had been through it was reasonable for her to be hungry. "We have to be quick," she said.

She cut off the highway and dropped down deeper toward the valley floor to Old Town where the big sign, PIZZA CAFÉ, was perched on top of a building. Here, too, were parked cars and pickups, and more working the streets. Because of the games, the loads coming in, and the excitement of the first big snow, people were out and about. Government buildings were down here, a hotel, and a hardware store built out of stone. Kate pulled in across from the restaurant. "We'll get it to go," she said. They crossed over, picking through the slush.

Inside, the place was steamy from damp coats hanging at the booths and ripe with the smell of sauce and baking dough. People sat in booths and stood in a line at the counter, filling the air with the din of talk.

"I'm going to the bathroom," Winona said. "I want pepperoni."

Kate glanced at the glass cases on the counter where already prepared pizzas were displayed, then spoke to Winona as if to a child.

"You'll be back in time to order. Get what they've made. You're buying."

"Oh." Winona moved off, mincing toward the restroom between the tables and around the toddlers in the aisles. Teenagers were chattering from one booth to another and young kids stood up in the booths to see. Laughter would rise, sometimes low and then erupt raucously. Just to Kate's right, a man was ranting about a coach: what the coach had done, had not done, what he should do. They'd lost a football game last night in the snow. He had a son named Joe. Joe could do this. Joe could do that. Joe could slice through the line. The man's voice chiseled through the noise. The father of an athlete, he had meaty features, and the aspect of there being absolutely nothing distinctive about him except the force he hoped to transfer to his absent son, who hadn't seen enough playing time. He passed the tailings of his force to the women in his company, probably the athlete's mother and grandmother, seated across from him, and at his side maybe the athlete's sister, sporting a tight booster sweater. She stared at a wall-mounted television broadcasting a college football game. The father thumped his fist on the table, and she jerked. "Joe's got the legs," the father said. "It's time the coach woke up."

Kate moved up in the line. Otherwise, an air of near jubilation filled the restaurant. She knew well the commonality of such gatherings, the shared concern for children, the good manners, and the mild gossip. She lost herself in the swirling voices and stared out the windows on her left toward the riverbed, considering how this place had come to be so: first the furs, later the mines and timber. The Canadian David Thompson had been the first white man to visit here, searching for pelts and measuring the world. An autodidact in "practical astronomy" and wildly purposeful, he used the stars to calculate position on the skin of the earth. Two hundred years ago, the world he charted, the long bolts of it running in all directions, must have seemed endless and inviting to the piercing of the eye behind the sextant. His presence, the trade goods he brought—beads, blankets, tobacco, alcohol, firearms— and the tendency of his men to drift toward fracases with Indians was what in Kate's business would be referred to as a "perturbation," the leading edge of the coming monumental disruption. She remembered that Thompson had left this place at the height of the spring thaw, battling his way back to the Rockies, eating his horses to stay alive.

Pizza had been brought to the proud father's table, and he'd fallen silent as he leaned forward on his elbows to feed. She looked back toward the river in the cut that had no salmon left in it, and smiled to herself as she thought of Thompson and remembered how Jack liked to play her against her presumed monomania: "How big is it? Is it big enough? It's got to be Godzilla-sized, right?"

He'd come home one day last summer after wrestling with the agencies over a bid he'd put in for a selective cut on state land. His bid had been entered perfectly in accord with regulations, stipulating a subcontract to a horse logger for erosion control on a steep slope, state-of-the-art restoration after the cut, and even allowing for a buffer zone on either side of a stream the state hadn't included in its plats . . . that is, informing the state of the existence of a riparian habitat that it hadn't accounted for. Considering that the land was going to be logged anyway, the compromise he'd struck between his scruples and his livelihood was to show how logging could be done profitably and with minimum damage, but he'd been bounced from one office to another, put off, insulted, and told that he'd added the stream to his bid to justify deflating the gross take.

"It's not in their paperwork," he'd said. "Therefore, it doesn't exist and I must be lying. We're supposed to be happy living in their imaginary world."

Kate had been stacking firewood in the shed behind the house. Travis had spent the morning splitting the wood and then gone around on the other side of the shed to pitch a bucket of balls into the mattress he'd nailed up on the wall. Every half-minute or so, the thunk of a ball reverberated through the walls.

Jack handed Kate a stick of wood. "You sort of expect that. What pisses me off is that half the time they don't know what the fuck they're doing, and on top of that they turn it around and accuse me of lying. Sometimes I think the extremists have a point about government." He bent to pick up a few more sticks to hand to her. "Those boys in their monomania." He smiled faintly.

It was late June. She and Abby had secured their grant, and Kate was flush with the prospect of going independent at last. The day had broken clouds, sporadic rain, deep shadow, and the sun flooding in shafts through the openings in the sky. In the woodshed, their labor kicked up puffs of dust. A horsefly circled her head. She waved it off and it buzzed heavily toward Jack, who snatched it out of the air and tossed it through the doorway while another ball thudded against the mattress.

"A person needs a big monomania to make sure the way gets cleared," he said. "Avalanche-sized." He scooped up an armload of wood and rocked back on his heels. Clowning with the anger he'd brought home, he said, "I'm talking about you. You've got it. You'll need to keep it big like a great fury, broad in the beams, so you can load it up and maybe stand a chance of slamming it into something useful." As if to punctuate his point, another of Travis's pitches thudded. Jack came beside her and began stacking in the row she'd been working on. "My wrangle is nothing compared to yours."

"They're the same."

"Yours is big brain. Big deal. Big trouble. Big excitement. Needs big craziness."

So thinking, Kate shifted her gaze from the riverbed to a stone building across the street, to the snow that dripped into sheets of water from its eaves, and to Winona coming back up the aisle. The purse swung from her elbow, a bill fluttered from one raised hand, and she cast her eyes at the people in the booths as she flitted by like a butterfly.

* * *

After a steep rise outside of Bonner's Ferry, the road became flat on the plateau, drawn true to the north through the woods. In the distance, the sky was black. Beneath the black lay mountains. Between here and there the midday sun shone through, and yet here it was snowing lightly. What she was wary of as she drove was the complication of silvery gray, the light, and then the black up in Canada. Snowflakes splattered against the windshield, while the inside of the car smelled of dough, cheese, and pepperoni. Wadded up napkins and the still half-full pizza box lay at Winona's feet.

As she chewed, she chattered. "You should see them eat. They're exactly the same. Like twins. Sometimes I wonder if they're both idiots, but Bud's smart and if you hear Zack talk, then you know. Zack likes to do everything the same as Bud. I hate sex. You sure you don't want another piece?" she asked, holding out a pizza slice.

When Kate shook her head, Winona ate the piece herself. "But its purpose," she said, "is to populate the world. 'The woman being deceived was the transgression. She shall be saved in childbearing.' It's the Jews. The Jews have brainwashed the nation. Who invented the birth control pill that made me barren? Who owns the drug companies to poison us? It began with fluoridation. It's their plan to make us mix with the niggers."

Exasperated, Kate said, "I don't like that kind of talk."

"Like it or not, it's the Jews who are the deceivers. Jesus withstood the Devil. The Jews are the ultimate hate group, but for us it ain't hate, it's real. We have to be real. If you've been brainwashed, you'll never be real until you receive the light."

Kate held her silence. At least Winona seemed to have given up on being taken toward Creston. She'd made a last pitch for it while they waited for their order in the restaurant, saying, "I'd be safer in Creston if Wayne's there. He'd take care of me. You want me to be safe, right?"

Winona had leaned her head back against the rest. Her eyes were slitted open. Kate was scrutinizing a luminous patch of beige at the edge of the woods a quarter-mile or so away. As the car approached, the color extended and took shape against the dark. It was a poised body, looking out at the road. Something in its stance told Kate what would happen. All the events of the next one or two minutes and of the final transient seconds were contained in the creature's bodily address toward a course to be followed, and instinctively, Kate lifted her foot from the throttle. —It's coming, she thought. It did so, moving clear of the cover. It was as if the timberline were water, as if a surface tension of the visible had been broken. The animal was a white-tailed buck, which Kate knew by the color and the arch of the neck and delicate carriage of the head under its rack. She lifted her foot to touch the brake and at that same instant a load of logs, two exhaust stacks, and a blue wind fairing appeared, looming out of the dip in the highway. The top of the cab rose before her, then the windshield. The deer dropped into the ditch.

The truck came into full view, silver and blue, blue cab, chrome. The buck emerged from the ditch, burst up the bank onto the shoulder of the highway, and there it stopped. Kate braked lightly, measuring the distance and speed to keep the Subaru back. She gauged the buck, and again by the address of its body believed she knew exactly where its mentality was lodged, hovering, terrified, giving itself over completely to its body which might or might not bolt and somehow not comprehending the speed of the vehicles. The truck advanced inexorably . . . wheels, chrome bumper, chrome grill, blue hood, a fang of a chrome hood ornament, windshield, blue fairing, chrome stacks, and the chestnut-colored load of logs.

The buck bolted. The truck caught it with the left edge of its bumper, tossing it upwards, and it roared by, slapping a glaze across the Subaru's windshield. Blind, Kate drove the Subaru right through where the deer had been, braked and eased onto the shoulder. She glimpsed the buck in her side mirror, at the center line, prone, its body askew, and pawing weakly with its front hooves. The scream receded behind her, and the load, black trailer edge, red lights, chrome, mudguards, and black tires vanished into the white mist. Kate flicked on her flashers.

Winona had turned in her seat to look. "Dog meat," she said.

Kate cracked open her door and stepped out.

At her back, she heard a screech from Winona, then saw another truck rising from the low stretch . . . red, chrome, chestnut-colored load howling in a white cloud. Kate made out the driver's head behind the window, turning to see her, then looking ahead. The buck pawed desperately at the pavement near the center line. The truck adjusted its trajectory and passed, barely missing the deer. A mass of vapor swirled over Kate, and the buck lifted its head several inches above the pavement. She saw the skin pulled back from its bulbous eyes, its distended nostrils, and its mouth open, panting. Listening for oncoming traffic and hearing none, she went to the buck, and saw the hindquarters shattered, one leg bent impossibly sideways above the knee-joint, and just above the hip a large protuberance, a swelling. –Kidney, she thought. Ruptured. She crouched before its midsection, thinking to pull it off the road, but not sure where to grab . . . not by the rear legs, which would hurt it, and maybe not by the front legs, either, because then it could hurt her with its rack. The buck woofed. Suddenly it pawed wildly at the road and managed to twist itself around. A tip of its antler caught Kate sharply on the shin and she jumped back.

The buck's muzzle sank to the pavement. Kate looked at it, thinking: All right, all right, you're done for, God love you. The buck seemed to regard her, its eyes glossy and too large around the dark rectangular pupils. It seemed to beseech her, and Kate felt something creeping up, a realization that something was there, something beyond her comprehension . . . inscrutable, not in words nor of the buck's own making, but of which it was a part, a retaliating sentience. Kate moved back to the car, opened the rear hatch, and as she straightened caught sight of a plowed out road entrance just down her side of the highway. She got back into the Subaru and pulled along the shoulder to the opening.

"The back's open!" Winona said.

"Be quiet." Kate drove past the opening, which she saw was a logging access, and backed off the highway into it. She walked around to the rear hatch again.

Winona twisted around and rested her chin on the top of her seat. "Now what?"

Kate rifled through her supplies for the emergency box and squeezed down its side past the chains and flares and felt what she was seeking— the old, serrated diving knife she kept there.

She pulled out and closed the hatch, and heard Winona's muffled voice: "Hey!"

To the north, over the screen of rosebushes and alders growing in the ditch alongside the car and just beyond the dip, Kate could see clearly the Y in the highway not a mile away, one fork going to Creston and points west, the other to Yahk, Moyie, and Cranbrook. She moved to the buck, again listening for the sound of trucks coming the other way and hearing nothing. The buck lay flat with its head sideways and its rack resting on the road. Blood oozed from its nostrils. Its ribs shuddered with each breath. Kate crouched and put a hand on its neck, the glands in it swollen with testosterone. Its rut caused a strong scent, the dank pungency of sex colliding with bile and blood. She slid the knife out of the sheath, went around and stepped on the rack, putting her weight on it. The buck didn't move. She straddled the buck's head, crouched and felt compelled to begin a prayer, what she knew was a response to the world, an animist succorance for it to accept the animal back into it. "Take . . ," she said aloud. "Take . . ." She couldn't say what she felt, after all. Her eyes welled with tears.

She adjusted her right foot, holding down the rack, and bent her knee to rest on the buck's head, put the blade to the buck's throat. The buck did not resist. She pressed and drew the blade up, opening a slit, and dug with the point to puncture the flesh. Cartilage popped as she probed and pressed against the handle with the heel of her hand. Suddenly, hot blood from the jugular spurted over the knife and her hand and sprayed up in a froth over her face and chest and down her pants. Quickly, she drew out the knife and stood straight.

Blood pooled on the pavement and steam issued from the incision. The buck quivered, lay quiet, then quivered again and let out a long guttural hiss. Kate's own breath answered in a shuddering exhalation. She stepped back and looked at her hand and the knife, drenched in blood and at her shirt—the fine, heavy, expensive, brushed-wool, doe-skin-colored shirt Jack had given to her, splattered down its front. She stepped quickly over to the edge of the road and bent to wipe her hand and the knife off in the snow, then returned the knife to its sheath, slid the sheath under the loose shirt and beneath the back of her waist-band. She was trembling. She inhaled deeply and shakily let air out again, went back to the buck, grabbed its rear legs, and pulled. The fractured leg swiveled crazily in her grasp. It took everything she had to drag it out of the lane and over the shoulder to the top of the bank. Jockeying it down the bank, she kept her balance in the snow by hanging onto the buck's weight. She got it clear, part way down the ditch, and stopped, panting herself now.

She climbed up around the buck, shoved the head down even with its haunches, grabbed its front legs with one hand, and put her other hand under its rib cage to roll it over once so that it lay nearer the bottom, nestled in the snow. For a moment, she crouched there, winded. She peered at her shirt. The splatters were absorbing into the cloth, turning it a deep rust color. She picked up a handful of snow and rubbed it at a corner of a blotch to no effect, except to darken the stains. The shirt was spoiled. She leaned forward, inhaling the buck's pungency. She fixed her gaze into the dense growth on the other side of the ditch. It was black and white in there, dim and yet suffused with light as if it were dawn or twilight, not midday. Out of an urgent need to ground herself, she called upon her habit of naming, that code: red fir, tamarack, a grand cedar, white pine, chokecherry, wild rose, alder, elderberry, the tips of the frosted, spraying Idaho fescue poking through the snow. From behind, she heard a vehicle pass, a pickup, maybe. A truck roared by. Ever so faintly, she heard her car running.

The buck lay still. Turned with its spine toward her, there was no movement of breath in the buck, whose head extended straight out from its body, with half its rack buried in snow. Large snowflakes that landed on him melted into the hair. Snow below the throat turned red. Kate's breath came out in puffs of vapor. Her boots and the cuffs of her pants showed dark dots of blood. Addressing the world, she attempted her prayer again, "Take this creature back." Then she addressed the buck: "Go back now," and suddenly the tears welled up and flowed, which seemed strange . . . hardly a sentimentalist, she was astonished to be so affected. Slowly, she reclaimed a sense of calm that seemed to arise not only from release, and from what could be named—cedar, cherry, highway, truck, her humming car, the elderberry and service-berry bush upon which the buck would likely have browsed, and the whitetail buck itself, Odocoileus virginianus—but also from the radiance of what now was inscrutable, the wild presence of the woods.

—We're almost to Yahk, she thought, wiping her eyes.

—Then I'm done with this.

She felt the thumping in her blood. It was as if she had passed into the eye of a storm, through the membrane of tumult into the quiet, leveling heart. It seemed to her that this was absolute anti-science, so pure it almost became science again . . . to see, to seek the detail, to become animal, and thus to enter into the arrangement of the world's mysteries.

—All right.

She knew this calm. She'd known it several times when one of her children was hurt or threatened. She'd known it diving, when her regulator malfunctioned, and the time she'd become entangled in the seine net, snagged by the control valve at the top of her tank and by the shank of her knife strapped to her ankle—the very knife she now had tucked under her waistband. Each of those times, and again when her mother died in the bedroom in her house in Demopolis, Kate had entered this luminous calm. It was the sympathy for death, the stripped away lucid calm at the portal to the end.

She heard feet crunching in the icy gravel a way up the road, and the thin, desperate voice singing out: "Where are you?"

A truck passed on the highway. Winona's shoes scuttled in the gravel, the sound amplifying with every step. Kate swung over to one knee and pulled upright, climbed the side of the ditch. About thirty yards away, four does picked their way into the ditch. They ascended and disappeared amongst the trees. They might have been the buck's herd. Twenty feet away was Winona, who had her back to them. Her shoulders were hunched and face wild-looking and wretched against the gray sky, completely absorbed into herself. "Where'd you go? You trying to scare me?"

8

This Fish

Experience has taught them the delicate
perceptions of this fish.
  —David Thompson, 1811

THE SIGNPOSTS FOR THE BORDER STATION came into view, then the open asphalt and the low buildings. "Listen," Kate said. "Don't say anything here. Don't open your mouth unless you're asked a direct question. If that happens, answer the question. Volunteer nothing."

She pulled up to the line in front of the station. A woman who looked to be Pakistani came out, dressed in a blue uniform, and leaned toward Kate's open window. "Where are you from?"

"Bayview," Kate said. "Down near Coeur d'Alene."

"Your reason for coming to Canada?" the woman said.

"Business. I am a biologist," Kate said. "There's a research station near Yahk and I want to check in with them. Fish."

"Fish," the officer said. She had a soft face, but did not smile.

"Sturgeon and Kokanee. Also Moyie Lake."

"I see. It'll be cold."

"You bet," Kate said.

On the other side of the lot was the U.S. border station, and beyond it the broad swathe cut in the woods that cleared out an observation space on either side of the line between nations. Swirling snowflakes danced in the dark cut that continued up into the mountains. "I'm coming back later today. But she'll be staying for two or three days."

She gestured at Winona and by her words gave up nothing. She was prepared to backtrack. "Do you know the forecast?"

The woman pulled away and looked up into the sky. "They say it's supposed to snow tonight. Most likely, you can get up and back under it before the worst hits." She glanced into the car's compartment. "Are you carrying fresh produce?"

"Leftover pizza."

The woman gestured with her hand for them to go ahead.

"Can you believe that?" Winona said acidly as they turned out of the lot toward the highway. "Gumbos on the border?"

A river that had snow on its banks—the Moyie—rushed alongside the road. Kate caught glimpses of it in its ravine according to the rise and fall of the road and the screening of trees. The river was bright in its tumult as it passed over the rocks. Above it the woods were dark, the stems driven into the white mantle. Canada. The road brought them near to what once had been the far reach of the salmon runs in the Columbia system, the coho, sockeye, and chinook swimming way up through Kootenai country into the Columbia Reach before they were choked out by the dams.

"It's still the Jews," Winona said. "The Trilateral Commission and the Communists. They want to do away with the border."

In the old days, eggs would have lain in the redds, the depositories where the spawning fish dug into the gravel of the river bottom.

"And the UN and the environmentalist Commies who're idiots to play into the hands of the Trilateral Commission and the Zionists like they are. The Zionists already get more support for their tiny little invented state than any other nation in the world," Winona said. "But they always want more."

And in time the eggs would hatch as fry to begin working their way downstream to salt water, their memory still attuned to every aspect of their ancestral home.

"So they put coloreds in the guard stations," Winona said. "It's Hebrew avarice. They got the environmentalists and devil worshippers in their back pocket. It's a Zionist Trilateral Commission plot to weaken the country."

"Which one?" Kate said.

"Which one what?"

"Which country?"

"Both," Winona said. "If you give up your distrust and self-defense, then you're going to fall. I know. I'm Canadian and sometimes we hate the U.S. I'm American, too, and sometimes we hate the Canadians. Distrust makes you strong."

Kate felt her eyebrows rising as she glanced over. Winona's cheeks had an actual flush to them, her lipstick had smudged onto her chin, and her mouth hung open, giving her jaw a hooked aspect like a fish. The frantic in her lay barely controlled. In the rearview mirror, which Kate found herself checking, the white billowed behind the car. There had been few vehicles on the road, and only two pickup trucks coming up from behind to pass them.

She had more than her share of intimate knowledge of the bad and deadly that was exchanged between the two sides of the border, but she hadn't been up here for several years and now recalled how much she loved it. As far as she was concerned, the border was pure political fiction. What could be more important, the water, the toxins in it, and also the passage of subterranean fluids, of terrestrial and aerial creatures, and of airborne flora, spores, bacteria, yeasts, insects, deer, elk, moose, wolves, bears, and in the natural history of the flow of glaciers and molten lava, even if measured by weight or volume, disregarding effect, dwarfed what human institutions had so far made out of the border. The border still wasn't checked carefully, not here in the interior, except for drugs and loads of logs or lumber. Contraband, weapons, and humans, including those expert in penetrating boundaries—Latinos and the Chinese illegals who'd done it for years, and over on the coast the occasional terrorist slipped across almost with impunity. On the right, the river crashed around a bend and plummeted through a string of short drops, throwing up feathers of white spray.

"Besides being stupid, Zack's sex starved," Winona said. "He'll do anything for me, and when Bud beats on me he gets upset, but he don't know how he loves me. Sometimes I see him out in the yard banging on something, a truck frame or engine case, or just standing there holding himself and rocking and desecrating himself like he's in pain. Do men feel pain when they're denied?"

Kate didn't answer. She rested her fingers lightly on the steering wheel, and found herself checking the mirror again. Nothing. They passed a sign that said that Yahk was ten kilometers away—ten minutes or so. She thought through what she would do then. It had been a long time since she'd been in close company with somebody like Winona, this woman deep in her trouble. Now, she was realizing that she would not be able to help Winona, certainly not on her own. She considered that ideas like Winona's, and especially the hateful ones, never went extinct but like opportunistic weeds kept springing up out of the barrens in human nature.

As if in answer to Kate's thoughts, Winona said, "'A foolish woman is clamorous. She is simple, and knoweth nothing.'"

Kate remembered where that one came from—Proverbs.

"I can be clamorous, all right," Winona said. Kate saw her tip her weight toward the window, lifting a buttock, then heard her fart. "It's the cheese. It gives me bloat." Winona giggled, then her voice deepened: "'Stolen waters are sweet, and bread eaten in secret is pleasant.' That's why the niggers. . . . The Trilateral are working both governments in secret, see, but those black scumbags should stay where they belong and not be coming up here without permission to take what ain't theirs. Stay separate and be equal and eat your own sweets."

When the smell of the fart drifted Kate's way, she cracked open her window. The chill, fragrant air sucked into the car. They crossed a bridge and next the Moyie was on their left shooting in riffles that forged white trails on the dark surface. "There's nothing to be gained from hate," Kate said.

"Independence is gained," Winona said. "It's a warning to the strangers. The borders created by man serve God. It can't be helped. They are God's borders built to make us strong in our righteousness and to keep us apart. 'Every place whereon the soles of your feet shall tread shall be yours.' Pastor Sutter says even Israel's false borders have their purpose because it's there that Armageddon begins. The final winnowing. Israel is the whore. Even an idiot can be tempted to cross over into the evil of this world, so I got to distrust all the idiots and keep my walls high and strong. You got to be ready all the time, now. It's coming! It's coming soon enough!"

The Proverb Winona was quoting from had to do with a prostitute who was seated outside a house in a city, beckoning to passersby. Kate remembered its being used in a sermon by a camp preacher at a summer retreat for teenagers down near Mobile. She'd understood that the text was directed mainly at Presbyterian boys, that it had the racist intention of warning them against the "Nigra whores," but that it was also meant to warn the girls, the "fair sex," against the menace of the "black beast." She remembered how the passage ended . . . "But he knoweth not that the dead are in there; and that her guests are in the depths of hell."

"We're almost to Yahk," she said.

"I've been knocked up three times," Winona said. "So, I ain't totally hopeless, but every one of them miscarried. That's God's way of making the curse of my barrenness clear to me, so I won't forget. The three souls lost . . . 'the three months to be destroyed . . . the three days the sword of the Lord, even the pestilence.'"

—First Chronicles, Kate thought. The Things of the Days.

"Close, but no cigar." Winona let out a high-pitched spasm of laughter. "Cigar. Get it? Like Bill and Monica? Talk about perversion. He's got a wart on him, too, right? Now we got Bush and Gore, but who cares? It don't matter except we're in the midst of confusion, which is good, Pastor Sutter says. Confusion and decay. More decay. More rot. Rot burns clean. The more the better to bring on the end for certain." Winona had turned toward Kate and her voice grew the more frantic. "It's like all my life I've been looking over the edge of an abyss, just about to fall in. We are meant to multiply. Bud wants a son. I am not a mother. Therefore, I am still a child myself. 'Every tree which bringeth forth not good fruit is hewn down and cast into the fire.'"

—Luke. The Third Gospel.

"I can't fix it. I can't fix what's wrong with me," Winona said plaintively. "'Many houses shall be desolate.'"

Biblical texts had not been driven into Kate as a child, but they'd certainly passed by her in quantity. Her parents had seen to it that her upbringing had been in the main a benign construction. It was as if she'd had her brain cells molded to hold a certain kind of spirituality. Since she'd worked to move large hunks of religion out of its digs within her, she still awaited the arrival of a new assemblage or a new activation, as if by a brain chemical moving in like a dye—catecholamine, maybe, an electrical charge washing over other cells and spreading its energy through them like the laughter of a crowd catching in a corner, then enlarging into mob laughter, a hurricane twisting around itself, magnetizing every niche, leveling the old and reshaping for the new. She would have liked to have the answers.

To the side, the river shunted back and forth as it wended its course around the protuberant granite, abandoning eddies in the backs of its corners, choked with ice-encrusted tree limbs and pieces of log—the river's junk. Above the eddies stood cutbanks and boulders and deep green firs with their black trunks implanted in snow. Green, black, white, beautiful blue frothing river where once the Kootenai had mounted their weirs and basket traps to harvest the fish. The car shivered as it flew forward on the gray snake that tracked the path of the river.

"He's coming! I can't stop him! He's coming!" Winona cried.

Instinctively fearing for some spooky emanation, Kate checked the mirror again. Nothing. She pushed back from the wheel, stretching her legs and took in air, then let it out. As a child, she'd been compelled to memorize a few verses and the order of the Books of the Bible. Other verses she'd heard repeated so many times in sermons, scriptures, and prayers that they became familiar. Doubtless, Winona knew many texts that Kate would never have recognized, a set of them selected by Winona's eddying pain. Kate had merely turned loose the trappings of religion as best she could, and was waiting to replace them with . . . what? . . . after science, whatever it was she was seeking, maybe a kind of chemically based animism she kept testing by chocking it up against her empiricism.

She'd been instructed by her father that the scriptures were mysteries of spiritual and historical truth, and so from earliest childhood, she'd learned that the truth had to be uncovered, that the Bible did not provide a road map. During her girlhood, the violence littered around her, the burnings and beatings and killings, was most formidable at the moment of transition from nascent anger to scheme . . . the knot of white men leaning over a cafe table, Sam McKinney among them, or standing at a downtown corner or on the lawn on the shady side of the church, talking softly and leaning conspiratorially toward each other when they struck upon a trail that would authenticate their hatred, as often as not guided by a scripture that validated the secession of the ungoverned self from reality. This was what Winona considered "independence."

Winona said, "I think you should take me all the way to Cranbrook. What if my friend, Lucy, won't help me?"

"Absolutely not," Kate said. "It's Yahk. Do you know where your friend lives?"

Winona's face was still as she leaned forward to stare through the windshield. The snowfall had picked up. They passed a ramshackle house with a loaded log truck in its front yard, the first sign that they were coming up to the town.

"And it's probably a good idea to call the police once we get to your friend's place," Kate said.

"No police. I told you that last night," Winona said, turning. Her eyes were slitted dangerously as they'd been last night when Kate came in with her purse.

"I'll leave you in town," Kate said, determining to call the police on her own as soon as she had Winona out of the car. "But whereabouts do you want to go once we're there?"

Winona snapped loose her seatbelt and clambered around to her knees to reach into the back compartment. Things clanked as she shifted them to get at her duffel bag. "I got addresses."

The false and hostile note in Winona's voice telegraphed something, as did her bodily presence . . . something . . . something shifting. Kate tracked Winona's movement in the periphery of her vision—the hip rising and pushing lightly against her. As Winona stretched to reach, she farted. "Well, excuse me again," she cackled brassily. The duffel bag hummed as it was dragged toward the seat. Winona's hip pressed as she dug inside the bag, and then the hip twisted away. The body straightened. The arm spirited by and in the passing hand that followed lay a glint. Winona swiveled and kicked her feet out and down into the junk on the floor. The glint moved to her lap, and then rose several inches.

Without looking directly at it, Kate knew what it was and instantly broke into a prickly sweat. She stared fixedly at an approaching bend in the road while her mind raced and her peripheral vision came alive with menace. On the left, the river cascaded down the grade. Straight ahead, the road disappeared and on the bank above its arc loomed a dark snarl of conifer and bush and the ghostly webwork of birch limbs. The road swung. Gingerly, Kate braked for it, thus attending to the details of trajectory and traction even as the shock of realization sifted through her. They crossed a bridge. The river now flowed on the right. The pavement stretched out before her. She moved her line of vision sideways and looked at it, in Winona's hands a heavy, brushed steel pistol aimed directly at her midsection.

Amazed by the steady sound of her own voice, as if disembodied from her, she said, "Please point that somewhere else."

"You've screwed with me long enough. We're going where I say."

Kate looked at her, above the gun and into the pale blue eyes lodged in the smeared eye-shadow. She turned back to the road. "What do you want me to say?"

"Say you get it."

Kate looked at her again. Winona's eyes were like glacial ice, that color, that pale, almost chemical blue, the blue born of tremendous compression, as if everything about her—the servility and wildness and meanness, helplessness, haughty ignorance, and all-encompassing fear—had been pressed into the space of two intensely blue chips. "You know you're about to get into much deeper trouble than you were two minutes ago."

"Take off your seat belt," Winona said.

Kate obeyed, disengaging the buckle. The slick fabric of the harness slid across her and spun onto its spool.

Winona turned so that her shoulder rested against the door, and let the gun settle into her lap next to the purse but kept it aimed at Kit. With her left hand she reached up and pulled down her own seatbelt. Kate heard the click when Winona inserted the tongue into the clasp. The Subaru's tires hissed against the pavement and the falling snow obscured the windshield. Kate switched on the wipers.

"This way, you'll get hurt, not me, in case you decide to crack up the car. Keep your speed up."

Kate dipped her eyes to the speedometer. They were on a long, gradual ascent, the road was clear and yet they were creeping at less than thirty. She depressed the pedal and brought the car up to thirty-five miles per hour, then forty.

"That's better," Winona said. "And just in case you've been watching the movies, this ain't no movie."

Hearing it so named, Kate felt as though she had stepped inside a movie, a world of make-believe.

"We're not stopping here," Winona said when they entered Yahk. She laughed gutturally, converting her usual twanging noise into a dire, deep-throated sound. "Go straight. I guess I don't know nobody here, after all."

The town was a short cluster of old dwellings and a saloon, the steep roofs heaped with snow. Icicles dangled just above the ground. Between the houses, there were glimpses of the river tumbling around ice-covered rocks, and just beyond the river the railroad tracks. The woods came close upon the town, pressing against the fences. Kate now wondered if Winona had a brother at all, or an estranged sister-in-law, or a mother somewhere. . . . She wondered . . . and this had become important . . . just how far Winona's capacities for sheer invention went, and thinking that, it struck Kate as they passed out of the town that there were people back there who might have helped her, that she might have taken her chances and careened into one of the driveways . . . maybe . . . maybe she should have done that.

Inhaling deeply again, she dropped into herself, so that for a passing moment all of her sat on the seat, touching the wheel, pushing on the accelerator pedal. They were headed northeasterly and behind them the sun dipped toward the trees. They'd passed under the edge of the black cloud cover and the intensity of the snowfall had risen another notch. If the sky had been clear, the Purcell Range would have been visible to the left and the Rockies lunging upward before them. Kate bent her wrist to see her watch. Travis's game would start in less than an hour, and soon after that she should be turning up at the gym. In her distress, she pictured Jack in the stands, watching, and the teams out on the court warming up, sneakers squeaking. The two bands would be assembling their equipment in the far corners of the stands. She could see Jack as if she were actually walking into the Sandpoint gym and scanning the stands for him, looking for him next to Gene and not far from the Grays, the Costas, or Joneses, people they liked but had absolutely nothing in common with except the children. He would be there. He'd be wearing a clean plaid shirt with the sleeves rolled up and his elbows on his knees, and he'd be casting his eyes toward the doorway to see if she had arrived.

The road grayed with wet snow. She slowed. When half-time arrived and she wasn't there, Jack would find a telephone to check the message machine at home. There would be no message. He might wait to the end of the game. But after that, it wouldn't take long for him to do something.

—We're survivors.

Trying to find herself in these events, she made herself think what at this moment she hardly believed: I am a survivor.

It was strange to consider the events that lined up to make the story: her car parked behind a screen of bush, the buck that chanced across the highway, the log truck that came the other way, the ferocious husband, the purse full of money, the duffle bag with a gun in it, the snowstorm and Winona having driven her car into the ditch, and her—Kate's—excess of sympathy, or misplaced charity, or her own slightly lunatic quest, and Jack's obviously correct denunciation of her intentions. Now this. Kate was sweating. Inside her shirt and the coat she'd put on back at the Y, her skin had grown clammy. Her head felt light and strange.

They crossed the Moyie on a corrugated bridge that made the Subaru's tires howl. Snow sifted down into the river, adding a bright sheen of white to the rocks around which the water ribboned, and up above the bank into the deep tangle of the woods. A fractured tree scissored off the bank and into the water. They were near the town of Moyie, a small place built on the east bank of Moyie Lake. As the highway bent into the town, Kate decided she had to take her chances here and stop, pull into a police station if she saw one, or off the road and into somebody's yard. She kept the car rolling above the speed limit, converting the miles per hour on her odometer to the posted kilometers, hoping they'd be stopped. A truck passed, slapping slush over the windshield. Kate flipped the wipers over to high, and back to low again. She felt the flush of her fear on her neck where the draft from the cracked open window struck it.

"Obey the speed limit," Winona said.

Kate ignored her. Down the way, a Shell sign appeared. Kate looked at the gas gauge . . . half full . . . then over at Winona. The makeup was smudged around her eyes, the lipstick on her chin, and her pupils had dilated inside the stony rings of blue.

"Keep your speed down," Winona said. "I don't give a shit. I'll shoot you."

Kate braked, making the car pitch forward. She'd set the gas station, which was now a block and a half away, as her mark. She had a gnawing in her gut and the intense clarity of the feeling that preceded risk. She had to do it.

"No tricks," Winona said. She shifted her feet in a way that seemed antic, lifting one leg to free her foot from the debris. The skirt slid up above her knees, revealing her spindly legs under the black body suit.

"We don't need gas," she said. "We're not stopping." She laughed eerily again. The Shell sign was a block down, and Kate fixed on the station, seeking the fastest entry into it. She'd jump the curb, if she had to, but then at her side an angular arm went up and Winona bent toward her. Suddenly, Winona grabbed the hair at the nape of Kate's neck, pulling herself close and making Kate's head jerk sideways, and Kate felt the muzzle of the gun poking just underneath her jaw, and Winona's lips brushing her ear as she hissed, "Do you think I'm kidding? Don't fuck with me here!"

Hanging onto the wheel, Kate instinctively pulled her head away.

Winona jerked Kate's head back and hissed again, her breath filling Kate's ear. "I don't care about you, bitch!"

"All right," Kate said, merely assenting, passing deep into full shock, and hardly amazed now, but merely taking in what was happening. The hand pulled her hair tight. They passed the gas station. Two cars and a pickup loaded with firewood went by, going the other way, swishing in the slush and oblivious to what was going on in the Subaru. Kate felt as though she were skating, gliding across ice and not manipulating the car at all, and she felt rather than registered what she saw going by from the centers of her eyes to the corners and then underneath the skin at her temples. She felt the cold between skin and skull, a sensory laminate of cold like the phloem of a tree passing down along her jaw to her neck where the gun barrel was, a brute of a thing pressed into soft flesh. The hand clutched her. She saw the blonde hair and one garish eye.

They passed a house with a big sign in the yard that said, BC JADE, INDIAN CRAFTS, WORMS, and a mercantile, then more houses, one with an empty log truck in its drive, and another with a lowboy trailer that had a skidder chained down to its bed. But for one house near the far edge of town, these places slipped through Kate's vision, sliding backwards along the walls of her fright while the car skimmed forward. As Winona released her hold, rocked her body back, and lowered the gun to the level of the dashboard, Kate turned to follow the motion, but shied from looking into the face. She looked past Winona through the snow. She poked up out of her shock for an instant, and in a wild flight of desperation drank in the one house in all its detail.

"Ain't no help for you there, neither," Winona said. She leveled the gun at Kate.

On the stoop of the house, two small children had stood on the bottom step. They wore bright blue snowsuits. Their knees were bent, their arms stuck straight out, and they leaned forward as if they were about to leap. Above them and to one side rose a picture window that had a bed drawn up to it. In the yard lay the garden, the stalks of the summer's corn bleached above the snow cover.

Kate's fingers held the steering wheel. Her neck hurt. Her legs ached. The woods on either side of the road flooded by the edge of her vision, but the image of the house which she'd absorbed in the instant of complete concentration stayed with her: the children poised to leap into the snow, the four poster bed mounted in the living room because the family lacked space. The parents probably slept there keeping watch into the deep of the night. Every spring the garden was planted for the hope of a crop burgeoning in the long days at the eye of the short summer which was sharply bracketed on either end by frost. It was the commonplace hope as she saw it that got to Kate. She'd fastened on it. She was coming out of the shock now, and slipping into panic. Her fingers had turned white from gripping the wheel. It was the hope in the garden and children, a stupendous exercise in hope drawn tight like a drumhead over hard times, that, and the vision of the refuge to which Kate now longed to return . . . her own home, the snow, the driveway, the shed, kitchen and bedroom, dog, husband, son.

She went into the panic as if into a fog. Her eyes filled with tears.

Winona sat upright, turned toward her, holding the gun with two hands and resting it on top of the purse. "I still got some power over Bud," she said. "In the moment when he comes to me and he's filled with pleasure he can't leave me. No matter how much he beats me, which I deserve, no matter what else he denies me, which I also deserve, he's mine. 'The womb shall feed sweetly on him.' Bud's just angry is all, and I'm angry at you for trying to mess with me."

—She's flipped.

Now, Kate forced herself to practice what she'd been schooled to do as a diver, to go ahead and give in to the panic, to thrash around in it for a moment, and then to arch against it, find her position, reach back, summon her resources, and seek her escape.

—She's a twisted primeval.

—But uncannily smart.

—Don't underestimate her.

"Bud wants the respect," Winona said. "He don't have a son, or even a daughter, but that ain't my choice. It's God's choice. He don't get the respect he deserves, neither, no matter that he's decorated by the army. He don't get respect from nobody, except a little from his so-called friends in the Brotherhood of Zealot. Mostly all he gets is envy."

Now, Kate looked directly over at her and wondered—Envy? Then—for the second time, Zealot? And—Decorated by the army? Him? She saw pale hair, pale, bony face afloat above the navy blue sweater, the makeup, lipstick, and feral eyes, the woman weirdly trans-lucent like an amphipod, a shrimp, a moon jellyfish frilly as a bridal veil, its mouth, gut, and gonads slightly more opaque and thus visible within it, the tentacles hanging down, swinging with the current, vir-tually shapeless, bedecked with electrically charged nematocysts. The woman was unpredictable and treacherous. There was a deep conun-drum within her nothingness, the mystery somewhere in her neurol-ogy of a dire contradiction that Kate could not decipher. Kate loathed her absolutely.

Winona stared back with her glacial eyes. "You asked where my people were from. It's Oklahoma, and before that Mississippi. My grandparents were fruit pickers up and down the Okanagan Valley just like the Beans they got in there now. Where are you from, honey, besides the lap of luxury?"

Turning to the road, Kate didn't answer, but she thought—Just so. And unable to stop herself from leaning back upon her Southern sense of caste, she thought again: White trash.

"If I got too strong," Winona said, "Bud would've killed me. I had to be weak for his wanting. But now I'm not weak no more, not for you, not for nobody. So, watch it."

Broken with rock and tangles of woods and cut by streams, the landform pushed up toward a high plateau. In the open spaces, the earth was brushed with white. The snow was unstoppable. Ahead, the road lay straight. Kate felt a bright, almost airborne tumult in her head like the fluff around a pod and in it the sharp seed of her contempt.

"Look," she said, keeping her eyes on the road. "I'll take you where you want to go."

"Oh, sure. You people are always happy to help when it suits you. A little while ago you could hardly stand hearing me talk. Now, you'd like to keep me talking, so you can find a crack to get in me."

"Put the gun away, and I'll help you," Kate said. "Or put me out and take the car. That way you'll be done with me."

Winona snorted. "And give up the fun of having a bitch like you around?"

As they drove further into the open, the wind rose and buffeted the car. Propelled by the cross currents, the snow curled up around the hood and sailed over the roof.

"A person like you should never mess with my kind, right? You've got your big house, wide-screen TV, stereo system, and your kid, the basketball player. Life insurance. But guess what, you can still be an idiot just like the rest of us. Look where you ended up. Serving me."

Cranbrook was not far away. Kate wondered what Winona planned to do there: Have her drive through the whole city with a gun at her head?

"Your life is important," Winona said. "Nice clothes. Big words. Answering machine. Computers. Your dishes match. People pay attention when you walk into a room. They love your good manners. You've got soap hanging from a string in your shower. You're top of the line."

"Maybe we should figure out what's the best thing for you to do," Kate said evenly. "This isn't it."

Winona laughed, her voice coming out in a low mordant again of guttural phlegm. "Honey, the best thing for you to have done was leave me in the ditch."

Kate revolved her head just enough to discern the outline of Winona's form and in the bleaching light to glimpse her besmudged, hook-like face, the blue, the gray, the red turning to a rust color. She remembered the bruises on Winona's torso and ribs, the black and purple, the old wounds turning yellow, and she sensed the inward transparency, the colorations pitched into the bright at the apex of the gradient that led to the diaphanous pale, and the fragility as if the chunks of her were barely bound together, as if the flesh of the woman was disengaging from sinew and prime to tear away from the bone. She saw her as a vivid fish in its spawn, but barren, and also lost in the barrens. Her homing instinct, her mortal monomania, was still powerful as she crept upstream, flickering in the riffles, and she snapped at whatever impeded her, but her delicate perceptions of scent and direction were thrown hopelessly awry.

Also marking the location of the gun, the bag, and Winona's hands resting on her abdomen, Kate considered simply reaching out and taking the gun away. She had been trained to coolly check off the hazards: faulty air hose, faulty regulator, embolism, nitrogen narcosis, tricky currents, tricky tides, cold water. She had survived a few things: a plugged hose, more than once, and the discarded fishing net.

—The knife.

She had it in its sheath still tucked under her pants. The ghastly possibility of reaching back and pulling it out before Winona used her gun became palpable. In her mouth, Kate could taste the prospect of using the knife, the metallic tang of her fear becoming anger. She might grab the gun and pull the knife.

Winona's fingers crept to touch the pistol's grip. "The world was created six thousand years ago," she said. "Six thousand divided by three is two, and three is the sacred number. First was Adam, then Moses came down from the mountains with God's commandments two thousand years before the birth of our Lord. In our time, we've come to the third two thousand year cycle, the second millennium, and the Second Coming. There are earthquakes all over the world, storms, volcanoes erupting. The wells are going dry." She tipped her body toward Kate and farted once more. "There's war. Race wars everywhere in the dark of the new world order oozing through the seams. Clinton's an Antichrist, bringing on the scourge. It don't matter. The corruption is a sign given to us. Soon, the imperial nation of ZOG in its blasphemy will collapse. The earth is heaving in preparation."

—Or I could slam on the brakes, Kate thought.

The stench wafted to her, then passed into the narrow current from the window.

—Maybe I could pitch her forward that way, then pull the knife. Or pitch her forward and deflect the gun. If I had to, I'd grab the muzzle of the gun. Maybe before we get to Cranbrook, I could do that, hit the brakes and slide, or at the first sign of Cranbrook, or maybe I should do it now.

The prospect, her nearness to it, and its unknown result filled her with fear.

The road steadied to the north. They headed into the wind. Snow flooded past the car. To the right the bed of the Canadian Pacific tracked the roadway. Toy-like, the rails and ties crested like a zipper in the white.

"The Devil's been released. He prowls the earth," Winona said. "We're going back home straight into the arms of Jesus."

They entered the west edge of a huge trench, what in summertime would have been a scrabbly, bright-looking furrow. It was the Canadian Kootenay drainage, what northerly by southerly had been left by the glacial arms that retreated fifteen thousand years ago, which in Winona's Bible Time had never happened. But for the snow, the Rockies would now be fully visible not far away to the east and north—jagged, wildly vertical, prodigious, and magnetic. Where they were driving was dotted with the scrubby, drought-resistant ponderosa pines. Farmsteads had been built with their backsides against the north wind and roof lines favoring the south. They passed a hay farm set a half mile back, then an empty log yard, and each had lanes onto which Kate was tempted to careen, but did not because the way was too far.

The falling snow had turned dry. It blew off the fields onto the roadway, eddying and surging like dust. It piled against whatever obstructed it—fence posts, rocks, tree trunks. Kate touched the lever on the left of the steering wheel with her fingertips and turned its knob to switch on the lights. Winona was watching her. The dashboard lights came on, also, and Kate looked at them in confusion, then amazement. Sometime during the morning, Jack had remembered to go out and put the fuse in the circuit box. The road slowly lifted. To the right, intricately eroded, beige-colored sandstone cliffs thrust through the white.

—All right, Kate thought, trying to poise and calm herself without giving any sign of doing so.

—Don't wait much longer.

—Slam on the brakes.

—Deflect the gun.

Carefully, Kate slanted her eyes and let them linger on Winona, who was no longer watching her, but staring saucer-eyed through the windshield. Kate looked back at the road. The car seemed insufferably warm, and something dangerous, an armature of Winona's wasteland, rose up like a fiend alevin coming out with its eyes protruding, a pair of absorbent, bulbous orbs implanted upon the mutational worm and tuned to its decomposing holdfast.

The highway carved a long bend and in the pale Kate picked out a culvert just ahead where the ditch was steep.

—There.

—Brake, turn into the ditch, let it slide, pin her door.

—Deflect the gun.

—Use the knife.

—Get out, or pile on top of her.

—I'm stronger. I can also outrun her.

Everything might have been changed if she'd driven the car straight into the ditch from the moment of her resolve, or if she'd spun the car around right there, or wrestled the gun away and let the wheel go where it would . . . anything . . . if she'd done anything in that flashing pivot of time. . . . She had her hands at the ready on the wheel and her foot on the accelerator pedal, just so, tensed for the brake. She sat there, rapt for a fraction of a second, filled with horrible wonder at what she was about to do, and in the corner of her eye she saw the steel, the weapon at the end of the arm, rising.

—Now!

Suddenly, the car filled with a roar. It slammed into Kate's ear and rocked her violently toward her door. She felt herself clutching the wheel and the car spinning and the snow whirling crazily past her. The car twirled full around and slid to a stop pointed in the same direction in the wrong lane. Her leg shook crazily as her foot dug into the brake. The engine had died.

Winona leaned toward her and screamed, "Get this thing going!"

But Kate was already doing that. Out of instinct, her awareness of a quite familiar, mundane peril—that she was stopped in the wrong highway lane—and even though there was not a vehicle in sight in either direction, she'd squeezed down on the key, restarted the engine, and set the car in motion. Knowing that she'd done what she'd intended, or begun it but had failed to finish it, that she was here and Winona was still there, Kate pulled the car rightward back across the highway, lined it up in its lane, and allowed it to creep forward. At the same time she was thinking through the parts of her body . . . legs, hips, belly, arm, shoulder . . . to discover where she'd been hurt. She wasn't hurt, except that her right ear rang violently. Cold air blew straight into her face. Her nostrils were filled with the scent of gunpowder. The window next to her had shattered. It was gone. All of this, Kate took in, and now also the piercing laughter at her right. Winona's form doubled up toward the floor, gripped by laughter, and then she straightened and leaned back, kicking up one leg, and twisted around. Again, the gun roared, and Kate's head recoiled, snapping sideways. The glint of the gun arched back, leveling on her temple. Cold flooded the car, entering through Kate's window and rushing out the second blown away window in the rear hatch.

"You're messing with me," Winona said. Her voice became husky and dark. "Don't mess with me, bitch. Fucking bitch. I don't care, don't you see? You don't matter. I don't matter. Nothing matters in this world. It's a zero. We're in the zero. All the forms of the earth are zeroes. Any path you think you could follow out of here is a zero leading back into itself. Everything passes into zero. The ground under the wheels of this car is a zero, crumbling away into zero. Only the Lord Jesus if he chooses can lift you out of this fucking zero." And laughing wildly, she said, "And He might not give a shit, either!"

Kate sat locked in place, not moving anything, not her hands that clutched the cold wheel, and not her right foot that stayed exactly where it was on the pedal, not even her eyes, which were fixed on the whitening ribbon of road as it slid under the car.

"Go faster," Winona said. "Stop thinking. No more thinking. Turn when I tell you."

9

The Moon Pool

WHEN THE DOOR from the observation wing opened, engine noise and cool air sucked into the *Bering*'s bridge. The captain stepped back inside and pressed the door shut behind him. A tall man in his thirties, he wore a blue polo shirt, white pants, and Nikes. He moved gingerly like an athlete with injured knees. His weathered face communicated an air of rectitude beyond his years. He picked up the handheld radio, came near U, and began speaking to the bridge of the approaching ship, the *Hermes*, the whiteness of which stood out against gray clouds and sea. Despite his beguiling drawl, the captain's instructions turned upon exact details: rpm readings, rudder angles, one after another.

U watched the *Hermes* adjust its course, and then he looked down at the shearwaters. They had the hue of soot mottled with white, a color changeable as the sea, but their breasts and the undersides of their wings were pale gray. When they turned in the distance to swing back toward the ship that was all U could see of them, the three rising to a trajectory that was never quite the same, making silver flashes in the shape of three crosses. As the *Hermes* nosed nearer, the shearwaters vanished and the white gulls that had been trailing the ship's wake filled the air like confetti.

The *Hermes* came abeam. The *Bering*'s hands cast the lines, and on the *Hermes*, the hands secured them. For a moment, the traverse pitch of the *Hermes* in the swells set it wildly against the gentle rise and fall of the *Bering*, which was held in position by a computer-controlled system that received its signals from satellite tracking stations. The system drove the propulsion props and twelve thrusters, designed to safeguard the drilling shaft that at this moment ran over a thousand feet through the sea and into the earth like an interminable proboscis.

Turning his head slightly, the captain spoke to the mate behind them: "Winches."

The mate spoke into the intercom: "Winch her in."

Below, the hands set the winches in motion, and as the *Hermes* pulled snug against the *Bering*, its motion was absorbed into that of the larger ship. U had felt the bump of contact and now faintly through the soles of his feet an accommodating growl from the *Bering*'s engines. A red-and-white ball rolled across the *Hermes*'s deck near to where Sophia stood, almost touched her heels, hung, then rolled out of sight. Sophia's face tipped up and U could plainly make out her features. By the strong cast of the brow, nose, and chin, he remembered the rest as it had been: the alert eyes and the amber color of her skin, and he remembered well the explosive force with which one expression could drive another from her face.

"Gangway," the captain said to the first mate.

"Gangway down," the mate said into the intercom.

The *Bering*'s hands swung out the gangway and cranked it down. Sophia disappeared behind the *Bering*'s trace. The shearwaters returned, riding the backsides of the swells beyond the *Hermes*. Gulls were strewn through the air. A solitary black-footed albatross appeared in the path of the shearwaters. Big, its wings seemed to nearly bridge the trough. It was also unusual for it to be in these waters at this time. When it ran up on the shearwaters, they banked against the draft and slipped into the next trough.

The captain set his radio down next to the binoculars. "That storm's coming on faster than we thought," he said. He touched U's arm, drawing him toward the instruments. The mate moved close to the window. The captain pointed at a radar screen. A dark, delta-shaped mass extended off the grid toward the high Arctic, but at its southern extremity it deepened to a bead. The captain ran his fingertips along the edge that ran northwest by southeasterly, the nearest to their position. "It's going to nail us. The system that blew through at the first of the week was nothing compared to what this one will be. The freeze'll come hard behind it, I figure."

U looked up at the captain, who was a full head taller. "How long?"

"Less than two hours to first blow. The pilot will want to move his chopper out or plan to stay awhile," the captain said. "I've got a supply barge coming. I don't really need it or the *Hermes* tied on in a gale. And certainly not the both of them at once, not when we've got the drill string down. I've been told not to pull the string yet, but we don't want to snap it off, either. The chief tells me they'll likely need another three days drilling this hole. Then it'll take a few days more to pull the string." Straightening, he took a brass bullet casing from his pocket, removed its cork, and tapped out a toothpick. He slid the toothpick between his lips, making it disappear, and slivered it out again at the corner of his mouth. He gripped the stick between two teeth and tipped the casing toward U. "Cinnamon," he said.

U shook his head.

"We might do it. The positioning system might hold us steady with the ship and barge tied on and not over-stress the string," the captain said. "It's not my first choice, you understand. To be honest, I'd like to pull the string right now and head out of here, but we've got directions otherwise from Houston. The barge would be smart to turn back."

U understood that because of the unusual weather the captain had been ordered to keep drilling well after the time these waters normally iced up, that having started the hole, abandoning it meant a loss of millions. Headquarters was playing true to form, pushing the envelope, having determined the likelihood of finding oil, and then gambling against the coming freeze. U's authority did not include instructions to ships, but he knew he was being made a witness to the matter. By law, it was at the captain's discretion whether to pull out or not, yet if he did he'd incur the company's wrath. Thus, he was not truly the captain of his ship.

"At this position, we'll be damn lucky if we don't get iced in," the captain said. "Then the company will have to come after us."

"The three of us could squeeze our business into a half hour," U said. "Then the chopper can leave with the security agent. But I need more time with Doctor Kopat. Perhaps the *Hermes* would let me go back with her."

"That's possible," the captain said.

A voice came through the intercom: "One aboard."

The captain stepped to the side and spoke back into the intercom: "Roger." To U, he said, "She's headed straight south to the passage."

U gazed through the windows down at the black helicopter lashed to four big staples on the yellow X painted onto the foredeck between two huge cable spools. A logo for Schtok Petroleum, which was emerging as Russia's second largest oil company, had been clumsily pasted over the old Soviet military insignia on the chopper's fuselage. On the outsides of the spools lay racks of drilling pipe. He and Carl Braun, the security agent assigned to him, had flown to the *Bering* from an elaborate installation on the coast of Siberia. Built by the consortium of oil service companies for Schtok, the city had been renamed Steklyányigórod—City of Glass. U sat on the consortium's board, representing his company, ZAQ.

The city was to be a storage and pumping center, and a shipping terminus, a central member in a new Siberian grid. It was being built out of steel, reinforced concrete, carbon fiber, space-age alloys, plastic, as well as quantities of insulated, high-impact glass calibrated to withstand the hurricane-force winds that blasted off the sea to the tundra. The city's buildings displaced their own weight and were anchored in water-saturated gravel to deep-set lead pods. They'd been assembled as modules in South Korea and Poland and been floated to the site under the tow of tugs. The city would be powered by geothermal and natural gas split off in its own refinery. It would have a fabrication plant, control modules, dormitories and recreation facilities for workers, a maze of access tubes, a desalinization plant to produce drinking water, an array of subterranean storage tanks, and pumping stations that were to be tied into the Russian lines and at the ready for the projected line across the Chukchi to Alaska, and then to the Trans-Alaska Pipeline System, which would be refurbished and ostensibly redirected. Other such installations were on the drawing board to feed the pipelines through China and Turkey.

Just yesterday, Schtok Petroleum's chief of security, Vasily Petrovich, had taken U and Braun on a tour of the construction site, built next to a landing strip. They saw the desalinization plant and partially built dormitories, some of the control modules, and one pumping station, all sunk into the permafrost. He said they had huge, adjustable pistons in their mounts to keep them level. Inside, baffles, fans, and vents created virtual weather, and, once they were installed, ultraviolet lighting systems would promote health. Some of the workers had already brought in soil and plants. One was growing lettuce in a corner of one of the buildings. Another was actually raising chickens in a cage. A well-padded man with small feet and hands and two Vodka-induced pink sears riding under his eyes, Petrovich led U and Braun past the chickens. He held up an imaginary egg in his fingers, and in his enthusiasm the stripes under his eyes deepened to crimson. "People here could survive anything! Even a holocaust!" he exclaimed in perfect English. His eyes grew wide. "Perhaps the end of the world!"

U had pondered the curiosity of human obsessions—to build such a city! He'd noted, as Petrovich's aide had driven him and Braun in from the landing strip one day and back out again the next—past the partially built edifices and the high gas torches set against the grim sky—that the route seemed devised to keep him from catching more than a glimpse of the ghetto-like temporary quarters made out of heavily insulated corrugated tin and surrounded by industrial debris and pools of oil, where the Russian workers now lived. Those workers were nearly destitute. They were marooned here because the Russian currency was in a state of collapse. The city's construction combined the American mania for mastery and result, adventurously applied by U's company, with properties from other minority interests: the British love for routine, the technical facility of the South Koreans, the manual force of the Poles, and the financial dexterity of the Japanese and the Hong Kong Chinese, U's own people. All parties levered savagely for footing on the feeding ground. The majority owner, Schtok Petroleum, had its own melancholy and often frustrated ferocity of ambition, its visionary, over-the-top aspect which it was incapable of ever fully escaping. The wildness of its dreams . . . U saw . . . rose out of Russia's interminable corruption.

Before seeing them off, Petrovich had looked around surreptitiously as if to make sure none of the workers was in earshot. He leaned near U and said that the previous president, Yeltsin, had been a testament to the advance of science, a walking, talking corpse, akin to the corpses of Lenin and Stalin preserved so long under glass for all to see. But Putin, Petrovich said, was vigorous, a master tactician. "Wait. You'll see. He's an athlete, a fighter." This was just a day before the U.S. election, and Petrovich had then asked, "And yours? Who will it be? Mr. Bush or Mr. Gore?"

U shrugged.

"If it is Bush, we will soon have the oil running, eh?" Petrovich said, holding U's arm. "Competition!"

"It doesn't matter which," U had said as he shook Petrovitch's hand and then he eased into the car next to Braun. They drove off.

Now, U touched his knuckles to the window on the side of the *Bering*'s control console. "South to where?" he asked the captain.

"I'd guess she'll go on to her home port in Seward," the captain replied.

In U's mind, a new plan broke loose: He'd be ashore later than expected, but he'd be on U.S. soil instead of Russian, which meant he could fly to Anchorage and go on from there through Seattle to Houston. Considering Russian inefficiency with its airlines, and the weather, he might well make up the time. He could satisfy his curiosity about Sophia, too.

"You'll have a sea before you reach shore," the captain said.

U remembered the *Hermes*'s four-second list in heavy water and the antic process of tacking the hallways to get around. The sea did not frighten him. He was its creature, smooth-bodied as a seal. He'd lived his boyhood almost in sight of the South China Sea and on weekends he'd gone with his friends to dive for shellfish in the shallows of a bay. When his time came to die, he'd often thought that the sea, the world of the unseen, the mystery, would be his chosen medium. "Can you radio ahead to the *Hermes* for me?"

"Consider it done," the captain said. "Have the pilot sent to the deck."

U went out. As he descended the three flights, the engine noise modulated into a low snarl. It was the positioning system and the revolve of the drill string at midships. He became rapt with that and slowed his pace so that he drew almost to a stop: the computer-driven thrusters used not merely to keep the ship in position, or not even mainly, but also to keep it from trailing in its own revolve the twist of the drill string that passed down from the two-hundred-foot derrick through a circular opening in the deck, the moon pool. The drill string turned in the center of the opening. The casing would pass through it later, and the cap, and eventually, if sufficient oil were struck, a pumping module and the line that would tie it into the system.

What he'd seen after arriving last night suddenly came back to him. He'd taken a turn on the deck, and beneath the derrick, he'd leaned against the guard rail to look into the hole at the sea. He had never been on such a ship before, and at first glance what he saw impugned common sense—a better than twenty-five-foot hole in the middle of the ship. It was as if he were aboard a big, buoyant doughnut, but, of course, the five-hundred-foot ship otherwise displaced its considerable weight, the tons upon tons of pipe, the machinery, the three cranes, the bunking space for its operating and research crew of fifty, the lab stack near the bow.

The circle of water reflected the rigging lights above and looked white like a moon. Seen from a certain angle—if he crouched a little—it even reflected the waxing moon in the sky, and in the shadow along the far edge, stirred up by the turning drill string, he could see faint traces of the cool, lime-white color of the bioluminents, plankton, krill. . . . He'd felt as though he'd entered an otherworldly zone: the two-hundred-foot derrick above him, the spools, winches, iron scaffolding, and ladders, the engine and compressor, the control platform and watchful, heavily dressed crew of four, the racks of pipe and casing, the drill string turning and passing through the water column to where it bored a hole through the sea floor, seeking out the trapped deposit, the combustible, deliquescent remains of Mesozoic kelp. Petroleum, the quintessential material substance that had driven all of the last century. There were also traces of bioluminescence near the surface, that life and, by implication, all the life teeming in the sea, maybe even kicked up crumbs of *Methanococcus jannaschii*, the microbial species of the newly discerned third Kingdom of life—Archaea—which sought the heat at the vents on the sea bottom. There was a slight stutter to the revolve of the drill string, the resistance of stone upon the teeth of the bit thousands of feet down. Everything in the world, everything humanly brilliant and powerful, and humanly delicate and vulnerable, or even hopeless, and everything in nature ponderous and beautiful and unknown seemed captured in the pool. In the brooding face of that, such singular architectures as the drill ship, a seabed pipeline, the rest of the pipeline system, and the city of Steklyányigórod seemed makeshift and frail.

He resumed his descent. At deck level he walked down the hallway and inside the officers' mess where the others awaited him. Sophia stood back from a table in the far corner, unzipping the top of her survival suit. At the table sat the Russian chopper pilot and the security agent, Braun. The perpetual erectness of Braun's military bearing had become irritating to U, as had Braun's attitude, a continual undertow of restiveness regarding the subordinate position he nevertheless filled to perfection. A laptop computer sat ready in front of him, and near it Sophia's aluminum case stood on its edge. U nodded to her as he came up to the table.

She said, "It's been a long time."

Braun's face lifted to look at U. Always watchful, Braun attended without comment to whatever arose—the degradation of street beggars, lavish banquets laid out in staterooms, the ornate curl of kiosks against a grim sky, or the sheen of dust left on a hotel window sill—but as to where his watchfulness led or how it was formed, what it became in his mind, and what, if anything, was done with it, there was no telling. U had come to distrust Braun. At times, he suspected that Braun had been engaged to watch him.

"You've met?" U said.

"Just now," Sophia replied.

She pulled her arms out of the survival suit, letting the top of it drape down beneath her sweater. She appeared older than he had expected. Her formerly impeccable posture had sagged, the lines in her face had deepened, her hair had silvered, and the flash of her dark eyes was echo of what it had once been. She had what appeared to be a surgical scar below her throat.

He turned to Braun and said, "You'll fly out for Steklyányigórod in a half hour." Then he gestured toward the pilot. "Tell him to prepare. He's to report to the deck."

"And you? You'll travel without security?" Braun said.

U let pass Braun's habit of interrogating by affirming the obvious.

As Braun spoke in Russian to the pilot, Sophia laid her case flat and popped open its latches. When Braun finished, the pilot, a stocky man with broad features, stood up and squared his shoulders under his flight jacket, which had the dispirited appearance of having had its military patches razored off. He nodded deferentially at U and left.

"And then?" Sophia asked.

"Carl?" U said. "Straight back to Houston." He addressed Braun, "Hopefully, you'll be on your way out of Russia today."

"Jones wants him to call Houston first." Sophia said.

"Oh?" He wondered why directives from his superior were coming through her. He paused, waiting for more, but Sophia was silent. To Braun, he said, "So . . . contact Houston from Steklyányigórod for your connections."

Braun had taken this in without changing his expression. "Understood."

"And yourself?" Sophia said to U.

"The *Hermes*. Then Seward. And Seattle and Houston myself."

She plugged one end of the cable into her computer, passed the other end to Braun, and opened her computer's lid. The intent was for her to transfer the preliminary scientific data and her recommendations to Braun's machine. She looked up at U. "I see."

"Coffee?" he said.

"Please."

He moved to the dispenser. Through the galley's serving window, he saw the chief steward dumping slabs of meat from plastic sacks onto the counter, while his helper loaded the dishwasher with lunch plates. U carried a creamer and cups over to the table and then returned for the coffee pot. He went back and began to fill the cups, finding it restful at this moment to be attentive and delicate in the way he poured.

He remembered Sophia on the *Hermes* over twenty-five years ago as it skirted the north of the Aleutians in heavy weather. He remembered the roll of the ship and sleeping with her, the rhythm of the sea articulated in the sway and stitched tight into a knot that encircled the blaze of their joining. He had, now, no sexual expectation, but simply the peculiar, chilled, voyeuristic curiosity over what being in her presence would reveal. In those early days, she'd been a zealous group leader on a research expedition and he an attorney on retainer for a venture capitalist, Arnold Hemming—"The Arm," he was called—who'd ferreted out a legal slit in the National Science Foundation–sponsored exchange with the Soviets during the era of deténte. Hemming had spread the slit into an opening that allowed him to get in behind the curtain, there striking bargains to supply technical support and equipment in exchange for cash and options on yet untapped oil reserves and unconstructed delivery systems.

At that time, the NSF and State Department had winked at Hemming's forays, while the CIA tracked him and the White House cultivated him as a confidante. ZAQ had evolved from the old, compactly woven oil service company into a full-blown proprietary middle-weight with its offices in a Houston high-rise, more field offices, its share in Schtok's Steklyányigórod, its drill ship, and its ranks of specialists, like

Braun. These days, ZAQ bore down hard on the fantail of debris left by the Soviet Empire and carried on an unending string of forays in a nether world of law and investment. For years, U's and Sophia's paths had wound around in the mounting shadow of money, and now, suddenly, they had intersected again.

He returned the coffee pot to the dispenser and came back to the table. In the galley, the dishwasher started up, throbbing heavily. "It's the storm," he said. He left it at that.

"I see." The computers were wedded. She snapped on her power switch and sat, positioning herself lightly in her chair. "This won't take long."

U sat opposite them. "There are no copies? Nothing by disk? And not in the air?"

Sophia looked up, arching her eyebrows. She took out a card, wrote on it, and passed it over to U. "Access."

U studied it . . . QNW2/PSZ. Out of habit, his mind exploded the digits. They flew out brightly, gathered in clusters, and twirled and regathered until they flashed into a form he could safe keep. "By memory only," he said as he pushed the card across to Braun, who was booting up his computer. Sophia typed on her keyboard. There was the clicking of the keys and the soft whirring of tiny fans forming a thin risible above the throbbing in the galley. From the galley, also, came a rhythm . . . a slap followed by a sharp thud, over and over again. The reverberation of the ship's engines made the steel legs of his chair vibrate. U felt himself enveloped by sound.

Sophia looked at him. "Did you get it?"

He said, "It's Q-A-Z- forming a bracket. It's backwards, and it has spawn in it backwards, too. The two is for the double A in the center. The slash is an erratic element. Or an anomaly." He paused, thinking: An erratic leads to a yet undiscovered source of order. An anomaly is an arbitrarily introduced element, presumably completely disconnected, though, truly, it is impossible for anything to be so.

She smiled wanly. "You haven't lost a step."

"I've lost several steps," U said. A wave of fatigue washed over him, coming from the unease he felt in dropping back so adroitly into what others considered his brilliance.

"Do you have it?" Sophia said to Braun.

"It's a cipher," Braun said.

U noted that he'd taken care not to reveal himself by saying too much.

As Braun bent to slide the slip of paper back across the table, U saw the pink of his scalp through his closely cropped, blonde hair. His face was a slightly darker shade of pink. He had thick hands, broad shoulders, a prominent jaw, blue eyes, and a neck almost as wide as his head. He wore a blue suit, pink shirt, and a tightly knotted, red tie so that his head looked like an ornament perched atop a garish base. U set the slip into an ashtray that said Harrah's Club on its bottom. He found a matchbook in his coat pocket and lit the paper. The paper curled into flame. A glutinous thread of carbon hovered above the flame, held aloft by heat, then settled on the table. U brushed it off.

Sophia tapped at her keyboard. "Ready."

Braun punched in his command. The two machines whirred and clicked at each other. "It's transferring," Braun said.

"The access code's in place?" U asked.

When Braun poked a key, Sophia glanced over at his screen and said, "Done."

She met U's eyes over the top of her monitor. Although the look between them began as a professional exchange, what he took as an unspoken affirmation that there was yet another previously set access code in her data, the look lingered on. When U averted his eyes, he saw Braun watching them. He averted them again to the wall above Sophia. The code they'd given Braun called up the files, which were now conjoined with his own files. The code Braun hadn't been given accessed the directory, which was designed as a failsafe shroud around the files, making it impossible for Braun to transfer them to anyone except designated parties. This also wearied U—the elaborate game, the scenarios and deadfalls mounted to keep Braun, or anyone, from breaking out from behind the masks assigned to them.

U sipped his coffee and ran through the protocol as it had emerged: "From here on, you'll send Doctor Kopat's data and your own on a secure ground line. Send it to Jones in Houston. The access code is not to be repeated on any medium. The rest is left to Doctor Kopat and me."

Again Braun nodded.

"Hard copy of the findings," Sophia said, lifting a packet of papers from her case and sliding it across to U. She took out a second packet.

"Parallel findings from the Beaufort, Chukchi, Prince William Sound, and Puget Sound. FBI files. McDuff and her partner, Abby Leonard, have published results and got a grant out of it."

U felt the ship shudder from waves breaking against the hull, and he looked at his watch. Twenty minutes had passed. "FBI files?"

"ZAQ needs to know exactly what they have. All of it."

"Why not ask to see it?"

Sophia snorted. "Why don't you ask her?"

There was a smoldering in her eyes, and as he was drawn into it, he thought . . . so now, here rests the vestige of the old loathing. He remembered that Sophia's eroticism framed her address to the world, that besides her daring, intelligence, and mendacity, she'd also had a pleasuring anima that luxuriated in all the engagements that the world might make with her, even the catastrophes of her own blunders. He remembered that once, long ago, she'd laughed and said, "Whenever I bewitch the world, its return is my beatification."

He gathered up the coffee cups, stood, and moved away, pausing at a porthole to look out at the rising sea, the growing edginess of the cut of white into the crests of the swells. "What is it?" he asked without looking back, and remembering Kate MacDuff's passion for principle. "The environmental damage?"

"Of course. But also design systems. Maybe contracts. Maybe the terms of production, maybe the permit to drill. This could be a serious breach. If those two have it all, then it's as good as out. Sooner or later someone else will have it. It looks like they've got the plans for the Athabascan tar sands, too."

U looked back, forming that in his mind.

Sophia turned to Braun. "Jones will want you to run a check on them."

U thought about the masks, how also one never knew just what they concealed or exactly from what quarter in the game the true animus emanated. He set the cups down on the dispensing stand and stood, gazing through the opening to the galley where two sets of hands coming out of white sleeves worked at the counter. The Jamaican steward's dark hands lifted a slab of meat from the bloody heap, slapped it down, struck it with a cleaver, severing it from bone, then tossed it to the pair of white hands that dunked it into a bowl. In a moment, after the first pair of hands slapped down another slab, the second pair drew the breaded cutlet out of the bowl, laid it on the pile, and the cleaver glinted down to the block again. The rhythm was the same, but it struck U that the sound alone told nothing about what the second pair of hands was doing, and yet once those hands were seen, the nature of what was heard was articulated anew. Paradoxically, a new, unheard beat was added to the rhythm that came from the two bodies in their address to food.

"And require them to turn over their data," Sophia said. "Under threat of lawsit. Then we'll know exactly what they have."

"Absolutely not," U said, coming back along the wall. "What do you think we are?" He addressed Braun directly. "Require nothing of either of them. You're to ask first."

Sophia leaned forward on her elbows and looked at him, while Braun waited, almost smiling. "The data is proprietary," she said.

"Maybe it is. Maybe it isn't," U replied. To Braun, he said, "Locate the labs and the researchers and report back. What we want is a review of what they're working on, what they have, where it's coming from, and if indeed it's proprietary. Do nothing more until you and I hear it from Jones," he said.

Braun again tipped his head and said nothing, which U considered insufferable.

He touched the packet on the table with his fingertips. Knowing that Sophia could muster all her desire to wax extravagant—in this case, apparently, her wish to protect company security as it happened to be tied to the promise of seeing an old adversary punished—U felt that he'd been maneuvered onto a stage. He moved away, remembering how much Sophia despised being thwarted. Then he remembered his fingers on her buttocks, digging in to pull him fast, her heels hooking around his calves, and then his hands on her shoulders, holding her flat against the mattress. A metallic taste came into his mouth as he remembered her voracity and how her mind reciprocated with its reveling body.

He turned back and brought the weight of his legal authority to bear upon Braun. "Do a full report," he said. "But until you hear otherwise, I want it drawn from public materials only, by permission, or from the review in process. I trust that's understood."

"Of course," Braun said, scrutinizing him.

Sophia scrutinized him, as well.

U looked away out the porthole and watched the stray white tatters of gulls wheeling overhead. The water in its chop was turning chalky beneath the darkening cloud cover. He closed his eyes. The hum of the ship's engine rose and fell and broke into the rhythm of the slap of meat and the thud of the cleaver with a snarl as the ship's systems responded to the uneasy sea. He envisioned the drill stem in the center of the moon pool, the metal passing through the luminous tension of the water. The shearwaters made silvery tracks in his brain, turning, hanging, flashing the forms of three crosses, and arching back against the ship's draft, the three of them passing again and again. He couldn't make the albatross appear in his mind. He saw Kate, her quick smile and the knife of her hair falling toward one eye. He remembered how years ago he had feared for the unfriendly waters into which her idealism might cast her.

10

Erratics

"... those ever watchful people,
ever alive to what is passing ..."
—David Thompson, regarding Piegans

AT THE FAR END OF THE GYMNASIUM, a double doorway opened to the lobby. Against the far wall stood a red-and-white Coke machine to which Jack's eyes moved repeatedly, drawn by the slightest hint of someone passing before it. Each time he looked, his alertness rose toward the image of Kate, the ghost-like sense of her that would materialize when she actually appeared.

Gene sat to his left, and next to Gene was Marlene. The gymnasium was cavernous and bright with its white walls, gleaming hardwood floor, and big floodlights. The place smelled of wax and cleaning agents and of the wet carried in: wet hair, wet wool, wet boots from stepping through the slush. At this moment, the gym had fallen under an uneasy hush . . . a murmuring, a subdued, restive hum like water moving under ice, pierced by the steady squeak of the players' sneakers against the floor. A mass of people sat in the center of the stands across the court on the Sandpoint side. There were fewer on this side, but considering the weather Post Falls hadn't brought up a bad crowd.

The game hung poised with the score tied at thirty-six. They had only eight minutes to go and the teams played like two separate kinds of animal, Sandpoint using its bulk against Post Falls, a smaller, quicker pack that whipped around. Now, Post Falls's point guard, Sam Gray, worried Sandpoint's guard at the top of the key. The Sandpoint guard eased back and passed off as the other guard rolled out behind him. Jack watched intently as Travis trailed the guard, broke a screen, and cut him off. Travis's face was flushed and his thick hair stuck straight up. He put a hand in front of the Sandpoint player's face. The ball went to the wing and back again to the point, and then inside on a wild bounce pass that ricocheted clear back into Sam Gray's hands.

The teams flooded down the court, their shoes thudding and then squeaking as Post Falls set its offense. Sandpoint collapsed into a double-team every time the ball went to Travis, who was a shooter, and left Sam alone on the outside, daring him to take a shot. Finding no one else open, he'd so far been shooting away vainly. It was as if the game had dropped into an entropy of errant passes, traveling violations, steals, and missed shots. The longer the stalemate, the deeper the crowd sank into an uneasy quiet. The Post Falls cheerleaders stood off in a corner of the court with their pompoms drooping at their sides.

Nothing at all was happening.

Across the court, the heads of the Sandpoint fans moved diffidently to follow the ball. On Jack's side, voices murmured, and then one from several rows behind emerged angrily: "Coach Chambers needs to get his head out of his ass." The voice belonged to Dick Petrie, the vitriol and the violation of the taboo against profanity at school functions being his habit. The basketball bounced, the players' shoes squeaked, and the ball came to Travis. When the double team collapsed on him, he passed off to Sam, who clanked a jumper off the rim. Sandpoint's center gathered in the ball and the teams flooded back the other direction. So it was.

Jack turned his eyes to the entryway, hoping to see Kate—hair combed close to her head, green coat open over her cream-colored shirt, and the rakish way she had of walking. He'd hoped she would be coming in with her face lifted, searching the stands for him. There was no one there. By now, even considering the snow, she should be here.

He drew his eyes back. Gene sat with his arms on his knees and a smile slid up under his grizzle of beard. His hawk nose stood in silhouette as he watched the game intently, and his head was scrunched down so that his ears almost touched the tufted fur lining of the sheepskin vest he always wore, no matter what the occasion. It was stained with grit and the damp, but underneath he had on a fresh white shirt. On

Gene's other side, Marlene held herself straight on the narrow bench, her plucked eyebrows raised as if the game astonished her. Despite himself, Jack smiled, too. He liked Marlene's way of pushing her absurdities into a style. It was as if the two of them wore masks: hers of unending amazement and Gene's sardonic one mounted against the perpetual pain he carried from his old fractures and shrapnel wounds.

Jack was glad that Marlene had Gene off the sedatives and alcohol and on her bitter-smelling teas. He was glad that Gene's son, Chris, had decided to move up from L.A. to live with his father while finishing high school, and that he and Travis played basketball together. Jack could see the back of Chris's head, the closely cropped black hair. A year younger than Travis, Chris was the backup point guard. Not yet as smooth a ball-handler as Sam, he was quicker and a better shot.

Sandpoint lost the ball and it returned to Post Falls's end in a rush of blue uniforms. Sam missed a shot. White jerseys swirled around the rebound and the ball went back again in another rush. Jack heard Dick Petrie's voice in a bitter curl of words. Here and there, other voices broke in . . . Max Costa, the grocer; Ernie Polk, a trucker who'd just lost his wife to cancer; and Nadine Gray, Sam's mother, crying out, "It's all right. Come on. Come on." Jack glimpsed Nadine's face, flushed and determined, set with anger against Petrie's taunt.

By being a part of the traveling entourage that followed the teams, or running into people at the cafe or at community meetings, or even from having gone to school with some of them, Jack knew most of the Post Falls parents. They were devoted to the kids. Though the town was changing, the parents were still rough-hewn, many of them, and this carried through to their children, the girls and the boys, who played a muscular, bared-teeth form of sport. A far-flung, largely rural school district that included several small towns, like Bayview and Rathdrum, the community dated back to logging and hay farms, and before that to mining. An old radical strain ran through it like a line of metal with its ties to Coeur d'Alene, Wallace, and Kellogg, to the Wobblies, bootlegging, prostitution, and gambling, and before that to tribes that had never been defeated, exactly, but surrounded. The most durable of agents had to be topography, Jack had long believed, so far subject to change mainly by what was called catastrophe. . . .

Extreme shifts in climate, and the advance and retreat of the glaciers.

The Spokane Flood, 14,000 years ago, which had buffed to a shine the rough cuts the glaciers had ground out.

Fire.

Dalton Bender, his ominous transformation of economy, and before him, the timber barons, before that the army.

The mines.

The railroad.

The fur trade.

An old snake was still lodged in the people, many of whom lived in mountain pockets, a diamondback, a living, commonly held relic of the hazard, brutality, and opportunism, and also of the common earth-bound competence with mountain weather, floods, hunting, fishing, with machines, and with raising the kids, keeping things safe, and putting up stores against hard winters. Jack rather liked the disorder this relic stood for, the high-spirited, sometimes visionary, and usually irreverent unruliness in the people.

But political discussions, both he and Kate entered with extreme caution.

Kate would have preferred more decorum, anyway, and sometimes she countered her unease with the people by lapsing into excursions of generosity, like supplying half the cakes for a bake sale or taking on the plight of somebody like Bud Willy's wife. She was less patient than he with the haphazardly stitched-together pieces: the vets like Gene, born-again Christians, Pantheists, Indians, gyppo loggers like himself, retired California cops, failed Hollywood actors, and county sheriffs, like Dan Painter, who differed from sheriffs in her home country of Alabama in his absolute incorruptibility but was similar in his love of talk. There were also the still working miners, carpenters, restaurant operators like Marlene, beauticians, aging hippies, marijuana grow-ers, government foresters, as Jack's father had been, teachers, naval researchers, and a handful of agency and contract scientists, like Kate, biologists, and geologists, heavy equipment operators, and outlaw bik-ers, like Joe Bliss.

Jack looked up, remembering that he had to be on the watch for Bliss, too, whose daughter played on the girls' team and who should be turning up soon.

The basketball game had fallen into decay. Jack felt for Travis, who was visibly tiring. Again, Sandpoint had left Sam alone on the perimeter, gambling that he'd shoot and miss, which he did. Sandpoint's center gathered in the air ball, and the ball went back to Sandpoint's end. A pass went around Travis and in to the center, who shoved his way through the opening and dumped the ball home. The Sandpoint crowd exploded into a shout, and their energy passed to their team, while the Post Falls players aimlessly brought the ball back. Sandpoint took it away and ran a break that ended in a lay-up, while the Post Falls defenders were still crossing the center line. Again, the Sandpoint fans erupted. Coach Chambers jumped up to the line, signaling for a time-out.

"There," Jack said. "He has to sit his starters down."

The scar on Gene's cheek bent upwards in a grin.

A buzz drifted across the floor from the Sandpoint stands. Both sets of cheerleaders began a chant and Jack dutifully rose to his feet but didn't join in. Gene stayed where he was. Marlene stood, clapping, although the Post Falls chant rang thin, barely hopeful, and within it the individual voices could be picked out as if it were a hymn sung by a very small choir—Marlene's voice, Nadine's, Ernie's, Max's, and Dick Petrie's cutting in and out in a harangue against the coach. Such as it was, this was the leading edge of the fourth, most true dimension of the game, the voices coming out of the tangle like an informing underworld of the offspring's enactment on the plane above.

Jack's eyes returned to the entryway. He too had a personal relic that had endured years of marriage and was composed of the missed connections with Kate, changed schedules, delayed arrivals, and the long separations caused by her work that at times made him feel powerless and vulnerable.

The coach substituted for everyone, bringing in Chris, backup wings, a center, and Randy Petrie. Small and wiry, Randy played like a dervish, frantic in his defense, but usually giving up the ball whenever he touched it. Jack could feel the father's joyless silence as hard as a bullet at his back. The Sandpoint coach fed in substitutes and the game got yet looser. Sandpoint ran its lead to eight points, but in the confusion Chris stopped and hit a three pointer. Marlene leaped to her feet and yelled, "All right, Chris!" Sandpoint countered, and then Coach Chambers signaled for another time out.

Jack nudged Gene. "Nice."

Gene grinned.

Jack touched Gene's knee. "I've got to go use the phone."

He picked his way down from the stands and walked along the mat at the edge of the court. In the lobby, a few kids scurried around the food concession, chattering on cell phones. The pay phone down the hall had a girl attached to its cord. Seeing Jack, the girl cast a sidelong glance from beneath her green eye shadow. Compliant like a child, but, Jack guessed, potentially defiant in her sense of deprivation, she wasn't about to get off the phone to suit him. He gave her room by moving clear of the lines back to the windows in the lobby, and searched over the parking lot. Big snowflakes twirled in the sky, piling on the roofs of cars.

He stepped outside into the slush, hoping that somehow his presence might conjure Kate's Subaru. He moved along, scanning the cars, then stopped and looked out to the east toward town, which was built around the north arch of Lake Pend Oreille. But for the snow, he'd have been able to see across to the break in the Cabinet Mountains where the Clark Fork River entered the lake. In the break lay the Cabinet Gorge Dam, built in the same place the ice dam had been ten or twelve or thirteen thousand years ago. Behind the ice dam had lain a great lake two hundred miles long, the water backed up deep into what was now Missoula, Montana.

Repeated ruptures had sent water roaring through the mouth of the Clark Fork, into Lake Pend Oreille, right by where Jack and Kate's house stood, across the Rathdrum Prairie, by Post Falls, through Spokane, and to the south and west over the lowlands and through the river channels, through the coulee country where Jack's parents had grown up, burying ten thousand square miles in all and converging in the Columbia gorge east of Portland. Sometimes it slammed into the narrows with such force that the cataract retreated hundreds of miles back into Idaho. Everything about the place between where he stood and west to the Cascade Mountains and south to Oregon was defined by these events, having occurred perhaps seventy-five times over several thousand years . . . how precipitous the canyons were, where the farmland became arable, where cities and towns came to be built in the broad bottoms, where the woods were, the lakes, rivers, and streams, where the outcroppings of basaltic rock lay exposed, what were called the "channeled scablands," and where the randomly placed, sometimes bigger than box-car-sized boulders loomed out of extraordinary

landscapes. The boulders had been transported through the gargan-
tuan eddies and dropped like pebbles to the bottom. Called erratics,
these hulks defied sense at first, for they didn't match the geology of
their surroundings. They and the floods that delivered them were a
reminder of the frailty of human action, even of humanly caused cata-
clysms and large-scaled perversities, and so the ultimate forgiveability
of human twists on the inexorable chanciness of the world. A positiv-
ist, Jack believed in God in this way, knowing that his life was nothing
more than an infinitesimally small thread in the big weave.

He returned to the lobby and heard the squeak of shoes and the
bouncing ball again. The phone was free. Jack moved to it, dialed in
his home number, and listened to the sound of air on the other end.
He disconnected, holding his finger on the collar, and dialed again. It
sounded like wind. He replaced the receiver, stood still, and thought—
But she's not here. She should be here. Since she's late, she'd have tried
to leave a message there, knowing I would check the machine. Then
he thought that Kate might be near, expecting to get here soon and
not wanting to stop to call home. Everything might be fine. But if she
were to be much later than this, she'd know he'd be worrying. She'd
leave a message. But the phone was out. There was snow. A line might
be down.

He dialed the operator and asked her to run a check. As he waited,
he listened to the squeak of feet going to the far end of the court, what
would be the Post Falls goal. He heard a whistle, and then quiet from
the stands. The operator came back on the line and told him that the
line was disconnected. "You mean the lines are down?" he asked.

"We don't have reports of downed lines in your area."

"The receiver could be off the hook?"

"No, sir," she said. "It's reporting a disconnect. It's probably inside
the house."

He hung up and moved slowly down the hall, thinking: Maybe it's
nothing. There's nothing for me to do except be where I'm supposed
to be. Beyond the windows, the dry, light snow swirled. He swung into
the gymnasium, spying Travis in the pack at the other end of the court.

He moved along the base of the stands and looked at the score-
board. The game had wound down to three minutes and Sandpoint's
lead had held steady. He climbed toward Gene and Marlene and saw
Joe Bliss way up at the top, leaning against the wall with his feet up on

the bench below and sporting his usual outfit: black boots, black jeans, black turtleneck, biker's vest to match his neatly combed, long black hair. Spots of bright glimmered on him: his rings, a necklace, silver conches strung from his vest. A tattoo emerged from his shirtsleeves. His wife sat next to him, nearly popping out of a lavender bodysuit. Jack caught Bliss's eye and raised his palms questioningly. Bliss smiled, his eyes watering, dazzled, and drugged. He gave Jack a thumbs up, which Jack took to mean he had his rig out.

Jack took his seat next to Gene and saw that Coach Chambers had put both Chris and Sam in the back court with Travis. The crowd was restive, its quiet broken by the occasional encouraging voice, rising like the caw of a crow.

"Three guards," Gene said. "It's an idea. Bliss says he cut a deal with Chuck Lamb to take his self-loader up and bring the logs down. He says Chuck's up there, now."

"Fuck," Jack said. He'd thrown Lamb off a job a couple of years ago for stealing logs. He guessed that Lamb owed Bliss something, or Bliss owed it to Lamb, that there was some entanglement between them that one of them was likely to draw him into. "I'll deal with that later," he said. "Our phone's disconnected."

"Disconnected?"

"The line's open."

Gene looked at him, squinting. It was the expression he took on whenever he studied something closely, as if he'd just rolled over a dead animal and was prodding it to see what had caused its demise. Jack turned his head back to the game. In the corner of his eye, he saw the moon of Marlene's face turn to Gene, her hand moving inside Gene's elbow and resting on his knee. They were interrogative and affectionate gestures, that was all, but they further piqued Jack's disquiet.

He tried to concentrate on the end of the game. It was a good strategy to have Chris in the back court with Travis and Sam, the ball passing among the three of them, and as the two, now—Chris and Travis—took the shots, it was clear that Sandpoint's defense was befuddled. Given time, the three-guard strategy might have worked, but Post Falls lacked someone to quicken it by countering the oppressive size of Sandpoint's inside players. Chris had Gene's eyes, cat-like and tuned to motion. What Travis had was steadiness and intelligence, not

Chris's predatory alertness. Chris sank a short jumper and pumped his fists at his teammates, urging them on as they ran down court, but the clock was ticking down. Even the shouts from the Post Falls side and Sandpoint's jubilation at the certain win seemed hollow and perfunctory. Post Falls could not tighten the score, hence the moves degraded to nothing more than a practice game with little happening except to go inexorably to the end. A shadow played against the Coke machine and Jack glanced toward the entryway. No one was there. His attitude toward the game came to be overwhelmed by his deepening worry. The elements peeled off to leave the essence, which for Jack was the sense of interior decay.

*　*　*

After the game, Jack asked the coach to let him take Travis straight home rather than ride the bus back to the school. "We've got a glitch in our schedule," Jack said, leaving it at that.

"Be good to him," Chambers said. "He played his heart out tonight."

"Thanks," Jack said. Normally, he would have offered more...they all played hard, or they're coming along, or we'll be ready next time...but he said nothing further.

He told Travis about the compliment as they pulled out of the parking lot. "We lost, though," Travis said coolly, a judgment seemingly leveled at a condition of which he was merely a part. Jack explained to him about his mother's not having come to the end of the game as they'd planned, how she was late, how the phone was disconnected. Thus, their drive through the snow down Highway 95 and easterly to the foot of the lake, which customarily would have had as its main feature a rehash of the game, fell into a troubled quiet.

When they turned off the highway onto their road, Travis asked, "How worried are you?"

"More than I like."

"Mom should never have gone with that woman."

"I think you're right."

"Why'd she do it?"

"She likes to help, I guess." He knew it was much bigger than that. He couldn't name it as one thing, but only in its parts: kindness, the capacity to take on another's trouble as her own, curiosity, indepen-

dence, and a sense of cause, of protecting another woman fallen vic-
tim to a hardship Kate herself had never experienced, and so possibly
even out of guilt for her own good fortune, and certainly out of moral
obligation, and then maybe out of an interior trouble in her own life,
something coming out of the shift to working on her own instead of
for a salary and having her last child soon to leave home. What had
come was an unsettling life-change not fully decipherable to Jack and
likely not to Kate, either.

When Jack nosed into their lane he realized—not naming the obvious and seeking an escape, maybe, into the comfort of routine—that
the snow would need to be cleared before it got much deeper. If he
didn't plow with the truck soon, he'd have to fire up the tractor and use
the loader. The way the lane was, Kate would have a struggle getting the
Subaru in, and then it hit him for certain: She wasn't here, either. He
pulled into the yard, turning hard and kicking hunks of snow against
the wheel wells. Only the van was there, heaped on its top with snow.
He barely registered the tracks that showed themselves as shallow furrows made several hours earlier, and already filling in with fresh snow.
He glanced at Travis, who sat erect with his hands resting in his lap.

"Mom's not home."

"Indeed." He hovered for a moment in the center of the turn-about,
holding down the clutch with his foot, his hand on the gear shift.
Something else was awry, something unfamiliar, an asymmetry, something off-balance. Jack scrutinized the house, still holding the clutch
down and easing the floor shift into reverse.

Travis spoke matter-of-factly: "My bedroom light's on."

Jack moved his eyes rightward. In the waning dusk, pale light
washed from the room behind the kitchen across the snow and into
the trees. "You didn't leave it on?"

"I always turn it off."

Jack eased the truck backward, then forward, inching up near the
walkway. He poked in the headlight knob, switched off the engine, and
withdrew the key—something he never did at home.

"See?" Travis said.

With the headlamps out, the wash of light from Travis's room into
the trees at the far side of the house was the more pronounced, then he
glimpsed light seeping from the barn. Jack tried to remember whether
he'd left it on or not. He thought he had. Berg appeared from around

the corner of the house and moved into the lawn and stopped, when normally she would have been dancing around the front of the truck. The pickup's two doors creaked heavily as they climbed out. They moved up the walkway, and Berg came to them, limping.

"She's hurt," Travis said.

Jack bent to feel her front shoulder. The dog quivered under his hands and began a dance around them, favoring one leg, winding back and forth from one of them to the other. It was as if the usual crazy dance she performed upon the return of her masters . . . or hosts, as Kate liked to say . . . had been condensed to a compacted circuit.

As they moved to the door, Jack saw through the window and in the dim light inside the end of the sofa placed askew . . . something wrong . . . and tacked to the door, a piece of curled paper, but he didn't fix on it because of what next he registered more clearly inside . . . something very wrong . . . the sofa turned completely around and a heap on the floor. "Shit," he said softly. Then he said, "Travis, step away from the door." Quickly, he went back to the truck, unzipped the bottom of the gun case he kept behind the seat, and drew out his 30/30. He found a box of shells, slid four of them into the chamber and went back to the door. "Stay clear," he said. He turned the knob and swung open the door. The door thudded eerily against the wall.

He stepped inside. Travis followed close behind. There was a small light on in the kitchen and from the foyer he could catch glimmerings in all the wrong places . . . pots and pans scattered over the counter and floor. He stood and listened carefully, hearing nothing but the silence of the house, his own breath, and the breath of his son. Between them stood the dog. Light from Travis's room pooled shallowly at the head of the hallway. He lifted the rifle a little, reached out and switched on the living room light, and waited a few seconds. Still hearing nothing, he took a step into the room. In the bright, the chaos rushed at him: chairs tipped over, cushions askew, and chunks of stuffing emerging, and at the far wall the bookshelf stripped, books dumped on the floor. The television was upended and the cabinets disgorged of their contents. Videos, tapes, compact disks lay wasted everywhere. The computer monitor hung from its cable and was turned on. Nearly upside down, the screen was filled with silver.

Perhaps a half-minute had now passed, but it seemed as if time had collapsed into itself and its immense, rapidly accumulating weight was dragging forward in tiny increments. Jack looked at Travis. Travis looked back. Travis's face was drawn flat with shock.

"Burglars?"

Jack softly repeated the word: "Burglars." He passed his eyes back across the shambles . . . things broken, cut open, things in mindless heaps. "Or jackals."

Berg circled them and put her muzzle into Travis's hand. She limped, but not badly. She'd been kicked, maybe. Jack went to the kitchen entryway. Before him lay more of the same . . . the contents of drawers scattered, over in the nook the table overturned, and chairs on their backs.

Travis came up behind him. "Jeez."

Jack stepped into the kitchen. His eyes went to the top of the refrigerator where he'd left his pistol. He couldn't see it, though a loaf of bread still sat there. He moved around the cooking island. Pans were strewn across the floor, and dishes, apparently swept out of the overhead cupboards and allowed to shatter on the counter. Jack's boots crunched on glass as he walked. Carefully, he picked his way to the refrigerator and stood up on his tiptoes. The pistol wasn't there. He saw that a piece of the telephone line still sprouted from the jack above the counter, near the sink. The line had indeed been clipped, then he spotted the telephone near the bottom of a heap on the floor . . . what had been emptied there from the drawers: knives and forks, screwdrivers, electrical tape, bundles of wire, a bottle of nails, hammer, poaching cups, spare batteries, broken down flashlights, old canning lids, cooking tongs, crayons, a card of thumbtacks, photographs, a chisel, a garlic press, a pizza cutter . . . things that had been allowed to gather in the drawers over the years, a mixed collection of still-used things and items that had assumed the quality of family artifacts together with the telephone. Jack felt a wave of outrage, and then suddenly spooked by an absence, he glanced over at the entryway. Travis wasn't there. He wheeled around, the debris at his feet clattering, and he called: "Travis?"

No answer. He heard footfalls proceeding up the stairs to the loft. Quickly, he stepped back to the doorway, through the foyer and into the living room. An eerie clatter of the dog's nails reverberated on the wooden steps, and he was spooked again. "Travis?"

He heard the muffled response: "Yeah?"

Jack moved to the near end of the hallway, which was open to the loft. Travis had turned on the lights in all the rooms along the hall. He looked up. "Are you okay?"

Travis's head appeared above the railing, his face inclining downward and picking up highlights from below like a planet. The voice came out clearly. "Yeah, but it's a mess."

"Come down," Jack said.

"Okay."

Travis turned away from the rail and Jack heard him shuffling around. "Come down now, son," he said.

"Okay."

Jack was aghast that he'd left Travis without telling him clearly and pointedly to watch out. It was the second time in the last twenty-four hours that he'd done something like this. He moved past the stairway, holding his rifle at the ready, and looked into Travis's room and then the bathroom and Kate's study, each of them ransacked and littered. He looked up the stairway. "Travis?"

He'd begun thinking about what might have happened to Kate ... he didn't think she'd had time to return here. But maybe she hadn't gone ahead after all. Maybe she'd thought better of it and come back. He wondered if she'd been kidnapped, and then wondered if she was being held somewhere on the premises. He felt a panic, then checked himself ... no, no tracks, the tracks he'd seen on the driveway were too old, and he went up to the window in Kate's study and peered out. He had a narrow vantage on the truck, its fresh tracks, alongside the other tracks two or three hours old. He pulled back and inhaled deeply, trying to get a grip on himself. "Travis. Now."

"I'm coming." Travis thudded down the stairs, the dog clattering after him. "They broke into the gun closet upstairs," Travis said. "There's not a gun in there. They broke the hinges and pried the door right off its lock."

"I want you to stay here with me," Jack said.

"Okay. But if they were after the guns, then why all the rest of this?"

"I have no idea. We're going to call the sheriff."

They went back to the kitchen. Jack laid the 30/30 on the stovetop counter and drew the telephone answering machine from the pile on the floor. He set it down next to the sink. Remembering that he kept an extra line in one of the drawers, he crouched over the heap, fished through it, and found it.

Travis was at the counter near the doorway, looking out the window. "The shop light's on, along with the light in the barn."

Agitated, Jack lurched to one side, drawing the 30/30 nearer. "Turn on the floods."

There was a switch for the outside lights in the foyer, and Travis went to it. Jack stood, removed the fitting from the answering machine, inserted the end of the new line into it, and set it on the counter. The flood lamps flared on and Jack gazed out the window above the sink at the illuminated yard and lane leading to the shop, hay barn, and corral. He pulled back, feeling exposed to whatever watchers might conceivably be out there. "We'd better stay away from the windows." With his foot, he shoved at the heap on the floor to clear a space to stand in; he slipped the other end of the line into the wall jack and then the plug back into the socket. The machine's operating lights came on. He picked up the receiver, put it to his ear, and listened to the dial tone.

"Did you see my room?" Travis said. He'd moved to the wall opposite Jack, over where he'd stood with Gene in the morning. "They tore my posters off the walls. That's all they did, except they took my new bat out."

Jack set the receiver back on its receptacle. His son's brow was furrowed. He was wearing a red "Bama" sweatshirt sent him by his grandfather in Demopolis and he had the hood folded back so that he looked like a monk, standing straight with his hands at his sides.

"And Mom's study? My bat's in there. It's broken. They must've used it on her file cases. Everything's dumped out. But they didn't take the stereo equipment, or the TV."

They paused for a moment, looking at each other and around the kitchen, and then back at each other. Jack shifted his weight, glass crunching under his boots. He felt the heinous violation of the act rushing at him like fire.

"And Mom's computers are sitting there like always, not trashed at all." He turned to face Jack directly. "Dad, where is she?" His voice broke. "Where's Mom?"

Again, Jack inhaled deeply and held the air. His breath expired shuddering. A pit yawed in his stomach, and his answer sounded hollow: "She could just be hung up somewhere on the road. She could have been trying to call. There's no reason to jump to conclusions . . ."

Just then, the telephone rang at his back, and he jerked violently. He lurched around and grabbed the receiver.

"The phone works," the voice said.

For a split second, Jack was completely befuddled, and then recognizing the voice, he said, "Gene?"

"If it didn't, I was coming over," Gene said. "Did you hear from Kate?"

Jack stared at the machine. It did not indicate that new messages had come in. "No," he said.

There was a pause, and then Gene said, "What's wrong, Jack?"

"Our house has been vandalized."

"What?"

"Wrecked." He heard his own voice crack. "The place is a wreck." His hands were shaking. He looked over at Travis, who was staring intently back at him, listening, and Jack then more fully registered the drawn and bewildered fright in his son's face, which must have been a mirror of his own. "Kate's not here. This place has been buzz-sawed."

"I'm coming over," Gene said. "Call Painter."

"Right."

"I'm coming over," Gene said. "Call the fucking sheriff and get his ass over there. It's Kate."

"What?" Jack said. "It's Kate what?"

He saw a new alarm dart into Travis's face. Jack raised a hand, meaning to signal to him that it was all right, or not that, not all right, that it was not anything new about his mother, but only that she wasn't here and they didn't know why.

"Kate's your first priority, right?"

"Right." The tone in Gene's voice had conjured up for Jack an image of his friend's face, like his son's alert face on the basketball court, taking everything in . . . ever watchful. Jack punched the message button on the machine. It began playing the first message left on the tape: Kate, two evenings ago, leaving word about where she was with closing out her project down at Dworshak and telling him when she'd be done the next day, and when she would set out—ahead of the storm, she'd hoped—and when she would arrive home. The sound of her familiar voice filled him with unfathomable pain.

"Who's that?" Gene said.

"It's the machine," Jack said. "It's an old message."

"I love you," Kate said on the machine. "Love to Travis."

The next message would be him calling from the warehouse to let Kate know he was coming with Travis, which Kate had interrupted by answering the phone. He would hear her voice on it, too, saying, "Jack? Do you have Travis?"

Berg was nuzzling at Travis's hip over on the opposite side of the island, looking to be petted, but Travis stood absolutely still, stiff-faced with apprehension.

Jack punched the OFF button on the machine.

"I'm coming," Gene said. "You stay put. Call Painter and be careful."

11

Zero

"**THERE'S A ROAD** up here on the right," Winona said. "Slow down."

Kate allowed the car to slow down.

"But keep it going. Not that slow," Winona said. "Faster."

Kate gave the car a little more gas. The cold rushed at her face and neck. She could hear the hum of the tires through the missing windows. Her legs were still shaking.

"Take that road," Winona said, pointing at an opening in the trees. "Don't stop."

The headlights played against the mouth of a snow-covered road. Kate turned the car into the softness. They'd already taken a left turn off the highway and come along the slowly ascending highlands toward the woods, and now the trees crowded close upon this back road, which stretched and wound before her in the headlights like a lamprey, smooth, glimmering, and swollen to a mound in its center.

They had turned before even reaching Cranbrook where by Winona's reports, garbled as they had been, her brother, possibly, and certainly her brother's estranged wife, Ruth, and her brother's friend, Wayne, and her mother, her mother's husband, and who knew who all else in the pack of them, were waiting to take her under their protection. Instead, the people in Cranbrook for all Kate knew were fictions, as the friend in Yahk, Lucy, must have been, as Yahk and Cranbrook themselves might have fed the fiction, plucked from the air as Hope, earlier, Skagway, Nadu, Tyee, and Dream had been. Now they were here, going where Kate had no idea, and whether Winona knew, Kate also had no idea. The woman had transported deep into her derangement where nothing was what it appeared to be, except the pistol which by the hook of treachery was what she clung to. In all Kate's life, albeit much of it passed in the midst of violence, she had never had a weapon held on her, nor anything near to it.

Kate had passed into a disbelieving state of alert over Winona's expectation that they would be able to go very far on this road. No one else had driven it since the snowfall had begun. If they stopped, if the car bottomed out and they had to make an exit, that would be it, Kate decided. She would run, never mind the snow and the night. If Winona wanted to shoot, that was fine. Kate had a furious vision of herself dodging back to the highway and ending up as Winona had been when she'd found her, hiding out in a ditch in the cold while she waited for someone to happen by.

The air rushed through the missing window at her side and streamed straight out the blown-away window in the hatch. She felt the chill against her neck and through her shirt and thermal top to her chest. The car plowed ahead, grabbing at gravel beneath the snow. Kate began looking for dips where the snow might have drifted and into which she could hang up the car, and then have to get out.

"Keep it going," Winona said. "You stop on this road, or accidentally-on-purpose put it into a slide, or do anything, I'll kill you. You know how to drive in this shit. Don't you dare fuck with me." She raised the pistol, leveling it at Kate's head. In the corner of her eye, Kate saw the barrel wobbling with the motion of the car.

The road went around an abutment. Before them loomed a rising straightaway. The woods pressed in on the right, and the left side was dark, as if there were an abyss. Kate had no idea what lay over the edge . . . a gradual slope, a precipitous drop. Here and there, a sapling scraped at the car's undercarriage.

"You're dead, honey, if this car don't make it," Winona said.

Kate glanced over. Winona's wrenched face picked up highlights from the dash, and her eyes glittered the same color as the gun that was poised four inches from Kate's face. Ahead, Kate thought she saw another turn. As she approached it, she thought she caught the flash of something behind her, a spark in the dark.

The light disappeared as soon as she came around the turn, which was extreme and steep. They were going up a mountainside. Kate had to give the car more gas to keep it moving. Her headlights swept over the tips of trees on the left side of the road. There was a slope there, and not necessarily a drop-off. The car shuddered as the wheels whirled and grabbed, and Kate thought it might soon high-center and if it did she'd have to duck down and go for it, open the door and jump, and go for the edge, taking her chances on whatever lay below, and then head for that light, or the highway.

She spoke. "I've got chains." She was thinking about that, too, maybe stop to put chains on, and run. "They're in the back."

"Keep it going, bitch," Winona hissed.

—She knows she'll have her hands full if she lets me out of the car, Kate thought. It's as if in her imbecility she nevertheless has a lit up rheotaxis in there somewhere making a map somehow in the wilderness of her brain that keeps her faced upstream and countering my every thought.

They came out on a second straightaway where the ascent grew more gradual. The light appeared again, playing faintly against the trees on the left, and then glimmered directly behind them. It was a pair of headlights. They glared for an instant in the rearview mirror as they passed, sweeping the dark, and then came back, steadying right behind the Subaru, glaring through the hole in the hatch window and refracting in tiny diamond shapes against the shattered glass at the edges. Winona's body jerked. She turned to look, then snapped open her seat belt and whirled completely around, looking. "Shit!" she said. She came back, thumping her knee against the dash and leveling the pistol at Kate's ear. "Faster." Then she screamed it: "Faster! Stay on the road!"

Whatever it was . . . a truck, judging by its headlights . . . and whoever . . . it was bearing down on them. Kate accelerated, but the car fishtailed and swung to the right. She let up on the gas, corrected the slide, and went ahead. The drag of the snow served to slow the car and keep it on the road. It promised that sooner or later they would have to stop. Kate saw that soon this was all going to end and become something else. She was sweating and her legs shook uncontrollably. The air blew against the sweat on her neck and chest and made her cold. There was another turn ahead, this one swinging left. They weren't going to make it to the turn before the headlights were right upon them.

"Faster!" Winona screamed.

"I can't!"

"Faster!"

—Where? Faster to where?

She said it: "To where? To where?"

"Nowhere!" Winona screamed. Her hysterical laugh suddenly filled the car. "Faster to Hell's fury!" She grabbed Kate's hair and yanked, jerking Kate's head to the side, then released her. The car skittered crazily. Winona screamed, "Go faster!"

The car fishtailed. The headlights at the rear glared back from the Subaru's rearview mirror so that Kate couldn't see ahead. They outlined Winona's form next to her—the havoc of her hair around her head and her arms raking the air. Now, Kate could hear the truck, the roar of it coming upon them . . . coming . . . too close . . . and then it slammed into the back of the car and drove it rightwards and sideways into the ditch at the base of the switchback. Kate's head lurched back and then forward when the car hit the bank. The truck's headlights bounced up. The car was tipped to the right. The truck's engine roared as it backed out, and in a flash Kate thought it was going to come back to pound them again. She braced herself against that, grabbing the wheel and struggling to pull herself straight. The truck stopped, its engine dropping to idle. Its lights poured into the Subaru.

Winona was scrunched half onto the floor and against her door, and she came up part way, brandishing the pistol. Kate saw the white of her face rising, the detail of the spittle on her lips, and her black pupils dilated to overwhelm the blue of her eyes, and around the eyes and down to the cheeks the discoloration like bruising. Suddenly, she began firing the pistol. The inside of the car thundered with gunshots, one deafening boom after another. She shot through the roof of the car, and then bringing herself higher, pushing up off the floor, she shot at the dashboard . . . four, five, six times. She emptied the pistol into the dashboard, and bent forward and huddling over the pistol, kept pulling the trigger so that the pistol issued a string of dry clicks.

Frozen in place, and astonished that she hadn't been hit . . . or at least in that moment, as the awareness of it flashed through her mind, Kate didn't think she'd been hit. How this had come to be dazzled her so that she felt like she could float away into the air . . . the clumsily and tremulously formed sense of what she would later ponder, what level of Winona's being it was that had willed her not to shoot at Kate, not even once, but to shoot up the car instead, whether a capitulation or surrender to the oblivion and the Hell's fury she'd named or a testament to the fact that she, Winona, driven by her mysterious mapwork and yet held in check by the cleaving in her being, or by the pool of profound innocuousness at her bottom nature, had never intended to shoot her, or couldn't have shot her . . . Kate didn't know.

Then all she could think was: Now! She's snapped completely! I've got to get out, now!

She tried that, pulling on the latch and shoving with all her strength against the door. She forced it open a crack, but it was stuck, or sprung, or jammed up against a rock, or held fast by the snow. The headlights from the truck glared into the Subaru. She tried to squeeze herself out through the crack, while Winona was hunched over the gun, still pointing it at the dashboard or engine compartment and still dry-firing it as if to further annihilate the car itself. Kate saw the midsection of a man sliding down next to her blown-out window. Hands grabbed the door by its edge and bent it up, making a heavy creak, and then coming near, the hands took her and drew her out by her shirtfront, and suddenly spun her around in midair.

An arm wrapped around her belly to hold her off the ground. She relented. The man carried her alongside the Subaru and dragged her feet up the bank. They moved along to the back of the truck, or van, and he set her down. Utterly bewildered, she stood still. But then she was staring dumbly at the truck . . . a panel truck, an old but shining, silver-colored, four-wheel-drive Dodge Power Wagon tricked out with risers, big knobby tires, spotlights, gas cans mounted in cages . . . and the confirmation of it, the complete inevitability of its appearing, was shocking, as was the man when she turned to see him . . . Bud. He had the smell and size of Bud, and his persona was affirmed by what he then did to her . . . he turned her back around and pulled her hands together and wrapped something tightly around her wrists. He reached for the rear door and swung it open, revealing a black space. Driven suddenly into a frenzy, she twisted violently and felt a shout tearing up her throat. She was grabbed by the shirt and the waist of her pants, jerked up, and heaved inside. A weight came onto her buttocks, a foot, maybe, pressing her down. She was shoved deeper along the panel until her head bumped something hard, the corner of something metal. The blow was sharp enough to daze her. It was dark. The cold seeped over her through the open door. The floor vibrated from the idling engine.

She lay still on her belly, fighting against blacking out, and heard Winona's piercing, faraway voice: "It wasn't my idea. She was trying to take me away."

Kate registered that, as well, the strange deceit, the fresh start on denials, what also seemed at once unbelievable and inevitable. It now became incomprehensible to her that she hadn't made her escape back in Moyie, or Yahk, or as soon as Winona produced the pistol, or something, somewhere . . . anywhere. As she lay on the panel, utterly still, barely sensible, she was galled by her stupidity.

She heard a man's voice rumbling, then a thud, Winona's voice crying out at the side of the truck, and the rumbling again: "You lying whore."

There was a silence and then the sound of a door shutting, what Kate recognized as the Subaru's rear hatch. The voices loomed nearer. She twisted around, but something else flew into the panel and hit her, knocking her back and rolling off beside her . . . Winona's duffel bag. She heard Winona's simpering whine: "She made me. I was ready to come back. I had a change of heart. I was wrong. The do-gooder made me keep running."

The rear door slammed shut.

Kate heard Bud's voice near the door: "You're a crock of shit."

There was another thud, and something slammed against the side of the Power Wagon. Winona wailed. A front door opened and shut, and the wailing voice came inside, sobbing now up front. In a moment, the other door opened and shut, and the sobbing dropped into gulps of words, what, when Kate thought about it later, she would see as more of the interminable, desperate, transparent shiftiness of her story made up on the spot: "I did the best I could. She wouldn't budge. I knew you'd find me. How could I not know that?"

Kate heard a sharp sound and a ricochet-like snap, and then Winona sobbing softly and moaning, "Oh, my God. I'm sorry. I'm sorry."

The floor quivered beneath Kit. She felt the Power Wagon pull back, and forward, and back again, and forward. Snow beat against the undercarriage. She kept still with her cheek pressed against metal. They were going back down the road. She saw two large bags stacked on one side of her, then, nearer, a pair of boots and ankles, and as she twisted her eyes upwards her body recoiled. A figure was seated right above her on the wheel well.

—His foot, she thought. His foot is holding me down.

She made out an ash-colored face shaped like a reptile head inclined toward her. It rocked with the truck. It moved, bowing toward her. She saw pale hands coming, felt them touching her near the spine, and then something was drawn out from underneath her waistband . . . her diving knife. She saw the hands, the pointed, pale face turned toward the hands, and the knife held up to be examined by the eyes in the face. The blade glinted as it turned in the off-gleam from the dash lights. As the truck careened around a turn and went downhill along the straightaway, the chains clinked, biting through the throaty purr of the truck and Winona's desperate sobs.

12

Dreamers

AFTER HE CALLED THE SHERIFF, Jack went out and followed the tracks to the shop. The tracks were footsteps, or mostly filled indentations in the snow. He didn't think anyone was out there, but he carried his 30/30 and moved warily. He passed beyond the reach of the storm light and into the evening dark, through the gateway and toward a faint light that flowed through the shop windows. Across from it a second small light had been left burning in the barn. The corral was there. He swung that way to check on the two dappled white geldings, entering the pungent aura of their scent. Ponderous and still, they stood alongside each other in the passageway to the low, corrugated metal grain silo that Jack had converted to a stable. One horse faced in, the other one out. Falling snow melted down their flanks. Hay lay piled in their crib, and their automatic waterer was working. All of it seemed eerie, to find these things just as they should have been.

He crossed to the shop, lowering the barrel of his gun. The door rasped when he swung it open. He stepped inside. A fluorescent fixture hanging above the benches was alight. He guessed he'd left it on, since otherwise everything appeared to be in order, with little heaps of disarray near what he'd last been working on . . . the routed-out sides of a wooden storage case for Kate, over in the corner parts for an old Harley. His hand tools were attached to pegboards above the benches, and Kate's spare diving gear hung beside them. In a line along the far wall stood the radial arm saw, power miter, table saw, router table, planer, metal lathe, his acetylene welder and the tanks, stacks of lumber, and the propane heater.

He edged along the bench on his right, still seeing nothing wrong, then stopped and looked back, passing his eyes over the room. The door to the cold room—where they stored vegetables and where he had hung the elk—was slightly ajar. The light within, what he was certain he had turned off, was burning. Near the doorway, the rack of old metal signs collected through the years had been disturbed. They were old stop signs, yield signs, road signs, and Forest Service signs picked up from junk piles. Most were still in the rack, but one was propped against the wall in the shadows on the other side of the door. It was a stop sign turned backwards and on it—in defiance of the fact that it was a hexagon—were painted the words:

Devil's Pentagram
Death To
EcoFascists

On the floor stood an open pint can of red paint. A screwdriver lay beside it and a brush was stuck into it. He turned full around, listening intently, and moved along the benches to the door to the cold room. He pushed it open with the barrel of his gun, waited, then stepped inside. Filled canning jars and cider jugs were on their shelves opposite him, and the salted down elk hide tacked to a sheet of plywood leaning against the edge of the shelf, the potatoes, beets, and onions on their racks to his right, and the apple crates stacked up on pallets. The skinned elk hung to cure from the sliding hook on the beam over to his left, hoofless and headless, its paleness, the meat of its apparition, drooping down to almost touch the floor. As he shifted to face the carcass he caught sight of a loop of rope hanging from the next hook over. His scalp prickled and he turned around to look behind him and back again before his mind registered what it was: the curl of blonde hemp. A noose, one of his ropes, wrapped into a hangman's slipknot and tied with a half-hitch into the hook.

His thoughts veered immediately to Travis, whom he'd admonished to stay in hearing distance and preferably in sight, but then he himself had ventured out here and left Travis alone. He set out quickly, not touching the door, and as he swung into the lane saw in the wash of light from the shop what he hadn't seen coming the other way—a fresh apple core lying in plain sight on top of the snow. He lurched, as if about to step on a snake. He bent to pick it up . . . the apple eaten right down to its seeds, fresh-looking, and then he looked closer, straining to see. Where the apple had lain was a cluster of paw prints. He looked at Berg, who stood several yards away at the edge of the light, looking back at him with her ears up. She must have nosed out the core. He glanced past the gate and the garden to the house, seeing lights sweep the trees, and hearing the grumbling of a truck coming up the lane.

He waited until it passed into view and he was sure it was Gene, then circled back inside the shop, cut across to the cold room, and now saw one apple crate just out of line with its stack. He tipped up its lid. Two rows, twelve apples, were gone. He lowered the lid and started back outside, passing his eyes over the carcass, the noose, and through the doorway, the sign on the floor, and going outside to the snow and the eaten-up apple. Both Gene's truck and the sheriff's SUV were in the lot by the time he reached the house. He went in, finding Gene standing between Travis and the stove and Painter surveying the havoc of the living room from the foyer.

"It's a lawless country," Painter said, as Jack moved past him. A tall man, soft in the jowls and paunch, he wore wire-rimmed glasses low on his nose so that he had a scholarly quality mixed in with his uniform and service belt to which were affixed a flashlight, handcuffs, and .38 revolver. He stepped to the edge of the kitchen and then came back to where he'd been before, poised at the edge of the living room as if at the lip of something rank. "They made a mess. I'm sorry, Jack," he said.

"Nothing from the wife yet?"

"No." Jack moved into the living room. He leaned his gun up against the wall. "They were in the shop, too."

"Tools?" Painter said.

"They didn't take anything except apples."

"You look like you've seen a ghost," Painter said.

"They left a message." To state the heinousness of what he'd just witnessed matter-of-factly like that seemed unnatural. "And a noose," he said. He glanced from Painter to Gene, who had bent to stoke the fire in the stove and who now looked up sharply.

"A noose?" Painter said.

"A hangman's noose made out of one of my ropes. And they repainted an old stop sign I had, so it says, Death to EcoFascists." He thought . . . they? Surely, not they. His teeth gnashed as he thought further, naming it to himself . . . he . . . Bud Willy. "I guess that refers to me or Kate, or the both of us."

Painter looked at him and spoke softly, "Listen, we'll get this thing for you." He touched Jack's arm. "I know you feel violated. Lose anything in the house?"

"Guns."

"Got the numbers on them?"

"Some." Then, thinking about where such records would be stored—in the safe they also kept in the gun closet upstairs and into which he hadn't looked for a couple of years at least—he said, "I think."

Gene had moved behind the wood burner and was rubbing his hands together over it to warm them. "It's a signifying, Dan."

"Right," Painter said. "To them the law's whatever they choose to make of it."

Jack had a queasy feeling, knowing Painter's proclivity for drifting into moral disquisitions.

"Sometimes it's an advantage, the lawlessness," Painter said. "We can pull most anybody over most anytime and be pretty damn sure they're breaking some law or another. Take you, for instance," he said, resting his eyes on Gene. "You don't think every badge in the county doesn't know the tab under the mud on your license plate is out of date? If we really wanted you, we'd just haul you in." Gene's hands came to a stop in their rubbing. He held them together over the stove as if he were praying.

Painter turned to Jack. "We'll put a trace on anything you know is gone. I'll need a list. First thing in the morning I'll send a team over to check for prints. We'll need some surfaces for them. Been in the refrigerator yet?"

"No, but the handgun I had on top of it is gone."

Painter crinkled his brow and studied Jack over his glasses.

"It was because of them," Jack said. He'd told Painter on the phone about Bud and Zack's visit and how Winona had been found, retracing the narrative, as Kate had it, back to Winona's phantasmal body materializing in a ditch beside her wrecked car. "When we first saw those two coming, I put it up there."

"We'll find some surfaces," Painter said. "One thing at a time. Nothing wrong between you and her?"

"Kate?" It was unthinkable to Jack, but an ancient horror rose, a primal paranoia coming out of something his body or his gender kept stored for him. "We had words over her taking the woman, but Christ, no. Listen Dan, my wife's missing and my house has been ransacked."

"I got to ask," Painter said, grabbing his belt and hiking up his trousers. "We had a missing person last year. Turned out it was a bigamy case if you'd want to call it that. She'd married two different men, and one of them was one of my deputies. The other was a marijuana grower, and he did her in over in Montana. We gave old Bill a personal leave and now I haven't seen him in a year. Heard he was down in Arizona. You got to keep a watch on husbands when their wives is missing."

"Meaning me or him?" Jack said.

"You ain't him. It's a lawless country where the least expected runs loose, that's all I'm saying. Inside every house there's laws being broken. A person has to make a lot of judgment calls. We've got the FBIs here enforcing a whole passel of laws I'd never heard of, and breaking a few, too, while they're at it. It's like a swamp we're living in made out of broken laws. Or pickup sticks. For every stick you pick up, you uncover three or four more. We got too many laws to break, if you ask me, and they keep on making them. It's hard to understand human nature. How much money did you say she was carrying?"

"Kate said probably several hundred," Jack said. "Maybe more. I didn't see it."

Painter looked around the room. "Well. So, we got money in it, too. Bud Willy's known to have associations with the Lord's Weapon people. I'll need to inform the federals, who are here in force anyhow since the Lord's Weapon is holding a conference, now of all times. We've got sympathizers rolling in, and certainly the press, too. Maybe counter-demonstrations. Law enforcement has its hands full and most likely I'll get called down there." Painter sighed heavily as he unzipped a pocket in his jacket and fished out a notepad and pen. "I don't suppose there's any reason for me to believe you two'd leave it to us."

When neither Jack nor Gene answered, Painter looked at Travis. "It'd be a good example for the young man." The wood stove ticked as it heated. Because of his increasing alarm and Painter's snail-like pace, Jack felt a gnawing cavern opening within him, and now that Painter had spoken of it, he realized he could last only so long before taking action.

"All right," Painter said. "I'm deputizing this one." He turned his eyes to Gene. "Consider yourself deputized."

"Hey," Gene said, lifting his hand.

"Put your damn hand down. What I mean is keep this fool here out of trouble," he said, nodding at Jack, and then he said, "I've put out a bulletin on her. Chances are she's just fine out there on the road somewhere. These two things may not be connected at all. Still, I guess I wouldn't mind having cause to get a search warrant for Willy's wrecking yard, which is in my jurisdiction. That compound is not, thank God." He pushed his glasses up on his nose, licked the tip of a finger, and flipped methodically through the pages of his pad. His pen appeared tiny in his big, blunt fingers. "Now," he said. "I want to know when you came in today. When did they come? When did you leave? Everything right up to now."

Jack told him all of that. Then they finished checking through the house and went out to the shop, Painter observing on the way that there were two sets of tracks besides Jack's. "Two of them," he said. "Or else one came out twice." When they got to the noose, Painter stood beneath it, gazing upwards, and said, "That's a pig of a message, all right." As he made more notes, the plundered articles and ravaged intimacies unleashed a deep turmoil within Jack . . . sign, rope tied into a noose, dislodged apple crate, and back in the house, books, silverware, dishes, furniture, and smashed-up filing cabinets. The house itself, which he and Kate had built, stone-by-stone, stick-by-stick, what they'd nurtured by the years of inhabiting it with their children, was encircled by malice. He felt as though he'd been stretched on his back, slit open, and had the bedlam of his beating heart laid out smoking on his chest.

"Best not disturb anything further in here for now," Painter said. As they walked back to where the vehicles were parked, Painter instructed them not to touch the gun cabinet, either, or the things in Kate's study. "Otherwise, go ahead and put things in order." Reaching his SUV, he swung open the door, slid in, and looked back at Jack. "And you should try to get some sleep, hard as it may be." He nodded at Travis. "The young man, too."

He left, and the three of them . . . Jack, Gene, and Travis . . . returned to the living room where Jack and Gene raised the sofa upright on its four legs. Travis carefully lifted the dangling computer monitor back up on the shelf. Jack stepped over a heap of scattered books and returned the easy chair to its place. "I didn't think he knew. Bud, I mean," he said, resting his hands on the back of the chair.

"That she was here? Me neither. Seemed like you and Kate got by with it." Gene picked up a blanket and folded it. "I guess he could have figured it out." He set the folded blanket on the arm of the sofa and gathered up another one from the floor. "But that noose and the sign don't seem exactly his style . . . Ecofascists . . . I don't know. That sounds like one of the Lord's Weapon boys, turning it around like that, and from what I've heard, what Bud said about his not having much to do with them anymore is true. Come first light I'm going down to their compound." Gene began folding the second blanket. "Dan'll put this on the wire, and he'll get the feds and the Kootenai and Boundary County boys working on it. He'll do his best for you, but I can just go down there and ask around. You never can tell."

"Come by here first. I'll go with you."

Gene gave him a narrow look. "Are you sure?"

"If Kate's not here, I'm damn sure."

Travis, who had gathered up a stack of CD cases, observed Jack with an inquiring expression. Jack could feel himself being measured by his son for what he would and would not do.

*　*　*

Jack kept the stove warm all night long. He'd tried sleeping upstairs, and then spent a couple of hours wandering the house, desultorily replacing scattered things, again thinking it strange how in some places the destruction was wanton and in others things had hardly been touched. Finally, he tried sleeping on the sofa in front of the stove, but kept awakening, imagining he heard the telephone ringing. Every sound from outside—the creak of a tree or the air moving against the eaves—he mistook for the sound of Kate coming up the road. At three in the morning, he pulled on his boots and coat, picked up the 30/30, went out and walked around the house, peering at the road and into the woods on the side and back of the house, and then on the opposite side, stopping at the end of the garden. The shovel handle stuck up out of the snow. Before him was the gateway to the unplowed lane that led to the corral, shop, and hay barn. The moon, a day short of full, glimmered through the veil of thin clouds. At that moment it was not snowing, but the message of the wind shaking in the cornstalks foretold the next wave of storm.

Berg followed, limping in his path. She approached to touch his knee with her shoulder as he stopped, but pulled herself erect when the voices of coyotes broke through the quiet. The high-pitched yipping and sailing glissandos wound around each other in a fugal knot, a brilliant and polished sound in the night. Such were their cries for a kill, emanating from the vicinity of the woods where he'd dumped the elk head and hooves. Berg whined and took a step forward, her body electric. Sometimes she would run out to chase them. The coyotes' call elicited a passing calm in Jack's otherwise distraught state, measuring the night as was their custom. Light from the exterior flood lamps merged into the quality of pearl where it passed into the cornstalks, beyond reposed dark trees, blue shadows, and snow the color of sea froth. The lane hooked into a skewed, two-dimensional world, and led to the tool shop. This time the coyotes howled from a different position, a swooping brightness to remind him that at that moment it was only the universe singing back at him.

He returned to the house, built up a bank of birch rounds in the stove, and slept fitfully on the sofa, his dread looming in his wakefulness and when he slept the nightmare pictures rushed in—noose, sign, Winona's garishly painted face, and a recurrent image of Kate's lonely figure straggling along the shoulder of a road. Finally, he gave it up, took a shower, and went into the kitchen to make coffee. He swept the litter off a stretch of counter into a bag, scuffed along pushing things on the floor into piles with his feet to clear passageways, and brewed the coffee in an old steel camping pot, since the glass coffeemaker had been shattered. The look of the kitchen with things broken and scattered, feeling shards still crunching under his feet, made him feel anguished. It was Sunday. Six in the morning. Kate would never have allowed so much time to pass without contacting him.

After 7:00, Gene arrived, bringing Marlene and Chris with him. In the foyer, Marlene grabbed Jack firmly by the arms and brought her face close to his. "I'm so sorry," she said. Looking past him into the living room, she said, "Oh, Lord." Then, as she headed into the kitchen, her voice took on a pained quality: "Oh, no, we won't have it like this. We're going to fix this. Chris?" Chris followed her, bending into the passage.

Gene had left his truck running at the end of the walkway, turned full around and at the ready. "Nothing?" he said.

Jack shook his head.

"The wrecking yard's still closed up. I looked last night and knocked on the door this morning."

"I'm going down with you," Jack said. "But I got to talk to Travis first."

They moved into the kitchen where Marlene had already put a broom in Chris's hands and found the folded-up grocery bags behind the refrigerator. She set three bags along the counter near the window, snapping them open decisively. One, she informed Jack, could hold what was destroyed; one, what was broken but redeemable; and one, what was intact but which she wouldn't know where to put. "Do you mind?" she asked.

"Of course not." Jack glanced at Gene, who smiled faintly.

Travis appeared, looking dazed, and wandered back out again. Jack found two cups, filled them with coffee for Gene and Marlene, and took his own out into the living room where Travis now stood in front of the stove. Jack sat down on the sofa in front of him. The sleeping bag, the same one Winona had slept in, the blanket, and pillow were heaped next to him. The loaded 30/30 lay on the rug. Travis's hair bent upwards on one side from where he'd slept on it hard. He wore a T-shirt and a pair of jeans, and his bare arms had sprouted goose bumps. Behind him the wood burner's glass window glowed with orange.

"Listen to me carefully, son," Jack said.

Travis's looked at him.

"Remember, Dan's sending a team down to dust for prints. Don't touch Mom's study or anything out in the shop. Don't even go out to the shop. Remind Chris and Marlene. Give them some help. If you hear from Mom, or from Dan about her, you're to get hold of me. Try calling the Compound, which is where we'll end up, I'd guess. I've got the number out next to the phone. If you can't reach me, if they don't answer or don't cooperate, if the phone's busy, anything . . . understand? . . . call the sheriff's office. The number for the line to Dan's desk is there. Or tell Dan if he's here, or any of his deputies, and get in the truck and come down and find me. All right? You know where the Compound is, right? There'll probably be police outside the gate. Tell them exactly what you're doing. Somebody has to come get me. Clear?"

Travis nodded without speaking.

Clattering and tinkling came from the kitchen, and the sound of water running into the sink.

"I wish to God I had a cell phone. But I won't go anywhere else without letting you know. We won't be long. Tell Marlene where you're going so somebody knows exactly where you are and when you left," Jack said. "Drive the truck. As long as I haven't heard from you, I'm assuming you haven't heard anything. Okay?"

"Okay. A cell phone might not get through to here anyway." Travis's face remained composed, but Jack knew well that there was a straining in the boy. What he didn't know was how long Travis could keep it as it appeared to be, roped up in his steadiness, or when he would have to let some of it loose.

"Don't touch the gun closet, either."

"Okay," Travis said. "You have to be careful."

"Right," Jack said. "You bet. I have to see if Bud's there or if somebody there knows where he'd be. I have to go see."

"What if he is there?"

—I'll draw-and-quarter the sonofabitch, Jack thought. Everything he could think of since he and Travis had come home from the game yesterday, or even before that from the time of his talking to Gene above Weaver's homestead and worrying about Travis driving down the mountain had folded upon itself into unreal disarray, like the kitchen itself. "I doubt he will be, but I'll do what I have to. I've got to do something. We'll be okay, son."

* * *

As Gene drove his pickup over the top of a promontory, a line of yellow laid by the dawn streamed above the woods. The lemon color traced the ridges to the east and had begun to seep out of the void into the gray sky. Snow piled in the woods and ditches. The road past the state park had been plowed during the night, but another deeply furrowed six inches had fallen onto it. The pickup rounded a curve and the road dropped into the woods. Jack shifted position and stretched out his feet over the toolbox on the floor. A chain saw rested between him and Gene. The dashboard was lined with plastic boxes that contained small things—tools and parts, coiled-up saw chains. A pair of rosewood dice with abalone dots and a lacy garter belt hung from the rearview mirror—articles of finery in the cab that otherwise had the character of a shop.

On the highway, which had been newly plowed, early Sunday traffic was sparse. Gene slowed as they approached the wrecking yard, where recent wheel tracks looped across the open space in front of the entry-way. "Those fresh ones are mine," he said, reading Jack's mind.

"We could go on back and check the house, I guess," Jack said.

"I think Dan's already sent somebody in. Maybe we'd best leave that to him. No telling what we might uncover back there . . . mangy dogs and more lunatics." A grin slid into the scar on Gene's cheek. Without taking his eyes from the road, he said, "What do you know, friend?"

Jack grunted.

Gene reached out over the chain saw and tapped Jack's wrist. "We're gonna find her."

Just as they entered the sprawl of Hayden and Coeur d'Alene, they turned off the highway eastward onto another county road, then took a right. The back end of the truck caught in a rut, and popped loose. Gene counter-steered and goosed the throttle. The front tires grabbed, bouncing the truck through the ruts that fanned out all over like a spokework. "This stretch's been hammered," he said.

Before them lay a straightaway. As Jack remembered, there would be a slow bend in the road through the woods, and then another long straightaway that passed down through a bowl in the landform. An observation tower would be visible in the woods on the right, and a bright red and blue sign with a heraldic swastika on it would jump out near the road. Clearly, the intent was for the Lord's Weapon to announce its presence as a warning or invitation to the curious, the hostile, or to pilgrims, and also to be able to spot all approaching vehicles at a distance. He thought it to be in character with the mix of those people—the tipsy balance on the knife edge between something like simple competence and total derangement.

After the turn, he and Gene would reach the steeply rising road-way, the gateway, and then the guard shack. Beyond it and behind the trees one side of the church would be visible. Jack knew all that. It was a looming in his mind, a cartography of what was to come as he stared through the windshield and tried to steady himself by finding the lit-eral answer to Gene's ceremonial question, What do you know?

He knew the earth, and internal combustion engines. He knew trees, how to cut them down, limb, stack, and load them, drive them to market, and how to leave them alone. He knew how to wait for an elk herd to pass. He knew the huckleberry, chokecherry, and wild currant. He knew his neighbors. He knew this snow. He knew how to live on his own, and how to love his children, Ron, Pamela, and Travis. He knew philosophy, or had known it from what he'd been instructed years ago, the sweep and idealism of its beginning with the suicide on principle of Socrates driving to the fragmentation through the centuries until the last one was reached, the coming apart, then, the systematic not knowing of modern times. Finally, that had caused in him a kind of ardent boredom and he'd exiled himself from theory to the stuff of the world. He knew the house he and Kate had built. He knew about the Spokane Flood and liked to think of himself living where it had been. He had his own obsession with water and he knew it, as well: the countering run of eddy lines, the maw at the heart of a hole, the surge of white froth. He knew how a river's flow articulated itself against the hull of a canoe and how behind every obstacle laid a void.

Kate entered his effort to steady himself through the personal catechism. She knew water better than he. She knew fish, fingerlings, eggs, spawning beds, current, tide, the sea bottom, and global currents. She knew rivers in detail. It was as if their spirits had met on the tensile surface of the water, his head in the air and hers in the deep, as if they twined that way in their long, loving search for meaning. She knew the voids behind boulders as sub-aquatic slack waters she could duck into for relief. He knew how she looked sometimes, doing that.

He thought about the time she'd dropped him off upstream on the Clark Fork with his canoe and he'd paddled down to meet her at a monitoring site. He'd come into the eddy and seen the bubbles next to a rock and then Kate, hovering behind the rock . . . black wetsuit, blue fins, blue buoyancy control vest, bright yellow tanks, and yellow goggles. She'd turned up to see him, peering over the gunwale of his canoe, and then she kicked and turned a slow half-somersault and came to a stop on her back underwater, spreading her arms as if to receive applause. She stayed there, floating.

Jack smiled to himself, lost for a moment, but by a trick of imagination he suddenly found himself staring down at his wife's corpse . . . arms spread limply, fins inclining her legs downward, on her back, her hair waving in the water. His body jerked. He stared through the windshield, inhaled deeply, and slowly let the air come out.

"If this doesn't feel right to you, I can take you back," Gene said.

"No," Jack said. "I want to go see. What about you?"

"Me?"

Jack looked over. "I'm sorry. It just occurred to me that this isn't a place you'd want to go into."

Gene looked back, and in the moment something was triggered from behind his usual thrust and parry, what revealed itself as somberness in his eyes. "You mean my so-called heritage? It's nothing. It don't matter and I don't care. They don't know. Up here, only you and Marlene do, and Chris, and maybe Kate, if you've told her."

They were on the last straightaway, descending gently. Down at the bottom, vehicles were parked on either shoulder of the road. To the right against the custard sky loomed the stand of trees, and in it Jack spotted the roof line of the observation tower, the deck with its rail, and the angular silhouette of a figure revolving slowly like an insect. The thin shaft of a rifle barrel glinted, and then disappeared. They passed the sign, the red swastika and crossed swords and crown against a field of blue. Gene's truck skittered as he pumped the brakes. A dozen or more vehicles were packed in close and four men, wearing slacks, rain jackets, and rubber boots, stood in a line. The uniformed Kootenai County Sheriff's Deputies hung behind in a group.

"Pistoleros." Gene said. "Watching over the fanáticos. Remember, we're only asking around."

One of the men in slacks began snapping pictures of the truck. Gene braked and the truck scooted to a stop. He rolled down his window. "What?" The one with the camera took a picture of Gene leaning out his window, and then Jack saw the camera adjusting to focus on him. "What is it?" Gene said.

"Federal agents," a second man said. The first man slipped the camera into a pocket. The four of them were different heights and wore different color jackets and slacks and hats, but still they looked the same with their smooth faces and straightness, formidable and shiny. The deputies comprised a far more motley group—big and small, fit and overweight. Jack recognized one of them—Bill Parsons, the father of a girl who'd been friends with his daughter. When their eyes met, Parsons nodded faintly at Jack, and Jack thought: In there somewhere behind that nod is Bill. The deputies and the line of agents suddenly seemed also unreal to him, like a charade.

"We're going in," Gene said. "But we ain't with them. Understand?"

The agent passed his eyes along the truck, taking in the dented fender, the broken grill, the Bungee strap that secured the hood. He returned his gaze to Gene.

"We're looking for Bud Willy," Gene said. "Or for somebody who'd know him."

Bending to see Jack, the agent said, "There's a bulletin out. There's a lot of people here and we didn't monitor the early comers, but I'd be really surprised if he slipped in."

Jack felt himself squinting. "You mean you know he's not here?"

"I think so."

Gene turned to Jack and raised his eyebrows. With his head, Jack gestured toward the entryway to the compound.

"I guess we'll check, anyway," Gene said.

"It's private property," the agent said. "They're letting the press come and go. It's up to them." He stood still. All four stood still. Behind them, calf-deep in the snow and hunched against the cold with their hands in their pockets, the deputies stood braced against the preposterous.

Gene popped his truck off the road to the twisting lane. They passed the gate and the barbed wire fence laced with razor wire, and a sign nailed to a tree:

WHITES ONLY ENTER

"I was white, once," Gene said in a low voice.

He pulled alongside the guard shack where a man stepped through the doorway and up to the truck window. "Morning, Gene."

"We ain't here to stay," Gene said.

The man bent and peered into the cab. "Doug Borrt," he said. He wore a black uniform, a dark gray trench coat, and had a pair of bright brass swastikas on the points of his collar and a military hat with a shiny black brim. Handsome, almost female-looking, his dark eyes flashed beneath deep black eyebrows and lashes, set off by his smooth white skin.

"DeShazer," Jack said. He'd put the face and the name together, as he guessed Borrt expected him to. He'd read that Borrt was under investigation, that he'd been an accountant before he'd received the "message." Now the Lord's Weapon security chief, the man's numbers—Jack guessed—had been converted from the effervescence of other people's balance sheets to the true grit of rightwing subversion.

When Gene said they were looking for Bud Willy, a smile pulled at Borrt's lips. He straightened so that all Jack could see was his belly and the buckle of a gun belt. He heard the voice: "Bud hasn't been around much lately. You're welcome here so long as you're respectful of the services." His hand gestured toward the slope.

Gene pulled up onto a flat, parked next to another truck, and they climbed out, coming together at the back of Gene's pickup. They moved by a television van, the presence of which Jack found reassuring. "Hell," Gene said. "These guys are just like me, lost wanderers on the earth. The only difference is I'm a deputy and they're full of shit."

Jack smiled grimly. What little he knew about Gene's sense of his religion had come like this in bits. In fact, he was relying on Gene's experience from the days of hiding out behind his tripwires and the perilous antics that had got him into trouble, the arrests for squatting on federal property, the drugs, and poaching charges that had caused him to be under surveillance and thus into backwoods association with a few of the Lord's Weapon types. Gene had once told Jack that he liked some of them well enough so long as they stayed off politics and religion.

The two of them brushed elbows as they walked across the clearing toward a raised platform. Gene said, "Probably, you want to be careful here."

"Right."

The detail before them, the mundane and ordinary—the platform, just beyond it three World War II–vintage Quonset huts, and to the left a dozen picnic tables in rows, fifty-gallon drums converted to trash barrels, rusted outdoor grills, a children's swing set, beyond it the scaffolding of the guard tower, and further up to their left the sanctuary mounted on a knoll—ran counter to the treacherous exotic Jack had imagined for the place.

They stopped at the platform. The snow that had been shoveled off of it lay in heaps on the ground. A table and a row of chairs had been placed there, and in front of the chairs stood a line of microphone mounts. Beyond the platform in the middle Quonset hut, figures passed by the windows. Smoke trailed from the hut's chimney. Another line of smoke rose from behind the church, a solid-looking white building with a blunt bell tower. The entryway was on the far side, and from within a man's voice could be heard rising and falling almost like singing. There was a flutter of motion in a stand of trees past the parking lot—children, boys. They carried sticks and ran in a compact formation through the snow, spreading out to sieve upwards through the trees and eddying back into a pack, then broke out of the woods and vanished. Up in the guard tower, a man in a black uniform and watch cap, holding a rifle, peered down at Jack and Gene. At the sound of a vehicle approaching from the distance, he turned like a praying mantis working its way around a stem, while the gun against his hip swung like a long antenna.

The gun was legal, Jack surmised. There was likely not much illegal kept here, only the suggestion of it, while the actual stuff, the stolen ordinance and bomb-making supplies, the fully automatic weapons, were cached somewhere else. The guard fixed his gaze up toward the road. On the ground, paths branched out everywhere and the ascending sun's shafts blazed furiously against the snow, making the mud in the trampled paths and the tower's outline seem dark. Except for the guard, the boys running through the woods, the figures in the middle Quonset hut, and Borrt down in the guard shack, Jack and Gene seemed to be alone. However, judging from the number of cars, and from what the agent had said, there must have been scores of people inside the church.

Jack felt the pit in his belly. It was fear, the same feeling he'd endured waking up in the middle of the night and again when they'd passed the wrecking yard. It was the panicky feeling he had cutting into a big tree he knew had rot, not quite knowing what it would do, or waiting for Travis to appear on the mountainside two nights ago. His knees felt disconnected as they walked him through the slush.

Gene gestured toward the Quonset huts. "I'll go that way. You look around back. I'll meet you at the church."

They parted. As Jack moved under the tower, he looked up at the heavy timbers and cross-beams. A ladder ran up the center to a trap-door in the floor. The derrick-like crosshatching of the tower pitched its shadow clear over the yard and bent up the wall of the first Quonset hut where Gene was trying the door. Jack followed a path around the back of the church toward the smoke. The young boys came into sight, six of them running into a field, sticks brandished against the sky, voices yipping, high-pitched and thin in the cold air. As Jack circled around the church, he saw three men working near a fire. Two of them carefully maneuvered stones from the fire into a pit. A pair of dressed-out pigs lay nearby on a sheet of plastic, and to one side he spotted a shallower pit with a grill placed over it. The third man, nearer to Jack, slowly wound a strip of burlap around the lower member of a large cross. He pulled the strip tight, fastidiously smoothing out its edges, secured an end to the wood with a staple gun, and looked up and grinned. He pulled off one glove and held out his hand. "Steve Green," he said. "Did you just get in?"

"Yes," Jack said, accepting the man's hand.

"I'm up here from Memphis," Green said. He kept grinning, exhibiting all his teeth and crinkling up his forehead around a quarter-sized patch of scar tissue.

At Jack's back, sounds issued from the sanctuary . . . a piano playing, and a noise like distant rolling thunder from people rising to their feet. There soared a single voice, followed by the unison of the congregation, and then the single voice again.

"Joe and Dave," Green said, gesturing over his shoulder. "They're cooking the hogs."

The two men used shovels to move stones from the fire to the pit.

"They're from Cleveland. There's folks here from all over. Some snow, huh?"

Jack murmured and looked down at the cross. It was a good fifteen feet long and resting on four low sawhorses. The lower member had been wrapped almost half way up to the cross-member. Underneath the wrapped portion, the snowy ground was dotted and pooled with a pink liquid—diesel fuel. From the church now, a different voice, a clear tenor sliced through the air.

"That's Reverend Palmer," Green said. "Out of Michigan. He's got the voice of the angels."

It came through a cracked-open window. A scripture was being read from which Jack could pick out words and phrases: "Spirit of infirmity . . . bowed together . . . woman . . . made straight . . ."

The voice went on, rising and falling. Steve Green and the other two men paused to listen intently: "Thou hypocrite . . . on the Sabbath loose his ox ... and lead him away to watering ... ought not this woman ..."

The voice lapsed, and the opening chords of a hymn were struck on a piano which clanked as if tacks were imbedded in its hammers, like a honky-tonk. Feet thundered again as people rose.

"His sermon's about the nation of righteousness within the nation of usury," Green said.

Jack thought about obsession, religion, counterfeit, weapons, armaments hidden somewhere, shooters on the loose, the eager light in Green's eyes, and his mind veered toward Kate, who feasibly was contained within that by which he felt threatened.

Diesel fumes cut through the air. Smoke from the pit wafted the scent of sage and cedar. Two military-style, five-gallon fuel cans stood in the muddied snow between the cross and the fire pit, and above them rested a pallet loaded with crates and freezer boxes leaking blood. Green's basin was filled with burlap, soaking in the chemical-colored diesel. Two cardboard boxes were stuffed with more rolls of burlap. Light and wiry, Green was dressed in insulated coveralls and a skull-cap. The other two men were tall, one with a pasty face and a belly that draped in loose folds between his suspenders, while the other, a thin man, displayed a huge, elaborate-looking belt buckle. Jack understood well enough that they were preparing to have a cross burning, yet he found it startling to be so near to what he'd only seen in newsreels or heard about from Kate.

"Diesel," he said.

"You got to do it right. You don't want to light it and not have it burn. You don't want it to burn too fast. You got to soak the stuff so it gets into the gut of the fiber and then wring it out just enough so it'll burn right," Green said. "Diesel don't fraction off like gas, but it fractions faster than kerosene. You want the inside layer soaked pretty good, and then wound tight over the top of it to keep the fuel in. You could soak the wood, too, if you wanted. They asked me special to come up and wrap it for them. It makes you look stupid if you light the cross and it goes out." Green laughed. "Or if it just explodes. Did you travel far to get here?"

"No," Jack said.

"You can go right on into the service, if you want," Green said. He pulled his rubber glove back on and turned to the basin, withdrew a strip of burlap, carefully wrung it out, and started wrapping the cross with it.

"I'm looking for somebody named Bud Willy. Do you know him?"

"I've met about fifty folks in the last twenty-four hours and I sure don't remember all their names." He spoke over his shoulder at the other two. "You boys know Willy?"

The two looked at Jack, taking their measure. "Probably inside," the thin one said.

"They're boars, actually, the hogs," Green said, working the burlap around the trunk as if he were bandaging a wound. "Peccaries from Texas. One of our members had them shipped."

The boars were small for pigs, it was true, elongated in the snouts, and muscled like runners.

"We got venison, grouse, and quail," Green said. "Wild meat. We got antelope from Montana to grill. The boars are stuffed with apples. I brought up a couple crates of Tennessee sweet potatoes."

"You going to burn the cross here?" Jack said.

Green's hands stopped and his eyes cut to Jack. "Tonight. It's a ceremony. Light. Light the cross," he said. "Burn is what the Jew media calls it."

Green bent back over the cross and now the other two were scrutinizing Jack. Jack turned and searched for Gene down by the Quonset huts, but didn't see him. He shot a glance up at the guard tower where the silhouette of the man was still poised toward the road. Jack turned back and looked out into the field. Six boys had spread in a wide circle, now swinging back toward the compound, their dark figures scampering in a ragged pack like six crows winging low upon the field. The hymn in the church finished and Jack heard the single voice speak in muted tones, then laughter rang out. The voice rose up out of the mirth.

"You ain't the press, I guess," Green said, looking up at Jack.

"I guess not," Jack said.

"If you was press you're supposed to wear a badge they'll give you at the guard shack."

"I'm not a reporter," Jack said.

"I hear this place is going to be crawling with press before long. It's already crawling with the damn agents. It's hard to tell who's who," Green said. The other two, holding the handles of their shovels with the blades spiked into the mud, kept scrutinizing Jack, the fat one's eyes like hard beads inside the folds of flesh and the thin one glaring at him sidelong.

"I'm looking for Bud Willy is all," Jack said. "Or somebody who'd know where he'd be. He owns a wrecking yard up on the highway."

"Probably inside," Green said.

"He's got a brother, Zack, who's . . ." Jack paused for an instant, seeking the right word for this edgy exchange. "Retarded," he said. "Bud takes care of him."

Green looked up at the other two men, who shook their heads. "Nope," Green said.

"We're all retarded here," the thin one said.

"So retarded we don't even know smart from stupid," the fat one said.

"Show him your Derringer, Dave," Green said.

The tall man let go of his shovel and pressed a button on his belt buckle. With a clicking sound, a tiny Derringer snapped out, pointing straight at Jack. The tall man held his palms out on either side of his hips and gaped. Jack stood still.

"It's a mechanical pecker," Green said, laughing voicelessly and wildly. It was all air gulped in and ejaculating out in puffs and making the scar on his forehead turn crimson. The other men rocked to and fro, sniggering softly.

"Yeah, everybody knows we're idiots," Green said as he bent over the cross. The tall man hunched over himself and pushed the diminutive weapon back into its nest inside the belt buckle. Then he and the fat man crouched to position one of the pigs on its sheet of plastic, while Green delicately and meticulously wound more burlap around the trunk of the cross.

The other two slid the first carcass to the edge of the pit. The slit in the boar's belly had been sewn over its load of apples. The fat man picked up the edge of the plastic while the tall one levered a ramp into the pit with the two shovels. The carcass slid off the plastic onto the shovel handles and hissed as it settled onto the hot rocks. A cloud of steam issued. The fat man dragged down the other boar while his partner manned the shovels, preparing to balance the boar on them.

"You don't want any hot spots," Green said. "You want everything to burn even and clean from the outside right down into the wood. This is no time to screw up, eh?"

"I guess not," Jack said.

"That's what I'd guess," Green said, drilling his eyes into Jack.

As Jack moved off, he felt the eyes of the three men on his back. He glanced down toward the Quonset huts and spotted Gene under an awning, talking to someone, then went ahead, walking by the church's open window where the voice toiled softly, rising, then ringing out: "The best men of our generation . . ." It faded again as Jack moved toward the front.

Jack came around the corner of the church and headed for the stairway. Water trickled from the eaves, rivulets of melt ran down the slope, and clumps of snow dropped out of the trees at his back. As he entered the church, he took care to shut the door quietly behind him. He found himself in a vestibule with shelves stuffed full of books and pamphlets. A basket rested on a stand for donations and against a wall extended a long table loaded with paraphernalia—flint fire-starters, dried foods, a model windmill, Vita-Mix machines, packaged jerky, soil-testing kits, knives, and night-vision scopes. Above the table hung T-shirts with "White Nation" slogans and a banner that asked, "Had enough?" A set of double doors blocked him from the sanctuary.

But the voice penetrated clearly: "And the ruler of the synagogue answered with indignation because Jesus had healed on the Sabbath day. . . . Ruler, the Bible says. Ruler of the synagogue! The ruler who failed to perceive a miracle as it was performed right before his eyes."

There was a silence.

He slipped into the sanctuary and moved along the back wall, searching for a place among the crowd. "The crooked woman," the man at the pulpit said. "What is there? What is there in the crooked woman?" By the time Jack found a place to stand out of the way, he was nearly to the far corner. He slid in against the wall next to a man with a softly whirring news camera on his shoulder. The pews were filled to capacity and the air was stifling. Jack's eyes scaled the line against the wall on his left and up to the pulpit mounted on a raised platform at the head of the sanctuary, where perched the stocky man with a smooth face, bald head, and squared-off chin.

Palmer looked to be in his fifties and bore the semblance of a chief mechanic, a construction foreman, lieutenant colonel, or farmer, someone in charge and clean, who did his work and washed up afterwards. He drew himself into the cradle of the pulpit, and his voice emerged, resonant, supple, and for the moment conversational: "We've all seen the like, the old in their wheelchairs or hobbling with their canes, the infirm, we call them, and people like this woman with one shoulder six inches above the other, twisted and bent. She can hardly walk. For eighteen years she suffered. For eighteen years she could not lift herself straight. What is there? What is there in the crooked woman?" Palmer stepped back from the pulpit. The silence in the sanctuary deepened. "And what is there in her healing by the Lord?"

Palmer took a red handkerchief out of his pocket and mopped his brow. "But we recall," he said softly, leaning toward the congregation. "We recall that this is the man who wrestled the Devil, who cast out them who bought and sold in the temple." His voice rose a little: "He demolished the tables of the money changers. The coins scattered across the floor. He cast the money changers out of the temple." Palmer paused and dropped his voice again almost to a whisper: "What is it? What is it about healing?"

On either side of the platform, near the front, stood two flags in stands—on the left the U.S. flag and on the right one that Jack had not seen before, bedecked in purple, red, and white, with a gold fringe. At the back of the platform stood an altar and mounted on it was a steel cross. From the wall, near the two corners of the platform, hung two pennants. He examined them, the red swastikas emblazoned at their centers, and looking back at the flag he made out the edge of another swastika. Just to his left, a nook built into a side wall revealed a large shield with yet another swastika, and two crossed swords, and at the top a medieval helmet, all surrounded by a crimson field, and then he felt something forming in the shadows of his fear, a gauzy thing slowly mending itself into a shape with the ribbons drawn out of his confusion, worry, and anger. It began to take form within the riddle.

"What is it about the blind man that Jesus healed?" Palmer said. "What is it about the ten lepers He cleansed? What about the impotent man, the boy filled with demons, the instruments of Satan who Jesus cast out? What is it about Lazarus? Or the crippled boy at the beautiful gate? The man with the withered hand? The crooked woman? Or what is it about the Lord Himself, who stilled the storm, fed the four thousand, and walked on the surface of the sea? What is it about this man defying the rulers of the synagogue?"

Jack was listening for the sound of Gene stepping into the vestibule. He ran his eyes from head to head along the pews, first on the left side, and working toward the front, also looking for Bud's close-cropped black hair on a square head, and the fold of skin at the neck.

"What message was he bearing?" Palmer said. "What is it?"

Jack glanced at the pulpit as Palmer took a breath and seemed visibly to expand. The congregation inhaled. After a pause, the words rang out: "The time is coming! The time is near! Our time is upon us! We want to be unchained from the wretched beast of the nation!"

A murmuring current moved through the congregation. Palmer rocked onto his heels, waited once again, and came forward and said, "Hollywood is the holy city of this nation. Millions worship the false idols on the screen. Sex, drugs, blasphemy, paganism, perversion. The military invites Sodomites into its ranks. Our cities are prowled by government supported thugs, the African tide of anarchy. The old and the frail cower in their rooms, the crooked, the lame, and the withered are afraid. A poison sweeps the nation, the bestiality born of the black and brown hordes. Children slaughter each other in the schoolhouse. Our nation aborts its unborn souls. Why?—the people are asking. The First Lady of ZOG shares her bed with usurers. Her husband spills his seed on the skirts of whores. Chinese devils and corrupt Islamite sultans buy and sell our elections. Laws are written by the Zionists. The sweat and toil of our people is a mockery. They're grinding us into the dirt! They want to strip us of our last defense! Let us loose . . . let us loose from the filthy bowels of this beast! We want out!"

The congregation sprang to its feet with a roar of approval. The cameraman next to Jack panned from one side to the other, and elsewhere along the edges a flurry of motion spread among the reporters. Jack's nerves jangled against the storm of voices, and within him, to the slowly forming gauzy thing, were now added the brute cries of the throng, the weight of each brought to unanimity: "Sieg Heil! Sieg Heil! Sieg Heil!" Several pews in front of him, one skinhead with a neck like a bulky stub and a blue swastika tattooed into the back of his skull, jerked his head with each word and raised his arm in a salute. Others joined in, their roaring chant making the wall at Jack's back pulse.

Palmer stood still, his face like stone, then approached the pulpit again and raised his hand. Gradually, people quieted and sat down. Pews creaked. Babies, cradled by their mothers, murmured. There were children of all ages and men outfitted in storm trooper uniforms. Jack had spotted Dick Petrie, too, just to the side of the skinhead, his presence confirming what Jack had long suspected. His face was flushed and sweat ran down his face. Most of the people were roughly dressed, as if they'd just come out of their kitchens and shops.

"The crooked woman," Palmer said softly. "The crippled boy at the beautiful gate. The withered hand. There's a message here. What is it?" He dropped his voice lower yet. "What's wrong with the crooked woman?"

The entire congregation in its anticipation leaned toward him yet again, and in his pause Palmer urged the people deeper into a pit of silence. Jack felt the thing taking shape, decrypting itself little-by-little under the sorcery of the sermon, the bedevilment of the listeners, and within the heraldic imagery of the place . . . red carpet leading to the altar, roughly built pulpit, crosses, flags, shields, crossed swords hanging on the walls, crowns, and swastikas everywhere in the room . . . carved crudely into pillars and the backs of the pews, dangling in the niches, draped in the windows. What was forming was wrapped with a winding assembled from shadows.

"What is wrong with us? What is it?" Palmer whispered. "Why do we bend to the Jew law-merchants, the judges, the Jew attorneys? Our nation has been corrupted and maimed to serve the barons of power, the infected pre-Adamite issue of Satan? What is wrong?"

The crowd waited, a few remaining on their feet, transfixed with expectation. Jack went back to looking where he'd left off, running his eyes along one pew, and the next, skimming over the closely packed men and women . . . the mother hushing her baby, next to her a man in blue suspenders, an old man in a suit coat shiny at the shoulders from wear. . . .

"This nation clamors for the fat dripping from the barons' chins," Palmer said. "The liberal elite, the blasphemers . . . Clinton, Hillary, Gore, George Bush, Jeb with his mongrel offspring. . . . Is it any wonder the nation can't choose? The Jew media poisons our children with perversion. False gods contaminate our children. Why? What is it? The temple was not blasphemed by money changers alone, but by the hedonist collaborators in filth and defilement, those taking the short-cuts through the holy place with their water vessels and kitchen utensils and doves for sale, those who carry on their obscene trade while the money clinks in the back rooms. And the rulers of the Temple would not allow the Lord to make straight the crooked woman, or heal the withered hand, or send someone to help the boy waiting at the gate." Palmer raised his hands questioningly. "Why?"

Jack's eyes passed over a large man in the far corner of a pew near the front, over to the extreme right and half-hidden by a post. It was not Bud, and yet Jack's eyes sprang back. It had to be Zack, slouched down on his spine . . . big head, short, crazily whorled hair, massive shoulders. Jack shifted to see better. There was no sign of Bud.

"Your cameras," Palmer said, passing his eyes along the side walls, and addressing the press. He gazed at the cameras near Jack, making Jack's skin crawl. "Vessels of a perverted culture." Zack's head rose from out of the throng and swiveled, filled with blank wonder, looking back because the others around him were looking. He engulfed a sandwich, pressing it into his mouth with his massive hand. His cheeks bulged when he bit down. Slowly, Jack viewed the people near to Zack, thinking that if Bud were here, Zack would be dogging him. If Zack were here and Bud was not near, then Bud was not present at all.

"We might dash your vessels to the ground," Palmer said in a conversational tone, "and throw you out of the sanctuary."

Members of the press corps shifted their feet. Several lowered their cameras and Jack felt the clear, rising, pleasuring antipathy of the congregation. Like a ringmaster, Palmer had summoned the congregation's hatred into the gap, shifting the atmosphere to raw enmity. As if attuned to the preacher's theatrics, Jack felt the thing within him gathering its shape out of the ribbons of his confusion. It composed itself in his body and rose to his consciousness. It was Kate. He saw her afloat above the congregation and on the level of the dais, but nearer than the pulpit, and she was looking at him. She was completely herself, dressed in her boots and corduroys and cream-colored shirt, and she had one hip cocked slightly in her way. Everything about her was exactly as it should have been except that she had a look of abject terror on her face.

Gripped by the vision, he couldn't breathe for an instant. The air grew thick. He rocked back to touch the wall with his shoulder blades as if seeking to pass down upon the firmament, then came back forward to the balls of his feet, and spoke softly to himself, "Hold on." The image of Kate disappeared.

—What is it? he asked himself, taking up the preacher's question.

Having asked it, he knew there was something he was registering but did not understand about this place, the depth of the depraved in it, which had become personal.

The cameraman next to him pulled away from his lens. A red crease encircled one of his eyes. "Hold on is right," he whispered, having recognized that Jack did not belong here. "This is crazy."

"Yes," Jack murmured.

Palmer wreathed his smooth, square, clean face with a beatific smile and made a sweeping gesture. "You are welcome to report that we are not the lunatic fringe." As quickly as he'd conjured the tension, as if from pure air, he diffused it into a ripple of laughter from the people. Jack heard the creak of the door between the vestibule and sanctuary and saw Gene appear and stop at the head of the center aisle.

"What is it?" Palmer said.

What it is—Jack thought—is it that they imagine in the beginning Satan corrupted Eve and compromised Adam and out of the first issue, Satan with Eve, or Lillith, came the mark of Cain and the corrupt tribe of Israel, the Jews, and everything follows from that. What's important is the conjured up beginning and then the preordained end, the locked-down system of thought to which everything adheres but nothing penetrates.

"What is it?" Palmer repeated.

—It's that their conception of the end is governed by what they imagine to be the beginning. A skewed myth, a fiery romance forming a brutal code, a fatally twisted idealism. And then Jack thought—Kate, knowing what she does about religion, would have grasped this instantaneously.

"'My house shall be called of all nations the house of prayer,' Jesus said. My house, the house of prayer," Palmer intoned. "My house, the nation. My crippled nation, waiting at the beautiful gate. The nation, the house of prayer."

While Palmer's voice was rising, Jack pulled forward, touched the cameraman's arm, ducked below his lens, and picked his way along the rank at the back wall.

"My nation, my house. Nation of prayer. Jesus will keep his appointment with us," Palmer said. He stepped out from behind the pulpit and stood with his arms spread. "My house the promised land, North America. With each miracle, throwing the money changers out of the temple, with everything he did, Jesus stayed true to all the appointments assigned to him by God. They are his preordained appointments."

As he moved, Jack marked the people straightening in their pews, felt the pooling of their emotion, and then suddenly Palmer let loose a string of rim shots: "My house! My nation! House of Prayer! Promised land! Crooked woman! Withered hand! The crippled boy at the gate! All the bloody classrooms! The blood running down the streets of the Holy Land! All the children of my nation waiting at the gate! What is it?" Palmer poked the air with his fist. "Jesus has appointments to keep! He's coming now, bringing his fire to our house of prayer, our nation!"

When Jack caught up with Gene, they turned and pressed on out of the sanctuary into the vestibule. The door squeaked as Gene opened it and as Jack eased it shut. They slipped by the books and pamphlets, banners, flags, bumper stickers, and the table with its buttons and packaged goods available in exchange for donations and consecrated by fury. The voice flashed through the doors: "Flood the Northwest with white babies! Leave no more question about whose land this is! That's our appointment! Our children are waiting at the gate! Our day of judgment is nigh! My house!" Other voices sang out with ecstatic affirmation, and his shouts punctured the rising flux. "My nation! My house! Promised land! Our new Eden! His appointment! House of prayer!"

Jack followed Gene through the second set of doors to the landing and down the steps into the glare of snow. Voices behind them grew more muted as they quickened their pace. From the southwest a thick bank of clouds rolled toward them, launching a chill breeze. Newly frozen snow crunched under their boots.

They hastened along, threading their way through the ranks of parked cars toward Gene's pickup. The man was still in the guard tower, leaning forward with his elbows on the rail and staring down at them, his rifle barrel angled up into the sky. In the woods to the left, the gang of boys clustered among the trees, and one voice wafted mournfully into the air: "I'll tell your Daddy. He'll take the strap to you." Nuthatches scurried up the trunks. A solitary magpie sailed overhead, cawing ominously. Jack felt as if he'd been twisted through time into in a strange, post-apocalyptic encampment.

"His house, my ass," he said.

"Yeah, they've got that bullshit piped into the Quonset huts so nobody misses a thing," Gene said. The bitterness in his voice made Jack look closely at him. Gene bent to light a cigarette. When he straightened, drawing deeply on the smoke, the intensity in his face and eyes, the humorless anger, was like what Jack had very rarely seen in him. "But I guess we should thank these assholes for being honest about what they think we are."

"I'm sorry," Jack said.

"You? Fuck no."

Gingerly, they stepped across a sheet of ice and over a low bank where snow had been plowed.

"Bud's not in there," Jack said. "I saw Zack. They've got her." Suddenly, his throat filled with emotion. "I mean, somehow, they or he's got her. It's because of how they think things begin." His voice cracked and he stopped, feeling deranged.

Given these people's way of imagining beginnings and of how beginnings preordain ends—he thought—then Bud would probably assume the spiriting away of Winona was a conspiracy against him, not just Winona's own idea for escape. What it is, is that they believe there is an original, pre-Adamite, God-given corruption, and seeing that, they rub up their romance against what they know is pain on this earth that's been chosen especially for them. They know they're in pain, and they're right about that. It's as if, lost in the fog of the uncertain world dissolving into one seeming fiction after another, they've countered by creating another one of their own, a true, great big fiction in which whatever they want is possible. They relieve their pain that way. Their pain governs everything. It's a priori. Bud's mind might well work like that, locking down in the same way according to his predilection for hurt.

Thinking that, thinking he had part of it, and knowing that however much on the mark it was, there was still something else in the riddle of it all. Jack choked through his emotion and said, "Bud would assume we're all in on his wife's escape."

"And he'd be right," Gene said.

They came up to the truck. Jack walked around to the passenger side and got in. The vinyl seat was cold and stiff beneath him. Gene pumped the accelerator pedal and started the engine. A cloud of blue exhaust floated past the cab.

"And you're right," Gene said, the smoldering cigarette jiggling in the corner of his mouth. "If what you mean is that they just make shit up."

"Nothing like it has ever happened to me before," Jack said, feeling himself smiling defensively. "It was like she was there, telling me they had her. It was like a vision."

"You mean Kate?"

"Right."

"Otherwise it's known as a gut check. You keep saying they."

"Him and whoever."

"That'd be right, too." Gene pushed down on the clutch and slid the shift lever into reverse. "I found Chuck Lamb down there. According to him, Bud's got his own group." He backed the truck out of the lot. "Lamb says he'll give us a line on Bud, but he wants to check it to make sure it's right . . . the Brotherhood of Zealot, or some such. Said he has something on it written down at home, but he won't go look until he's free here, and then there's the ceremony. Maybe at six." He shifted into first and looked across at Jack.

—Zealot? Jack thought. Isn't that what he is?

—Lamb. Petrie. Who else?

"It sounds like he's stalling. Why?"

Gene gave Jack a pained expression. "It's Lamb. He wants a piece of the action."

"What action?"

"Your action."

"What?"

"Easy," Gene said. "Money. He wants to go back to work for you."

"What? He thinks I'll negotiate something like that now?"

Gene pulled the truck forward. Jack gazed toward the lane and guard shack where Doug Borrt would be, and from the bottom of the lane at the federal agents and deputies, and then as they started out along the county road he peered deeply into the fog.

Gene said, "Look, Lamb's a groveling asshole, but I picked up something about Bud. He might be a mercenary."

"What the fuck else is new?"

"No, Jack. A mercenary. Do you understand? He hires himself out. Maybe he's his own mercenary out for hire."

Jack tried to absorb this as the truck shook through a maze of ruts.

He knew he'd been too cerebral, that he seemed only to understand through the back door of his philosophical observation . . . beginnings preordaining ends, a priori, fictions . . . and this when he'd just observed the fiasco of fascist metaphysics.

13

Cannibals

SEVERAL OF THE SCIENTISTS had come out onto the foredeck for a look at the drill ship before the *Hermes* cast off. One young man wearing a white sweatshirt with an image of a hooded man and under it the words "Free Chiapas" bounced the red-and-white ball on his forehead, soccer-style. He sent it into the wind. It sailed back. He sent it out again off his forehead, and again, finally catching it with his hands and setting it down on the deck. The ship, still tethered to the *Bering*, rocked to starboard and dipped forward, and the ball rolled in a French curve to the tip of the bow. The scientists watched the helicopter rise from the deck of the drill ship and strain against the wind, the heavy thunk of its blades reverberating as it plowed into the clouds, taking Braun away.

The scientists went inside, while U lingered at the portside rail. The lines were freed and the *Hermes* cast off, its engine rumbling as it initiated what would be almost a complete 360 to head it southward past the *Bering*'s stern. Because of the sudden pitch of the ship, U found himself clinging to the rail. The wind tore at his windbreaker and brought tears to his eyes, and he felt invigorated by the prospect of heading out in such seas. Next to the *Bering*, the shearwaters glided out of the trough and back, and out, and back, and as the *Hermes* drew away, they grew tinier until they were nothing. The gulls were gone. The albatross had disappeared. Soon it would be dark. Up high and small through an alight window at the *Bering*'s bridge, the captain's silhouette could be seen lifting a hand. U returned the salute, then picked up his luggage—a bag and his attaché case—and made his way to the steel door that led within.

He walked along the hall in the direction he remembered led to the ship's mess, entered it, and moved down the aisle toward Sophia. At a nearby table sat the scientists, including the young man in the Free Chiapas sweatshirt, which reminded U of something he couldn't place and brought a fleeting sense of probing an old ache, like the feeling of touching the tip of his tongue to a socket left by an extracted tooth. U sat down opposite Sophia, placing his luggage on the floor. He heard the scientists mention Nome, and then Seward. As the ship finished its turn and came broadside to the waves, its list increased. Suddenly, the scientists rose and swerved through the doorway, lunging past a man seated on a stool in the shadows. U recognized him from his last voyage on the *Hermes*—a man named Peter Totemoff.

"They're heading back to their racks," Sophia said. "It's the sea."

U glanced at her, and then at Peter, who didn't appear to have aged in the least. Small and wiry, an Aleut, Peter had coal black hair and a face the color of an almond. He was smoking, and he stared down the length of the galley toward the ship's stern. Though he now possessed an air of repose, a passion smoldered just beneath the surface, as U remembered it, a volcanic quality that could erupt if Peter were provoked. Another doorway at U's back led to the afterdeck. Peter gazed out the window in the top of the door at the spray that broke across the deck with each portside pitch of the ship, probably measuring the reach of the white spumes. His body swayed, countering the motion. The smoke from his cigarette undulated while the ship swung like a rocker arm, pivoting around it.

Just above U's head to the left was a porthole. As the ship slid down a swell, then dipped toward the coming wave, he could see the top of the gray laced with white against the darkening sky. It was as if the ship paid its obeisance by bowing to each looming swell.

"I might not last too long, either," Sophia said. Her mug of tea had slopped over and made a pool on the table.

U didn't remember her being prone to seasickness.

From the galley just on the other side of the serving counter, a mixer ran, utensils chattered, and something savory wafted. Peter snubbed out his cigarette, rose, waited for the pause at the center of the ship's motion, and walked in a straight line down the aisle to the serving counter where he leaned into the galley. "What's for dinner?" he asked. The reply came out as a squawk and a violent clattering of pots.

Peter straightened and looked directly at U, smiling wryly. "I remember you," he said.

"Long time," U said.

Peter looked at Sophia, and back at U, and in the traverse of his eyes lay the intimation of memory, the mildly scandalous liaison the crew back then had certainly gossiped about. His eyes marked that U and Sophia were here together again, but how he felt about it, or how he would judge it, what heaviness of portent or what lightness of comedy his personal knowledge held, was absolutely concealed. "The Chukchi and the Aleutians," he said.

"Yes."

Peter gestured upwards with his thumb. "We've put you in 2-C, one flight up." Poising himself, he waited for the dead spot in the ship's motion, then turned, darted up the aisle to the doorway, and slipped out.

Sophia swallowed two pills with her tea. "I hate this."

U wanted to tell her that she would feel better if she made herself conscious of the ship as an instrument that probed the sea, that it might help if she stood up and looked out the window or even went outside where she could see the waves coming. There was a rhythm to it, and the trick was to find that steadiness deep in the sea's heart. He now remembered, since Sophia had put him in mind of Kate McDuff, how those had been her words for it . . . "the sea's heart."

The ship moved southward toward the *Bering* Strait. Once through the strait, they would swing eastward. When they entered the lee side of the Kenai Peninsula, the seas would likely improve, but that was a day and a half away, and before then they might well be negotiating the forming ice. Presently, the ship's course was set at an angle of about 30 degrees to the trajectory of the waves, so the shearing force of the sea against the ship was felt more at the stern than the bow. Each pitch of the ship to one side was followed by a slight sternward twist. With each twist, the countering effect of the ship's ruddering system could be felt. They were seated near the stern.

"You didn't used to get seasick," he said.

"You're telling me?"

"You've been too long away?"

"I'm afraid that's not it."

U himself had never been seasick. "Think of the sea as a rippling skin," he said. "The molecules roll upon themselves and break into froth. The ship cuts into the sea's resistance. You can soften the effect by making yourself of a piece with the ship."

"Please spare me your pedantry," Sophia said.

U pulled the two packets she'd given him from the side flap of his bag and set them on the table.

Sophia touched the top sheaf. "That's what Jones sent on Leonard's and McDuff's research. And Braun does not quite have all of it as I'm sure you guessed."

"I didn't guess," U said. "Why would Jones give information that might be proprietary to Braun?"

"You don't trust him, right?"

"I don't trust anybody." U smiled. "For example, Kate McDuff was your protégé. You had a falling out. So, I don't completely trust even you."

This was a sounding. In the diving incident between the two women, Kate had dressed Sophia down on the *Hermes*'s afterdeck—just outside the doorway next to where they now sat—and in the presence of a half-dozen American and Soviet scientists. To Sophia, for whom the image of her faultlessness shielded the strangeness of her interior clockwork, whose powerful will had always ticked away behind the bright lens of her presentation, it was a public breach.

What U remembered—and now again that he was in Sophia's company, this was coming back to him vividly—was the two women clambering out of the inflatable and up the ladder to the deck of the ship, shedding their tanks and pulling off their hoods—the one just a few years out of school and considered privileged to be allowed to dive with the other, the great one who was already an internationally recognized authority, a known personality. Kate had addressed Sophia directly: "You left me. It's a cardinal rule, in case you've forgotten, never lose sight of your partner. And certainly not for fifteen minutes." Startled, Sophia had swayed back and her face visibly dropped. She'd said, "I knew where you were." "No, you did not," Kate had said. "You went ahead and lost me. If we're to dive together, we've got to keep the basics straight." Sophia whipped away and vanished through the doorway. From the others, there'd been a silent, astonished homage to Kate's nerve.

"McDuff was the most athletic and smartest young female diver I'd seen," Sophia said, her voice taking on a knowing tone that suggested she was being charitable. "She could read the water. She could have broken my depth records. She gave up the opportunity of a lifetime."

U permitted his body to cant slowly one way and the other to counter the ship's roll. At the time of the incident itself, Kate, once she'd spoken her mind, had gone about her business. He recalled how she'd looked: her wet hair clinging to her cheeks, green eyes, dimples, a small mole on one side of her mouth, and red drysuit folded down around her waist. U had admired her contagious high spirits and good manners, the shine of her idealism. It was her generous nature, together with the fact that Sophia in her possessive mentorship had let down her defenses, which made the exchange on the deck so telling.

A couple of nights later U and Sophia had been in her quarters while the ship steamed northward toward another dive site in the Chukchi. Sophia, dressed in purple sweats, sat cross-legged on her bunk. She'd showered and had a bottle of skin cream open on the bed next to her and was rubbing it into her arms. U sat still on a chair, intoxicated by her imperious beauty. Each of them was dizzy from the sudden ascendancy of their careers, and in the way of shipboard isolation, a romance had tricked out between them.

She confided to him her version of events. She'd seen the net and gone around it and when she looked back she saw Kate coming around it, too, and that then she, Sophia, had been distracted by an oil seep, an iridescence on a shelf, a faint bubbling, yet only for a minute, she said, and that was the rub. Truly, how long was she distracted? She said she'd then realized Kate wasn't with her and she went back to look. "I found her in plenty of time. I suppose I should have known she'd be upset, but she could have spoken to me in private." Sophia's damp hair clung loosely to her shoulders and her skin shone. She picked up a tissue to wipe the oil from her fingers. Her black eyes snapped and her lips moved like a mechano's, releasing the words. "She shouldn't have done that. She had no business trying to make a fool of me."

That hadn't been all. After the two women had resumed diving together under a cloud of chill cordiality, and then when the *Hermes* headed back to its home port, Kate had the temerity to decline Sophia's renewed offer—given out of her obsession, perhaps, a last test of Kate's devotion—to continue as a member of the team. Later, Kate sent an assessment report to the National Science Foundation that questioned the safety procedures and the number and depth of the dives Sophia had scheduled. The report caused a mild sensation as it leached into rumor, the science-world gossip driven by the fact that Sophia was a star. Kate's report had revived questions about a diver who'd been lost under the ice on a previous expedition in the Arctic, and Sophia was called before the governing board for "review."

Now, U found himself gazing at Sophia's chalky skin, set off against charcoal-colored sweater, and then again at the scar on her neck. Age spots had collected beneath her temples, and her eyes had a glaze to them. "That was long ago," he said, shrugging.

"Being reacquainted with her obstinacy brings it all back."

"Her obstinacy?" U said.

"She got married and had babies," Sophia snorted. "A person of her talent building a nest in Idaho? Her husband's a logger, for God's sake. Can you imagine?"

"Yes," U said. He could easily imagine that the young woman he'd encountered would include a husband and children in her life. As to the husband's occupation . . . who knew?

"I heard she was crawling along river bottoms doing agency counts," Sophia said.   The ship slid into a trench and seemed to pause. U sat still. Sophia had married an engineer who designed deep submersion apparati according to her specifications.

"And that's what you have to say? That in your opinion she's wasted her life?"

The ship pitched deeply. A wave slammed against the port side. White spume foamed at the porthole above U's head and the ship's superstructure groaned. Not answering, Sophia raised her hands to hold the edge of the table. There was another squawk from the galley and a shadowy, bear-like emanation lurched by the opening. Something heavy clanked in there. U picked out the salt shaker from the shelf of condiment bottles at the end of the table next to the wall and fingered it idly.

The salt shaker had a spring-loaded lid. All the bottles were packed in and corralled by a little fence to keep them from flying across the galley. The table, too, had a one-inch lip, which Sophia was grasping. The chairs were bolted to the floor. The serving counter had a lip and all along its front were wire bins where items could be kept. U looked up at the dripping porthole. It was dark outside. Saturday. Still Saturday and the lens of the abbreviated northern day had squeezed shut.

"Look," he said. "The problem with having Braun engaged in an inquiry is that it's Kate McDuff's data base. Or others she's been given access to. It's hers and her partner's to release for peer review when they see fit. Some portion of it is surely public already, since you say they have a grant. Did anybody consider that this might be an absolute waste of company money, sending Braun off on a wild goose chase?"

"The détente documents are certainly not hers," Sophia said. "They've been classified for years. What's more, ZAQ had one of the principals at McDuff's old employer do some consulting for us. She might have current data, too, also classified. I told you, there's a leak, and some people think it's a treasonable act."

U studied her skeptically.

Sophia lifted her chin and looked askance at him.

"You're saying she stole the files?"

"Who knows? It looks like she's had the old ones for years."

"Accusing her of treason is a little extreme, don't you think?"

"I said, 'some people.' Hemming is bouncing off the walls over this."

U pictured Hemming, to whom he was to deliver the documents in Houston, probably via Jones. Hemming, the company founder, was a small, excitable man with big ears. Prone to hyperbole in his rackety, buzz-saw way of speaking, Hemming's use of the word "treason" was not inconceivable; whereas Jones, the executive vice president, was large and methodical, a disarmingly soft-looking man given to chuckling whenever he had to parse Hemming's vitriolic edicts into workable instructions. U parted the top of the sheaf and looked at the heap of papers. The possibility of contracts and blueprints breaking loose was always an anticipated risk, since in the United States the classification of information as "secret" was ubiquitous. Most of the time, security classifications merely carried matters into a hinterland, the interminable fog where government and industry stood around with their hands in each others' pockets. The whole of Hemming's ZAQ deal going way back into the détente era would still be covered by a veil of secrecy. Certainly the new arrangements between ZAQ and Schtok—brokered by the State Department—would be, too. Such secrecy allowed officials to lie with impunity about the facts in public. The real question was rarely whether materials were in fact "classified," but instead whether anyone was willfully playing the leaks and breaches to put an adversary on the defensive.

"So? What is it? That she'll use the agreements to spike an environmental argument? And then others will jump in? The better possibility is that everybody will just ignore her?"

"It looks like she and Leonard are using the pipeline tie-ins, offshore sites, and shipping channels to project spills and toxicity rates," Sophia said. "They'll argue that the whole North Pacific fishery is going the way of the lower coast. They'll use oil as a tweak on top of the rest of it . . . the PCBs, radiation from Point Hope, nuclear waste dumps at sea, toxic runoff from Siberia and from the Athabascan and Peace Rivers in Canada. We need to see exactly what the two of them have. There is a die-out going on now in the Arctic. Some think the *Bering* fishery's about to crash, but nobody has fully documented the causes yet. It would be like McDuff to try to show that the whole of the north is one besmirched habitat. She'll let politics drive her conclusions. You'll see. She proved long ago that she's oblivious to consequences."

U well knew that the stock and trade of company science was to divide the findings of adversarial science into pieces and to question the evidence bit by bit. Finding a flaw or two, company science had its own ways of using the courts, politics, and the media to tear apart the whole cloth of a counter argument. What struck him now about Sophia's account was the absence of self-irony. He answered her cant from under the cover of his own: "Steklyányigórod's up out of the ground. Schtok is negotiating the Chinese and Turkish pipelines. We just left a ship that's drilling a test well in the middle of the Chukchi. We hope to be laying pipe. Everybody knows there are stringent environmental provisions, especially for anything coming into the U.S. If we have to, we'll trade the Arctic Refuge back to the environmentalists again."

"Of course," Sophia said.

"Classified is academic. Damage control is part of doing business."

"Exactly. This is damage control. I'm telling you, we can't allow McDuff to continue on with this."

In his view, the position of American environmentalists was made hopeless by their dependence along with the rest of humanity upon resources. It was as if they were cradling the infant of their dreaming. They had to hold the infant close while they fought to protect it from being ripped to shreds, but at the same time they themselves nibbled at the infant, tearing away bits of its flesh to sustain themselves in their combat. It was so that the Arctic National Wildlife Refuge, the Alaska Maritime Refuge, or Lake Athabasca could be threatened by industry over and over again, and then handed back in part or in whole over and over again as the spoils of battle, while in the meantime industry lopped off hunks of the world somewhere else. It was like a wei chi'i game in which the adversary repeatedly displayed the same weakness, was repeatedly encircled by the same stratagem, and was always forced to give up new stones elsewhere in order to hold onto the stones it embraced. U was fatalistic about the future of humans on the planet. The game's outcome was always predetermined, no matter how dense and convoluted the maneuvers, because human rapacity was nonnegotiable and inexorable.

"Look," Sophia said. "So far as Hemming is concerned, the environmental issue is far from the top rung of this little feeding chain. Somebody . . . according to Jones, Hemming believes it's Mobex . . . somebody used a magazine to front a Freedom of Information request. We got some of those materials, including work-ups of FBI files on McDuff and her husband. There's next to nothing on her partner." Sophia pushed back from the table and stretched her legs. A foot glanced off his ankle. "What Mobex is trying to get is the agreements, all of them going back thirty years. Somehow, McDuff seems to have these. We know they're out there, and Mobex knows, too."

"Mobex." U drew himself up, feeling his iron being struck. Mobex, a petroleum behemoth with a reputation for brutal efficiency, had already tried to breach ZAQ protections over the lease and service agreements. Given access to the documents, having the proof of them, Mobex would try to lever more information out of the government, snarl ZAQ in a political wrangle, and tie up ZAQ in court on charges of what U had always known was a ZAQ vulnerability—unfair access to markets going way back to the Nixon and Carter administrations. It might well end with Mobex taking on ZAQ holdings.

"It's Hemming's theory?" he asked.

Sophia's reply caused him to seek further into what should have been obvious. She said, "No, not his theory. Hemming is convinced of it. There's a mole."

"I see," U said, and then cogs dropped into place. "Braun?"

"Could be. Jones wants him to do the digging, trusting he'll either find the leak, or show himself to be it. But you insisted that he work with public materials only. Listen, Freckles . . . Braun's out there, now."

Thus, she struck another kind of iron in him. "Nobody calls me that anymore."

She examined his forehead where the mass of freckles ran. Russet-colored and pronounced in his youth, the irregularity of pigmentation he'd inherited from an unknown father who'd availed himself of his unknown mother's willingness in Hong Kong, had paled through the years and almost merged with the color of his skin, that of dried leaves.

Sophia dropped her eyes to his and the melancholy in her tone surprised him. "I forgot. Apologies."

He gazed at her. "You're feeling better?"

"It comes and goes. It's not just the sea." She tugged at the neck of her sweater and revealed more of her scar. "They've given me a pacemaker. My body doesn't react to things the way it used to. Sometimes, it doesn't even feel like my own body. I don't dive at all now."

This gave him pause. "I didn't know."

"I love the sea," she said. "But this is my last voyage."

"I'm sorry."

It was a moment in which their shields edged downward. He thought: Her life has dramatically changed.

"Yes," she said. "Listen. We're both to report to Jones. Me on what we're getting from the science and you on Braun, on what you think they'll get from the agreements, the legal implications of it. They being whoever . . . McDuff and Leonard, the media, and Mobex. You're to keep track of Braun, so hopefully he'll stay in touch like you told him to. Probably, Jones would have liked him kept on a shorter leash, but under the circumstances there was no other way to do it." She paused. "There's a lot at stake."

U certainly understood that. Futures, careers, egos, people living or dying, international politics, corporate preeminence, all of it was defined by the main thing, money, billions upon billions of dollars. He understood money, although it was hardly personal to him. He sported the jeweled ring of his Brotherhood, his Rolex, and his glasses had gold-plated frames, but his clothes were plain and inexpensive, like the wool trousers he now had on, the polyester shirt, a sweater, and the windbreaker he'd bought on sale. His habits were ascetic. His business was to keep the accounts of fabulously rich corporations in balance and within the confines of law. Money was like water to him, as molecular as water. It moved in waves and transported loads of debris like water. It had surface tension like water. In its brightness it ran hard in the channels and sought out the fingers and pooled in the eddies and estuaries and piled up on itself in places. It could convert the goods of the world—trees, crops, stone, or petroleum—into itself, and it fed upon itself. A great loss was as fascinating to him as a gain. Because of the absence of personal greed in himself, which was actually a disinterest, he knew he was considered incorruptible. Money could be counted. It arrived charged and departed charged. That was all. He knew that in his way he was an innocent, or even an idiot, when it came to reading the twists of human passion.

Sophia sat still with her eyes closed. "It's coming back."

U glanced at the two folders, the portals to a distasteful world of detail. He had what others considered a perfect memory. They thought it so in accordance with the standards of the age that placed the highest value on the ability to hold and manipulate letters and digits, which in its infancy had invented the word "photographic" and in its maturity had invented a machine to store minutia in endless quantities. From his boyhood, U had displayed powers of retention many considered phenomenal, and beginning with the sisters who first educated him, he had been set apart. He had no idea why he was this way . . . an ample, highly oxygenated flow in his arteries, maybe, or an excess of cells in his brain, a peculiarity in the reach of the dendritic paths between the cells, maybe an extra mutated gene like Wolfgang Mozart was said to have had, or a neurologically induced disorder that allowed him to absorb the ever-heaping data dots, the ever-widening fields of the absolutely mundane. He did not carry his own computer, which would only have widened those fields.

The sea rose, its rhythm intensifying. Swells broke against the hull and sent a soft thundering through the mess hall. Something slammed in the galley, and suddenly the cook appeared in the opening above the serving counter. "Shit!" she said, causing Sophia to jerk. In one hand, the cook held up a glass baking pan that had a rubbery substance in its bottom. "Cake," she said. Well over six feet tall, the cook had a wild halo of frizzy brown hair, penciled eyebrows, and dark lipstick that made her look like an extra-large incarnation of Madonna. She wore a green flannel shirt rolled up to her elbows and her voice crowed like a rooster's. "Lasagna. Nobody's eating lasagna tonight. I made chocolate cakes. Look at this. It's fudge."

She put one hand on her hip and with the other tipped the dish precariously toward them, and at the same time swayed perfectly in rhythm with the ship's motion. It was like a circus trick. "What happens if I get sick, I ask you?" As abruptly as she had appeared, she vanished, and in a far recess things bumped and slammed.

U looked at Sophia. A green tinge had appeared at her temples.

"I have to go," she said.

What he held in his memory, what was also called eidetic, and which so far as he knew was everything he'd ever read but with large quantities of it, the tiny digits stored deep in piles in the nether reaches of his brain and likely to be retrieved by chance provocations, had lately caused in him a deep confusion. The sisters had told him it was a gift from God, but now it seemed a curse, and at some deep, adult level, he had grown afraid. The accumulation of material had left him with a vast detritus that sifted here and there like ash. He could never sweep it clean. It rose in billows, and blew away to collect elsewhere. It sifted through his fingers. The reason why he had watched the shearwaters with such attention, had been so keenly conscious of the motion of the ship, and had taken pleasure in the violence of the sea, was to relieve his mind of the weight it carried. He would have happily eaten lasagna. He'd have been pleased to dig out the collapsed cake, as well.

"Is there anything I can do for you?" he asked Sophia.

She shook her head and closed her eyes. The ship rocked. The condiment bottles rattled. At his back, spume hissed over the rails onto the deck and, from deep in the galley, more things thumped. Metal pots rang. The unseen cook emitted a sound that curled into a war cry, then dropped into a roil of muttering and cursing. The scientist's sweatshirt—the image of Subcommandante Marcos—emanated in U's memory, swelling sinuously through the litter. Kate McDuff had always worn a T-shirt under her drysuit, on it an image of the bearded Ché Guevara and under it the word Ché!

He remembered finding Kate standing in the bright sun at the rail on one side of the foredeck not long before the *Hermes* had put into port years ago. Three Russian scientists were at the point of the bow, talking in their language. The end of the voyage, the prospect of homecoming, and the fine summer weather had created high spirits on board ship. He and Kate had spoken of their plans after disembarking: He was headed for San Francisco to close out some business, she to Seattle to get married and look for work. When he'd observed that she must not therefore be continuing with Sophia, Kate had replied, "She lost a diver on her last voyage. Maybe it wasn't her fault. Maybe he was pushing himself too hard. But now, she could have lost me. Technically, she's an incredible diver, but there are too many tricky situations with her. You need some easy dives mixed in with the hard ones for the fun of it. To be honest, I've even wondered if she meant to leave me behind. That's how much I've lost confidence in her. I will not work under her," she had said.

"She has influence," he'd said.

"Yes," Kate had said softly. Her face became somber. "I'm giving up the advantage of her influence. But the more by far," she said, looking across the water, "it's this I might be giving up." The landform toward which they were headed had appeared at the horizon, the deep blue hump of peninsula enshrouded in feathery clouds across the glassy sea. "But there'd be a lot more hurt the other way."

U had asked her why she wore the T-shirt.

"Oh," she'd laughed. "I always dive with Ché."

That, too, he had found surprising—that the high-spirited, cultivated, well-mannered, and talented woman with the beguiling southern accent would take on such a figure as a patron. He'd been unable to make sense of it, and yet now the thought that Kate's idealism might have made her, first, dangerous, and second, marked, and vulnerable to being manipulated by directives emanating from all across the globe, was sparking through his mind. This other woman before him, on the other hand, was one he had once acquired in his role as a ritual figure in her ceremony of preeminence. But as he gazed at her now, he saw she was changed . . . the mask of pain, the waxen pallor, the implanted battery and diode, and her darkness as of a root in the clammy earth.

"I'm going to my cabin," she said, taking a shuddering breath.

"You're sure you don't need help?"

She waved him off and swayed out of the booth, then picked her way along the aisle, grabbing at the backs of stalls for support. She was hunched like a crone. When she reached the door, she set her weight to pull it open, and disappeared.

He stood up, tucking the two sheaves under his arm and picking up his bag and attaché in either hand. He tried to copy Peter Totem-off's method by waiting for the ship to roll to its center and moving quickly down the aisle, staying within the trench of the ship's motion as the ship itself occupied a trench in the sea. He could ride the heart of the trench like a shearwater, then climb up the slant at the door, but two-thirds of the way along, the ship pitched and threw him flat on a tabletop. He dropped his bag and then the attaché, which bounced and skidded along the floor. He hung on, clinging to the table edge as the two sets of papers sifted from the sheaves and scattered.

The cook's frizzy head thrust through the serving space. "Gotcha!"

He waited for the pause in the ship's list, then, still hanging onto the table, tamped what remained of the papers back into the sheaves. He crouched, and as the ship began to swing, crawled down the aisle, retrieving the pages. The cook leaned out, grinning down at him. Once he had the pages, he crept back to the table and made a pile out of them. The ship rocked. The cook vanished. When the ship paused, he grabbed his bag and thrust the papers back into its side pocket, retrieved the attaché case, and waited for the next lull. When it came, he lurched to the door and made it into the hall. Carefully, he pressed his weight against a rail and mounted one step at a time toward the next level. Waves boomed in the closed space, and the ship's engine growled as its prop screwed into the sea. The higher he climbed the more extreme the roll of the ship felt, as if he were ascending the neck of a bottle.

14

The Pre-Adamite

COLD.

Her breath vaporized in front of her face. She watched it to assure herself that air still passed in and out of her lungs. Each column of vapor spread into a diffuse cloud, and thinned almost to nothing before she exhaled into it the next column. Everything else in the room was a blur. When she closed her eyes, her head reeled and then settled upon a black dot.

Cold.

It was cold in the room.

She was handcuffed. And her legs, cuffed to the legs of the chair.

Her hands were cuffed behind the chair.

Her shoulders ached. Her thighs ached. One knee ached.

Slowly, she realized that she had blacked out and was just now awakening.

Pain under her chin like a line of fire.

A figure that blotted out the light.

When she opened her eyes, the white room swam before her. She turned her head to the right toward a shiny thing. Two of everything. Her head throbbed. The images came together to make one and she saw a heating register. It was made from brushed aluminum, as was the window casing above it. Outside, a snowbank crept a quarter of the way up the glass pane, pressing against it. She saw the snow, but the room was almost dark. In the light from a storm lamp, she saw snow-flakes swirling and sifting to the top of the bank.

The storm lamp had not been on at first.

Through the upper part of the window and some distance away as if they were floating in the air, she saw two lines of purple lights.

"Keys," someone had said.

"What keys?" the other had said.

Two.

Two of everything on either side of the dot as if her eyes had been jarred loose.

Cold.

Snow.

"I need the keys to open with," the one had said.

"Bring them back," the other said.

Equipment barn. They dragged her out of the Power Wagon in an equipment barn. Machines, the smell of oil and diesel, and the lime smell of concrete in the cold.

"In there," the other one said. "Take her in there. I got to plow the strip."

Bud Willy. His voice rumbled when he spoke.

"Piece of shit!" the woman said with her voice like a bray.

Counting Winona, there were three.

"Then shovel the walk," Bud said.

She heard the voices in her head, detached from their bodies.

Winona screamed.

She was shivering, staring at the window, at the snowbank below and the light above it and in the distance floating purple lights.

Everything repeated itself.

Her knife.

Now, it was almost dark in the room.

"Keys."

Ansel. Or Hansel.

"In there."

She had obeyed, passing out of the equipment barn through a door to the snow and out of the snow into a house and around two corners to the dark. A light came on. Then dark. He shoved her into the dark. A carpet thick against her shoes. Snow pressed against the window. Snow melting from her cuffs. A white light came on outside. Purple lights came on.

A line of pain like a blaze.

The light came on in the white room. He pushed her into the chair and went behind her, loosed the rope but grabbed her arms. She felt the steel coming on her wrists, tight, first one and then the other.

He came to the front and hunkered, hunching to one side and then the other and tied her ankles with the rope, each to a front leg of the chair by wrapping it around and yanking it tight. His oily hair hung from beneath his black cap. Before her stood a desk, behind it a chair, and to her left another steel door, which was closed, and to her right the window.

Her shoulders ached. Her legs ached. Her neck ached. Her knee ached. Her shirt was stained to a rust color and into it fresh rivulets of red had soaked.

Winona screamed.

A figured blotted out the light.

Now, she closed her eyes again. In the darkness the dark streams of her brain converged upon a black dot.

He had stood, hovering over her. He walked back to the doorway. The light went out. The door shut. Boots squeaked on the floor outside the room.

Cold.

Her own knife.

The door opened. The light came on. He closed the door. Far away inside the barn, she heard an engine start. He stood above her. His lips snaked sideways, carving a slice in his face.

"Scared yet?"

Ansel. Or Hansel.

His voice mostly air with a rattle in it like peas in a pod.

She was shivering.

Her eyes were like a loose spark, darting all over him. Thin, he wore a black pullover sweater and the black cap, his baggy camouflage pants tucked into his black boots that dripped melted snow onto the pale blue carpet.

His teeth were yellow. The pale blue irises of his eyes floated in corneas the color of phlegm. Yellow teeth, streaked yellow hair, yellow pockmarked face, long hands, blue and yellow eyes. He took a cigarette out of his shirt pocket, stuck it between his lips, and lit it. He pulled a sheath from his belt and bent toward her.

Her sheath. Her knife slid out of the sheath.

Blood had sprayed from the buck's throat to make the rust color on her shirt. While she'd lain in the back of the Power Wagon, this man put his foot on her back, pressed his weight on her, and took her knife. He'd been like an insect, poised and still on the wheel well above her. His face was like an ax catching light from the dashboard up front where the others were and the light from the headlamps glancing off things and washing back in the long ride that brought them to this place. Now she remembered that part, her fright on the floor and the ax-face above, not speaking, and the smell of him, and Winona's frantic talk breaking into sobs.

"You got everything you wanted," she'd heard Winona say.

"Shut up," Bud said. "You tried to run."

"Not from you. At first, yes, I did. I changed my mind. I didn't know what I was doing. She made me keep going, the temptress. But I knew you'd come."

"You're lying."

"But I went where you knew how to find me."

"That's because you're stupid. Shut up."

The man dropped the spare tire on her, the weight of it knocking her wind out. Bud told him no, take it off, leave her be. They drove twisting down the hill, then on interminably while she lay still with her head jammed against a metal box, traveling fast in the long, furious quiet. Winona started in again. Bud told her to stop. The chains rang. The floor shuddered. They began to climb. The Power Wagon jolted and swung on the turns. Brush scraped against the sides.

The equipment barn.

The cold.

And Winona: "Where? Jeez, Bud, where is this?"

Then here in the room, not moving but merely straining against the cuffs, pulling every muscle in her body tight as he bent toward her.

He drew the knife out of the sheath, undid the top buttons of her shirt, and poked the tip of the blade through her thermal undershirt to the skin of her chest. Cigarette smoke trailed into her nostrils, overwhelming the rest of his smell . . . anise, sweat and anise, the scent of sweat and anise seed under the cloud of tobacco. Enraged, she stared over the top of his head at the white wall. He began cutting, holding the collar of her undershirt with one hand and sawing open a slit with the knife, then put his hand in, holding her breast and pinching her. He rocked back on his haunches and stared. She felt the dot of pain on her chest. Not moving, her body strained. The dot passed into an incensed knot that tangled through her body and jerked tight. The dot became a dot of mind as she rose up in herself to think:

—Whatever else I have to grant this man, I will not grant him an ounce of compliance, absolutely nothing out of my terror.

The diesel engine had passed not far from the room. She felt a vibration in the floor under her feet. She saw light in the corner of her eye, small outside the window as it passed across and disappeared. Before her was the dot of her consciousness, everything of her own matter that she could force into it.

"Not bad for an old broad," the man said. He opened the cut in his face beside the cigarette so that it made a wedge-shaped hollow in the yellow with the smoking coal at its edge. She stared straight at him as the light in the corner of her eye went by in the opposite direction.

"It's the time of the Serpent before Adam," he said. "It's the prior time. Lilith out of the original chaos making the true order of men out of the seed of the prior time come back now to make a mess of things." He brought the blade near her face.

"Get away," she said.

"She talks." Slowly, he waved the blade before her face and whispered: "Out of Cain the soulless horde and out of Rebekkah for mating with Satan and out of his seed, Esau, the new progenitor, the wound of the beast, the mongrel parasites living off the production of the Adamic race, and worst of all the traitor whites like you."

She stared back at him, holding fast to the dot of her will, emptying everything into it, thus telling him that no matter what he did she would never bend to him.

He cut her, slicing under her chin and up along the edge of her jaw. "Bleed a little more, bitch betrayer," he whispered.

He slipped the knife in the sheath, tucked the sheath back under his belt, and bent, bringing his face close. Smoke curled up into her nostrils. The light in the corner of her eye passed again, going back the other direction as if the light stitched the dark out there where the purple was. She stared firmly straight into the dot, hanging onto it, not giving in.

"I'll be back," he said.

The words hissed out of her mouth: "Fuck you."

His body cocked itself. Suddenly, he lurched at her and everything went black.

Cold.

She was shivering.

She could feel the lump swelling above her temple where he'd hit her.

She felt the line of fire from where he'd cut her.

Everything about her ached.

The door was open now and the light in here was off.

There was light from the room beyond the doorway and light glimmering through the window from the storm lamp outside. A pale cast in the white room allowed her to see the vapor of her breath passing out in columns and diffusing into small clouds. It was night. Slowly, she was coming awake into the lunatic pieces.

She had dreamed something. She remembered that Jack would be waiting for her, and thinking of how distraught he would be filled her with anguish. The blood from the cut had dripped down her shirt, the new red darkening the rust color from the buck. The coagulation in the cut crinkled when she bent her head. She had the feeling of what she'd dreamed, laying out the space it occupied in her body, not articulating itself, yet raising an overwhelming longing.

—Where?

—Where am I?

Winona appeared, bending as she looked through the doorway, the angularity of the figure and hook-like head outlined in the light at its back, and then the skirt snapping like a fin as she turned to scream.

Two of her.

The shout came out raggedly from her throat: "Bud!"

The massive figure filled the doorway.

Two brutes in the two doorways, filling them side-to-side and ducking in their combination to clear the tops of the two jambs, darkening the light in each, and looking in at her, then pulling away.

She shook her head to make the twos collapse into ones, and hung onto the black dot that was stuck like a pin in the light on the far side of the doorway. She heard voices out there: Bud, and the other one. She saw a white wall out there, and a polished wood floor reflecting a straightedge of light thrown upon it at an angle. She shook her head again. It hurt to move her head. She looked out the window at the snowbank and above it the line of purple lights, which were on a hill. She had seen lights from a machine going back and forth, moving by the window and out of sight on either side. Clearing the space marked by the purple lights.

A figure hurtled across the opening of the doorway and slid across the floor until it hit the bottom of the wall, and another figure agile as a bear sprang after it and lifted it up.

Bud pressed the other one, Ansel, or Hansel, against the wall by the neck and grabbed him by the front of the shirt and held him. The other one's feet were off the ground, kicking like an insect. She heard his choking, and from somewhere over on the other side of the doorway, Winona screaming again, the sound of her voice terrified or ecstatic: "Bud! No, Bud! Bud! No! I love you! I love you! I love you, Bud! No! No!"

Bud pulled back. The other one thudded into a heap on the floor. One leg moved, slowly stretching out. The dot of her suffering was on him like a spike.

Bending over him, Bud jerked him up by the shirt. "Fucking keys," Bud said. He dropped him back on the floor. "Fucking knife." And then opening the door to the outside and throwing him out. "Fucking motherfucker."

15

Written with the Heart's Blood

THEY DROVE OUT OF THE COMPOUND, past the officers, and started along the back road. It was snowing heavily, the flakes driven by the wind into near whiteout. They reached the highway and turned onto it. To the east, the hills were veiled in white. It was past noon. Gene kept to the right-hand lane, falling into the cautious pace of church and Sunday shopping traffic.

He said, "But you've got to remember that Kate's survival instincts are fucking strong."

Jack murmured.

"Zealot," Gene said. "Besides the obvious, I got no idea what it means . . . or is. Lamb says they follow the fourth philosophy, whatever the hell that is." The bite was back in Gene's voice. "Lamb said Zack was dropped off yesterday for some of the women to watch over. He says Bud does that at times."

Jack said, "So, it could mean he came back to my house after Travis and I left for the game. Not finding Winona there, he trashed it, then dropped Zack off, or dropped Zack off first, and took off after them? It's a lot of steps."

"Right," Gene said.

"And it's Lamb telling us all this," Jack said.

"Yeah, maybe it's all bullshit." Gene looked closely at Jack, pursing his lips. "I told Lamb you had business with Bud. An engine. Meantime, Lamb says he got the paymaster at the mill to cut him a check for Bliss's load."

"He what?"

"He claimed Bliss said it was okay. He had to have the money, he said."

"Fuck," Jack said, lifting his feet over the toolbox. "Bliss told me Lamb owed him the favor. The paymaster's got no business cutting a check against my account."

"Yeah," Gene said. "But who's the bigger liar?"

"Lamb."

A tractor-trailer rig roared past them, slamming a sheet of slush against the windshield. Gene switched the wipers to high and leaned forward, peering through the glaze. "I told Lamb I'd make it right with you."

"So Bliss is supposed to pay you back for the load he didn't deliver, but what was delivered by somebody else who owed him, and you end up owing me?"

"I told Lamb he might consider his debt to Bliss settled, that if he comes through for us we'll cover it."

Jack thought about Lamb—a little man who liked tall women and big rigs and engaged in endless small-time dirty dealings in an effort to trim the world down to his size. "What we want to know is where Bud went."

"This outfit of his is tied into a B.C. group, according to Lamb. It's international, he says. I guess he means there's a few like-minded idiots on two sides of the border."

"B.C.," Jack said. "Yahk. It's where Kate was going to take her." With his outward calm, he was trying to fight off his inward panic.

"Yeah." Gene blew smoke, then reached to tap his cigarette ash into the ashtray. His face was grim looking. He had the cigarette between his fingers, his hands on the wheel, and the smoke trailed upwards, mushroomed at the ceiling, and shot out the window.

They were drawing near the turn-off. As they drove by Bud's wrecking yard, their heads turned. It was exactly as before, with the red CLOSED sign in the window just visible through the blowing white. There was a rapt moment like a trepidated prayer.

"I was raised Orthodox," Gene said. "Do you know what that means?"

"Strict."

"Like what you'd call Holy Rollers, almost. My folks owned a furniture store in San Diego and we lived in a town called National City, south of San Diego, if you can believe it. A navy town. Navy town in San Diego county in the fifties and sixties?"

"Strict, too."

"And white and paranoid as hell about the Kikes and Beans. We kids were told to stay quiet and keep our religion at home. When I had my Bar Mitzvah, I only had one friend at school I dared invite. So, I took it seriously, the assimilation, married a wasp, got drafted, had a kid, got divorced, and came out here to straighten myself out after the war. I got pretty assimilated acting like a redneck, but that place today rang my bell, I'll tell you."

"I'm sorry," Jack said.

"No. I'm just all of a sudden pissed off, that's all, the way those turkeys are so self-satisfied, strutting around with their heads way up their asses." He drew deeply on his cigarette as he slowed to turn off the highway, balancing that motion against the motion of turning and at the same time lightly pumping the brake, then making the turn and cutting the wheels against the slide in the slush. He punctuated the maneuver by blowing smoke and tapping his ash in the tray. The truck straightened on the paved road that would lead past the state park.

Jack gazed at the shoulder of the road near the corner. It was where he'd last seen Kate and he could still see the partially filled tracks of where the three of them had parked. He felt a wave of despair. He wanted to take away the moment. He wished that what he'd said—"It's a fucking bad idea."—had been much more direct, that he'd broken ranks from their longstanding matrimonial agreement of granting each other room and instead laid down a stiff enough ultimatum to make her stay, or else broken down completely and begged . . . any-thing. He remembered his misgivings as the Subaru pulled up to the intersection, turned right, and headed north. When he drove to the intersection, he had watched the Subaru until it dwindled to a dot.

"Let's say Lamb is stalling," Gene said. "In hopes he'll wangle a con-tract to haul for you."

The truck jumped in and out of a rut. The driven snow blew at them from the left. Jack put his feet back on top of the toolbox so that his knees were up in his face while in his belly the elements of his dread wound around. "We're still not sure it's Bud."

"Yeah, but I say offer Lamb something. Blackmail's not legal tender."

Jack said, "He said six?"

"Yeah. He thinks he can make a run to his house before the ceremony. I'm hoping it's like you were saying. These guys' sense of how things end up is completely fucked. Lamb doesn't know what the shit he's doing, but we might get a little something out of him, like where is Bud likely to go in B.C. Anything to draw a line between the dots. One more thing . . ." Gene had both hands on the wheel and was driving steadily in the sideways blowing snow. The cigarette dipped and swung in the corner of his mouth. "I can tell by looking at you that what you're about to do is jump in your truck and go chasing off. Pissed as I am, I can't be one hundredth as pissed as you are. Don't do it."

* * *

Gene ducked straight into the kitchen, but Jack stopped in the living room where Travis stood waiting behind the couch, his face pinched. From the kitchen, Jack heard voices and the oven door creaking. In the living room, all the furniture had been put back in place. The lamps stood in their correct spots, but one had a crushed shade. Berg lay curled up at the side of the wood burner, slowly thumping her tail. Jack turned his eyes to Travis. The mutual gaze said everything, which was that they had nothing.

"No calls?"

"Not from Mom," Travis said. "Not about Mom. Except Pamela. You're supposed to call her right away."

"We didn't make much headway down there, either." Seeing Travis's face tighten even more, and the house on its way to being put back together but still visibly a wreck, Jack felt himself about to plummet yet deeper into despair.

He gestured to Travis that he'd be right back and moved to the cloud of aroma in the kitchen. There was bread which Marlene was coaxing out of its pan onto a rack on the counter next to the stovetop by drumming the pan's bottom with her fingertips. Gene stood near her. They'd been talking when Jack came in, and now the two looked across at him. Chris was over in the corner behind the table, sweeping a pile of debris into a dustpan.

"Oh, Jack," Marlene said, her face filled with sympathy. "I lost somebody once." She stopped and her eyes welled with tears. "Oh, God, I don't mean that. I mean I have an idea what you're going through. She's going to be all right. Nobody would dare hurt Kate."

Gene had a complicated expression ... his lips slightly upturned, his brow furrowed, and his cheeks drawn, rendering him faintly amused, exasperated, and worried all at once. Jack knew that Marlene usually said exactly what was on her mind. He was grateful for her concern. That was all.

Chris dumped the dustpan's contents into a paper bag and carried it past Jack over to the counter where he set it next to the other bags. The kitchen was clean, the refrigerator and all the counters wiped down, the drawers and cupboard doors shut, and the table in order.

"Thank you for this," Jack said.

"Don't be silly," Marlene said. "I made bean soup. There's salad. And bread."

"Thank you," Jack said.

"We're going to take Chris to basketball practice," Gene said. "We can take Travis. It might not hurt him, if he wants to go."

"No." Travis had appeared in the opening to the foyer. "I'm staying."

Marlene rocked forward, her face brightening, then responding to the apparitional look on Travis's face, she settled back close to Gene with a worried expression. Chris hiked up against the counter next to his father, dug his hands deep into his pockets, and scrutinized Travis, engaging him in the thoughtful center of male adolescence. Chris's sympathy hinted at the shared bewilderment to the strange happenings of the adult world. Travis sighed and shifted his feet. Jack caught Gene's eyes flicking from Chris to Travis and back to Chris. Through the east window and on the lee side of the house, where just yesterday Bud and Zack had stood, snow swirled unrelentingly

"You need to eat," Marlene said. She gestured toward Jack and Travis. "And you," she said to Chris. She took a stack of bowls and plates out of the cupboard and began ladling soup. No one moved. "I mean now. There's coffee and juice." She hoisted a pitcher. "Glasses are on the table." She looked at Jack searchingly. She was still embarrassed by what she'd first said.

"Thank you," Jack said.

Chris and Travis moved to the food.

Gene said, "After practice is over, we'll go back down and talk to Lamb."

Travis shot a glance at Jack. Jack lifted his head, meaning he would explain it.

"But one of us should let Painter know," Gene said.

"I'm calling him," Jack said. "Did he come?" he asked Travis.

"His deputies were here taking fingerprints. We can touch whatever we want."

"Did they find anything?"

"They acted like maybe they did."

The food tasted flat on Jack's tongue and even Travis ended up poking idly at the beans in the bottom of his bowl. The quiet gave the meal a funereal pall. Afterwards, Marlene and Gene washed the dishes gathered for them by Chris, and Travis headed disconsolately back to the living room. "You got to talk to that kid," Gene said in a low voice.

Jack put the clean dishes away, then trailed Marlene, Chris, and Gene to the front door. "I'll be back," Gene said. Jack eased the door shut behind them and turned to Travis, who was crouched next to the stove, rubbing the dog's ears. Jack moved to the other side and stood. The fire crackled, radiating into the continuing pause. Through the windows out in the sheen of driving snow, tree boughs sagged deeply.

—This thing has actually happened, Jack thought.

Travis spoke: "The deputies said Dan Painter wants you to double-check the tool shed for anything that's missing. They dusted for prints out there, too."

"Okay," Jack said.

"And Pam," Travis said. "Don't forget to call her."

"What did you tell her?"

"What was happening. She's worried."

Jack didn't want to call his daughter yet, not because he wished to keep anything from her, but because the talking would confirm the hurt of what he could not explain. And then there was Ron up in Alaska, and Kate's father down in Alabama.

"The deputies said Sheriff Painter wants a list of what's missing."

"Okay," Jack said. "We can start on that."

He went into the kitchen, found a pad and pen in a newly arranged drawer, and returned. He set the pad and pen on the arm of the sofa and stood back beside the stove, the momentary resolve to act decaying into a lull.

Travis hadn't moved. "I plowed the lane."

Looking at his son, Jack felt himself filling with anguish. It was the haunted expression and yet the pride in taking responsibility.

"I saw," he said. "Good. Did you feed the horses and check the tank?"

"Yeah. And Abby Leonard's assistant left a message for Mom to call. Abby's coming back from a research cruise in a couple of days."

"Abby's assistant will have to wait."

"Don't you keep your short crowbar in the tool shed? We found it upstairs. It looks like they used it to pry open the gun closet."

Jack thought he'd had the crowbar in the shed. "You didn't find the .38?"

"No."

Guns. He had another pistol, a .45 in the glove box of his truck. The 30/30 carbine lay where he'd left it on the floor in front of the sofa.

"Dad," Travis said. His voice had a plaintive sound that made Jack turn to him. Travis's hands came up to make a gesture, and then dropped to his sides. His eyes glistened with tears. "What's going on?"

Jack felt a surge in his chest and his own eyes brimming. His durability and disinclination to draw attention to himself crumbled in the face of his son's emotion. He looked down at his boots as the tears welled to his cheeks, put the butts of his hands into his eye sockets and pressed, and ran his hands over his tears, then straightened and inhaled shakily.

"I'm afraid," Travis said. He stood and pulled a red handkerchief from his back pocket and wiped his eyes. "This isn't like when she's late, or when she gets hung up in an airport somewhere. This isn't like anything else."

"I know, son." His voice broke and the tears came up again.

"Why, Dad?" Travis passed the handkerchief over to Jack. The thump of a log shifting to the bottom of the stove and the ensuing crackle of sparks rising up the chimney accentuated the deep quiet of the house. "What has she done to anyone? Or why did they break into our house? For the guns? Then why the rest of it?"

It struck Jack as he dried his eyes that in his self-absorption, and parenthood, in the fog of his obligation to be protective, in the smolder of his rage, he hadn't considered that Travis might form his own inquiry. Berg stood up and nuzzled Travis's knee. Her hip pressed against Jack's leg. She was like a lightning rod bridging the tension. It was a moment like none other that he and Travis had ever known.

"I don't know. Not for money. Or not much of it, anyway. And we still don't know if there's any connection between Mom's . . ." He paused, seeking the word.

"Kidnapping?"

Startled by the naming, Jack said, "We don't know that."

"Come on, Dad. It's like what you always tell me. Look for the obvious. If the car won't start, first check the battery. Don't assume it's the starter or the engine."

The dog stood with her ears upright, watching Travis.

Again, Travis's voice thickened. "We should never have let her go off like that."

"Believe me, I've thought that." Jack stared out the window, then drew his eyes in to the lamp with the shade ruined into the shape of an egg. Next to the lamp stood the red easy chair.

"Or is it you? Have you thought of that?"

It was a new idea. He looked down at his feet and thought: Who the hell am I? An itinerant gyppo logger and desultory leftist. I make things—fences and, once, shakes—and sometimes I've made trouble for the Forest Service, the planning commission, or the school board. An out-of-date philosophy major still trying to find a way to bind together a life and the broken-up world in a way that makes sense. But mainly I am nobody to anybody except myself, my wife, my children, and my friends. I've got nothing of value except a few machines and a house. I think too much. All I've got out of it is a couple of good ideas about how to log in a way that won't hurt yet keep people working. Anybody can have these ideas for the asking.

Berg took a backwards step, barked at Jack, and looked at him with her ears up.

"She's not limping," Jack said. He marveled at how Travis, even as he urged him to examine the obvious, had leapt right from the most obvious to the true. The room was rife with raw emotion and Berg knew it.

"I don't think it's you," Travis said. "I just wonder if the stuff in the shop could have been meant for both you and Mom. What I think is we need to find the one thing that'll make the connection."

"Bud's rage is the first candidate."

"You mean he saw the purse and figured that Mom took Winona?"

"Something like that."

"And then what? That he's caught up to them, somehow, or knew where they were going and now he's got the both of them?"

That was what had been unspeakable, almost unthinkable—that if Bud had somehow caught up to the women and was keeping them, or intercepted Kate on her way back, he might have hurt her . . . or worse. Jack again saw her as she had appeared in his vision, her horror-filled face hovering, then flickering away. He ran his eyes across the room from the black dog, sitting on the hardwood floor in front of the steel blue sofa, and on up the other side to the hardwood shelves loaded up with the monitor and the yet disarranged books and videos, shelves mounted on the white interior wall. He looked back at the askew shade on the wrought-iron floor lamp, which threw an elongated, yellow egg-shape high on the wall. Jack hadn't looked up there in a long time . . . the basalt up near to where a beam was mounted to tie the walls together, stones chiseled into shapes by his own hands, secured in the nests of mortar, and when he'd been working from a scaffolding, the stones and the mortar loaded by Kate into the cradle he'd devised and attached to a pulley system. He remembered working on that place in the bright July sun, their second summer here after moving from Seattle. He could feel the shaky scaffolding under his feet and the desiccated mortar on his hands, and could see Kate below in her shorts and loose shirt. There was a parallelogram-shaped, steadying hunk of granite up there beneath the beam. The mica within glittered in the light from the lamp. A story was attached to the granite, which he'd found in an extrusion in a spring bed.

—My house.

"Why are you and Gene going back there?" Travis asked.

"It's Chuck Lamb. He's going to see if he can find out where Bud would go."

He'd given Travis a shadow, not the flesh and bones of it, not the bizarre heat of it all, the twisted ecstasy, not the mercenary sanctuary with its loathsome iconography, certainly not his frightening vision of Kate, nor the questions about Bud's group, B.C., and Lamb.

"I know a couple kids whose parents belong. At school that place is a joke."

"That'd be correct," Jack said, thinking about how kids carrying on in their theatrical ways as if they had nothing at stake—boys in their cowboy hats, driving their jacked-up pickups, guns in the racks, and girls with their bare midriffs, haughty eyes—and yet how in the rightness of their clean perceptions, would see the Lord's Weapon for what it was, a twisted, dark comedy of the woods.

"Still," Travis said, "Strange as Bud Willy was when he was here, he seemed like he was under control to me. You know what I mean?"

Jack didn't quite know. "And?"

"He's taking care of a brain-damaged person."

"It's a strange world," Jack said. "Sometimes it's pretty surprising, like a respected businessman who looks smooth as silk in public, but at home he's abusing his wife."

"That's what I mean. That's the way we think, but what if it's the other way around with this guy. First, what if what you see is exactly what you get . . . his nature, I mean. A bully who's taking care of an idiot. The bad and the good in him perfectly obvious. Next is something else we haven't seen yet?"

"Where did you learn that?"

"It's one of Mom's rules. It goes with your rule of looking for the most obvious thing first. But never assume there's not another piece of information out there that won't change everything."

"That's not bad."

"And what about the money?" Travis said.

"It's hers, or it's his and she ran off with it, or it's somebody else's, or it's counterfeit. Or something. Who knows?"

"Yeah. Maybe it's a hate crime."

"Meaning?"

"If it's a hate crime, then whoever did it hates something. What? People around here know a little of what Mom does, but everybody knows who you are. They know you go to the board meetings and raise hell sometimes. Remember when you accused the superintendent of making racist remarks about the Indian kids? It was all over school. That's why I started wondering if it was you. If somebody's hate is strong enough, there's no telling what'll tick them off, right?"

Jack stood still, listening and looking out the window. He spotted a porcupine creeping up the trunk of a tree just off the lane, its coat of quills frosted white. It would eat around the bark near the top, girdling the tree. At another time, he might have gone out and shot the animal.

"And if it's not you, and maybe it isn't, or if it's not just because

Mom helped the woman get away," Travis said, "or not both of you being made into some kind of example, then what is it about Mom somebody would hate? I'm just asking."

Jack was moved by how Travis's willingness to inquire brought into balance his own lack of steadiness. "Okay, son," he said. "Maybe we should start our list and see where it leads."

"Or maybe it is random," Travis said. "That place Sutter has down there is full of ex-cons, right? It could be. It could be anything."

In Travis's expression, Jack saw an easing of the haunting. Outside, the porcupine disappeared among the tree limbs, making the tip of one tremble and shake snow loose. "Since when did you get so smart?"

Travis grinned wanly.

"Nothing's gone from your room?"

"Just the bat. Except for that and the posters, my room wasn't messed up like the rest of the house."

Jack sat on the sofa. "Check your room again, then go on to Mom's study. I'll check upstairs and call Painter." He started the list and found a little calm in that, too, as if the naming of items laid down stones on which he might position his feet.

The blued and walnut-handled Smith and Wesson .38 that had been on top of the refrigerator.

And from the upstairs closet . . .

The Winchester 30.06.

Weatherby .338.

Holland and Holland .375.

Browning 12-gauge automatic.

Ithaca 20-gauge SKB double.

Ugartechea 10-gauge double.

Remington bolt-action .22.

Remington semi-automatic .22.

Guns . . . in his case a small armory of sporting weapons given him by his father and left by his grandfather, and in the main rarely used but merely held. He stopped for a moment, remembering that he needed to get the serial numbers, which should be in the upstairs closet. He'd have to check. To the list he added:

Twelve Fuji apples.

*   *   *

Jack checked out the tool shed one more time. He found nothing new, and came back to the kitchen to place his phone calls—first, the sheriff's office. Painter wasn't in. When Jack told the secretary his name, her voice softened. "He's working on your case, Jack. I'll have him contact you."

He dialed Pamela's number. Her voice came on, chiding him for not calling her immediately. "Don't do that to me again," she said. Then once he had run through it all, Pamela groaned. "Oh, God, Travis told me that. It's Mom still trying to save the world."

He recounted how their place had been vandalized, guns stolen, and how he and Travis were doing an inventory. Yes, the police were involved, yes, he was taking precautions, and, no, they didn't know if the things were connected.

"According to Travis there's a husband," she said.

"One of the Lord's Weapon boys, maybe."

"What!" she said in a way that made him wish he hadn't mentioned it.

"But it may not mean anything," he said.

"I'm coming. I've got a ticket and I'll be there by eight. I'll rent a car. If the planes aren't flying to Spokane, I'll drive over."

"It's bad here," Jack said. "Big snow."

"I'm coming." It was an attorney's caveat delivered in her mother's tone, telling him not to bother arguing that point.

"I'm going to call Ron, now," he said.

"He's away. I've tried him."

Jack tried anyway and listened to Ron's message announcing that he'd be away for the weekend. Ron had gone back to school in Fairbanks, financing it with summer fishing. He had a cabin in the bush, a relationship with a woman Jack and Kate had yet to meet, and at times he could be very hard to reach. Jack left a message saying they had a problem and to call as soon as he got in, then stood for a moment, his mind completely blank.

Snow flooded by the window above the sink, obscuring the outlook to the gateway, horse corral, hay barn, and the tracks he'd made a few minutes ago leading to and from the tool shed. He walked back to the hall and stepped inside Kate's study, where Travis was sitting before an alight computer screen with his hands hovering above the keyboard. "I can't see anything missing from this room," Travis said, "Except maybe disks and CDs. But there's something funny here."

In a lower corner of the aquamarine screen, the creature of the Zamiatin game—Boo—rolled ponderously, and the center almost up to the top was filled with a school of fish. Travis clicked a key and a box appeared on the screen, a transept. He clicked the mouse several times, isolating the box and increasing its size. In the box, fish teemed and roiled in a slippery tangle of silver. "It's the pinks coming back again," he said.

Jack moved closer to see.

Travis clicked a key. The screen returned to its first conformation. He clicked another key and a chronograph appeared. It said:

4:17:32
Year 6
Month 7
Day 22
13:53.29

Jack was not nearly as adept with computers as Travis. He knew Kate had dated the beginning of the run 1999, that the system was set to turn into future time so as to project a host of interfacing effects, including toxicity and mutation, and that the visual mock-up on the screen was a playful attachment. The program was running, now, in the projected year 2005, and the pinks were rushing back to spawn.

"There should be more disks," Travis said. "Maybe she has them in the car. And there's something wrong with the way her program opened up."

Jack eyed the shelf where Travis had gathered up the disk and CD cases. There were a half-dozen. Over the last few months, Kate had been seriously setting up shop in here, and he was sure she'd had thirty or forty of them in two sizes. "There absolutely were more disks. A lot more. They're nowhere else in sight?"

Travis revolved in the chair to look. Papers from the filing cabinets had been dumped and the cabinets themselves pummeled with the baseball bat, which lay near the far wall, broken in half. There was a window in the wall, which opened to the woods where the snow persisted in curling toward the window. It did seem odd, the way the room had been ransacked . . . to the left cabinets destroyed, and then maneuvering to the right, things dumped from shelves, but the long desk and computers were hardly disturbed, not even the patch of wall above the computers where she pinned up pictures of her parents and kids and other images that struck her fancy, landscapes, fanciful renditions of salmon, a postcard of Frida Kahlo with her mustache.

"No," Travis said. "That's all."

Jack crouched over a pile of scientific offprints that had been spilled from a filing drawer and restacked. His eyes came to rest on the topmost article. It was about the Chilean temperate rain forest, notes written in Kate's hand filled the margins, and his emotions pitched at the evidence of her:

... perturbation, offshore drilling ...

and the interior ... tar sands ...

floral interface with North American Coast ...

hemispheric mirror image north and south. ...

He remembered a conversation with Kate about how the two temperate rain forests at the far extremes of the Pacific Coast shared species known nowhere else in the world, and the look on Kate's face as they'd talked, the radiance in it. No matter how disturbing her findings might be, she always retained a girlish pleasure in the act of discovery.

Travis was studying the screen again. "The animation's acting weird, too."

"Did the deputies check it?"

"Yes ... for fingerprints."

Jack gazed at Travis's poised head. Though his three children were each absolutely themselves, still Jack saw them as parts of a shared life, he and Kate and the kids joined softly even through distance and trouble like cloves of an orange to a stem. The plaintiveness, the haunted look, and the pride he'd seen in Travis, the lucidity, the steadiness Travis had instinctively offered when it was required, and now the acute concentration would be shared by the other two. Jack felt better, having talked to Pamela, and leaving a message for Ron seemed like throwing out yet another guy line to steady his ship.

"I'll be back," he said.

He climbed the stairs to the chaotic bedroom in which he'd tried and failed to sleep last night. Clothes still lay in heaps across the floor and piled at the opening to the clothes closet. He moved into the center of the room. A photograph of Kate's parents hung askew on a wall. In it stood the spare, wispy-haired man dressed in his clerical robe, and the intense-looking woman Jack had never met. Other pictures had been dashed to the floor, books and magazines dumped from the shelf near the bed. There, the edge of the room picked up the arching rock work of the main house. Next to the bed, a window looked out onto the lane, the county road, the wooded drop toward the lake. The falling snow now taking on a metallic glint in the dwindling light. To Jack's left were the clothes closet and the gun closet built next to each other to make a corner in the room. The door of the gun closet, popped off its hinges but attached on its other side by a padlock, leaned cockeyed into the room, and just below it lay the short crowbar.

He began picking things up, and found himself holding a pair of Kate's sweatpants, underthings, and a skirt. Confused by the smell of her, he stopped. He was standing under the wall-tie that emerged from the bracket mounted above the hunk of granite in the far wall of the living room and extended across the house to here. The tie, bolted to another steel bracket inside the closets, had encrypted its own story. That tie, the very log, had broken loose from the gin pole as it was being raised for mounting and almost hit Kate, who'd been standing below holding Travis, then a baby. It was a brush with horror born of his error that still made his blood run cold. He forced the memory away.

His mind was trailing what his body did and he'd completely lost track of why he was here. Then he remembered—to get the serial numbers for the guns and see if anything else was missing. He set Kate's things on top of the dresser and moved into the gun closet, pulling the string to turn the light on. He looked at the empty gun rack installed against the stone wall. Every gun had been taken. All of his cleaning and reloading equipment remained on the shelves above, and maybe half the boxes of shells. It looked as though they'd taken the guns and just started in on the shells. Maybe they'd got tired of carting things downstairs.

The box where family documents were stored—birth certificates, passports, titles, and deeds—had been upended and dumped on the floor. Jack set the box straight and thumbed through the papers. Everything seemed to be there, including lists of serial numbers to the guns and electronic equipment, which he folded and slid into his hip pocket. His eyes gravitated to the hunk of granite on this end of the wall-tie, up near the ceiling in the corner of the closet. Next to it was a piece of pumice, and with a start his mind bumped up to what his eyes were

227

perceiving. Behind it were hidden the originals of all Kate's disks. The pumice was undisturbed.

He'd made the opening after the ties had been mounted, the sills and the roof put on, and they'd moved into the house. He'd hollowed out a cavity beside the granite and cut a hunk of pumice to be pressed to fit as a cover over the compartment. Now, he reached and gently worked out the pumice cover, set it down, reached up again, slid out an old military cartridge case he'd put there for Kate, carried it into the room, and opened it. A good two dozen old floppy disks were in it, wrapped in plastic, and a thick wad of envelopes—letters from Kate's mother, he remembered. A floppy disk case and several four-and-a-half-inch CD cases were squeezed into the end. He opened up one of the CD cases and looked at the labels: chukchi1–chukchi8, chukchi9–chukchi16, chukchi17–chukchi23. . . . The labels were dated six months ago, written from when she'd come home from the DDM office for the last time. He saw that the older disks had a code name—cdec—and were also numbered and dated to years ago—1981. He looked at them, puzzling over the name.

He remembered when she'd first put the floppy disks into the case along with the letters, how later she'd copied the old disks onto CDs and added them to the collection downstairs, and then returned the floppies to the case. And he vividly remembered the new CDs she'd brought home, copying everything onto three-and-a-half-inch disks downstairs just this last May. And upstairs . . . here . . . he envisioned her inside the gun closet, straining to push in the case. He'd been sitting cross-legged on the bed, waiting for her. The case chunked softly when it struck the end of the cavity. "There," she said. "Safe."

The closet light had been the only light upstairs. Down below the living room was dark. Travis had gone to bed. Kate was silhouetted when she pulled back to inspect her handiwork, and she leaned in again to press the pumice in place over the opening. Outside, there'd been a hard gale that made the window next to the bed shudder, and she turned to him. "They're copied, now, all the originals," she said. "I can't believe the permutations that came out . . . are still coming out . . . of that one trip years ago."

"A couple good things, too, as I recall," he'd said.

"It's true."

The trip was the one years ago when she'd been a research associate on a voyage that took her to the Arctic Ocean, the Beaufort Sea, thence to the Chukchi, and afterwards to the Kuriles. It had changed her life and Jack's, since she'd been offered and turned down a permanent research position by the woman whose name he well remembered— Sophia Kopat. Kate had almost lost her life diving in the Chukchi because of the woman's negligence.

Jack remembered their discussions about that back when he and Kate still lived in Seattle, just before they'd married. She had an apartment near the University, he one on Capitol Hill hardly a mile from where Pamela now lived. They had questions to resolve: He'd been encouraged by a professor to continue his studies toward a PhD in political theory. Kate had been offered an opportunity that would have thrown her onto the international stage in her field. Each of them was filled with the sense of options which at the time they were about to renounce, a luxury granted by the vigor of their youth and the blown-open aura of the early seventies.

When he asked why she was giving up her chance, she said, "I'm ready for something else, that's all. Even if I wasn't, I wouldn't take that position."

They were standing out on the balcony of his apartment after an afternoon shower, as shafts of the mid-summer sun broke through the clouds. Cars hissed by on the wet pavement. The sun was soft on the rhododendron leaves in the garden below and against the pastel two-story homes across the way. Far to the west, the slopes of the Olympic Mountains glistened in the washed air. Kate had been back for just three weeks since the voyage, and had been wrestling with her decision.

"The die was cast for me, anyway," she said. "I shamed Sophia in front of her crew. With good reason, but I shamed her nevertheless." Jack felt her body straightening next to his. "Honestly, I still wonder if at some level she left me caught in that net on purpose. Abandoning me like that. Jesus!" She turned to him, the color rising in her cheeks. "I wrote up my assessment of the cruise this morning. When she sees it, she is really going to be pissed."

From Kate's talking about her, Jack had formed his own image— skinny, pallid face, feverish eyes, and wild hair. "She scares you," he said.

"Yes. Her power and her incompetence. I may be looking over my shoulder for years, but I'm not going to spend the rest of my life pleasing the likes of her, or having no life at all! I know from watching my father what being invited inside can do. As soon as you take one tiny step in, you're done for. I can't do that. That's not why I became a scientist. There have to be other ways."

It was 1972. Jack looked down the street at the corner where two billboards were mounted. One advertised an upcoming George Harrison and Ravi Shankhar concert in the Arena, the other was a psychedelic Seven-Up ad with a great big rainbow and the words, "Get The Message." In response to the Viet Cong Easter offensive, Nixon had mined Haiphong Harbor. George McGovern was gaining on the Democratic presidential nomination. Martin Luther King and Bobby Kennedy had been dead for four years. George Wallace had been shot. The Watergate burglary was about to happen. "You've got to be sure it's not a challenge you should accept," he said.

"I have to go another way."

When he grunted his assent, she leaned against him, turning a little so the front of her leg ran up the side of his. He put his arm back around her. They were quiet, looking down at the neighborhood. A Volkswagen bus with flowers and a large black peace sign painted on its side drove by, trailing a line of dark smoke. At that time, the business strip on Capitol Hill already had a meatless restaurant, a gay-operated poster shop, and stores specializing in occult philosophy and drug paraphernalia. Jack liked the neighborhood, and Kate came to, because of the divergent passions and the clouds of crazed righteousness. He himself was not exactly a participant in that world, nor was she—too reserved, too purposeful, too independent.

He was working as a bank teller, having temporarily parlayed his master's degree in philosophy into a job that required a tie and coat and that allowed him to dream his way through rudimentary numbers for eight hours a day. The hippie van turned the corner and behind it appeared a squad car with its flashers on. They both disappeared. He liked living on the edge of high energy, as if the anarchist strain in him needed something to feed on. He raised his gaze to the city, and then to the clouds carried in from the Pacific. He pleasured in the feel of Kate against him, her leg against his, her shoulder.

"Me, too," he said.

"Hey." Kate nuzzled him. "Let's get married."

Her face was brimming. They'd intended to marry, but he had yet to hear her state the need of it with such decision.

"I'm ready," she said.

He remembered his mood brightening, the amused and slightly ironic feel of the smile moving onto his face. "And I'm the answer to your state of readiness?"

"Right," she said, turning him toward her. "A little later, for a long time, and soon, too. I mean right now."

"Aren't I supposed to put the proposition to you?"

"Okay. Do it."

He remembered bright eyes and pale red lips, white teeth, the mole on her cheek, sharply cut hair, the firmness of her belly, her hotness and her willing dedication to such pleasure. Because they were of the old school, regarding love as a compact, the act they were about to perform would become the prime ceremony of their lives. They'd married before the summer was out. A year-and-a-half later, Pamela was born. Three years later, they moved into the woods of the Idaho Panhandle. And it was afterwards that she'd brought the floppies home, many years later the CDs.

*   *   *

Upstairs, Jack had sat on the end of the bed while she came out of the gun closet and told him what she'd only intimated at dinner with Travis—that she'd discovered yet more information in the files, hence the CDs she'd brought home. Also, she said that Sophia Kopat had recently been named to sit as the science director on the board of the oil development company, ZAQ, and that she'd abruptly reentered Kate's life. Sophia had submitted a petition for censure before the National Academy of Sciences because Kate and Abby Leonard had published the articles with information in them from the old Chukchi cruise.

"But what we used," Kate said, "amounts to nothing. We could have accessed nearly identical data from other sources. They were very discrete perturbation rates, that's all."

"Does it jeopardize your grant?" Jack asked.

"That's the first thing that came to my mind. I called the foundation. I don't think there's going to be a problem, but it means we have to send in the other data. Sophia's claiming I breached scientific ethics by using proprietary information. She says ZAQ has grounds for a civil suit but prefers the less disruptive request for censure, all of which is just corporate bullshit." Kate flushed with outrage. "Less disruptive! Can you imagine? The information we used is not proprietary!"

"So what does it mean?" Jack asked. "That really she has nothing and the company's just trying to scare you off."

"No. Well, yeah, they're obviously trying to scare me off. Or she is. Or she's mucking around in the old bad blood. I spent all afternoon picking through the files, re-sequencing and copying them, and while I was doing that I discovered more files had migrated to my DDM machine in Spokane. New information and parts of it probably are proprietary. Updates of the old blueprints and project proposals. All the little fuckers are in there, now," she said, gesturing back at the closet. "And you'll never believe what they contain. Transaction documents between Schtok Oil, the U.S. Department of Energy, and ZAQ. New contracts, financial documents, environmental impact findings, and permits issued. The Alberta tar sands are in here."

"Wait a minute," Jack said. "You're way ahead of me."

"I had this old Chukchi Sea stuff in my files all along, remember? How or why, I was never sure. Probably it was sent to me as a member of the research cruise. And probably by mistake. Now I think someone at DDM . . . maybe it's Massey . . . has been doing work for ZAQ. There's more stuff in the system. I had a feeling something was annexing itself to my Chukchi Sea files because it seemed like they were taking up more space, but I never looked at them until today when I found a copy of Sophia's petition waiting for me."

Jack said, "Wait. What if the documents were planted?"

Kate smiled. "I thought of that. The paranoid's dream." She was dressed in her traveling clothes still. She pulled off her sweater and stood with it draped over her arm. "But I don't think so. I've been racking my brain over this. I got the new files somehow, probably because of the DDM work for ZAQ. Or maybe Drainier still has access and he's done something, some incredible blunder that drives the information to me. I hear he's in the early stages of Alzheimer's. And now, Sophia, on behalf of ZAQ, she claims, has asked for a censure of Abby's and my work because of the old data we used. The petition is a bluff. Most likely, Sophia knows Abby and I got our funding and we're gearing up for the study. ZAQ's not going to want to provoke too much public attention for the likes of us. At worst, they'll be intimidating on general principle, but Sophia saw a chance to grind her ax. And back in the seventies, ZAQ defied international agreements, and now Schtok Oil is opening up fields for private development from American oil companies, like Mobex. The big companies would do anything to shut ZAQ out of what little it has in the Chukchi, or Alberta, or wherever. Yet ZAQ still has a permit to drill in the Chukchi."

Jack rocked lightly on the end of the bed. At his back, the window was open, letting in the cool night air. Near to the house came a hoarse, croaking owl-like hoot. "They'd kill to protect their deals, I'd say.'

She lifted one foot, pushed off her shoe, dropped it to the floor, lifted the other foot, standing balanced for a moment on one leg, swathed in her moral outrage. "Of course, anyone of them will, and not just animals, either. They kill all the time, moving into undeveloped places and depriving people of their livelihood. Wars are fought over it." She let the second shoe drop.

This was becoming another installment of the decades-long conversation they'd been having about politics, money, and science as they'd aged out of their previous life, perched on the radical fringe in Seattle and then passing into the legitimacy of raising kids and wearing their masks in this patch of hinterland. Even as they seemed more and more to belong in Bayview, their sense of not really belonging had run within them like a strengthening underground river.

"These companies act in concert when it comes to dealing with Congress, or the public," Kate said. She pulled off her knee-high nylons. "So, of course the knives come out when they're competing for a site. You're right. They'll stick each other, too, at every opportunity. Before I left I wiped out all the files left on my office machine." She dropped her nylons to the floor and began unbuttoning her blouse. "What I figure, scary as the data on environmental damage is, which after all is what Abby and I are working on, that'll have a fraction of the effect that exposing the contracts, options, blueprints, and permits would have on stopping oil development."

"Or on slowing it down," Jack said.

"You're right. Maybe slowing it down. Science is not sexy." She stopped for an instant and smiled. "This other thing is politics and big money. Politics and big money in the view of the world are very sexy."

"And dangerous," he said.

"If my getting the rest of these documents is a screw-up Sophia doesn't know about, and I don't know how she would, really, then her petition is still just a bluff, a shot from cover. I guess what she'd like is for me to be discredited."

"So?"

"So, I'll respond to the petition. It'll probably go away. Then I'll sit tight and do my work. There's got to be a limit to how far Sophia will stick her neck out." Kate finished unbuttoning her blouse. It sparkled with static as she slid out of it and draped it over the arm of the chair. "I'll stay quiet about the new information. If something in the environmental impact data looks like it would be useful, we can seek confirmation of it elsewhere. Otherwise, maybe I'll just think about a way to use the other stuff later on. That's another dimension, a dirty little high explosive inside the bomb. I'd need my own cover for that."

"Good," Jack said, feeling relieved and hoping she had it all right. He was impressed by his wife. "You'd be a persona non grata for sure if you were to do that." He gazed at her as she stood in her bare feet, skirt falling from her hips, inviting-looking belly, her strong swimmer's shoulders pulling the bra straps tight, and her intent, vibrant face. The way she looked accentuated his hunger for her. Again the croaking hoot sounded near the house and in a moment it was answered from some distance away by a more deeply pitched croak.

At that time—and now ever more so—the petroleum juggernaut was splitting into conflicts in the Persian Gulf and out into Turkey, Afghanistan, Azerbaijan, Chechnya, the old Yugoslavia, and Alberta. Because of her idealism and ecological passion, this had fixed itself in Kate as a personal horror. For Jack at that moment, his erotics seemed a fixative of a different order. Watching and talking with her, he became giddy in the atmosphere of discovery and intrigue and keen middle-aged sexual yearning. What he said next was meant to be part cautionary rebuke and part playful banter but later—and now, as he stood there in the disarray, holding the cartridge case—would seem chilling in its innocence: "Don't ever forget that ZAQ could stick you."

"We'll have none of that." She dropped her skirt, lifted out one foot, hooked it with the toes of her other foot, and flipped it onto the chair.

"You need to be sure about what you're doing. You need to be awfully goddamned careful, Kate."

"But when it comes to science, dirt is their game." She unsnapped the bra, shook it down her arms to one hand, and turned to him. The lack of reserve expressed her lack of anxiety over who she was in his presence, and at the same time offered an invitation to him to be who he was. "Dirt is not my game," she said, smiling impishly.

She pitched the bra over to the chair and reached for the dresser, pulled out the white cotton nightgown, put her arms into it, turned back, ran her hands down the nightgown's hems, drawing them inward, and began buttoning from the top. She stopped. "Still, I'd love to find a way some day to blow the whistle on the assholes."

Something heavy landed on the roof just outside and there was a scrabbling sound like claws and a string of very close hoots. Jack twisted to look out the window, filled with the black of the woods and the pale froth of the waxing moon in the sky. An answering call echoed nearer their house this time.

"They sound like snowy owls," Kate said.

Another burst of scrabbling noise at the eave, then a ponderous beating sound. He strained to see and just picked out the white arch of wings flying away.

"Down here?" he said.

"Sometimes they come this far south," she said. "Maybe they're measuring what's left of the night between them for their kill."

He turned back. "You're going to have to watch out, if you ever do blow the whistle. Times change. It's not like it used to be. If Bush is elected, he'll be all over the Arctic Refuge and the rest of the offshore stuff. People get hurt trying to live up to what they think they should have done at an earlier time." He arched his back and grinned. "Hard as it is to imagine your possibilities being diminished in any way."

"Is that so?" she said. "The blueprints on one of the CDs have schematics for a tie-in from Siberia across China, and another one in the Chukchi to the Alaska pipeline. Another for a pipeline from Alberta down to the Gulf of Mexico. Can you believe that?"

"It figures."

"Persona non grata," she said, bending to finish buttoning her nightgown. "Not acceptable. Not welcome. You betcha."

"You could have skipped that part."

"What?"

"The buttoning up."

"Oh?"

He swung his feet around to the floor and moved to put his hands on her hips. Her warmth came through the cloth, her pelvic bones and beneath them the softness, and in the warmth the quality of her skin and in himself a hungry liquidity filling his throat.

"Are you going to stick me now?" she laughed. "Wait." She went back into the closet, checked the pumice one more time, pulled the cord to switch the light off and came out, shut the door, and snapped the padlock shut over the guns. They moved toward the corner of the room near the window and next to the bed. She backed up and arched her neck, lifting her face to him. He spread her nightgown and ran his hands up her ribs. She reached down and wrestled open his jeans, and gasped as he pressed her against the wall.

That was then, what they'd been denied yesterday, which through the years of being together had become an ever more excursionary inquiry into their natures, even in their increasing softness, greater stiffness of joint, and brittleness of bone. The act was never quite the same, and yet at its root it was always the same. Now, as he stood holding the metal cartridge case, his loving, sensual recollection was cruelly supplanted by a vision of her as she'd appeared to him in the Lord's Weapon sanctuary . . . dressed in her corduroys and cream-colored shirt and her face filled with terror, the skin stretched taut around her eyes and her mouth open as if she were about to scream . . . and in the midst of it, through the window, he glimpsed lights coming up the county road and heard Gene's truck, and then Travis's voice . . . what made the hair on the back of his neck prickle . . . calling him from downstairs . . . "Dad!"

It was as if he were living inside a mind that was his own—and in it were Kate and his children and all his material memory—and yet also living within a mind bigger than his own, bigger than he could manage, a mind awash with the heart's blood, wild with electricity, and thudding with a big, sonorous, and passionate mystery through which he must find his way.

16
Snakes

JACK CAME DOWNSTAIRS to the study, carrying the cartridge case. Travis stood over the computer with his hands poised. On the screen, columns of digits broke up and spread apart. "Something's really wrong," he said. He tapped in a command that blinked the system over to the mock-up. The monitor changed from silver to aquamarine. "I'm positive somebody's been into this." Travis pointed at the chronometer where the minutes ticked by. "What I remember from when I looked before going to the game is that it was way back somewhere in year two. Mom doesn't let this thing run so fast."

Jack heard the front door, footsteps, and Marlene's voice singing out, "We're here!" Cupboards and drawers opened in the kitchen. Marlene came in with a stack of plates, followed by Gene. Jack studied the monitor, the upper portion teeming with twisting, silvery fish. At the bottom lay the off-white creature, which had expanded into an eerie, dragon-like shape that took up a third of the screen. The silver fish broke up into bits that slid toward the margins of the screen and vanished, as if they'd been sucked off the edges of the world. The white thing flexed and expanded more, metamorphosing into one bigger and more grotesque dragon shape after another. Suddenly, it filled the screen with its limey color. There was a popping sound and the screen went blank.

"Whoa!" Travis said, quickly draping himself over the computer and reaching to tug at something. He straightened, holding the end of a cord. "That was Boo."

Jack smiled faintly. "But what happened?"

"I disconnected the modem."

"I can see that. Why?"

"I don't exactly know." Travis laid the cord down and stared at the monitor.

Chris came in, carting three pizza boxes with a row of Cokes balanced on top. He set them on the desk next to where the plates were. Berg trotted in, sniffing the air.

"Boo?" Gene said.

Chris leaned near the monitor to look.

Travis stared intently at the computer. Jack heard the hiss of Marlene's synthetic jacket as she moved. "Something's wrong," Travis said. He typed in another command, opening a file, but those digits also instantly broke apart. "Christ!" he said. "Shut it down." He poked off the power switch, and stood for a moment, watching as the silver in the screen condensed into a dot, then he turned around. "Either somebody's hacked the system, or else something's really screwed up." He glanced at Chris. "Or Boo just took the whole thing over, the whole North Pacific and Arctic. It's acting like it's crashed."

"Wait," Jack said.

There was a pause. He couldn't figure out what he wanted to ask, and no one else spoke. Travis took a slice of pizza out of the box and crunched into it. Marlene passed out plates and ended up standing next to Gene near the battered filing cabinets. Travis picked up the open box and held it out to Jack, who absently accepted a piece. As Chris opened the other boxes, pizza aroma deepened. Berg had settled on the rug with her muzzle on her paws, her melancholy eyes moving from one person to another. There were a lot of bodies in this small space, five of them along with the dog. Jack still held the cartridge case. Directly across from him was the window, through which he detected falling snow. It neared dusk and he became aware of the room's penumbral hues. He reached to switch on the lamp on the shelf above the computers. A green cast from the lamp's shade was thrown to the ceiling and down to the floor with pale yellow in its center like a yolk.

He stared directly at the lamp for a moment . . . undamaged . . . and the computers beneath it, also undamaged. "You can't tell which it is?" he asked.

"I think this is over my head," Travis said.

There was a pause again, and then Gene said, "What the hell is Boo?"

"Who, Dad. Who is Boo," Chris said. "It feeds on poison. When there's no poison, it gets smaller. You know the fish in the mock-up, and the weird-looking snot-colored thing usually hanging out in the bottom?"

"Yeah, maybe," Gene said.

"I saw it," Marlene said. "I didn't like it."

"It's the bad and the ugly," Chris said. "It eats poison and reproduces inside itself."

"You mean it's alive?" Marlene said.

"If you took all the poison away, it'd die," Chris said. "But you can't ever do that, so Boo lives forever. He's got a mind of his own."

"You mean it thinks?" Marlene said.

She and Gene scrutinized Chris, Marlene's eyes round and wide under her thin eyebrows, while Gene's chin scrunched low into his vest.

"Maybe," Chris said, glancing at Travis.

"That's what I mean," Marlene said. Her body straightened the more and a hunk of crust fell off her plate, which Berg's tongue snagged from the floor. "No wonder!"

"It's kind of like a cartoon, that's all, except it's a real measurement," Travis said.

"It's made out of numbers," Chris said. "It represents the count Travis's mom's program is making, so it's just numbers, like in a way you could describe us as so many valences of our atoms if you wanted to."

"I don't want to. I don't like it. We are not in a cartoon here. This is bigger than you think," Marlene said.

—She was right about that, Jack thought. He said, "Travis, you're telling us somebody's been in Mom's system through the Internet?"

"In the Gateway, yeah, I think so. But not this one." Travis turned around and disconnected a line of plugs from the power strip, leaving two of them in, and reached out and switched on the IBM. "So far as I know, she's never hooked this up directly to the other computer or to the Web. She uses it as a reservoir, sort of, just to hold stuff." The IBM clunked. The menu flickered onto the screen. Travis tapped at the keyboard, bringing up a list of files, and leaned to scrutinize the monitor.

"The thing is, it looks like somebody's been in it, too. There are not enough files in it." He gestured at the Gateway. "Either someone's been in that one here, or they hacked into it, or both of those things. Maybe they were hacking when Boo accelerated. This other . . . they'd have to be here to get into it."

Jack looked over at Gene. "The computers weren't trashed."

"Maybe they had to leave," Gene said.

"Maybe." It made sense as an account of what was before them.

"Or maybe somebody was screwing with the computers for the hell of it while somebody else trashed the place," Gene said.

Jack grunted and moved to the desk and set the cartridge case between the pizza boxes and the Gateway, snapped open the latches, and took out the three-and-a-half-inch CDs. "These are disks that Mom kept stored away."

Jack took out disk cases, removed the disks from them and fanned them across the desk. The labels were written in Kate's hand . . . *Hermes*: Dives 1–10, Sectors 1–4; Dives 11–16, Sector 5; Beach Surveys, Sectors 5–7, Analyses. . . . More had place names like Long Beach, Glacier Bay, and Puget Sound. The largest group, some twenty in all, had the volume name, Chukchi, and individual numbers.

Travis looked at them. "I recognize them," he said, turning to the monitor. "They were in the IBM. They're not there, now."

Taking out another case, Jack extracted the floppy disks with the code name cdec. He spread them out and stared at them, his mind fumbling again with the name, and then he remembered what the code was for . . . Canyon de Chelly. It was the name of the canyon in Arizona that Kate loved, and it had opened up an emotional passage that was transposed to him from her. She'd told stories about living in Arizona for a year and a half with her brother and mother, who at the time, according to Kate, in some never fully clarified way, had come to be "estranged" from her husband while he bore witness to the racial deconstruction of Alabama. Canyon de Chelly or the nearby town, Chinle, was an ancestral home of Kate's mother's, and from it arose an enormous irony of lineage that one had to be a southerner to fully appreciate. Her mother was one-quarter Navajo, a source of fascination for Kate and another of the horrors out there, but one that was lodged in her almost as a horror of affection, an invitational suffering. "How about those?" he asked, touching the floppy disks, then bending to look at the three-and-a-half-inch CDs. "I think she copied them."

"They were in there." Travis picked one up. "They've got a weird name." He leaned toward the monitor and scrolled the list of files. "But they're not in there now."

Jack was grappling with a mix of detail and feeling—the name of the file and what Travis had discerned about the computers, and the feeling for what he knew about Kate and her mother. All through Travis's life when the family was together at night, riding in the car, or at the dinner table, and more lately when it gathered for holidays, stories were told about the parents and grandparents, slowly weaving together a whole fabric out of reminiscences: Jack's memory of his own short history of immigrating ancestors that disappeared suddenly like a blip over the horizon three generations back, and Kate's much longer, far more ornate history for which Travis and his siblings had developed fascinations. It was Kate's odd and turbulent background that most held the kids' attention, that and the way she had nosed through the turbulence to end up here.

"It's pronounced Shay," Jack said. "Canyon de Shay."

"Oh, yeah," Travis said. "I remember that." He picked up another floppy disk and held it out.

"You're sure they were in there? The machine still takes them?"

"Files with those names, yes."

"You might've been right about there being a third possibility," Jack said. "It could be your Mom's work." He turned to Gene and Marlene. "What we're talking about is research that Kate's been gathering for years. It's just lately that she's been able to get serious about putting it all together. Because of the grant. And most of the disks she kept in this room are gone."

"All Bud Willy's got on the counter in his wrecking yard is one grimy adding machine with a crank," Gene said. "I doubt he did the computer end of this operation."

To Gene's and Marlene's right, the window was nearly dark, but white, carrying a tincture of the green from the lampshade, flowed by it. The computer monitor glowed, while Gene and Marlene had grown obscure back in the corner of the room. Jack took another slice of pizza. "Then Bud wouldn't have been alone here. If he was here at all."

Gene murmured assent.

Jack gazed through the window into the mobile silvery sheen passing into the black. He had an angry metallic taste in his mouth, cutting through the cheese and dough. He peered at his watch. It was after five. Snow was piling out there in the dark, wherever Kate was, and in whatever condition.

"Did you hear from Painter?" Gene asked.

"I think they called him down to the compound."

Marlene broke her silence: "He should be here."

Travis said, "Maybe Bud's fronting for somebody."

Once again, he'd gone to the obvious. Jack glanced at Gene, who looked up, his black eyes glistening as crumbs of pizza crust tumbled off his beard into the light on the floor. —Can it be? Jack thought. The other Boo, the actual one out there living off the poison, traversing the earth's great space, and parasitizing all the vile little pockets of canker like the Lord's Weapon and Bud's brotherhood and then making its sinister entry into my house? It seemed unreal, absolutely as nasty, outrageous, and fantastic as Boo was to Marlene.

"Mercenaries for hire," he said.

"I guess you'd have to say it's possible," Gene said.

Jack was thinking not just that, but the other half of it. —Was it conceivable that somebody would hire them and, if so, what did that mean?

"They like money," Gene said.

"Winona," Jack said.

"Yeah," Gene said. "Where the fuck did that wad of money come from?"

"She said it was hers."

"We're supposed to believe that?"

"I guess we don't know."

"Oh, my God," Marlene blurted out. "I told Kate it was a good thing she had money. I told her to take that woman somewhere safe."

"Marlene, it's not your doing," Jack said.

"I should've come over. If I'd come, maybe I'd have seen."

"You didn't know. Nobody knew."

Chris, who was leaning against the edge of the desk with his hands stuffed deep into his pockets, watched his father and Marlene over in the corner. Travis stared at Berg lying in the middle of the floor with her ears flat.

"Maybe Lamb will give us some help," Gene said. "Maybe he won't."

"No," Marlene said. "I don't want you going back there. Neither one of you. Look what's happened already with people doing things on their own."

In the unease of Chris's face, the aghast and formidable look Marlene had taken on, and the sharpness of Gene's face, Jack felt the thudding of the splintered unanimity the three of them longed for. Marlene had her admirable project with Gene and his returned son. She was bent upon doing her own stitching together of the mismatched hunks of quilt. Her mothering impulse was strong, perhaps too strong as she reached out to rectify and heal and pull everyone inside her good wishes . . . Gene, Chris, most every troubled woman she came across, and now Kate, and Travis, and himself.

"Marlene," Jack said. "It's not your fault." He took out a CD from its case, what he thought was the lead one of the bunch Kate had brought home last summer. He held it out to Travis. "Try that in the IBM."

"I'm so sorry," Marlene said, her words lingering in the air.

Jack shook his head, meaning to reassure her, and moved close behind Travis. Travis slipped the CD into the IBM and tapped out commands until the computer beeped and the heading for the disk came up—I. Chukchi—and below it a list of files, 1 through 8. "I think it's a copy of what's on the first floppy disk."

"Open it up."

Travis did so. It read: "National Science Foundation, U.S. Department of State. Terms of agreement for scientific exchange between the government of the United States of America, National Science Foundation, U.S. Department of State, and the Union of Soviet Socialist Republics." It was followed by the opening clauses of a contractual agreement. Jack leaned past Travis, pushed the scroll key, and concentrated on the material that flooded onto the screen: the terms of exchange, permit numbers, crew list, drilling notes, core samples, and several times the name ZAQ, followed by columns, paragraphs, pages of ledgers, accounts of money expended, page after page of graphs, maps, design schemata for drilling sites, tie-ins to refining and support plants, pipelines, pumping stations.

Jack straightened. "Okay. That's the old set of documents." He picked up the second CD and handed it to Travis. "Let's look at this one."

While Travis tapped at the keyboard, Jack glanced behind him. Chris had slid along the desk nearer to the computer monitor. Gene had come out to crouch next to Berg. The dog threw her head back, tossing a scrap around in her mouth. When Gene reached out to scratch her ear, she growled softly at him. Gene bent forward and growled back and her ears shot straight up.

Jack turned back to Travis, who had opened up the other CD, which listed the copied cdec files 17 through 23. Thinking of Kate's methods, her meticulousness, he said, "Open up the last file and go to the end of it."

Travis hit a key, the computer thumped, the file appeared, and he scrolled to the end of it. What Jack saw was the bottom of a paragraph, a curious phrasing ". . . the people who lived there . . . Canyon de Chelly. The living must allow the dead to strengthen them."

"Back a few pages" Jack said.

Travis scrolled back a page at a time, going through ten or so to a line break.

"There," Jack said, and he began reading carefully, growing rapt, as Travis sat still on the chair next to him, reading, while the others in the room held their silence.

The written matter began: "The material in these twenty-three files includes at the outset data from the research ship, *Hermes*, as it was received by me via computer transfer in the DDM research labs in Seattle, Washington. I neither solicited nor in any other way sought the material, but concluded that it came to me because I was a member of the research crew aboard the *Hermes*. The financial and contractual material in the early files reveals that ZAQ, the Interior Ministry of the U.S.S.R., and the National Oceanic and Atmospheric Administration under the auspices of the U.S. Department of State entered into an agreement for oil exploration in the Chukchi Sea, the Arctic Ocean, and off the Kurile Islands in violation of U.S. law and standing international agreements. This conclusion is reached on the basis of the terms of the exchange, thusly . . ." It then started in on the specifics.

Jack scrolled forward toward the end of the section: ". . . as the later files through 2000 have come to me, seemingly annexing themselves to a site in one of my programs. I surmise from someone at DDM, probably Bill Massey, who heads up the environmental impact statement for American interests, including ZAQ, on the development of Siberian and Chukchi Sea oil extraction. The environmental impact state is prefatory to a test drill site in the Chukchi, and feasibly the construction of delivery systems to ports by pipeline . . ."

"Okay," Jack said, reaching for the scroll key and taking the file to its end again, and reading what was on the final page, what he took to be a kind of free-form editorial reminder, or journal that Kate had written to herself. He knew that as she put research material in order, she had the practice of drafting the like at the ends of documents and occasionally in the midst of the dry data. She'd told him it was a way of keeping herself alive as she worked, and of remembering the big picture: "The singular brain of the oil interests seeks to compel the far more asymmetrical and disorderly brain of the people in the world to submit. For my own purposes, I named these files Canyon de Chelly because the spidery labyrinth of canyons complicated like fractals tens of thousands of times in detail, compounded endlessly from the big twists and defiles to the small alcoves, benches, caves, and the myriad of circuitous hand-and-toe-hold trails, all according to the principle of irregularity, the very brain of the people who lived there . . . Canyon de Chelly. The living must allow the dead to strengthen them."

"That's enough," Jack said, straightening. In the care taken with what he'd been looking at, and in the language of what he'd just read as it gathered around the hazard of meaning, in her evocation of the place, and the appearance of the word, the usage of which he and she shared—brain—he absolutely recognized Kate. In her research, he knew, Kate had tried to create a receptacle of understanding that would accommodate what she believed to be the unending, vibrant, and never dying complexity of her subject, and so to be true to the world. At its root, her fascination was guided by charity, humility, and the belief that the world would resist the falsehood of simplification that oil interests demanded.

Jack picked out the first CD they'd looked at. "Let's make another copy of the one in there now and of this one. For safekeeping."

Travis began doing that, while Jack, attempting to ground himself by attending to domestics, gathered up the remaining disks from the desk. He rearranged the letters in the bottom of the cartridge case as padding, and paused again . . . the letters, which he'd never read, but portions of which Kate had read to him, written by Kate's mother in the months before her death. Jack wished he could have met her. He knew that her troubled life and passion and what he took to be her incisive thought were powerful forces upon Kate. The old school penmanship in blue ink on the envelopes, rounded and clear and straightforward, was not unlike Kate's handwriting. Carefully, he placed the old disks back in the cartridge box and turned to Marlene and Gene.

"What we have . . ." he said, moving back against the wall. "Or what the files have on them is government and oil company information that could make Kate into a whistleblower. It's possible somebody knows she has it." Once more, he paused. "They surely wouldn't want her to have it." Uttering that much of what he suspected made it now seem like a certainty, and at the same time he was thinking . . . it's still not just that, it's also her nature, something anthropological and historical and psychological and biological and analogical she's pursuing in her research . . . that's where the real danger in her is, and they might sense that but would never be able to name it because it would entail a complete revision of their way of seeing the world. He took a breath, feeling a surge in his sense of Kate and a deep unease over what he knew to be her preoccupations with political force, consumption, and extinctions. In his state, he felt an even more powerful sense of foreboding over her notion that the living must accept the strength of the dead, which he couldn't help but take as a warning, an ominous promise of what Kate would expect if she were to die.

He forced himself back to the matter at hand. His voice sounded remote to him: "Just know that much. Know that no one in here except me has any idea what it is. No idea. You especially," he said, touching Travis's head. "Forget the little you do know."

"Okay," Travis said. He'd put the two CDs in their cases and passed them to Jack.

Jack put them into his breast pocket. "I'm keeping these on me for now." He gestured at the cartridge box. "Those I'm putting away and nobody but Kate and I know where. Nobody will find it." He looked at his watch. It was a quarter of six. "Then I'm going back down to the compound."

Gene's expression grew into a pugnacious query. Chris was watchful. Jack felt Travis's eyes on him.

"Honestly," Marlene said. "I know Gene will go with you. This mountain-man mentality gets a little old."

"I have to go," Jack said. "At the moment it's all I've got. Besides, Dan's gone down there, too, and I need to talk to him face-to-face."

Marlene looked at the floor.

Jack softened a little. "Marlene, if there's a chance Lamb can tell us where Bud would go, I've got to pry that out of him." He looked over her shoulder at the sheen of snow in the window and beyond into the black. Soon enough, the drift forming there would come up to the level of the sill. He felt his own coldness, the leveling of his emotion in the face of something akin to doom. "I can't let it rest."

"I got to go with him," Gene said.

Marlene sighed. "I knew it."

In the distance through the rooms, Jack heard the phone ringing. He wheeled and lurched out into the hall, groping his way in the dark between the sofa and stove to the kitchen, and around the counter to the red dot of light on the telephone machine, amazed by how quickly he was flooded with hope . . . that it would be Kate, that she was all right, after all.

When he answered, a voice said, "Yeah, it's Jim."

Hope decayed into a wave of dismay. "Bliss?"

"Yeah, listen, Lamb's picked up that load and he took payment for it, but he owed me. He picked up the damn load to pay off his debt to me. Now, the asshole's taken payment for my load and he's wanting to get the other logs out of the woods up there. He says he'll work off the extra for you, but that's my damn job and it's my money, double what he's got. Fuck him."

Bliss's tenor voice was strained with anger. Jack had to grope for his meaning. "Look," he said. "The paymaster shouldn't have cut a check for him."

"Damn straight, he shouldn't," Bliss said. "Lamb owed me, plus what was owed you, not me him, and how the fuck did Gene Scratcher get into this? What the hell!"

Jack leaned back against the cooking island and let his hand sink to his thigh, still holding the receiver. He closed his eyes.

He heard the voice like a woman's in the distance calling him. "Jack?"

He lifted the receiver. His habitual and what seemed at that moment lunatic sense of good manners held sway. "I'll straighten it out," he said, but wondering: How? How am I going to straighten it out? I don't give a damn. He said, "I'll call you back."

"Okay," Bliss said. "He's got your money what you owe me. He stole it. And I got a deductible on insurance I got to pay right now to get the rig back on the road."

"Jim," Jack said. "I'll call you back. Later."

* * *

Jack returned the cartridge box filled with disks to its hiding place upstairs and slid the box into the cavity within the gun closet. All of it seemed transmogrified by a weird serendipity of design: Kate's mother's last letters kept safe there, and the disks added, and then more disks. Maybe somewhere along the line the letters in alien companionship with the disks had occasioned the name Kate gave the Canyon de Chelly files. This was mere speculation, but the core truth of it he felt sure was right, the thing in Kate's nature he could never fully understand because it was hers, not his, what in his sympathy he merely knew was there, a fearsome and complicated psychic totem forged from warring, intertwined elements: her beloved, austere mother, her compromised father, the class-infested, violent little town she'd grown up in, and the other place emanating in the inscrutable desert because her mother had told her she had to visit it before she died. He pressed the hunk of pumice into the opening, securing a tomb alive with potency, the touch of his fingers on the stone keen with his own reverence and trepidation.

Once downstairs, he instructed Travis to stay alert to the phone, to watch for Pamela who should be here in an hour, to try Ron again, or get Pamela to try him. He and Gene left, taking Jack's truck this time along back roads to the highway and then to back roads again. At the bottom of the lane to the Lord's Weapon Compound, they came upon the enforcement, the plainclothes police and the uniformed ones, cars with the stroboscopic back-and-forth lights on their racks, a van, and an armored vehicle. To the right of the road, behind the compound's barbed wire fence and washed by the lights, Lord's Weapon men in their uniforms, military-style helmets, and trench coats stood in a row like a string of cut-out men. Up behind them, an orange glow reeled into the snow-filled sky. A distant voice crackled out of an amplified system.

Dan Painter emerged from a cluster of police and walked along the shoulder to Jack's window. He bent to look in, his face fringed by the fur of his parka hood. "I was about to call you. Listen," he said. "Kate's car with two women in it crossed over going toward Yahk. The Border Patrol and the Canadians are working on it. So is the FBI. There's an alert out. But it's a blizzard up there."

Snow blasted into Jack's face. "What does that mean?"

"The alert or the blizzard?"

"No, Dan, why the fuck didn't you call me right away? Where did they go?"

"I'm telling you now," Painter said. "I'm sorry. We're on it, and on this bullshit, our own blizzard of fools. It's a record of their crossing the border, that's all. The Canadians put out an all points on her."

Jack placed his hands on the steering wheel and pushed back into the seat. The engine of his truck hummed. He felt cold to the core. Next to him, Gene was still and watchful. "What about Bud Willy?"

"Nowhere in sight."

"You checked his house, right?"

"Wrecking yard and house. They're under surveillance."

"We're going in here."

"I wouldn't," Painter said.

"If you'd called, maybe we'd be driving to Canada, instead. Look, Dan," Jack said. He told Painter how somebody had been in Kate's files, how there might be compromising information in the files, and how Chuck Lamb might know where Bud would hole up. "We're going in here to find Lamb."

"Files?" Dan said.

"Computer files. Government files," Jack said, cinching down the baroque tangle of it all into a tight little knot.

"And Bud?"

"Good question. What about Bud?"

"Lamb, you say?"

"That's who we're going in to find."

The usually distracted quality of Painter's face had drawn tight. "Well, then," he said. "There's no law against your going in, but we're expecting a busload of protesters any minute now. We're just your elected idiots protecting the liberties, including everybody's freedom, defamers and anti-defamers alike, to be idiots, and your freedom to join whatever assembly you choose, and everybody's freedom to pack as many goddamn weapons as they like. I expect you've got a couple of them, too."

"One, you bet your ass."

"I want to know when you'll be back out."

Jack tipped his watch toward the dashboard. It read: six-forty. "By seven-fifteen."

Painter drew back, rubbed off the lenses of his glasses with his gloved fingers, trained a flashlight on his watch, and looked at Jack. "I wouldn't."

"My wife is missing. Until she's back, I'm in your damn face, Dan."

In the starkness of his silence, Gene had yet to move a muscle.

Painter pushed his parka hood back on his head and leaned into the window. "Tell you what," he said. "Why don't you two get a couple of signs that say 'I'm not an asshole' and strap them across your chests." He drew back. "That way we can tell you apart from the rest of those clowns."

They pulled up the lane, slowing for the guard shack across from the WHITE'S ONLY sign. A hand appeared from the darkness of the shack to wave them on, and they drove up into the lot that was jammed with half again as many cars as there'd been in the morning. Jack found a space by the trees, switched off the engine and lights, and bent to reach across Gene to get his .45 out of the glove box. Gene grabbed his wrist. "I'm carrying that." He opened the glove box, slipped the gun out of its case and held it between his knees, cocked open his door to switch on the dome light, snapped out the gun's clip to check it, climbed out of the truck, and inserted the gun into the back of his pants under his vest and coat. When Jack got out and shut the door, Gene said, "But I'm damned if I know where we're supposed to find those asshole signs."

They moved through the snow at the end of the parking lot. The guard stood in his tower, leaning against the rail and looking toward the glow that seeped from behind the sanctuary. Burning diesel fumes cut through the chill air. A faint hiss of fire could be heard, and the stentorian voice of the Reverend Palmer snapped through speakers mounted in the trees, as if big birds were perched on the limbs, all of them crying in unison the same indecipherably arcane song: ". . . with many a light, floating the livelong yesternight, shifting like flashes darted forth by the red streamers of the north, I marked at morn how close they ride."

Gene said, "What the fuck?"

They walked past the elevated stand, under the guard tower, around the end of the building toward the clearing where Jack had met the three men earlier, and approached the rear of a crescent-shaped pack of scores of onlookers. Several balanced news cameras on their shoulders. Firelight licked across the snow-laden ground, shooting between the legs of people and glimmering against the snow-saturated sky.

"Hope Dan doesn't come slamming in here before we're done," Gene said.

Jack grunted.

They swung rightward and paused. In the center of the clearing fires blazed in ten-gallon drums, and two men in robes and hoods moved from either end of a line of drums between the circle and the onlookers, also lighting those drums with torches. Fires flared up one at a time, flames deep red at first within the clouds of oily smoke, then bursting into orange. Palmer, decked out in a white robe with dark sashes and a peaked white hood and brandishing a lit torch above his head, stepped into the center of the circle. He stopped in front of the yet unlit cross, which was held upright by cables. The two men, their torches aloft, moved to their places beside him, and in the wash of light, all of a sudden, Jack spotted Zack off to his right, the unmistakable tousled head towering above the others, his presence marking the absence of the other. Palmer's voice boomed out of box speakers on either side of the circle, echoed from below by the squawking trees: "The fires lit by the Dragon of the Night. The hope of the future."

A file of seven hooded men bearing unlit torches materialized from the darkness. Palmer led them in a counterclockwise circumambulation outside the drums, and then threaded them into the circle, announcing, "The officers of the Klan have entered the Sacred Circle." The men dipped their torches into the fires and raised them above their heads. Ten torches burned in the air, making a second circle within the circle of burning drums.

Jack and Gene touched elbows. Gene's face was a study in concentration—lips set beneath the aquiline nose, brow furrowed, and his scraggly beard glistening with hoar as his eyes moved to take in one thing and the next. Jack felt aghast and cold and vengeful. What he was witnessing, the nasty little cobbled-together mummery flimsy with numerology and icon, part Masonic, part church camp, part Boy Scout, and part Halloween, had insinuated itself into an actual insult.

"The Klansmen and the initiates enter the Sacred Circle," Palmer intoned. Another file of men ghosted out from the side of the sanctuary, and moved counterclockwise outside the blazing drums. Jack scrutinized them, recognizing more than one familiar face, including Chuck Lamb and, coming nearly last, Dick Petrie. As the men in the outer ring paraded around, the men within circled again, this time clockwise. Rings of fire threw jagged shadows of the men's draped forms helter-skelter in all directions across the trampled snow.

"Our light came from the cross. To the cross it shall return." Palmer's voice crackled and popped. "Ere yet abroad, the cross of fire should take its road." He bent toward the cross, applying his torch to its base. Small blue flames crept up the beam to the cross-members, along the members to their tips, and on up the spine to the top. Palmer stepped away. "First he essays his fire and speed, he vanished, and o'er moor and moss sped forward with the Fiery Cross." There arose a hiss, and the booming gasp of combustion. Long flames lapped up above the tip and threw out heat even to where Jack and Gene stood at the edge of the throng.

Palmer's voice rang through the compound: "Speed forward with the fiery cross!" He gestured to the men with unlit torches. One at a time, they turned, moved between the burning drums into a veritable inferno, touching their torches to the cross, and returned to their places. They held their torches aloft. Jack examined Chuck Lamb taking his turn, and then Dick Petrie, whose eyes flashed jubilantly, and he feared for Petrie's son, the marginal athlete compelled to enter the blazing ring of his father's hallucination.

"We welcome you to the Sacred Circle," Palmer said, after the last of the initiates had lit his torch. "You are Brothers, tied by a sacred bond." He paused, then led the file of nine officers along the line of initiates, shaking their hands. Shadows of the Klansmen twisted across the ground and rose up on the side of the sanctuary. Snow dropped from the black sky into orange-like sheets of blazing copper. At the edge of the fire's halo, light faded to a deep burnish as it passed into night, the woods, and the field that extended out from the rise.

From far off sounded a chant . . . the anti-defamation protesters, their voices like coyotes yipping from a faraway hollow. Here, the people became still. Gene leaned forward. He'd raised his coat collar around his neck and he glared steadily into the fire with glittering eyes, all his energy fused into an implacable core. He turned and started down the slope. Jack moved with him, reaching under his coat to touch the cases in his shirt pocket, making sure they were there, the digitized relics, and all of a sudden a disturbing realization broke out . . . Abby. Abby's assistant. She'd called. What if Abby's lab had been messed with, or worse? For all he knew, she had everything from Kate's files in duplicate. What if Abby was also in trouble? He'd forgotten that. He should have called. "Goddammit," he breathed to himself.

The speakers crackled: "Mothers, wives, and sisters of these men, hold them close to your hearts. God gave us fire for light. Fire to cook our food. Fire to warm ourselves. Fire to shape metal. Fire at the heart of our lives, the cross of His crucifixion turned to fire." There was a pause. "Roll away the boulder from the tomb!"

Jack glanced back and saw the torches being doused in water, but the cross and the burning drums were left to burn. The crowd swarmed in upon itself, spread and collected in bunches. Some moved down the slope toward the parking lot, among them the news people, hustling to get out with their stories. The Klansmen circulated amongst the crowd, joining their friends and families. Jack could hear the casual parlay over the snowstorm. The intimate air was reminiscent of churchgoers from his own childhood, the correctness of good citizens in their self-certainty, the temporary muting of their troubles, the simmering absorption with themselves and even their kindliness, their troubles expiated by ceremony, their gladness like reprimanded children safe for a fleeting moment in the denouement of their sojourn on earth, all their necessary fallacies confirmed. Jack even second-guessed what he'd always believed to be the solace of the quiltwork of associations in this place, those friendships with dissimilars. He felt as if he'd entered another dimension, parallel to his own, but alien, demented, and crawling with snakes. The world, heavy on its edge with everyday deceptions, tipped crazily under his feet.

He looked around for Lamb but couldn't find him. He trailed Gene out of the spreading gyre further to the edge where they came upon Zack standing alone.

"Gene!" Zack said.

"Hey, boy," Gene said.

"Gene!" Zack cried, bouncing up on his toes. His coveralls were encrusted with ice nearly to the knees, and his sweatshirt darkened from the shoulders down across his chest by melt. His Redman hat was soaked.

"Where's Bud?" Jack said.

"Not here," Zack said, staring vacantly over the top of Jack's head. "Fire," he said.

Jack looked into Zack's face. "Where is Bud?"

"Not here." He took a string of red licorice out of his pocket, bit a hunk off. As if he were capable of focusing on the manifest but not upon the absent, he produced another licorice string and held it out while looking directly at Jack. "Want one?"

Jack took it. "Thanks."

Zack's forehead screwed with worry under the brim of the cap. "You're welcome."

"Right," Jack said. "Thanks."

"Not thank you. You're welcome," Zack said.

Jack was supposed to say it, so he did, "You're welcome."

"Thank you," Zack said, bouncing up and down. "I'm glad. Tell him, Gene," he said. "Gene?"

Gene was looking toward the remnants of the crowd. Clusters of men remained near the outer ring of burning drums, while others filtered away.

Zack reached out and tapped Gene's shoulder.

"Hey," Gene said.

"Tell him," Zack said. "Get it right. Not backwards. Backwards hurts. Not thank you. You're welcome. Thank you. Get it? Gene! Bud's gone," he said, sounding desperate. "Thank you! Gene!"

"Easy, Zack," Gene said, reaching out to grasp Zack's wrist. "You need to get in somewhere warm. Go in the church."

"Jesus is here," Zack said. He revolved his large body, shuffling his feet in sliding motions through the snow. The seat of his coveralls was also soaked, and with what, Jack dared not consider. Zack ended up facing them again. "Gone. Bud's gone. Jesus is here. Get warm. See you," he said, abruptly walking off toward the ring of drums and blazing cross. "Fire," he said, spreading his arms and weaving inside the drums and stopping to look up at the cross, silhouetted hugely against its light. "What a fire!" he cried as he marched in a circle around the cross.

Gene gestured down toward the Quonset huts. "We're supposed to meet Lamb down there." As they picked their way down, Gene nudged

Jack. "It's amazing how solid that guy, Palmer, is in his lie. Smart as Zack is dumb. But what's the damn difference, except that Zack won't hurt you?" They moved out of the firelight and into the shadows.

Snow sifted, heavily and steadily. Cars and pickups were maneuvering out of the lot, their headlights splashing over this side of the sanctuary, the legs of the guard tower, and the Quonset huts. A line of taillights flickered and bounced while motorists crawled down the lane. From the road at the bottom, Jack heard a woman's voice shouting indecipherably through a bullhorn and the voices of other protestors calling back. Through the trees shone flashes of twirling police lights and the white glare of a quartz-iodide flood lamp. He considered Dan Painter and the others straddled between the edges of two tricky, irreconcilable worlds. He and Gene passed by the picnic tables to the middle Quonset hut and entered to its warmth. They were alone.

The hut's walls were lined with tables, and on them stood stacks of pamphlets and books, a computer and printer, an old mimeograph machine.... The arching walls of the hut were covered with pink insulation and viscuine. The vertical walls at the two ends had been paneled with fake wood. At the far end stood a refrigerator and double sink, a counter with a Vita-Mix machine, and in the corner a stubby oil-burning stove, the source of the hut's stifling heat. On their end and below a window, posters plastered the wall. Through the window, he could see the ring of drums and the cross, standing out as if lifted into the sky. He considered the posters: one for the Yakima Militia; one for the Militia of Montana; one with a screaming infant and the words Abortion, The Globalist Plot; one that said ATF, Armed Tyrants and Fools; one with a heroic-looking couple leading two tow-headed children up a hill toward a sunset that said White Pride; another with a caricature of a woman posing provocatively on the steps of the capitol building and surrounded by dark-skinned men that said Jewess Whores, Islamic Dogs. Yet another portrayed Jesus in flowing robes smashing open bags of money with a sword while fat, cigar-smoking men in suits scattered for cover, and still another said Holocaust, Zionist Lie. Jack leaned to peer at a glossy black-and-white photograph. A black man, naked, had been hanged by a noose from a tree and his head lolled down over his chest. Scrawled with a red marker were the words Nigger Gelding.

"Shit."

Gene's voice was hard. "Keep looking. It gets worse."

The door creaked open and Chuck Lamb appeared with his robe draped over his shoulder. He knocked the snow off his boots against the sill and stepped in. "Gentlemen." His little round belly recapitulated his oval face. Pale hair frizzed out from beneath his blue watch cap. Jack remembered how when Lamb used to work for him, he'd been seized by a mysterious, inexplicable urge to crush him.

"I guess I should switch off the mike," Lamb said. He moved down along the table at the wall to where the audio consoles were stacked. "We run the PA from here." He flipped a switch and punched several buttons. Strains of a Strauss waltz could be heard outside, emanating from the trees. Lamb walked toward them, saying, "It's something, ain't it?" He looked out the window at the cross on the hill which still blazed as if pinned onto the dark.

"That thing'll burn all night long," Lamb said.

Neither Jack nor Gene had spoken a word, but stood stone quiet, leaning against the edge of a table behind them. Jack scrutinized Lamb, drawn into alertness by the way he'd turned to look out the window—something oddly pliant there in his body—and now by the way twisted to face them with a theatrical swagger, and by his face, the softness of it, the curling lips, a bit of downy beard on his chin, and the brightness in his eyes as if he were on PCP.

"Gene says you know where in B.C. Bud Willy would go," Jack said.

"I can help you with that," Lamb said. "But you got to help me."

He drew the robe off his shoulder and laid it on the table by the door, revealing a holster attached to his belt, and a pistol. Beneath him, Jack felt the table shift as Gene's weight lightened on it. Jack regarded the pistol, displayed along with the swagger, as an aid to Lamb's transfiguration. Lamb reached into his back pocket and produced a folded sheet of paper, which he spread open.

"I had this drawn up. It's what they call a letter of agreement," he said. "You and me can do something. The assholes at the mill laid me off. They got the Mexes working in the woods. Meantime, they're laying off the white fellers and the drivers. You got to fight fire with fire is what I believe."

"I want to know where you think Bud would go," Jack said.

"Cut me in and I'll tell you."

"Sounds like you already took a cut." The hope Jack had arrived with, fragile from the outset, was ripping into ribbons. The man was mad. He could feel his madness, and he wondered how he'd imagined that this degenerate fool . . . now sporting a letter of agreement, trying to nose out a small-time deal way down with the dregs of the world . . . could possibly have been of help.

"We'll be partners," Lamb said, exercising his delusion. "I know what the future is."

Jack looked to Gene and saw uncertainty growing on his face, but at that moment, the door swung open, letting in the waltz music and a man—young, tall, tanned, and wearing a Gortex windbreaker. The man pulled off his gloves and unzipped his coat, the scent of cologne wafting through the Quonset hut. He moved toward Jack and extended his hand. "Jack DeShazer?" Jack didn't move. The man withdrew his hand. "Dick Troop," he said.

Lamb's hand, holding the paper, sank and his face stiffened. The door opened again and banged shut behind another man. He had a thick jaw covered with a stubble and a rangy, wolf-like carriage, and he wore a heavy pea coat. Next to Jack, Gene rose fully from the table.

"This is a private meeting," Lamb said.

Troop ignored him and in a smooth voice, said to Jack, "I'm with Watchcap Security. I talked to your wife a couple days ago."

"Oh?"

—Two. Two days. Friday. When I was on the mountain, trying to get home.

"At her lab. I'm afraid this little fellow's out of his depth here," Troop said.

"Hey," Lamb said. "What do you mean depth?" He passed his paper from his right hand to his left and back again. His chin with its wisps of white beard thrust up and his lips puckered into an indignant snout. "You just jumped into the wrong mud hole, buddy."

"I think we can help you," Troop said to Jack.

Gene stood poised. Without moving, he was suffused with the concentration of his musculature and of his attention tuning to a dread alert. Jack felt that—Gene's vigilance several steps ahead of him.

"Who you work for means nothing to me," Jack said, but he was thinking—Wait!

"Right," Lamb said. "Me neither. And who are these assholes?"

Gene spoke for the first time: "Chuck. Back off."

"The hell," Lamb said.

The rangy man swiveled malevolently toward Lamb, looking like he'd just as soon stuff him down a rat hole.

To Jack, Troop said, "The last I heard, your wife is fine."

"I think you better get a lot clearer than that." Jack felt his legs tightening. He still was thinking—Wait!

"Hey!" Lamb said, passing the paper to his left hand again. His eyes bulged, and when he spoke his voice cracked. "The hell. Security? Do you know where the fuck you are?"

Troop said, "His shooting off his mouth isn't helping."

Gene spoke again: "You, too, pal. Ease up."

The eyes of the man in the pea coat steadied on Gene, then returned to Lamb. Troop did to Gene what he'd done to Lamb, which was to ignore him pointedly. This made something click in Jack. Out of his sense of who Lamb was and who Gene was—the one a complete and dangerous fool because of his machinations, loose wires left for people to snag themselves on, or some deviously misplaced piece, a gnat-sized demon that could cause everything to seize up, while the other, Gene, was anything but a fool and, if provoked, ten times as dangerous coming at you—Jack marked a failure of perception in Troop. He displayed his idiocy, despite having the other one with him, a henchman, it seemed, and his own shine and polish and pricey coat and bulked-out classy look. That glimmered at Jack, as did another thought, a story in the new weird modality that flashed toward its end faster than he could make sense of it—that Troop was about to confirm what Travis had deduced about his mother's disappearance, and what Jack had been guessing about the Lord's Weapon all along, that it and Bud Willy, or some other extension of it, were connected. Now what had been poised to happen was happening before his eyes, that someone or some thing—Watchcap Security or DDM, for God's sake, whatever Kate had been afraid of or whatever Troop's buggery covered (or tried to hide)—was a competing, second interest, and whatever agency it was had crossed the line and hired mercenaries, the mercenaries themselves having slipped the traces of their dogma to allow themselves to be hired for the money, and all the while Lamb, who had caught just a whiff of what was going on, the stink of it, and frantically wanting money himself, was turning his own little screw deep inside the wheelwork. As Jack leaped wildly from one strand of this thought to the next, and even as he hoped against hope that somehow what Troop said about Kate might be true, that they might get her loose, even as that played appallingly on his emotions, freezing him . . . Wait! . . . the elements of the story were driving at breakneck speed toward their conclusion.

"She is in B.C.," Troop said. He turned his eyes on Lamb and gestured at the door. "You'd better leave."

"What?" Lamb said. The paper he hadn't known what to do with floated to the floor. "I don't think so!"

An apple appeared in the other man's hand, and he looked at Jack, turned it in his fingers, and took a bite. He wiped his chin with the back of his hand. Jack knew the apple by its size and color, a Fuji.

—My house!

Gene—knowing, too, and acting well ahead of Jack—said, "Get out of here, Chuck."

Lamb went stiff. The man in the pea coat held the door open. Cold and music streamed into the hut. In a flash, Jack saw perfectly that Troop was a liar under his sheen, only a more complete one than Lamb and thus to be distrusted the more completely. He saw the thumbs of Lamb's hands hook into his belt and the fingers of his right hand reach back to release the strap that passed over the butt of his pistol. The predictability of the stratagem, and Troop's obliviousness to it, amazed Jack for a split-second. Lamb's eyes turned glassy, and the rest of him, as he stood still, ripped apart into ever more narrow ribbons before Jack's eyes. He thought again: Lamb is mad! Jack was frozen in place while everything spilled over him, hearing the music outside and down at the end of the hut the refrigerator humming and the fire hissing in the stove, and the crunch of the apple again between the man's teeth. He passed through the gibberish of what was happening right in front of him and went deep into the babble.

Lamb's fingers slipped around the pistol butt.

Gene's energy coiled at Jack's side, and he thought: Gene's just ahead of me. He saw this coming. I did not. I'm also an idiot. And these others didn't see it, either. They don't know the depth of the panic a person like Lamb lives in. They're looking at Lamb as if they still expect him to walk out the door.

Jack, unable to make his muscles move even while his mind flew off, saw Gene moving, bending a little and reaching back under his coat in one lithe motion. At the same time, Troop stumbled backwards toward the refrigerator at the far end of the hut and the other man released the door, letting it bang shut, and reached inside his coat, coming out with a revolver just like the one Jack had left on the refrigerator at home. Lamb's gun came up. The gun Gene had shimmered out. Gene's leg came up sideways into the air to kick him, and then Gene went down to one knee. Lamb's gun waggled wildly. The hut was filled with a deafening roar, followed by the soaring melody. The waltz rang in Jack's ears as he lurched sideways, trying to keep his balance against the searing in him. He glimpsed through the window the burning cross up on the hill, and something else out there, crazily bouncing beams of white and red light coming near, and he heard shouts and beheld Zack's shape dancing around the cross. Another roar came, deafening in the hut, and another, and yet another as he fell slowly like a tree. His chest thudded. He lost his breath. Blackness passed over him like a veil as he pitched toward the floor and hit it with his face.

17

Rechercher

BUD HAD NEARLY KILLED THE MAN, holding him against the wall until he
choked, then letting him drop to the floor, and bending over him and
cursing, taking the hoop of keys out of his pocket and the knife from
under his belt, and lifting him and dragging him away fast. They disappeared. Winona appeared on the other side of the doorway, shrilly
screaming after the men, "Don't kill him! Bud! Don't! What'll we do
then?" But the way she sounded, ecstatic, and the way she had her
hands up before her, as if they were wanting a pair of pom-poms as
she went after them, she might as well have been screaming, "Do! Oh,
please, do!"

The front door could be heard opening and Bud's voice, speaking
into the chill outside: "Shovel, asshole."

She had heard the other one's voice rising: "Hey, it ain't nothing. I
ain't done nothing." She heard a sound bright as of two hunks of pipe
being knocked together, and a thud and a moan, then the shovel scraping against stone or concrete. She sat still, listening. From farther away,
she heard Winona's twangy voice and Bud's voice, the rumbling bursts
breaking in. The shoveling went faster. She heard Bud's voice again,
and then Winona minced through the doorway to the room where
Kate sat, bound and handcuffed, shivering, groggy from the blow.
"Well, good Lord," Winona said, putting her hands on her hips. "Look
what he did to the bitch."

The front door shut. Heavy footfalls approached, and he came, filling the doorway with his bulk and dipping his head to clear the jamb.
He took a single step into the room and glowered at her. His brow

knitted clear back to the top of his head, plowing furrows into his close-cropped black hair. Holding the hoop of keys, he came toward where she sat not moving a muscle. He had the knife . . . her knife . . . and he sorted through the keys on the hoop until he found what he wanted, a tiny steel thing that he held up to see between his thumb and index finger, and then he looked down at her again, examined her with an expression she'd seen before . . . eons ago, it had seemed . . . the fierce, inquisitive look he'd had in her kitchen. His lips formed a straight line, his eyes glittered, and again she sensed the intelligence lodged in him, a bright sliver in the bruising hugeness of his person.

At his side, Winona looked as though she'd been attached to the ceiling by a rope, as if in her frailty she needed that to keep her from collapsing. Bud came near. He smelled of the outside, like an animal . . . the dank wet, the trees, and diesel, unlike the smell of his brother, the idiot, the stench of urine and old sweat. Bud moved around her and in the corner of her eye she saw his bulk descending, a moose at her back, kneeling to the floor. She felt his callused fingers gently turning her wrists, and then the one hand holding both wrists, and in her bones she felt the snap of the handcuffs releasing, first one, and the second, and then the two hands gently guiding her hands around to hang at her sides.

Kate lifted her hands and laid them on her lap. The wrists were chafed. Her shoulders hurt. Her head hurt. Bud was behind her. He woofed softly as he shifted his weight, and through the rungs of the chair she felt something being sawed at. He rose and came around, holding the handcuffs and a length of rope in one hand, which he stuffed into his back pocket. He now knelt before her, bending to the ropes that tied her ankles to the chair. One ankle was freed, then the other. She'd found herself looking at his shoulders from the top, first one and then the other under his plaid shirt, and she was amazed by the size of them. Each time he freed a foot, he firmly and gently slid it away from the chair leg in a nurse-like gesture.

He lifted his upper body, staying on his knees and yet coming up so that his head was even with hers, and looked closely at her injury. She, looking back, saw the dark stubble on his wide chin and cheeks, his broad, flared nose, the faint scar running from above one eye socket toward his ear as if someone, once, had tried to scalp him, and the over-sized pores in his skin, the thick eyebrows and long eyelashes, everything too big as in a dream, and far too near. When he raised a hand and reached out to touch her face, her dot of fury formed and placed itself on him. She would not be touched. She said it, "Don't touch me."

To her surprise, the hand descended. The torso eased back, the butt resting on the ankles, and in one motion, a synchrony of separate, large gestures of the body, he rocked farther back, balanced on the balls of his feet, rose up to tower over her, and at the same time swung his head leftward to peer down that way, and he spoke: "Make her an icepack."

Kate rubbed her chafed wrists and moved her feet to stretch her legs.

From Winona, whose hands lifted as if they, also, were affixed to strings, emerged an indecipherable, half-disputational, half-moaning sound.

His voice rumbled: "I said make an icepack. We don't want her looking like this."

"Oh sure, yeah, help her now," Winona said. "I've been hurt, too, you know."

His body turned toward her, not menacingly, or only so by its size and habit of dominion. "Do what I say. And get some blankets. We got to take care of her."

Winona stood still with her hands at her sides, while her body steadied itself, and her face, garish with its smeared makeup, tipped back. "Where?" she said.

"Try the refrigerator, cheese head. Check the closets." He revolved his head to look around the room. His eyes fixed on a far corner, then dropped back to Kate. "There's a bathroom back there, it looks like," he said.

Kate rose up a little in the chair, straightening herself. It was apparent that he was not familiar with this place. She remembered that coming here he'd several times asked directions of the other one, Ansel or Hansel, as the Power Wagon pitched this way and that on what she'd taken to be back roads in the woods. Near the end of the journey, in the deepening twilight, the limbs of trees had scraped the roof. From her position, still and terrified on the floor, she'd seen sheets of snow sliding down the windows. The lurching grew wilder. The tire chains clinked and the engine revved as it pulled the weight through the ruts as if the Power Wagon were a pig, forcing its snout through the heavy brush ahead of its body.

Here, facing Bud, she put her hands in her coat pockets to warm them and found her scrimshaw salmon, which she clutched in her right fist as if to gain a holdfast. Her mouth was dry from breathing through it. "People are going to be looking for me," she said.

Instinctively, she was searching out the same space she realized Winona sought in his momentary reserve, as something in his being passed or stepped back from his own precipice and left an open ledge. His shirt still had the store creases in it, and he had on new jeans, a shining belt buckle, and freshly oiled boots. She remembered the green parka he'd worn when he'd pulled her out of the Power Wagon from where it was parked in the equipment barn. The parka had fur at the collar and the factory smell still in it.

"Let them look," he replied. He turned to Winona. "Now, move. Get her the icepack and some food, too."

"Oh, all right," Winona said. The blue skirt Kate had given her to wear was torn, and under it the black body suit was ripped down one leg. Her knee had bled from where she'd scraped it, most likely, when she was thrown to the floor of the Subaru. Kate reached up and touched the front of her own shirt, stiff with dried blood. Winona moved to the doorway, saying, "What about me?"

Bud spun around, agile as a bear, and though he was going away from her, Kate cringed. Winona slipped through the doorway. Bud stood for a moment, then turned back to Kate, his brow knitting as he mastered himself. "It's no point trying to get away. But you got to be treated right." And then he said something that Kate merely took in, numbed and confused as she was, although as she thought about it later, it seemed deranged, not because Bud presumably believed it . . . indeed, later, in his strangely governed brutality and in his disappointment with the support he got, he would seem the only one among the group who was not deranged . . . but the concept, the tactical concept that had made itself available for his use: "The way he treated you is against the rules of engagement."

He was gone, leaving the door open. Kate sat still, listening to the sounds that came from what she took to be a kitchen to the right of the doorway. She heard the crack of ice being broken out of its tray, then cupboard doors opening and closing, and Bud's voice rumbling. Outside, the shovel scraped at the walkway. Bud's shadow crossed by the doorway, passing into what she thought was the sitting room through which she'd been brought in. There were easy chairs and a sofa there, and two more doors leading somewhere else. She thought she heard the front door open, and a second door, and in a moment she felt a draft swirling around her legs. She heard Bud's voice from that direction, then the two doors closing one after another.

Winona came back, carrying a towel wrapped up around ice cubes, and thrust it into Kate's lap. "Here." She hovered over Kate. "You look like shit."

Kate lifted the icepack and pressed it against her cheek.

Bud passed by again, heading into the kitchen.

"He's something, ain't he," Winona said. "Dropped the asshole like a bag of seed. If Ansel screws up again, he's dead meat. So are you."

—Ansel, then, Kate thought.

"Don't mess with my husband." Winona stood with one hand on her thrust-out hip. She had her doll-like face cocked. Her lunatic eyes narrowed. "He's mine," she said. "And the window's wired, in case you're thinking the way you like to do about getting away. Forget that. The whole place is wired and booby-trapped. Booby. Get it? That's you, honey. You'll never get away from here, neither one of you, you and Ansel, and it won't just be me after your ass."

As she went out, her—Kate's—skirt snapped when she jerked to the right.

From the kitchen, Kate heard the sounds of cupboard doors again, and the voices going back and forth.

She heard Winona: "I'm telling you, I didn't mean nothing. I'm sorry. I would've come back. I got lost in myself is all."

Bud said, "Hush."

"I was trying to come back. You don't know what I went through. It wasn't supposed to snow like that. It's that you hurt me. I shouldn't be hurt so much, but it's God's will for it to come out like this. How did you know I'd run this way?"

Out of the rumbling of Bud's voice, Kate picked out: "Cranbrook," and "cabin," and then, "Pay." She heard, ". . . they said they'd pay."

"How much?"

"Hush."

There was the sound of metal, a pot, perhaps, clanking against something else, and the hum of something running that sounded like an electric can opener. Kate conjured up the space made out of what she'd glimpsed—the yellow walls, a stove somewhere, a refrigerator, counters around the edges, overhead cupboards, and now the two of them moving in it, alone together with their bizarre rapprochement.

"Look at that thing," Winona said.

There were footsteps in the kitchen, receding and returning.

"It's funny how things work out, ain't it," Winona said. "But where are we?"

Kate sat still, pressing the ice pack against her cheek and listening intently for the answer to that one.

There was a squeal and a thump as if of weight shifting suddenly, his voice rumbling, and then an animal sound from her, a moan, or a rattling like a cat. Kate envisioned Bud shoving Winona back against the counter, his weight upon her, but to what purpose she could not imagine ... his way of reprimanding her, or silencing her, or some brutishly rendered affection. Whatever it was, Kate believed it arose from the desperate contradiction of Winona's love coming out of whatever long history of abuse she'd suffered, and his acceptance of her self-loathing, the twisting in her, and of the interminable lies that were known by him to be so, all of it merely a repeated domestic rerun that included her flights away from home and his finding her and enforcing her doom. As to what might be made of what she'd heard him say ... they said they'd pay ... Kate had even less of an idea.

She chastised herself for not remembering from the start that the likes of Winona projected injury as an intimate violence against someone else.

It was a truism of such women.

Of such men, too, she guessed.

And as to herself? How had she put herself in this position? What outcome of herself was being theatricalized for her? What did it mean?

Her fourth answer to Jack ... something invitational in corruption and suffering ... the ruin.

After a moment of quiet, she heard silverware and dishes, and what she thought was a refrigerator door sucking open and shut, water running into a steel sink, and then footsteps coming. Kate stood up. She felt dizzy. Winona entered, carrying a bowl and plate and a glass, which she set on the table. The bowl had soup in it, and on the plate was an opened tin of tuna, a few slices of bread, and a couple of other things in wrappers. "Hope it ain't beneath you," she said.

Bud followed, carrying a stack of folded blankets, which he set on the chair behind the table. He turned to the wall where there was a thermostat, and when he adjusted it, the registers clicked on. He turned back and stood next to Winona, his brooding figure dwarfing hers. "You'd better eat something." He gestured with his chin toward the cot at the rear of the room. "If you've got any sense you'll get some sleep, too. Nobody will wake you."

"I want to be taken back out of here," Kate said.

"Later," he said.

She felt on her face how she must have looked, pressing her teeth together, her jaw set, the muscles drawn tight, swollen nose and bruise on her cheek, and her eyes glaring at him.

"Now," he said, dipping his head toward Winona. "Out."

They left, shutting the door behind them. Kate heard a key turning in the lock on the other side of it, the sound of the click of the latch monstrous. She went to try it, gently twisting the knob in each direction and wondering if the others were listening on the other side. She stood for a moment, filled with fright and insult. She went to the door at the back of the room and pushed it open. It was a bathroom, white tile, white fixtures, a shower stall, and equipped with soap and towels that looked as though they'd been hanging there for months. She sat on the stool to relieve herself and felt a stinging sensation. —Water, she thought. Drink water.

She went to the sink, turned on the tap, which spat air, then water, and she bent, gulping out of her hand. Straightening, she glimpsed herself in the mirror above the sink and recoiled from her image, worse than she'd imagined: disheveled hair, swollen cheek, bruised around the eye, the line of red beneath her chin, and stains on her neck and profoundly down her shirt. She went out, moving to the backmost of the windows. Like the other two, which overlooked the hump of a hill lined with purple lights where the bulldozer had been pushing snow back and forth, this window was barred from the outside. Under each window was a stainless steel heating element. There were little night-lights in the room as if for a child, one plugged into a wall socket behind the table, one in a socket in the wall near her. A lamp stood on the table.

Through the window she could see the steadily falling snow and the form of Ansel in the faint light from the storm lamps, hunched over a shovel as he worked his way along the arching walkway. She leaned close and saw one alight window at the back of the equipment barn where the Power Wagon was parked. There was a doorway at this end of the barn, she remembered. Still dazed and frightened, she was nevertheless trying to piece together everything she could think of to offset her confusion . . . the barn there, the house here, between them the curving walkway, and down below and out of her sight, the road they'd bounced along through the squeeze of tree limbs.

Inside the equipment barn, as she'd noted when they let her out of the Power Wagon, was a flatbed truck, a tank truck, a crawler tractor with a snow blade, a pair of snow machines on a trailer, and a drum stuffed with cross-country skis. . . . There was a generator, she remembered, roaring after Bud started it, and between the barn and house, the snow-filled walkway and set of low stairs winding through two turns that the man . . . Ansel . . . had jerked her along, having been given the keys by Bud and told to take her inside. She remembered Bud saying he was going to plow "the strip," and now suddenly realized what that might mean . . . the dozer going back and forth on the rise above the house, the line of purple lights . . . a landing strip.

As she looked at Ansel shoveling the walk, her teeth ground with fury. The bright of her anger lit up an array of smaller lucidities that were like bits of stem and seed stuck to the hide of a creature crawling out of its den. She went to the table and stared at the austere array—a tin of tuna with its lid pried open, bread, a bowl of oily-looking soup, and two Hostess cupcakes in their wrappers. She did not feel in the least like eating. She looked at her watch. It was after midnight.

She had to sleep.

Drink more water.

She had to get warm.

She should make herself eat.

She dug a chunk of tuna out of the can and put it on a corner of the bread and ate it. She carried the plate with the other things on it and the bowl of soup over to the register under the first window and set them down on the carpet, went back to the chair at the table, took a blanket and draped it over her. She stood still for a moment, looking at the locked door and listening, hearing nothing from the house, only the slow scraping of the shovel outside. She went back to the register and sank to her knees. Coming as near as she could to the heat, and holding the ice pack against her cheek with one hand, and hunching over the plate and bowl like an animal, she ate everything.

* * *

She sat in the chair where she'd repositioned it near the back of the room next to the second window. She had tried to sleep once already, covering herself with the blankets, and she knew exactly how it would be when she tried again, fitful and frightening as the images she willed into being engaged in their chancy game with the other images that rose up on their own out of the dreams that awaited her: a fire on a moored barge, a net drifting in the sea, a pair of legs in neatly pressed khakis leading down to a pair of shined loafers that followed a cane as it tapped along a sidewalk, a peeled log dangling from a boom, her mother, Xaviera, sitting in the bow of a boat, and Jack's voice repeating over and over again, *rechercher, rechercher, rechercher,* and Jack as he'd actually been on the side of the road, reprimanding her for her refusal to bend to his wish: "I fucking hope to God it's not a big deal." Then there was the prospect of what she'd begun to dream in the shadowy twilight of her lingering wakefulness, the sense of a horrifying puzzle awaiting her which she attempted to stave off by envisioning her escape: finding a weapon and holding it on the others, slipping away and fleeing on foot into the woods, or better, starting up the Power Wagon or one of the trucks, and driving it straight down the road that had brought her here.

Near the white wall opposite stood the small wooden table. To it, she'd returned the plate and bowl and empty tuna tin. Behind the table was a straight chair like the one she sat on. There was a floor lamp there, too, which she'd turned off. Enough light to see by came through the windows from the storm lights, reflecting from the snow, and from the nightlights. At her feet, the towel in which the ice had been wrapped slowly leaked into the carpet. Fully dressed, and having draped one of the blankets over her shoulders, she began to sweat. She could now breathe through her nose, but her head still throbbed, her wrists ached, one knee was swollen, and she had a strain in her back. Her hands were in her coat pockets, and in the right one she held the leaping scrimshaw salmon. She ran her thumb along the arch of its belly as if to summon its power.

Outside the window, persistent snowfall collected on a rising bank that pressed against the glass. Holding out her left hand, she tipped her watch toward the window. It was three-thirty in the morning. The house was absolutely silent, but she decided to take a shower in order to get clean, to do something, to be ready.

She flipped on the bathroom light and shut the door, pressing in the lock button on the knob, then thought better of it, went out and got the chair, brought it into the bathroom, shut the door, slid the white bathmat under the chair's rear legs, wedged the chair back under the doorknob, and depressed the lock button again. She stripped, setting her clothes in a pile on the toilet seat, and extracted her shirt to inspect it. The bathroom was bright with its fluorescent light glinting off the white tile. The front of the beloved, buckskin-colored shirt was stained almost black with her blood and the blood of the buck. The stain curled in whorls and paled to ochre toward the sides and spattered along the arms. Up near the collar, the blood was caked around the bone buttons. Dried blisters of it flaked off at her touch. She listened to the house again, hearing nothing, then ran the cold water into the sink, set the plug, and put her shirt in it. As she kneaded the shirt, the water turned pink.

She turned on the shower, waited for it to heat, found soap and a washcloth, stepped inside, and scrubbed. Moving from her toes and ankles up to her head, she gingerly bathed the cut under her chin, her nose, and the bruise around her eye. She washed her hair and rinsed it, letting the water stream over her, and turned and stood as long as she dared in the gush, letting it warm her and beat against her back. She looked at her puffy knee. Turning the shower off, she stepped out to the tile and dried herself, but despite the locked door, the chair, and the other locked door that led out of the room, she was suddenly spooked by the actuality of herself, stark naked, and the image of the like which the sound of the running shower, if heard, might provoke, even in Bud for whom she suspected rape was daily, if matrimonial, and certainly in Ansel.

The thought of his hatchet face, stringy hair, and cruel eyes made her shudder. Holding the towel around her, she stopped to listen. Hearing nothing, she pulled on her underwear, thermal pants, the torn top, corduroy trousers, and socks, disengaged the chair from the knob, opened the door, peered at the room, and then walked into it. Everything was as before, three ghostly windows, the cot with its tangled covers, and down at the other end the table, chair, and lamp. She carried the chair from the bathroom, returned it to its position next to the cot, picked up the towel that had held the icepack, took it to the bathroom, wrung it out, and hung it over a rack to dry.

Leaving the bathroom door open behind her, she drained the water in the sink, refilled it with cold water, and worked at the shirt with the soap, drained the water, rinsed the shirt, washed it again, rinsed it, drained the water, then spread out the shirt on the edge of the sink. There was an overhead hot air blower, which she switched on. She looked at herself in the mirror, allowing herself that, tipping up her chin to see the cut, the line of the slit through her epidermis. Leaning forward, she scrutinized her eye and cheek. She would have a black eye. It was so that her thoughts flickered back and forth between the paltry acts of doing something—her grooming and ablution, makeshift laundry, a minor healing—and the incomprehensible insult of her imprisonment. With the former, she strove to harness her horror. She gazed at her shirt. Where the stains had been worst, they would be lightened somewhat, but it was likely that from soaking in the bloody water, the shirt would now be stained everywhere.

Kate wanted nothing at that moment except to be home with her husband. Looking at the shirt, something in her snapped. Jack had given it to her for her birthday. She remembered the pleasure in his face and in Travis's eyes in his taciturn, watchful way, as they sat at the kitchen table and she took the shirt out of the package. It was the spirit behind the gift that now pierced her. She tried to stifle the noise she began to make in the bathroom, and yet at the same time her sobbing turned out of control. She put her elbows on top of the shirt, on the edge of the sink, buried her face in her hands, and tried to tighten herself around the despair as her body kept knotting in paroxysms. She felt hopelessly lost, her hands pressing into her face, the sink digging into her elbows, her bare feet on the tile floor. Something loomed, and glancing into the mirror, she glimpsed what she thought was a shape, an apparition struggling to rise up from the floor behind her. A guttural grunt wrenched out of her chest and she whirled around. No one was there.

She edged into the room. Nothing was there. Her body felt tremulous and light. She took in a deep, shuddering breath, let it out, and walked the length of the room to the main door and tried the knob, gently twisting it each way. It was still locked from the outside. She went back to the bathroom, got her coat and boots, and shut that door, then went to the cot and sat on the edge of it, listening. She heard nothing. She set her coat and boots at the ready on the carpet next to the cot, piled the pillow against the wall, lay back with her head propped up, and drew the blankets over her.

After a time, she began slipping in and out of a drowse. Each time falling asleep, her mind teemed with the stuff of dreams. Each time emerging into wakefulness, she tried desperately to form the meaning of what she'd seen, but before she could she fell asleep again . . . thousands of fingerling fish streamed by, the drifting seine net encircled her, there was a tapping as of a cane, her dying mother sat in the bow of a skiff as they plied the Black Warrior River. Her mother's back was to her and of Canyon de Chelly, she said, "You must see it before you die! You must! . . . Before you die!" Her mother's off-kilter back became Bud's as he adjusted the thermostat. Then he loomed behind her. His voice rumbled, "Nobody will wake you." All avenues of escape were closed off by the floating net. She began clambering up it. The strands of plastic changed to rock hand-holds and toe-holds and the sound of the cane resumed . . . tap, tap . . . as she climbed a long crevice to the mesa at the top where she saw Jack, his face filled with terror. Over and over he repeated, ". . . *rechercher . . . rechercher . . .*" He had the cane. He tapped a stone with it. The shirt he'd given her whipped from his hand and floated away.

She fell deeply asleep for a time, and then at first light it seemed she awakened and saw Travis standing beside her. She said to him, "Please help me." She saw his grave face exactly as it was and heard him reply, "Have you considered confession?" This, too, she struggled to understand as she listened, still mostly asleep, to a throbbing sound that approached from the distance. A huge shadow leaped across the room. The noise passed away, and then returned, a heaviness through the air that made the glass in the windows vibrate. Suddenly, Kate was on her feet and at the window. The thing came into sight, dipping out of the cloud cover, a thick mono-prop, steadying its wings as it dropped to catch the line of purple lights.

18

Hagia Sophia

U, **WITH HIS MIXED ANCESTRY,** unknown parentage, and the orphan's education given him by Catholic missionaries, soon learned that he had no one but himself to be familiar with, his own strange mind through which his experience of the world was filtered. The Sisters had told him they discovered his brilliance as soon as he began to talk, as if he were a geode dug out of the ground. They cracked open the chalcedony and there he was, luminous and crystalline. There was no explaining it except as a gift from God, they said.

He himself came not to be religious, for he set to riving this "gift" with his analytic powers until it was in splinters, but one or two of its horrors clung to him. He would never forget the Mother Superior taking him aside when he was ten and reminding him of the moral precepts, the rules, and of how waywardness—going outside the confines of the orphanage without permission, arguing back, telling lies—would result in punishment. These might come to seem to be small things, she said, but he should practice obedience. Because of his great gift, she told him, he was capable of a great sin and for this he might burn in Hell forever. Later, as he grew up, he doubted this account but never succeeded in shaking it entirely. He was sent off to Yale, to London, and brought back to Yale to study law, and then put to the service of the Pacific trade where he continued to stay within his confines by fulfilling the stereotype of the prodigious, ever-obedient, prestidigitating China Boy, and he became hollow, a zero, outfitted with ready-mades to avoid the great sin that subliminally terrorized him.

He developed a fascination with death and killing. He'd been responsible for killings enacted just outside his authority . . . assassinations, guerrilla attacks, and multiple deaths occasioned by political displacement in newly oil rich places . . . Nigeria, for example. The deprivation of the Russian workers in Steklyányigórod might evolve into another such case. He was sure he was not a sociopath, but he developed a libidinous fixation with the modes of assassination . . . knife, gun, bomb, sabotage, poison, strangulation, poison. Instruments of death appeared in his dreams, yet he had never fired a gun, nor, aside from kitchen knives, had he ever possessed anything resembling a weapon, and he had never come near to what Sophia had done, what he construed as the willing negligence of allowing an actual net, like the miles-long train of a deathly wedding gown, to unfurl under water and descend, unbeknownst to Kate.

*   *   *

He sat cross-legged on his bunk in his cabin. The ship's engine murmured steadily, rising and falling with the pitch of the sea. He'd been reading through some of the papers Sophia had given him . . . Kate's records, her education, employment, selected writings, reviews of her research, and information released under the Freedom of Information Act to an industry journal, Energy Futures. The raw FBI files were not included, but taken from them, it was said, was a biographical work-up in which Kate's father was mentioned as a Southern civil rights organizer during the early sixties, and her mother described as ethnically mixed, which made him stop and look up at the wall as he conjured Kate's face in his memory . . . maybe . . . maybe there was something Asian or Indian in the squaring of her cheekbone and jaw.

Her husband, DeShazer, was said to have radical associations. They had a daughter who was a Seattle-based immigration attorney, a son a student in Alaska, and another son still at home in Idaho. "Dedicated worker. Pro bono work for liberal causes," it said of the daughter. "High school athlete. Leftist lifestyle," it said of the first son, and of the second: "Athlete. Student leader." Kate was portrayed as "likely to defy authority on questions of personal principle," "given to extreme independence and capable of insubordination," "not a team player," "an ideologue." Her husband was described as "a leftist intellectual" and associations were listed that had become arcane through the passage of time . . . an SDS member, possible ties to the Weathermen. He'd held positions beneath his expertise, "perhaps as a cover," and was known to frequent "elements of the political fringe. Possible drug abuse. Possesses multiple firearms."

Among Kate's writings was an opening assay on bodies of material drawn mainly from the North Pacific. It focused on the passage of pollution through generations of coho salmon and the lodging of toxins in the internal organs of fish, causing "sublethal effects," including chromosomal damage. Other animal mortality rates were cited: those for seals, sea lions, and orcas and terrestrial animals ranging from lemmings to polar bears, and bird populations, some of which Kate claimed had grown all but extinct, such as yellow-billed loons and common murres, and others, such as owls, that showed signs of serious habitat fragmentation. . . . Near the end of the article were five sentences, tucked adroitly into the text: "The incidence of land-based pollutants carried to the seas by rivers, such as the Peace and Athabascan in their flux to the Arctic Ocean, and of marine-based pollutants deriving from the Chukchi and Beaufort Seas, have increased exponentially. These are now entrained in the systems, lodged in benthics, and can be expected to rise as additional petroleum exploration and production systems in the far north are put on line, joining with other land-based and air-borne pollution sources. Such systems are likely to follow initiatives entered upon more than twenty-five years ago between the U.S., the then U.S.S.R., and several petroleum companies. The companies, once their positions in newly capitalized oil fields in Siberia, the Ukraine, the Caspian and Baltic regions, and various off-shore sites are formalized, and then the states, for which the companies are surrogates, will operate at times independently and in fierce competition with one another. And at other times, especially as delivery systems are constructed, they will operate as a functional monopoly with the power of life and death. In addition, the foment of civil conflict within the newly independent, resource-bearing nations is presumed."

The like, in the harangues of the political fringe with which Kate's husband had supposedly brought her into contact, was a commonplace, but the difference was her authority. In her articles she referred to the need for an assessment of the interconnected marine ecosystems of the north . . . the North Pacific again, the Arctic, the far north of Alberta, the Caspian, Baltic, Black, Beaufort, and Chukchi Seas, including geophysical and meteorological analyses. U was impressed by her boldness, thinking she had wasted absolutely nothing in her experience.

He read through the remaining materials, then made his own notes, including Sophia's fascination with Kate. He opened his attaché, using the combination to release the locks, and placed the two sheaves together with his notes on top of the documents, the stiff papers, archaically beribboned, perforated with old world stamps and insignia, and kept in archival envelopes. He closed the case and slid it under the bed, put on his pajamas, and slipped between the sheets. After a time, as the storm reached its highest pitch, his cabin came alive with twitching and rattling things. The attaché skittered around, skated out from under the bunk, bumped against the wall, and slid back. The ship itself creaked and boomed, yawing with each crash of the waves. He had never been in a storm of such violence. Once, he got up to stow the attaché in a closet, holding himself steady by clutching the little table that was fixed to the wall. He peered out his porthole. It was impossible to distinguish between the black of the sky and the black of the sea except by the faint, lightning-like whips of white froth. As the ship listed heavily toward the water, he stared straight into the profundity of the deep.

He built a set of embankments on his bunk out of pillows and stacked-up blankets, leaving a cavity in the center, then climbed back in and lay still with his arms folded across his chest as if in a coffin. He slept fitfully, drowsing in and out, while the reeling ship raised in him an animal ecstasy. It was as if a tongue had shoved up through the gridwork of his machinations—now, the findings from the Chukchi, Beaufort, and Arctic, the benthic analyses, mapped out transepts, logarithmic charts, the species counts scurrying like ants to build new heaps of numbers, and the endless contracts and letters, memos of agreement, legal briefs, and permits granted comprising the vast webwork that extended through decades and across boundaries into scores of nations and hundreds of corporations. It was a net from which there was no extrication he could foresee, not even by civic revolution, but perhaps only by world-wide catastrophe, killing on a massive scale. He wondered if Kate understood that the economies of the earth, the hunger of its people, and how the end-of-century rise of corporate nations had caused the environmental argument to become quaint.

—I myself have never had ideas like hers.

—It's breathtaking.

—It's because I truly have believed there are no ideas, except as cobbled together out of the chaos, an amalgam of ready-mades from the wobbly, orbiting world.

—Or, there is only one idea and that is the idea of our death which will ultimately be revealed to us as yet another material fact that finally disassembles the last of our illusions.

—It is so, truly, that Sophia and I are kindred souls.

Again, he fell asleep inside his nest of pillows and blankets in the darkness of the cabin. The image of the shearwaters returned, their looping rhythm as they foraged the troughs, the infinite complication of their adjustments in the eddying wind, the glistening, tremulous crosses made by their bodies, the yang of their image to the yin of the sea. He slept well into the morning and clambered out of the bunk, put on his robe, and made his way along the hall to the shower. In the narrow stall, he soaped himself down while the heaving ship tossed him wildly back and forth between the stainless steel walls.

He went for breakfast . . . oatmeal, eggs, bacon, and coffee . . . a ballast in his belly. A few of the science crew were in the galley, stragglers like himself, but there was no sign of Sophia. He needed to try to call Jones. After placing his dishes in the bin at the counter, he went to the hall and started up the ladder, clutching the rail as he climbed into the increasingly extreme pitch of the ship, then came out into the bridge, a place sumptuous with instruments and hardwood cabinets. A crimson rug lay on the floor.

Peter Totemoff stood to one side at a window, panning to the northwest with binoculars. The captain stood behind the wheel, but set to autopilot the wheel adjusted itself, turning several degrees back and forth as the ship rode the swells. U introduced himself. The captain, Leroy McCaine, had a similar air of rectitude as the captain of the *Bering*, was equally tall, older and sparer in build, and was a black man. It gave U pause, the ultra-modern aspect of the race mix in the wheelhouse, something unreal and heroic. McCaine's hair was grizzled to gray at the temples. His face was angular and bony with deep vertical lines creased into the cheeks. U grasped the rail at the side of the instrument panel to steady himself.

"You've been aboard before, I understand," McCaine said.

"Long ago." U looked beyond the bow. The violence of the swells rising to the ship's rails was far more visible from the vantage point of the wheelhouse than from below. The red-and-white soccer ball rolled into his sight at the tip of the bow, then shot toward starboard and vanished. Cloud cover was a darker shade of gray than the sea and the two were separated by a pale line of light at the horizon as if the force of the sun seeped through from a nether region.

"It's a sea. It blew fifty knots last night, but she's a fit vessel," McCaine said. "The wind will let up once we're through the strait." A smile played at his lips. "We might even beat the ice. I hear they're not letting the *Bering* out yet. She'll be lucky to clear before the freeze."

U asked if he could radio out. McCaine glanced over at Peter. "We can try."

Peter set the binoculars on the console and led U into the chart room at the rear of the wheelhouse, picked up the handheld mike, made contact with the marine operator, and passed the mike to U, who, remembering that it was Sunday, gave the operator Jones's home number. To his surprise, the call went straight through, and Jones barked back, "Where the hell are you?"

"At sea," U said. "I'm with Sophia. There's weather."

"There's weather everywhere," Jones said. "With Sophia Kopat? Did she give you the papers?"

U affirmed she had, and explained how he'd come to be on the *Hermes* and when he expected to put ashore. He pictured Jones seated in his den in the leather studio chair with his knees apart, leaning forward, soft belly, the church-going white shirt and red tie, a cordless receiver next to his pink face, the desk before him clean except for the green blotter pad and a large calfskin-bound Bible open at its corner. On the wall at his back were photographs of himself from years ago as an Oklahoma football player, and to the side the picture window overlooking the Houston skyline and the distant haze.

"McDuff has our information, right?" Jones asked.

"She has something."

"You've read what I sent?"

"She must have the old agreements."

"Is Braun still with you?"

"Braun's going through Steklyányigórod, then on down to Houston."

"He didn't report in. There's no answer on his cell. Listen, U, we have to locate him."

U had given up on his own cell phone several days ago, and then, as he was about to explain the obvious, that cell phones were useless here, the connection with the marine operator began to break up. He wondered—How? How can I locate Braun from here? He heard the words: ". . . brief . . . Mobex . . . tracking device . . . Hemming." Then Jones's words came through clearly, as if he'd stepped out of a fog, and he named what U himself had conjectured would soon happen: "Mobex is filing in federal court and they're after McDuff's records. And what the hell is Zealot?"

"Zealot?" U shouted, thinking—A fanatic? Then he thought: Did I hear him right? "What?"

Another wave of static had expanded into a cloud, washing through the line as the broken-up voice went on. U strained to decipher the words. Twice he heard, "Open wire," and then, "McDuff" and "Kopat."

"Can't hear," he said. "What?"

Peter Totemoff's head jerked into the opening to the bridge. "Clear the line."

U heard words from Jones: "Braun! . . . bloodsuckers! . . . can't be on his own . . . ashore."

"Clear the line now!" Peter's face wrenched angrily. "Do you hear?"

U snapped off the connection. Peter lurched back into the bridge. U hung the receiver on its hook and followed, finding Peter at the window, glassing the sea with the binoculars. McCaine stood at the helm, holding the wheel with one hand and leaning toward the radar screen and at the same time twirling the dial on the radio before him. U positioned himself between the two men, shifting his weight from leg to leg to counter the ship's pitch.

He was rattled and he took a deep breath to calm himself. He presumed Jones was afraid Braun had gone ahead on his own, and that he—U—was to call back on a secure line as soon as the *Hermes* put ashore. In the distance, an ocean-going tug and a barge came toward the *Hermes*, which U supposed was the drill ship's supply barge, far behind schedule. Loaded with colored containers, the barge rode the swells in a rearing motion behind the tug, like a loosely attached wagon.

"It's the *Lucky Lady*," Peter said to the captain.

Something was very wrong with the pitch of the barge. Once, it seemed almost to stand up on its edge. The tug that pulled it swung violently in one direction and then rolled into the trough. Frothy noise flooded from the receiver and McCaine, still hanging onto the wheel, spoke into his mike, "*Lucky Lady, Lucky Lady*, come in." He paused, and then resumed. "This is the *Hermes* off your bow. *Lucky Lady*." He lowered the mike and said, "Peter."

Peter turned to the captain, and then looked back out at the barge and tug. The captain looked. U looked. The two vessels rode up another wave. Again, the barge tipped, standing as if on its edge and hung there, then slapped back down. The tug was foundering.

"She's going down," Peter said.

McCaine spun the wheel. The *Hermes*, shuddering heavily, sharpened the cut of its arc against the waves toward the tug and barge. U clung to the handhold at the side of the instrument panel. A binder slid off the sill, scattering papers across the floor. "Call up the crew," McCaine said. He had both hands on the wheel, holding it fast and looking straight ahead into the *Hermes*'s new trajectory. "Roust the First Mate and send him up."

Peter vanished down the hatch. Scarcely a hundred yards away from the *Hermes*, the tug and barge rode up the slope of the next wave. Two small figures in orange suits appeared from the tug's cabin and clambered along the rail toward the stern. The barge stood on end.

"Lord Almighty," McCaine said. "Turn it loose."

The tug lurched sideways. The barge fell on its edge, slicing through the surface of the water. The tug's bow reared, dragged by the weight. The two figures crouched at the stern. They were tiny looking, clinging to the rail, their arms and legs wrapped around it. The *Hermes* came within fifty yards. When it rode up on a swell, the tug rode down. The tug slipped sideways into the trough, listing heavily. It began ever so slowly to come back to center, but it was hit broadside by a wave, and in what seemed a split second, the tug simply vanished from the shiny trough. On the surface a few colored things bobbed crazily, yellow and orange and green and bright blue . . . boxes, containers, maybe the crew.

"Lord Almighty," Captain McCaine said again. He had one arm hooked into the wheel. With his free hand, he reached over and flipped a switch on the intercom, and bent to speak into that onboard mike. "Ready the lifeboats!" He looked back for an instant, his eyes wide, the pupils and irises dwarfed by the bloodshot whites, and his lips, at the bottoms of the long lines in his cheeks, flecked with spittle, and then in a fleeting gesture of acceptance, or approbation even, he raised his eyebrows at U and almost smiled, as if in relief that the worst possibility had at last made itself evident and that they were now entering the center of the horror. His expression raised in U a strange, ecstatic terror. McCain turned away. With his back to U, he spoke calmly toward the window, "We might fish them out."

*   *   *

The captain of the tug, *Lucky Lady*, and one of his crewmen perished. In U's world, the two would be of no more or less importance than the tug itself, or the barge, or the barge's cargo bound for the *Bering*. The lives of the seamen were of less value to U's company than the tug's cargo, and all of those of far less value than the *Bering*, and the *Bering* a tiny fraction of the value of an offshore oil strike, and even that not for the value of the well itself but for the foothold it would give ZAQ in Chukchi Sea futures.

The survivor, whom Peter Totemoff and his crew had hauled from the drink and onto the circling *Hermes*, provoked a striking feeling when U saw his expression—the hood of his survival suit pulled back, the drenched hair, blue lips, and the look in his gray eyes, steely with terror, amazement, and even exultation. The young man nearly toppled from the chair he'd been put in, but Peter caught him. Two of the scientists were there in the galley, along with Peter and a deckhand. The one who wore the Free Chiapas sweatshirt, a medical officer, took command, instructing the others to get the young man out of the survival suit and into something dry.

As Peter opened up the suit the young man suddenly went rigid and his voice came out raggedly: "I told him. I told Lewis to zip up his suit. I told him."

The scientist stepped past the others and cradled the young man's head in his hands. "Easy," he said. "You can't help that."

"I told the captain not to take us back out," the young man moaned. "I told him. I said we can't go out in that. It's crazy."

"Easy. We have to get you warm," the scientist said, looking up and running his eyes over the others. He said, "Get blankets."

While another scientist went to get blankets, Peter worked the crewman's arms loose and then pulled free his legs. U surmised that in the violence of the storm and in the expectation of ice, the tug had turned back, but had been ordered out of port again to supply the *Bering*. There was also remorse in the crewman's expression . . . the sting of remorse for having survived, perhaps, and fury for the cause of the sinking. The strong passions wove in and out of the man's face as he emerged from the suit, and then from the wet clothes he wore under the suit, leaving him with the white of his own skin. His hands wrenched into a knot in his lap. His legs and shoulders shook violently. He looked up at the ceiling, holding his jaw clenched to keep his teeth from rattling, and then a look of beatification filled his face as if everything drained away, leaving in their wake an awful emptiness. "Oh, my God!" the young man sobbed.

The blankets appeared, the crewman was wrapped in them, and he fell still, clenching his jaw around his chattering teeth. U made his way across the galley and climbed to the bridge to where Captain McCaine was. He stood next to the captain while the pounding in his heart slowly relented. "The crewman looks like he'll make it," he said. "He's cold, but all right."

McCaine murmured. The ship rode the swells, yawing port to starboard, and recoiling with a little twist. "The Coast Guard's on its way, but we need to get clear of here," he said. "We're getting some ice." McCaine gestured with his grizzled chin, and U saw a distant skim of pale out there, slicing through the gray. "I hear the *Bering* struck oil," McCaine said. "So, I guess everything's right in the world except for those two poor SOBs in the deep."

After a time, U took his leave, descending through the hatch to the ladder. Remembering his attaché in the closet, he went to fetch it and made his way to Sophia's cabin. When he knocked, he heard her call from within. He entered, and she looked up from the pages that lay before her on a table. Her expression grew searching as she revolved in her chair to face him. "What is it?" she asked. She wore a dark brown sweatsuit, the top of which was partially unzipped over a black camisole. Above her head, white spume dripped on the porthole glass.

"A tug and supply barge went down." He ran his palms over his wool trousers and moved from the door to the table, stopping a couple of feet away. Her scar passed down below her collarbone, disappearing under the camisole. He set his valise down and eased into the chair opposite her. The two of them swayed, countering the rock of the ship, he in his rounded body and she in her scrawny one. This was the same cabin as she'd had years before, the oversized quarters reserved for the chief science officer. Two pillows stacked on top of each other stood at the head of her carefully made-up bunk.

"Yes," she said. "I heard one man made it."

"The tug shouldn't have been out. The *Bering* should not be where she is, either. But the captain says she made a strike."

"We got something then."

U gazed at her. The strike would open the floodgates from the coffers. Optimism would suffuse the grid. A chute would open and money would rush toward the next thing . . . more drill shafts, maybe, floating derricks, the pipeline.

She said, "So, what is it? The two men lost in the drink?"

"It was the expression the survivor had. He looked like a saint. Beatified. I've never seen anything like it." He paused, then said, "I reached Jones. He says Braun's out of touch. But then the connection broke up, so I don't know what else he wanted."

They rocked to and fro. He shifted his weight from one leg to the other and Sophia's motion mirrored his. He regarded her, finding his eyes resting on her crone's breasts as they draped limply within the silky camisole and sweatshirt. He looked up. She smiled. He felt her presence in the air, what might actually have been the chemistry of everything she said and did, every gesture as it was directed by a transmission from her world.

He allowed his eyes to drop again and rest bleakly on her scar. The wound had a pink color merging into the white seam. He remembered that he'd always felt baffled by her sudden shifts from charm to animosity, thoughtfulness to ruthlessness, and by her bursts of sexual appetite, what he'd supposed were moods, but from her they came powerfully amplified. In the old days, she had filled his emptiness with whatever called her, her vapor subliming into his chill.

He looked into her face. Her gray-streaked hair framed the rose appliqué on her cheeks. He remembered that her name was Czech. Her upbringing had been strict, even cruel. Her father had been a surgeon. She herself, as he'd known her, was strict, quick-witted, and venomous. For her, all things gathered around the sacred strategy of the self. "Look," she said. She pushed her sweatshirt off one shoulder and pulled down the top of her camisole so that he could view the scar passing along the inside of her breast. She looked down and ran her fingers along it... intimately absorbed unto herself. "My life is changed. I told you my heart is regulated by battery and diode. I'm on heavy medication. Everything is different. I've been this way for two years, which is about as long as my cardiologist said it could last. I'm on a transplant wait list, but I don't know if I want it."

U kept his quiet, thinking that in the old days she'd enjoyed what flooded his emptiness when they made love, a rage to match her own.

*   *   *

Oh, my traveler! The misery of your endless wanderings upon the world!

*   *   *

"You see," she said, readjusting her camisole. "I no longer care about Kate McDuff in the way you think I do."

"In your message, you said, 'Breaches must be eliminated.' The files on her show that somebody's been kicking the wheel to keep it spinning with damaging innuendos."

"I was asked questions. I answered. Not innuendos, but facts." She shrugged as if to say there was no way of countering such perversities of the world. "And it was 'breaches,' I said. If it's true that McDuff's twisting in the wind... after what she did to me... I'd say she chose to play hardball. But really, I no longer care."

U wondered if the delusional parts of her were now peeling off into shards. "Yet it sounds as if your grudge is still alive."

The old haughtiness came momentarily into her face. "Grudge? She has material she shouldn't have. She and Leonard will use it in a way that's dangerous. Your friend Petrovich is powerful, but there'll be trouble once the higher authorities realize he's been overseeing imperialist oil exploration ... greasing the skids for western companies. If Braun had been sent in the beginning with instructions to get McDuff's records and pull her up short, we'd have preempted her. As it is, we're all left guessing."

"We're running a sting on Braun, then."

"Maybe. But it's McDuff who made him necessary."

U's own voice seemed distant inside him, as if someone else were speaking. "And it makes her vulnerable."

Under the camisole, Sophia's ribs cut chevrons on either side of the pad of her belly. They heaved when she leaned forward and laughed, making a sound like the caw of a passing raven as it winged through the night. "Vulnerable? Coming from you, that's comical."

He felt a click in himself, what might have been rage, or the circuit opening to let the rage come in . . . who did she think he was? Yet he spoke calmly. "I can see that you've changed," he said. "Except for the one thing, which is that I still have no idea what to expect of you."

"Look," she said. "I could die tomorrow. It's an existential life. Everything is immediate like during a dive. If I had my way that's how I'd choose it, to do one last dive and die that way in the deep. But of course there's always this damnable will to survive. Every morning waking up, I'm amazed I've been allowed to pass through one more night."

In a way, U envied Sophia her proximity to the end.

"Before, you asked if you could do something for me."

U murmured.

What he had anticipated in his meeting with Sophia—that he would become a voyeur upon the old days—had narrowed into a voyeurism upon this moment. He felt an intense familiarity with Sophia, yet what was new in her, the acceptance of the shakiness of her own existence, made him feel remote. Upon this feeling was drawn the ramshackle skyscape of the workers' slum in Steklyányigórod, the desolate streets of Moscow, the scaffolding of oil rigs in Kazakhstan and Azerbaijan built next to bomb craters, the corruption of resurrected fascists, the killing, deprivation, and opulence . . . Mercedes Benzes, Armani suits, caviar, guns, trip wires . . . and the endless milking of such aberrations by ZAQ and the others. He and Sophia were two demigods cast far away in the rocking ship near the top of the world, left to their own resources, while down below the arrangements they'd aided pitched along inexorably toward their final ends. A wave slammed against the ship's hull. Creamy froth dripped down the porthole. Before him, Sophia came to seem etched against the wall . . . dark hair, hag's jaw, piercing eyes, starved-looking ribs, and surgical scar. He exalted the heinousness and wonder of her being into a form of prayer. The nether reaches of everything he held in his memory . . . digits, details, columns, words, codes, contracts, schematics, even his own notes . . . began to curl and burn like the pages of a book.

She leaned toward him. "I'm weak. I feel what little fortitude I had left has been taken from me. I'd like to go out on the deck."

He understood that he was to accompany her. "Of course."

19

The Cane

FIRST THERE WAS THE UNMISTAKABLE SOUND OF IT, the low rumble, and she went to the window to catch sight of a plane descending from the sky. The Power Wagon materialized and pulled to a stop at the edge of the rise next to the runway, and the plane, which had passed out of her vision, returned to it, now taxiing back on skis on the skiff of snow left by the plow. It passed between the purple lines and nosed out of the nimbus of swirling fog and snow dust in the pale of dawn. The stubby looking red-and-white plane, what she knew to be a DeHavilland Beaver from her bush flights in the old days, stopped not far from the Power Wagon and cut its engine. She took a deep breath and watched as the prop slowly came to a stop.

The pilot's door swung open and a man clambered down, moving to chock up the wheels. A tall man emerged from the other side, and then Bud, wearing his green parka, came out of the Power Wagon and high-stepped through a snowbank to help with the baggage. The three men climbed into the Power Wagon and drove away. In a few minutes she heard voices in the house, passing near her door. She heard them in the kitchen along with clattering utensils, and then she heard nothing. After a time, they came near her door again. Something jingled... keys. She stood frozen in place. Winona's voice issued from the other side: "Are you in there?"

Kate heard a key in the lock and the door opened. Winona entered, carrying a tray and nudging the door shut behind her. "Why, here you are," Winona said. She was wearing insulated boots, purple ski pants, and a lemon-colored turtleneck, and had redone her make-up, which meant she'd been carrying her own all along. The colors of her mask were altered to a metallic silver, now, under the eyes, and her eyebrows penciled in blue, and orange rouge on her cheeks that clashed with magenta lipstick. She looked garish as ever walking to the table on her stick-like legs.

"More food." She gestured with the tray, causing its contents to rattle, and set it down. "Be not forgetful to entertain strangers, for thereby some have entertained angels unaware." Winona twisted toward Kate and laughed shrilly. "How could this happen to you? How can you get out of here? What's wrong with this woman, you're asking." Winona batted her eyelashes. "Me, I mean, being an abomination of the earth."

Winona left. Kate heard the key turning. She waited, and then went to try the door. It was as she had thought, locked, and she moved to the table and looked at the food—stale bread, apple and slices of withered carrot, juice, more soup. Again, she compelled herself to eat, facing the door. For some time there was no sound from the other side of it. She moved to the window, carrying the soup. The snowbank outside had risen another six inches against the pane, and in the half-hour that had passed since the Beaver had landed, the better part of the ground fog had burned off. She picked out a fringe of woods alongside a cut in the earth, what looked like the channel of a stream down below the end of the landing strip. Behind the Beaver lay an expanse of earth littered with snow-covered boulders, a moraine that tilted gradually at first, then in the distance precipitously ran up the skirt of a deeply gouged mountain to the toe of a glacier. She bent to see the top of the mountain. It was wound around with glaciers beneath new snow covering. By the light slanting in from the south, she judged the mountain to be north of the house. It would be cold out there.

She'd been thinking this place was in the foothills, but saw now that it had to be well near the Rockies and at the upper reach of the timberline. The Power Wagon, she thought, must have driven up here alongside the channel, and she wondered: What stream, what river, or what reach? What mountain? She tried to envision a map of the region and to measure the distance traveled from the highway . . . coming from Cranbrook, and then on the highway northward for maybe an hour, up the logging road, and back down again in the Power Wagon, and more northward in the dark, maybe four hours, or five or six. The general direction had to have been northeasterly.

She looked back at the door, listening for voices. She was on ten-terhooks. She wondered what the arrival of the plane meant, and what the men were doing, but again managed to distract herself, finishing off the soup and conjuring a cartography—the flatlands rising, the Shuswap Highland, the Scrip Range fronting the Columbia Mountains, and to the north and east the Rockies. This was perhaps west of the Rocky Mountain Trench, deep into Kootenai country. She could not remember names of the small settlements, or the tributary rivers. She tried to calculate the best way to go if she managed to get free and suddenly she went to the cot, sat on the edge of it, pulled on her boots and laced them, and put on her jacket over her thermal undershirt. She needed to be ready.

Outside, the shadow of the house made a parallelogram on the snow. As the morning advanced it compressed, the far edge sliding nearer and nearer to the house in accord with the quickened arch of the far northern sun. She felt she'd been left to worry and to twist, impaled upon her narrow hope. She went into the bathroom to see to her shirt. It was nearly dry on the front, though deeply stained. She turned it to its damp side, stretching it out on the edge of the sink and leaving the ceiling blower on, and went back out and sat on the edge of the cot. From this position, gazing through the second window, she had a better view of the cut in the earth lined with aspen and birch, what was unmistakably a watershed. She checked her watch. The minutes were excruciating as they passed by so slowly. Being left here brought her terrifying dreams of the night back and cast them against her deepening despair.

The sense she'd had, slipping in and out of sleep, of being isolated amidst a tumultuous population of actors was still alive in her. All the actors had mysteries to play out and all were familiars, but the stories were broken to bits. She was waiting for her mother. There was a Coca Cola sign. She thought of Ansel leaning toward her, and her outrage was reawakened. Travis's words blazed in her mind: "Have you considered confession?" He had appeared exactly as he was, brimming with life, so that she felt he'd actually been there, and yet what he said—hardly trained as he'd been in religion, or only in Kate's and Jack's cobbled-together rendition of old-time morality and new science, a quasi-agnostic animism, and certainly not taught to think of confession as an exculpation of guilt—was completely unlike anything she'd ever heard him utter. She doubted that the word "confession" was in his vocabulary, and wasn't sure that the word "guilt" was either, certainly not the systematic guilt of the Calvinist theology she'd been taught. She wondered what it meant to have Travis appearing as himself, or even as she could vividly see him now, and pronouncing what her own history supplied to him.

Her body tensed when she heard the key in the lock again. She rose to her feet and watched the knob turn, then the door opening. The tall man, whom she recognized as the one who'd gotten out of the plane, entered. He left the door ajar, which she marked, and inclined his head in her direction. "Doctor McDuff?" he said, and she immediately felt a displaced cognition . . . of course, McDuff . . . her professional name . . . but McDuff! She felt everything sliding as if to one side of a ship, and then the ship listing crazily. Certainly neither Bud nor Winona had an inkling of that name. Everything she'd thought took on a new meaning, running ahead of her ability to decipher it.

The man moved to the table, pushed the tray to the edge, and positioned the chair behind it and sat. He wore wool trousers, a white shirt, a dark brown V-neck sweater, and a bright red, tightly knotted tie. He placed a black valise on the table and gestured at the other chair in the center of the room. "Won't you sit?"

She didn't move.

His scalp shone through his close-cropped blonde hair, and his ears stuck out from the sides of his head. He looked straight at her with bright blue eyes. "I'm Carl Braun," he said, and she judged its spelling by the way he pronounced it. "They told me about Ansel. I guess you don't always know what you'll get when you hire help. It won't happen again."

She remained locked in position, staring at the ajar door, and thinking—Hire! Hire him! Hire a predator!

"We don't want to make you afraid. In fact . . ." He stopped, rose to his feet, moved to the doorway, and said, "Bud, bring in one of those soft chairs for Doctor McDuff, will you?"

And that name he used for her, the professional appellation again, and the genial, educated cadence in his way of speaking. It came as a startling probe into the half-subliminal, half-conscious world occupied by her science, now stirred up. There was a rat, nosing through the cargo that had slid to one side of the ship.

Braun returned and sat, resting his elbows on the table and his chin on his fists.

She spoke not to the heart of what she felt, but to what she saw had become a detail of that heart's effect, and in the meantime startling herself with the clarity of the words that emerged from her mouth. "What you mean is that you weren't aware he'd victimize a woman. It was a different order of victimization from what was intended?"

Braun shrugged. "He's being sent away."

Kate turned her head and looked out the window into the glare of snow lit from over the top of the house, then looked back. "Don't condescend to me. Who are you?"

Above his knuckles, his lips moved as if he were about to smile. A large blue chair appeared in the doorway and beneath it Bud's legs. The chair tipped sideways, came through the opening, and tipped back, the weight of it managed as if it were nothing. Bud carried the chair near Kate and set it on the floor.

"And take that out, will you?" Braun said, flicking his fingers toward the tray of dishes.

Kate watched for a reaction, but Bud picked up the tray without speaking. Pinched in his hand, the tray looked tiny. He wore the same plaid shirt, jeans with his key case on his belt, and, now, a folded-over holster out of which stuck the butt of a pistol. He looked somnolent as a bear, averting his eyes.

This, also—Kate supposed—a rule of engagement. Beneath the mask, she expected, lay a volcanic seething, and for the second time, she had the peculiar sensation of seeking a foothold of trust in that man—Bud—whom she absolutely despised. He left the room, pulling the door shut.

She stayed where she was with hands in her coat pockets, her right fingers stroking the scrimshaw salmon.

"I'll be straightforward with you," Braun said. "We need your data."

She looked at him steadily without speaking.

—My data?

And then, tagging what he'd said as if the words themselves were specimens—That!

Braun's manner of speaking consisted also in his bodily address, a stiff, self-satisfied, and vaguely military occupation of the air. The type was familiar to Kit. His way of manipulation and his look, the crew cut, protuberant eyes, his clothes, the wool trousers, and ribbed, richly dyed sweater fitting loosely over his rawboned body were all familiar. She knew his ilk, his excessively long arms and clean ugliness and his bony head stuck on top of the shirt collar and red tie like a trophy on a pedestal.

—Mechanical engineering, she thought.

—Maybe geology.

—Or maybe it's military.

—A mid-grade officer.

"What data?"

He folded his hands before him on the table and looked at her inquiringly.

"Whatever it is you want," she said, "I've not been asked. I've been abducted."

He raised his eyebrows. "You could have talked to Dick Troop when he sought you out and saved everybody a lot of trouble."

Troop? The rat prowled, overturning a can of garbage. The ship listed more deeply. And Bud? What could a right wing enclave possibly want with her beyond taking its revenge on her for spiriting away one of its women? Why Winona in the first place and how did a man like this come to be joined with them? And . . .

*　*　*

. . . through affinity or habituation, going through a process of elimination much like what Jack had gone through but more rapidly than he, and yet coming to a stop short of where he, at that moment, beset with turmoil, had been standing in their upstairs bedroom holding her sweat pants and underwear, and drawn to go into the gun closet, had been about to come to . . .

*　*　*

. . . she had also thought, as Travis had, and as Jack had, that it might not even be her, but something Jack had done, or somehow maybe the two of them. He was by far the more likely to run afoul of the Lord's Weapon, so she, even as she'd been held under a gun, tossed into the back of the Power Wagon and bound and assaulted, had kept herself from passing fully into this dark arcanum where the rats now called out the snakes, thick as arms, and the cargo from the containers heaped up in disarray, the only real reason Kate had ever had to fear a threat of this nature . . . the disarray, the unwinding of everything. The snakes gently knotted and entwined upon each other, making snake balls. Kate saw them now, sliding their bodies and arousing more to twist out of hiding. They hissed. It was certainly she.

"That man, Richard Troop, did not tell me what he wanted. He was otherwise obviously lying, and a fraud, as you certainly are. What you call trouble hardly covers this situation, and what Ansel did to me is nothing compared to what you're doing."

"Oh?" Braun said.

Despite herself, Kate felt a flicker of hope, though she sensed that her hope was only a piece of meat to him, turning on his spit.

Braun closed and opened his eyes. "Once we have what we need, you'll be released."

"I bet. First, I need to contact my husband."

He leaned back in the chair, crossing his long arms. "We want your raw data."

"What raw data?"

"Long Beach, Puget Sound, Vancouver Island, Glacier Bay, Prince William Sound, the Bering Sea, Beaufort, the Arctic, the Chukchi. All of it."

He thus named it, and the rest was coming, she was sure. Having been named, she felt the shadow of it, the grim fascination she'd carried for years, the doom of the earth and its creatures, the doom of its manipulation, and the inescapable doom that politicians, agency officials, and professional scientists had contrived to deny even as they built their rickety scaffolding all around it and gathered like carrion eaters to render it up. Now, with a sickening feeling, she realized she had been little more than a watcher and by that had put herself and her family in peril.

*   *   *

As a child, four-years-old, standing outside the screen door of a grocery and reaching to hold the tin Coca Cola sign that made the handle, she'd seen the legs in khaki and the swinging cane come toward her.

Her mother was inside, settling the bill, and Kate was looking down the sidewalk, then, too, watching, transfixed by the thin cane with its steel tip. It swung and tapped the concrete, and alongside it the feet in shined loafers scuffed softly. She looked up at the man, Louis Dufay, as he came. He wore a blue shirt, and his eyes stared stonily straight ahead out of his shining face, not seeming to see her. Three men carrying ax handles appeared from across the street, walked single file between two parked cars and onto the sidewalk. Her mother emerged from inside the grocery, pushing open the screen door and stopping as the white men surrounded Louis and forced him back the way he'd come. There was a snapping sound and a piece of the cane flew out, clattering to the concrete. As the ring of men lurched around the corner into the alley, an ax handle reared up and came down with a thud. Kate's mother clutched her grocery bag, grabbed Kate's arm, and hustled her off the other direction. Knowing only that something was terribly wrong, Kate learned later that Louis had defied the city ordinance against Negroes carrying canes inside the city limits, and the more, he'd committed the violation on the main street.

Later, when Kate was thirteen, the year of the Freedom Riders, she heard from the resurrected talk about Louis Dufay, a precursor to the "present trouble," that he'd also been "sodomized" with the butt of his cane before being killed and left on the riverbank south of town. When she asked what that meant, her mother curtly said, "Katherine, no. You're not to remember that." Her father, in his mildly arrogant, bitter, and Calvinist way, spoke as much to his wife's sense of insult as to his daughter's bewilderment, "Those lost souls did not invent themselves. They were cowards, also. The ordinance, the municipal law, was born of the fear of the insurrection they knew was coming, that the field hands would come into town just as he did, but perhaps by the scores carrying canes as weapons as they deserved to do. It's a poison and now we all pay for it, but only a few realize what the nature of the guilt is. Others want to escape knowing, and when they do the killing they are trying to remove the presence in God's eye that insists on payment in spirit. What they don't perceive is that the Black man in this nation is never passing away. The poor will never pass away, nor will the disenfranchised. The nation will pay."

*   *   *

All Kate remembered at this moment was the cane, the clattering and its attachment to Louis Dufay in her dream, while the whole of the recollection was hidden and entwined there in the twilight of snakes coursing over the cargo between dream and wakeful thought. She went on to remembering Travis: "Have you considered confession?" A glimmering recognition came to her that she was therefore supposed to find a way to confess everything, that she was to disgorge herself of her life of petty alliances, of her fellow-traveling safety, of all of her privileged flirtation with action, the tempering effects of ambition, and of the prideful and fatalistic doom she'd been born with. Standing before Braun, she had a very strange, obscure, and yet exact sense of relief because now the nominal guilt was present, rising to come out into the light, and at the same time she felt a quickening in her blood, the will to survive, and to protect those she loved.

She sat down in the straight chair, not the soft one. At last she named what she'd come to in her tangle. "It's oil," she said.

Braun appeared amused.

"You forgot the Aleutians, in particular Amchitka, the tar sands of Alberta, and all the rest of the North Pacific. It's oil, right? But what interest does somebody like Bud Willy have in that?"

When he smiled, his cheekbones became bullet-shaped protuberances.

She said, "And I'm supposed to have this information with me?"

The table creaked when he leaned back.

"Or I'm supposed to direct you to it? Let me talk to my husband and he'll hand over everything. It's what, the disks that you want?"

"Not those disks." He opened his valise and raked out a heap of disks. Kate recognized them by the color coding of their cases . . . green cases, yellow ones, black ones, white, blue, red, and transparent. She felt her breath growing shallow as meaning became clear: They'd been taken from her house, or already given up by Jack or Travis.

Braun looked at her closely. "Your husband and son are fine."

Shaken, but clutching at hope and her composure, she thought that if Jack were loose, he'd have Dan Painter. Painter would have access to the Border Patrol and FBI. "If you have those, you have everything."

"Not quite." He ran his hand through the pile, separating several disk cases held together by a rubber band, and looked up. "We downloaded your machines, but still don't have it all."

"How would you know?"

"Please," Braun said. "It's not just what's on these disks, interesting as it is . . . nicely presented, cross-referenced, projective, and interfaced. It's quite a system. And your abstracts are like invitations to the ball." He paused and nodded at her. "A woman of principle. But just what is it you believe in, ecological anarchy, like Murray Bookchin?"

She was thinking there was no way anyone could have combed all of her system and the disks in the time that had passed. They must have been searching for something in particular and she feared she knew what it was . . . the original disks that included the bundle of agreements, the contracts. She was still mystified by how Bud Willy came into it. What she knew of the extreme right wing's use of science was that it was housed in illusory conspiracy theories, such as the notion that the Alaskan DEW Line was a device to control the earth's weather, though the reasons for the like—a religious faith in the disorder of weather as a revelation of God's purpose—was at bottom not so far removed from what she'd come to believe.

She felt the gyre of doom again, at once spewing things out from its extreme and drawing her into the center of its whirl. She remembered the peeled log in her dream, dangling by hooks in the air, how it fell from the gin pole and might have killed her if Jack hadn't pushed her clear . . . that one, a brush with death in their early life together, and the same log that he lifted again and placed on top of the wall to make a tie, one end of it entering a bracket inside his gun closet. Within the closet, behind a hunk of pumice, inside the old cartridge case, along with her mother's last letters, she'd stashed the disks that contained all the information, old and very new, the original and her redrafted versions, and including the documents of exchange between the U.S. State Department, the U.S.S.R. and later Russia, the National Science Foundation, and the oil companies, the memoranda of agreement, the ledgers, accounts, and the blueprints for the Siberian refinery and pumping station and the pipeline tie-ins across China, Turkey, and the tar sands sent down a pipeline across the United States, and along the Chukchi sea bottom to Alaska. Why the new and information kept gravitating to her files, she didn't know, but believed it came from Otis Drainier . . . an oversight, or failure of perception, a function of Alzheimer's. She did know that it was a political ace-in-the-hole from which she'd kept shying away. She hadn't been able to stop it, or muster the will to bring it out into the open, not even for Abby, but only telling Abby that she had it, and then she thought—Abby! She hadn't considered her safety. And just now, as this realization shot through her, she thought—Don't say it . . . don't say her name to him!

"Surely you don't think I'm associated with the Lord's Weapon," Braun said.

She turned her face to him and at the same time tried to discern what disks he had. She thought he didn't have the ones she'd stored in the gun closet, but she didn't want to give herself away by looking too closely. She said, "Then who are you associated with?"

Braun shrugged.

She was thinking, ZAQ Petroleum. She told herself—Don't say that name, either!

"As to Willy," Braun said, "besides retrieving his errant wife, who had a change of heart and then a change in plans at the last minute . . ." Again Braun smiled. "Did you know he's a decorated army veteran? He's had you under surveillance. He was available to us and he's proven most useful."

A chill passed through her. She tried assembling that version of the story . . . surveillance, something she hadn't been aware of in the least. For her anxiety over her project to have made her oblivious after all to the actual fact of the danger she'd put herself in . . . and then Winona in the ditch, and Bud, seeing his plans going awry because of a change in Winona's . . . in the scheme of things a small thing . . . Winona thinking momentarily that she might break loose from him, him looking for her, and Winona making away, and then . . . What?

"I see you're beginning to understand," Braun said. "You should know, too, that it doesn't matter whether I tell you this or not."

She amazed herself with the certainty of what she next said, what covered what he'd just said and a host of other things, too, including her outrage: "Then you're planning to kill me."

"Oh, no." He chuckled outright. "It's that you've really never been here. You drove that woman across the border and disappeared. God knows what you were doing with her and her husband. An odd liaison for a woman of your cut, wouldn't you say? Who would believe you? For us, this place doesn't exist."

"And Bud Willy? He also doesn't exist?"

Again Braun shrugged. "He's rewarded for his work."

Outraged anew, more outraged than her circumstances allowed, she said, "If it is the oil companies, then they have the resources to fight off whatever I would print. They have their lobbyists, lawyers, spin doctors, and government ties. I'm not so much of a fool as not to know that." She went on: "I'm just a scientist. Whatever the effect of what I find is beyond my powers to forecast. I am not a politician. And I'm not a Bookchin, who's an idiot. What are you?"

"Information Specialist, Watchcap Security," he said. "MS in sonar technology, Oregon State. Lieutenant Colonel, Army Reserve, which is how I first became aware of Bud Willy. But none of that means anything to you."

"I know what Watchcap Security is. And I see you've had enough science to understand what I do . . . form hypotheses, mount research designs, reel in the findings, and put them together to make sense. I said I'm a scientist. That's all I am."

"Good," he said. "But you're hardly just a scientist. Doctor Kopat says your ability to work the edges is considerable, which is what gets you into trouble." He looked closely at her when he said that, and then went on. "You regularly walk out there to the brink where you're not supposed to be. You're running your findings into a state-of-the-art computer synthesis. You've got a very advanced program, projective time grids and all. You and you partner . . . Abby Leonard, is it?" He paused. "Since she's institutional, her files were much easier to access. The two of you want to show that the composite effects of fishing, drilling, development, and transport have taken the North Pacific, the Chukchi, *Bering*, and Arctic to the brink of collapse. All that's needed is a tweak to snuff out the Bristol Bay and *Bering* fisheries. They'll go the way of the Oregon and Washington Coasts. No?"

She sat rigidly still, having marked the irony of his tone, which was overt, and his evocation of Sophia Kopat. Her mind entered into a kind of tortuous, leaping Ukrainian dance, landing on this thing, and then, way over there, on that thing, which was Sophia, and beneath it all turned the snakeball of terrors and her dread over Jack and Travis, and now Abby, too. She felt desperate and near tears, which she fought off. She said, "It's not a question of what I'm trying to show. It's what the data shows. The world that made the data will still be there. Data merely names what is happening. Somebody else will find it."

"Come now," he said. "You've crossed over into advocacy."

"Advocacy!" she said, feeling the flash in herself as if from a detonation. "And what is this, kidnapping, assault, and larceny, if not the extreme of criminal advocacy?" She pressed on. "If you've got all that, if you've got those disks in front of you, then you have everything."

"Those are copies," Braun said.

"Those are my copies," she said. "You want originals? What are you talking about? The originals are somewhere else entirely. What do you want . . . to wipe out all trace of the information, including what's already been composed for dissemination by me or anyone?" She passed her eyes over the disk cases scattered across the table. Certain that the disks from the gun closet weren't there, she went on, taking the chance. "And how could I possibly prove that there aren't any more copies of those disks floating around? It's impossible to prove a negative."

"We know how you work. We know what's out there. You and Leonard have kept this close to your chests. We know you have more and that you haven't even passed it all to your partner. We know you're obsessed with back-ups. It's part of your fanaticism. We know that there's an original that someone has pegged . . . a mole, it seems . . . for further information to gravitate to. We want what's not here."

"You should try somebody else for that, like Doctor Kopat. Maybe she knows," she said, mounting her own irony, and again startling herself by what she said, an instinctive lucidity, something triggered by his raising of Sophia's name and by the photograph of the long-ago science crew she'd pinned up in her study, the fact that she knew Sophia worked for ZAQ, Sophia's petition, and most of all by the image of entrapment she'd dreamed . . .

* * *

. . . the net!

. . . abandoned and all but invisible, dropped down on her from nowhere, and tangled on the regulator at the top of her tank. Sophia swam on, receding into the chalky, silt-laden water like a ghost unemanating itself to a black slit, while Kate twisted to free herself. The net caught on the handle of her knife, which she kept in an ankle sheath. The net shifted, bending her backwards and at the same time arched upon itself in the currents, suspending her upside-down with her head pulled back so that she looked through the chalk-color into the deep. Fastened by the ankle and behind the neck, she groped for the knife but couldn't reach it, and in a rush of desperate grappling, twisted further into the net. Then stopping, stilling herself, hoping that Sophia would miss her and return, Kate remembered that a hazard of underwater panic was the instinct to load up the blood with oxygen, causing one to gulp down the very air that would define the margin for escape.

She willed herself into a calm, waiting as the cool moved like a curtain from her brain to her limbs. The net curled, bending her the other way. Above, the chalk-colored water lightened into a sheen near the surface, and she could see the huge white seine coiling upon itself, stretching like an enormous train downwards, loaded with creatures: hundreds of fish, octopi, squid, not far above her a still-struggling halibut picked up from the bottom in the net's wanderings, a half-eaten-away seal. Bent another way, she was able to grab her knife and work it loose, freeing her foot. She reached behind her head, sawed through the filament to free her regulator, then sawed an opening in the net to go through. She swam out cautiously, holding the knife, and rose toward the surface. Sophia reappeared, the slit re-emanating through the chalk-colored water, and seeing the net, veered to avoid it, and rose behind Kate.

Kate challenged Sophia on the deck of the ship, not so much because of what she had done as what she did next, setting her tanks down for the deckhand to take, dropping her weights, pulling off her hood, and beginning to pace up and down as she barked out further instructions. She ordered the crew to do this and that with the tanks and the specimens, to prepare the skiff for the next dive, to tell the captain to adjust the itinerary, and coming back to Kate to tell her to get her gear up for the dive three hours away. It was as if nothing had happened. It was her obliviousness, and the way she filled all available space with her will that made Kate stop her short.

"Now listen, Doctor Kopat," she began. "You left me. It's a cardinal rule, in case you've forgotten. Never lose sight of your partner . . ." She gained strength as she saw the support in the faces of the others, likewise even the supernumerary who'd come to be among them, the small, round man—Clinton U. His face lifted as Kate went on. Behind his glasses, thick as bottle bottoms, his magnified eyes steadied on her.

Kate had always wondered if Sophia had seen her trapped in the net early on and if, driven by an evil dispassion, had moved away, figuring that Kate would get loose, or ought to, or if she was even glad to see her jeopardized. Now, seated across from Braun, Kate also had to wonder if Sophia had the gall and cruelty of imagination to work her own edge, to arrange this present outrage.

"You and Sophia have a long history, I understand," Braun said.

Kate didn't speak.

Braun picked up his valise, held it open to the edge of the table, raked all the disks into it, and set the valise on the floor. The table creaked as he leaned forward on it. "This goes far beyond Doctor Kopat, and beyond Arnold Hemming's little drilling and oil services company. ZAQ?" he said. "You're right. The environmental argument doesn't have a chance in hell of convincing anybody at this stage. But if it comes laced with legal questions, then that's another matter, isn't it? If it's loaded up with diplomatic snarls so hot that they threaten to destabilize the government of the host country, or to compromise Putin, or Schtok Oil, or our own national security, not to mention our leases and permits, present and future, then that's obviously another matter, right? What do you think the American interest in the Russian holdings is about? Do you understand that the northern hemisphere is realigning? Are you a fool or is it a form of intellectual terrorism that you intend? Do you know what patriotism is? Or treason?"

Still soft, weirdly mellifluous yet increasingly intense, his voice sounded disembodied. He himself, with his tight-skinned face perched above his lanky shoulders, seemed unreal. "We have to take care of the loose ends," he continued. "You're a loose end." He leaned forward a little more. "You're in possession of classified material. We want all records, written, computerized, scientific, and otherwise, the template and software for your program, all things printed or drafted to be printed. We want the contracts, financial statements, schematics, and letters of agreement that fell into your possession. We want you to tell why information is gravitating to your program and bring it to a stop. Everything. Is that clear?"

She was more than shaken, now. She was stunned. "You have everything."

"I don't think so," Braun said. "And you are walking contraband. We want you to publicly correct your findings." He smiled again, the bullets in his cheeks forming. "Do you understand that. We want you. We can arrange for honors and grants, entitlements, seats on reviewing boards, and a handsome consulting retainer."

"Or what?" she asked. "You'll eliminate me?"

"Far too messy," Braun said. "I told you, you'll be released. I suppose these bumblers we engaged do that kind of work, too, since they believe nothing compromises them. Steal for money, hire themselves out as mercenaries, and kill, too, I'd guess. But we want to keep you safe." He raised his eyebrows.

"You will eliminate him, then."

"Who? Willy?" Braun lifted a hand and passed it though the air as if to wave away the possibility of Bud Willy meaning anything at all. "Imagine what could happen if Watchcap and a company like, say, Mobex unleashed their resources. We'll impugn your character. Your father was arrested in the sixties. You have a history of political sedition. You and your husband took cover in the Idaho Panhandle, notorious for its militias. What can this mean? You're in possession of classified files. You're a bandit scientist. You disappear in the company of known right wing extremists. You're dangerous, unpredictable, and seditious. And if that doesn't work . . ." Braun snapped his fingers. "Well. . . . Listen, all we want is to destroy your information and neutralize your effectiveness. What I'm saying is there are friendly and unfriendly ways for you to reenter the world. It's a classic scientific error you made, isn't it? Holding information secret for too long, waiting for the opening. Hubris, isn't that what it's called?" He smiled. "Pride. Self first. The fatal flaw. It's such a simple error."

Genuinely fearful now, or terrorized, and resentful of the intimidation, she took another chance: "We have nothing more to talk about until I'm put in touch with my husband."

He stood up. "The longer you stall, the longer your husband's out there twisting in the wind."

Kate sat absolutely still. "Then you'll have to kill me."

Saying that, pitting herself against him that way, so skewering her deep distrust of him, made her feel as if she had begun to confess.

He picked up his valise and nodded at her. "It would be a shame to lose a woman of your gifts."

Kate's arms and legs ached from holding position.

"Think about it."

He pivoted on his toe and left, pulling the door shut behind him until the latch clicked. The key turned in the lock.

She stood and went to the window. The sun was setting and the shadows were long. The DeHavilland stood on the flat and behind it the upper portion of the glaciated mountain gleamed. To the left and closer to her were the trees that led into the watershed, Engelmann spruce and fir, alders and birch. The house was silent. She went into the bathroom and stared at herself in the mirror. Beneath her eyes dark circles had appeared, her corneas were bloodshot, the creases in her face deepened, and her hair was matted. It seemed strange that she was the image in the mirror, even impossible . . . the mother, the researcher, the old self under there loaded up with all its familiarities, including, she'd have to grant, pridefulness, but caring, too, and the feel of the road she drove every day, the ticking of the bush against the kitchen window, the sound of Travis thumping his barbells against the floor at dawn, and Jack, his grave face and way of rocking back on his heels when he smiled, his way of beckoning, and his touch when she answered his invitation. Was it her . . . was it really her standing there?

—It is a great love, she thought, as her eyes welled.

Her shirt was dry. She put it on, tucking it in her trousers, and looked at herself again, her beleaguered face above the buckskin-colored shirt that was smeared dark with blood.

She went and sat on the edge of the bed. Her body ached all over. The room was bathed in the dusky whiteness from the early rising moon, the chill of it reflecting off the snow. She felt as though her brain were resting in it, her brain floating in a white bowl. She loosened the laces of her boots. She moved to the center of the cot and lay there, straight as a board, mustering all her strength to think clearly. When she closed her eyes and concentrated, the same dreams began to take shape, vivid and frightening, this time along with the image of Braun's bony face. What she would dream or think . . . there seemed to be no difference, now . . . would be what had always been within her and would always be with her in the body where she lived inside her husband as he lived inside her, and everything that was happening was inside both of them, too, like a river within rivers.

Well after darkness, she heard the whine of an engine, unmistakably not the DeHavilland and not the Dodge Power Wagon. It faded away, and then returned, its engine hacking and burbling. She rose and saw a single headlamp playing against the bank this side of the flat where the DeHavilland was parked . . . a snow machine, bouncing up the bank and swerving across the flat. She heard a rifle report, then another. The snow machine veered wildly and disappeared around the watershed and behind the trees.

When Winona came in, bringing food, Kate said, "I want to talk to your husband. Tell him, now."

20
Sea Ice

THE *HERMES* PASSED within the relative calm and fierce cold at the tail of the storm, skirting the Seward Peninsula and heading for the passage at the tip of the Alaska Peninsula, which Captain McCaine believed he could make. The freezing of the sea could be heard, even from deep within the ship. Ice shrieked and cracked as it adhered in the cold, thrusting parts of itself upward. At times, a "growler" bumped along the length of the ship's hull and the engine could be heard throttling down against the friction. U set out from his cabin to see to Sophia, but first, carrying his attaché, he climbed to the bridge. Here, the noises, the cries and murmurings, were more muted, but came eerily from all around, and indeed the ship's progress, as it had ceased to pitch and now ran more or less erect, seemed strange . . . dark water, dark sky, pale, moonlit ice.

He asked to make another call.

"We can try," Peter said. He led U back into the chart room and contacted the marine operator.

U's murkily formed intention had been to try Jones again, but instead he gave the operator Kate's number, which leapt to his mind. Then he searched frantically for what he would say if she answered. The operator put the call through. Out of the static U heard faintly a woman's voice on a message machine, then the beep.

He spoke into the mike: "This is U. It's Clinton U." He paused, wondering if she would remember him and still amazed by what he was doing. He was shouting: "Tell Kate to be careful! Tell her! Kate! It's U! I'll call back!"

He hung up. Ice bumped against the ship's hull and the deepening vibration of the engine came through to his feet. Suddenly, he had no interest in calling Jones. When he returned to the bridge, Peter studied him solemnly. The captain smiled. Perhaps misconstruing what he'd overheard, he said, "We're going to be fine. Don't worry."

Bewildered, U climbed down the ladder and walked to the door to Sophia's cabin where he stood still. At the end of the hallway was the lab where several members of the science crew were at work. No one looked out at him. What he remembered relishing as he stood there, looking back through the years as if through a long line of doorways, was the instant in Sophia's bewitchery when the hardness passed away from her eyes. The ensuing softness set him and herself momentarily free. There lurked enough of the animal in her to allow the passing relinquishment as a broker to her pleasure, and when it appeared as burning warmth in her eyes he'd known he was allowed to come into the hoop. He remembered this. He also remembered how when she pulled him close, the pulse of her body quickened as if she had ascended to a place where she was indifferent to his presence. He recalled how that used to confound him.

He felt the pound of the engine as he stood there, and the screech of ice on the hull, and resonating against his skull a crack and wail. He thought grimly of the raised seam of the surgical scar like a zipper, and the lump of her apparatus. He had always mistrusted Sophia, but now he wondered if the diode and battery had become items in a growing reliquary of herself. He wondered if she was that ancient a being, in repose in a garden of cruciforms.

As to Kate, he could hear her voice more clearly now in his mind than he'd actually heard it a few minutes before on the message machine, the soft lilt of it nearly lost in the static.

The telephone call had been his cry of profound confusion.

He passed within Sophia's cabin.

Sophia was there, seated in a chair at the table. She wore a blue coat. On the table were her gloves, papers, and a prescription bottle. He moved forward and stopped, arrested by her motionlessness. Her complexion was the color of ash and before her on the table lay her hands white as gulls. She looked at him and slowly nodded. He came nearer, tipped the bottle and read, Alprazolam . . . a tranquilizer.

"It calms me," she said.

"I see," he said.

She took air in and let it out. Hardly a sigh, it amounted to nothing, a mere transpiration. She put on her gloves and said, "I've been waiting."

He grew courtly, extending a hand, which she took. She rose, came around to him, and slipped her arm inside his. He still had his attaché case which he set down for a moment to open the door, and then picked it up as they went out. She felt light against him, yet her hold was firm. Once out into the hallway, she paused to survey her science crew, tightening her hold the more. Several were bent toward the monitors of their computers. A young woman, her dank hair concealing her face, peered into a microscope, seeking instruction from something gathered and now seen through the scalpel-like lens of the machine . . . small crustaceans, maybe, an amphipod, maybe a slice from the liver of a fish, or maybe Methanococcus janasschii, the microbial feeder of the deep sea aromatics . . . methane, benzene. . . . U's memory readied to supply the possibilities to him, but he stopped it.

The scientists labored as if their chief might appear at any moment to press them, yet no one looked up. They were rapt with their work. Sophia did not speak. The two walked along in the other direction to the T in the hallway that led to the ladder well. Here, U unlatched and heaved against the heavy door. They squeezed out into the cold and picked their way to the stern. A lifeboat hung overhead. Icebergs loomed in all directions, huge, ponderous, and raggedly shaped, glowing in the moonlight. They cruised slowly, seeking to join with the crying-out ice of the sea's own making. A ship had passed, headed the opposite direction to the northeast, its wake limning a stretch of parallel milk color to the churning wake of the *Hermes*.

U looked to Sophia. "Icebreaker?"

"I guess so." Before them was a steel fence with a railing. She placed both hands on the rail. "It's going up into the Chukchi to cut a channel for the *Bering*."

He set down his attaché, securing it against the fence, and ducked under the bow of the lifeboat to see the icebreaker better. As it receded, its running lights and mast beacons became like markers on the points of a kite flown low to the horizon. He relished the sound of soft thundering as it rode up against hunks of ice. Something nudged his feet from behind . . . the ball, still rolling loose on the deck. He turned and kicked it toward the stern, and he thought then that he heard something, a soft splash, which would grow in his memory to something distinct and horrifying, a terror he should have anticipated.

He ducked back under the lifeboat again and found Sophia gone. He looked around, down along the fence where the ball was spinning, thinking she would be there. She was not. He turned back and with a jolt saw Sophia's body slipping into the wake of the ship, resurfacing in the froth, which was alight with startled bioluminents. The wake, aerated by the turning screw, bobbed her up and she penetrated to the dark. Something shiny was beside her, and instinctively he looked down for his attaché. It too was gone. He looked back into the water and picked out the black case . . . that which contained Sophia's report, the intelligence file, and his own papers, the contracts and irretrievable, stamped documents in archival wraps. The attaché gleamed for an instant, disappeared, and after it went Sophia, her body outstretched like a knife blade, and then she vanished, too. He began to shake uncontrollably.

The ship sailed across a huge amphitheater from random sectors of which resounded the howls of ice transmitted hundreds of miles through the cold air. The sky was cleansed and clear. He looked up and began to pick out constellations . . . Hercules, Draco, Ursa Major, Cassiopeia. . . . He stopped himself and simply beheld the whole of their overwhelming numbers. Here and there, they were so thick as to make curls of white. A green and pale yellow aurora throbbed in the far north. The moon was out, a day short of full, hovering low above the kite of the icebreaker, hardly muting the astral display above. It threw a widening channel of reflection upon the gently chopping sea, where, as if it were a huge bathtub, the white nightmare shapes floated.

The ship tacked this way and that, skirting gigantic glacial matter. Even the lights of the icebreaker were gone, leaving only the sea with the *Hermes* in it, steady in the arch it carved toward the Pacific, along with the craggy icebergs and submerged bergy bits, following the beckoning of currents, the nudge of wave trains, or the rising and falling hydraulics of cold and warm from the deep. Such trajectories were invisible to the eye, and yet they were filled with the latency of motion that would continue even after the Arctic lens closed over the sea.

Still shaking, U inhaled deeply, sucking the cold into his lungs. He could see where Sophia had stood, the footprints left by her warmth, and where she'd grasped the rail and flung his attaché over together with its documents, and then herself, the last traces of her presence already glazing over. He was quite free to stay at the ship's stern and freeze, even to join Sophia by pitching himself into the drink. His feeling of horror sank into a grieving melancholy he couldn't understand. His fingers went numb on the freezing rail, his eyes stung, and the cold crept under his collar to his shoulders. He couldn't fathom what lay before him in the going away world, the sea, black and sometimes whitening in the moonlight where the skim of its frazil had begun to form, and not the muscular, green and lemon-colored aurora flexing across the sky, not the stillness, not the stars, not the music of the wrenching ice, the moan and the song of it, not its percussion coming at times in succession like a string of yells, and at times separated by long silence, sometimes sobbing across the distance, sometimes near. It was like a serial music with an unintelligible code all around, shrouded and obscure.

21
The Killer

EARLY IN THE MORNING when she'd been sitting on the cot—still half-dazed, desolate, and beset with her dreams—she heard Bud and Braun in a room removed from her own. Though voices were muffled, it was clear that the two were in an argument. She moved to the door, straining to make it out. She heard the name, "Ansel," and words repeated several times, "trace," "cash," "exchange." After a few minutes, she heard the front door opening and shutting. She heard an engine running outside and what she presumed was the Power Wagon pulling away, and then silence. In a while, it returned, or some vehicle did. Two engines were echoing against a wall. The front door opened and shut, and again there was nothing.

She waited another hour, sitting on the bed, pacing the room, sometimes staring out one of the windows at the snow so brilliant as to make her eyes ache, the bright going up the mountain and glittering on the glacier that wound out of the mountain and down toward the distant snarl of woods. The storm had passed and the sky radiated the color of cobalt. She considered crashing a chair against the window, despite the alarm system, the imbedded wire, and the heavy glass, but then what?

The sum of her dreaming had told of an uncommon history in a chaotic time, interlaced with episodes from her life and together with wild projections, the ephemeral gliding soft as breath into the palpable, the palpable back into the ephemeral, night into day, and day inhaling the night. Jack's repeated exhortation . . . *rechercher* . . . *rechercher* . . . called her out to find a way to see the world as it had come to be. Jack was always in the history, as was her mother and her mother's childhood home, Fort Defiance, Arizona, and her father, the sanctuaries of Kate's own childhood filled with scriptures, and the black sanctuary down the road from her father's church, its walls swelling with Gospel, the net, the clattering cane, Cañon de Chelly, which she had since visited following her mother's last exhortation on her deathbed, and Drainier, her old mentor, who in a burst of insight she thought had somehow (in his dementia perhaps . . . that part of it she couldn't fathom) keyed her files to receive endlessly the documents of agreement between Schtok, Mobex, and ZAQ, the National Science Administration, the State Department. . . . Her daughter, Pamela, was in there, and Ron, Travis urging her to confess, and fingerling salmon spraying like ice particles, spawning fish struggling against the current and seeking out the slack water with their disintegrating bodies, and numberless ghosts of animals and people gathering in clouds to float above the sites of destruction and sterilized barrens.

The whole of the dream was a disturbing version of her ventilated Mexican fence. Everything she had ever known or imagined rushed through the crevices and under the cactus spines, revealing a meaningless clamor of winds, a rhapsodic cacophony of cymbal, brass, and hushed strings, a tale told by her in her dream-idiocy, filled with flurry, gale, and squall.

Without being cognizant of it, she was desperately fatigued.

She went in and out of her dream state, which kept spinning around an instruction that brought tears to her eyes:

—Serve life. In this loving service, die well.

She heard footsteps crossing the floor at the far end of the sitting room, and she stayed where she was on the edge of the bed with her elbows on her knees, listening intently. When she heard the person moving toward her door, her body tensed. She heard the key at the latch, the click of the lock, and saw the knob revolving. Coming out of her daze, she stood. The door swung open and Bud entered, holding a tray of food—juice, oat meal, and boiled eggs. Closing the door behind him, he moved to the table, set down the tray, and turned to her. His head followed the motion, swinging in the path of his body.

"What?" he said.

She put it to him directly: "You've got to get me out of here. And yourself. He will have you done away with."

He glowered at her. He'd changed his shirt to a red one, which spread in a blaze over his torso, and he wore the same oiled boots, trousers, and brass belt buckle. His hands hung at his sides, turned slightly back. "That'd take some doing."

"Look," Kate said. "Whatever wrong you think I've done to you, I'm sorry for it. But it's nothing compared to what is about to be done to all of us. Surely you understand what we're up against? This man, Braun, and the organization he works for?" She gambled on what she'd overheard earlier. "A million, or two million is nothing to him, and he'll use what he has to cut to the quick. He's paying you what?"

She'd struck a note. He pursed his lips and drew down both of his cheeks, which, with his massive stillness and impassivity, made his mouth like a fissure opening up in the earth.

"Braun doesn't care about you," she said.

"And you do?"

"It's oil," she said. "Everything in the world moves for oil. It's powerful. Braun works for interests we both hate."

"What do you know about hate?"

She paused. There was truth in what he said. In her life of privilege, by her nature, and no matter what-all she'd witnessed and to whatever extent her research was driven by effects she despised, she still knew far less than he about the in-roads of hate, both directed outwards and coming back at him, the long-held weight of a world of hatred. "There are probably some things we agree on," she said.

"I doubt it," he said. "Anyway, this ain't about agreement." He lifted his hands to his belt and jammed each of his thumbs through a loop, causing his key ring to jingle.

—Whatever soul a person or creature has, she thought, is known by its exchange with others in the world. She had to find that in him. "We live in the same place. We probably drink the same water. The coyotes probably run from my place to yours. We share enemies, I'm sure, like the county commissioners."

Bud loosed a longer string of words than she'd yet heard from him, his lips moving in his otherwise immobile face. "You're all our enemies. If the enemies are turned against each other, that's fine. If we can pick up a little of the slop they leave around to further our cause, that's good. Big as they are, they're careless and soft. If you pinch their butts, they squirm, and loose change falls out of their pockets.

The difference is your kind kisses their ass to get it."

"Then why am I here?"

He turned his head and gazed out the window to the side, where the mountain towered, lit by the midday sun. In that gesture of body, she detected something disconsolate, but he said, "Any coyote I see on my place'll never make it back to yours."

"Listen," Kate said. "I had no reason to stop when I saw your wife standing on the highway in the cold. You'd do that, too, for somebody."

He turned back and seemed about to smile. "I got a contract with the county for that, the fools. And as to my wife, you hid her in your house, then drove her off away from her husband."

"She might have died out there."

"I'd of found her. I always do. She's a tougher bitch than you'd think." Now his lips slid into a grim smile. "But this time I get paid for bringing her back."

That piece of the causative confirmed Braun's version. "I was being followed?"

"She didn't tell you it's her brother's cabin up that hill? All I had to find out was which way you was headed. Half the time, Winona's predictable as a cow. Open the gate to the feedlot and she goes through it. She knew I'd find her there. She has to have the crooks bent back out of her once in a while. Your kind only twists her up."

"I see," Kate said.

"No, you don't. She tries to get away, but then once she starts she realizes she don't want it. It happens again and again. Besides, we got our purposes," he said. "It ain't about the Jews or the Niggers with us. The Lord's Weapon had its purposes, too, but we ain't part of it. Sutter's an old man and it's just bragging with him. Our reasons ain't the same. We'll do what we have to in our own way. Neighborly as you'd like to think you are, good manners from the likes of you don't mean squat to us. It's just another of your tricks for getting us to do what you want. This is a war of independence. When we're done, North America will be cleaned up and re-sized."

For a moment, they stared at each other from their distance of ten feet or so. Highlights from his red shirt reflected up into the blue-black of the stubble on his chin, which was scarcely any shorter than the stubble that ran over his head. His eyes were hard again. As the moment distended with the intractability of their differing identities and her sense of his outrageous illusions, he seemed to grow larger. The room with its white walls and blue rug, awash in the brilliance from outside, grew small.

"My husband," she said. "Jack. Is he safe?"

"Last I heard he had a basketball game to go to."

She was appalled by the image that came again of Jack in the stands looking out for her, as she knew he would have been, and of the torment he must be going through.

She reverted to her first, simple request, convinced that Bud was the only one capable of granting it: "Get me out of here."

"Since we're talking money and since you say he's got millions, what would somebody like you give me back for such?"

"How much or what do you need?"

He kept staring at her for another few seconds. In the impersonality of his scrutiny, Kate realized again that she did not consider him a physical threat. Even her foreboding of him had the neuteredness of an unnameable, unlike Ansel, even Braun. He was an alien force, a complete stranger, and yet beneath his immobility, she thought she discerned something moving . . . what, she had no idea . . . a small click like that of closing pincers deep in his shadow world of apparitions and conspiracies and as far beyond her apprehension as were his hatred and his so-called war of independence.

"The way this worked out, you chose to put your husband and son at risk, what no woman should do." Swinging his head toward the table, he said, "Eat that." He then left the room.

In the time that followed as she passed through the day in its interminable, anxiety-ridden boredom, several vehicles came and went outside, the engines and closing doors reverberating against the walls of the buildings, and there were well more than the original number of people entering and leaving the house, their footfalls sometimes landing in bunches outside her door. Several times she picked out the muted sounds of commotion, and once or twice Winona's voice in its way of arching up out of indecipherable exchanges. Kate heard the engine of the DeHavilland turning over, but not starting, yet turning over again and again, the starter motor grinding as the batteries wore down. Through the window she saw the pilot clambering up the side of the nose and lifting the engine shroud to peer inside.

Braun appeared, unlocking the door and coming in when she was at the window. "Have you decided to cooperate?"

She turned to face him and did not answer. The whole of it, his question, his insolence, hurry, and taut voice gave the impression that as he passed by at that moment he'd remembered he was obliged to hector her.

He said, "Don't forget what I told you. You don't have much time."

Not speaking, she focused the dot of her will on him. She spoke it silently to herself—I will not comply.

"I'll be back. Make up your mind or we'll make it up for you." He jerked out, shutting the door. His footsteps went rapidly away.

And then again, not long before dusk, the lock clicked. The door swung open. Winona entered, and right behind her came Bud in his fiery shirt, carrying a shotgun in one hand. He shut the door with his foot. Winona held a stack of clothing, and advancing toward Kate, began talking: "They didn't live up to their bargain, the assholes. They're like everybody else, their word ain't worth a damn."

Bud followed, saying, "Hush."

Winona lowered her voice. "Everything's screwed, thanks to Ansel. He flipped." She sniggered and then said, "Maybe it's you. Maybe you flipped him with your lures."

Bud grasped her arm. "Shut up."

She shied when he released her, but what was darkly ebullient in her kept bubbling up. "'And love no false oath . . .'" she said, leaning away with one leg bent and her back arched in a tango position. She'd changed again, now dressed in yellow leotards, a pink skirt, and a loose, flowered blouse heavy with azaleas and crocuses. Her face was painted like an exotic bird and around it her blond hair, to which she'd applied a gel, was like a clamshell. Looking meekly at Bud, she spoke softly, "'. . . for all these are things that I hate, saith the Lord.' It's the end. The lie is the end. We're in the midst of the last lying."

To Kate, Bud said, "You've got three minutes. Be fast and keep her quiet."

The tip of the gun barrel traced an arc as he swung around. The stock clicked against his keys. The keys jingled as he moved off. He filled the doorway and went out, closing the door behind him.

"'Keep me quiet,' he says," Winona said. "I bet you'd like that."

She thrust the pile of clothing at Kate—polypropylene long johns, socks, pullover rain trousers, Kate's own blue sweater, gloves, a parka with a hood, stocking cap, a small pack, and a pair of cross-country boots. Astonished, Kate picked up the boots.

"Fast," Winona said, deftly pulling out the long john bottoms from the pile that Kate was holding and letting them dangle to the floor. "'Be fast,' he said. Hey," she said, tipping her head near to Kit. "Wake up. He's turning you loose. Put as much of this on as you can is my advice. I'll be glad to see the end of you."

Kate sat on the edge of the cot, barely thinking, but making her body move. She pulled off her boots, stood and skinned out of her pants and pulled on the long john bottoms, and put her own pants back on and the rain trousers over the top of them. She wrestled out of her shirt, and put the long john top over her own torn one, the shirt back on, the blue sweater that smelled pungently of Winona. As she did this, Winona leaned over and whispered, "They're trying to screw us over. They say they won't give the rest of the money over until you're disposed of. 'Disposed of' . . . can you believe it? They're fucking up. They don't understand Bud. They don't understand that he doesn't care what they think. He'll get the money anyway. That man wants to keep our money and pay us later. He says he has to deal you off first. He thinks we're idiots."

Kate sat back down on the bed and pulled on the socks, hardly caring what Winona said. She was flooded with hope and panic.

Winona picked up the boots from where Kate had set them and held them out.

Kate took them. "In these?"

"Ain't that what you people do? Drive up and down the highway in your SUVs with your skis just so on top?"

She bent double, laughing voicelessly, and Kate, as she was leaning to tug on the first boot, saw the wild colors jumble up in the corner of her eye.

"Ansel snuck back here last night." Winona chattered on, holding her head sideways near Kate's face. "He stole a key, so maybe Bud screwed up, too. Everybody's screwing up. Everybody's fucked. Bud shouldn't never of let him go, the disloyal punk. Ansel sugared the gas tank. He stole his gun back and a can of gas and snuck back out and sabotaged the airplane, can you believe it? Nobody heard him. Tricky devil." She straightened when Kate stood. "He cut the wires in the plane. They don't know what's next. They say they've called in the specialists. I bet," she said, raising her eyebrows. "He's dead meat, no matter who gets his hands on him. The pilot's on the phone. It's screwed. They're screwed. We're screwed. Braun's screwed. Everything's screwed. The world is fucked." She looked at Kate's feet. "Do they fit?"

Kate flexed her toes. "Yes."

Winona's eyes, afloat in the many colors of her face and decorated all around their edges, were like two pale blue clouds. "I thought so," she said, taking a step back. "You'd be my size, honey, if I'd get a little fat back on my bones. Personally, I'm glad you're leaving. Bud's a hard man, but he's mine." She held out her hands palms-up. Her filmed-over eyes looked joyless as if the remains of her inner being had also been sabotaged, shut down, while her doll's mechano had been wound tight to keep her marching on. Kate took it to be her doom, the route she'd chosen from the start. So strong was the pull of Bud's gravity upon her lightness, the fissioning of her core, the endless breaking apart, there was nothing in her that Kate could see to rescue her from the final end. She had come all this way upstream to the exact same barren.

—The ruin.

"'At her feet he bowed, he fell . . .'" Winona intoned.

The door opened and Bud was there, motioning with the shotgun for Kate to come. "Lock this door," he told Winona. "If he comes out of his room, distract him."

"I can do that," Winona said, placing a hand on the pink skirt at her cocked hip. "'At her feet he bowed, he fell, he lay down: at her feet he bowed, he fell: where he bowed, there he fell down dead . . .'"

"And shut the hell up," Bud said.

Kate followed him out, across the sitting room to the front door and into the silvery twilight air along the shoveled walkway. She'd put on her own coat and the parka over it, and she zipped up the parka as she went, looking furtively across the yard, which was furrowed with vehicle tracks. She saw a gate and the mouth of the roadway, deeply rutted. They went around the dozer, Power Wagon, and a pickup truck to the side door of the equipment barn. The shotgun looked like a toy in his hand, a stick gun. He let her in the barn, stepping to the side and looking back at the house, and then came in after her and nudged her toward the back wall to a bin filled with cross-country skis. "Choose," he said.

She touched one uncertainly, making several of them rattle.

"Quiet. Do you ski?"

"I can."

"Listen," he said, as she began picking through the skis. "If you get home, check on Zack."

She stopped and looked up at him, taking it in, then, understanding his meaning, her eyes were drawn to the metal case resting on the floor. She thought the case was the one she'd jammed her head against riding in the Power Wagon. A padlock lay on the floor beside it, and the lid was open, revealing greased gun barrels, and a row of fist-sized things wrapped in cardboard with wires sticking out. Four hundred-pound bags of fertilizer lay to the side of the case.

Watching her as she looked but without turning himself, Bud said, "That's right. I knew not to trust them so I came prepared. Listen to me. This is what I want, and I don't mean take him in. You don't want him and he don't want you. I mean a person in your position can make sure he's being treated right by somebody."

The generator, which had been humming at idle, suddenly throttled up, making Kate jump. Bud did turn to look at that, then he turned back to gaze outside through the open bay. Kate wasn't sure if he'd heard something, or if he was just looking, or thinking, but in the motion and in the ever-so-slight shift in his expression, an infinitesimal tightening of skin at his jaw around a sag, she glimpsed once again the disconsolate thing in him. The twisting, heavy motion of his head raised in Kate an unexpected sadness for him. Suddenly she understood that Bud was making final arrangements.

"I don't want him locked up in a hospital, and not chained up in some fool's back shack, neither. Understand? If it happens, get him loose. Get your husband to help."

"Okay. It's Zack," she said. What he was asking seemed like nothing. "I promise."

"That's right. Zack," he said. "And that's all. Except it could be you need to know Carl Braun's trying to trade you off for his own profit, or some such."

"I see," she said.

"Now choose."

She found a pair of waxless skis.

"You'll go back that way," he said, pointing at the door behind her.

In full alert, now, and strangely lucid, she moved to the door and peered down to the yard, then across at the house, marking that it was made out of concrete, which gave it the strictly serviceable look of a government building. The snow had slid off the metal roof, piling deeply under the eaves. She again looked over at the pickup next to the Power Wagon, realizing that others had to be here, somewhere. . . . Who, or where they were, she didn't ask.

"You'll go that way."

"What way?"

He lifted the shotgun from his right hand to his left, moved near her and leaned through the doorway, looking out. She felt the gravity of his bulk, brooding with the smell of wool and sweat and the chemical repellent on the canvas of the parka he wore over the red shirt, and of his competence and blunt masculinity, and above all, Kate would soon see affirmed, the self-certainty of a zealot. But at that moment, she needed him. She would even consider what she felt was a reverberation of what drove Winona to him. He pulled back. "All right. Now, when I say, walk up to the plane. Get past it. Then you can ski."

"Ski where?"

His words were like clods lobbed at her. "Past the plane then up over the mound there. That way." He gestured with his head in the direction of the landing strip. "Don't double back to the road. They're all over it and I'll be done with you. You have to keep your part of our bargain. Understand?"

"Yes," she said.

"Go a little north. Then west. Mad River. It's down in the draw. Go through the draw to Mad Lake. The North Thompson. Tracks. There'll be train tracks to cross. Blue River. It's a town."

She'd looked to where his head almost touched the door jamb, concentrating to take it in, as she understood she was only going to hear the directions once. "How far?"

In the shadow of the doorway, his small black eyes were glossy. He was like a Silenian bust, the layers on him of girth, muscle, and thickness, the forbidding demeanor, had opened to reveal the small, buried, stone-like thing at the center that housed his rapacious intelligence, united with the code of his filial love for an idiot. A moral pin had been struck in him. She had the skis and a set of poles over one shoulder. He leaned near again, looking out. Her skis chattered against each other as she edged to the opening. He touched her elbow lightly from behind and she heard his breathing near her ear.

"Maybe twenty miles. The pilot's on the phone in the house. The others will come back. Maybe you can make it. There's food in the pack. Watch out. Straight across and up past the runway." He gave her elbow a push. "Now go."

She went, heading straight out along the shoveled trail, up to the landing strip, and around the DeHavilland. She looked back once at the house with its frosted roof and saw Winona in the yard, squirting toward Bud. Kate went on, glad for the cover of the DeHavilland once she put it between her and the house. She then set the skis into the snow, and the toes of her boots into the bindings, crouched to clip each one true, and stood and slipped her hands through the loops of the poles. She set out, skiing tentatively at first up the hummock, shocked by the cold on her face and in her lungs, and astonished yet again, amazed that she was here. And next she went faster in a frenzy, nearly out of control. Next, she simply jogged as fast as she could up the slope, making the ski tips clap into the snow.

She went over the top of the hummock and almost fell, but caught herself, and then heard what sounded like a shotgun report carried through the cold air. In a few seconds there was another blast, and then a string of them, the differing sounds of various weapons. Pausing to peer from behind the hummock, she saw the crippled DeHavilland down below, beneath it the low house with light in its windows, and to the side the equipment shed, between them the storm light, the now small shape of the bulldozer, the Power Wagon in the yard, a pickup beside it, and yet another vehicle with its headlights on. She had no idea what the gunshots meant . . . that Bud and Winona had been shot, maybe, or maybe it was Braun and the Pilot, or Ansel, venturing back yet again, and shot, or maybe he'd come back shooting.

No one was in sight.

The last traces of the sunset etched a red line around the distant mountains to the west. Stars were already out, and the pale, full moon was rising from the southeast. There was a glow to the snow, what she expected would be a night-long suffusion of twilight.

She started down the other side of the hummock, entering the large swail-like cut, and found that she could glide in the deep snow. A hundred yards below lay the tree line, and she eyed it, instinctively wanting its additional cover. But to reach it, because of a sudden drop she suspected lay directly between her and the woods, she first had to angle upwards along the moraine and then circle around. She started in on that, compelling herself to ski more steadily now. Out in the open, traversing, she made out the toe of the glacier to her right and, in the tricky whitened light above the toe, the glacial flow that passed from the mountain. She looked down and leftward again toward what in its horizontality, like that of a large dam come upon from upriver, had the appearance of a huge crevasse. That was what she wanted to avoid. It could be what the "little north" part of Bud's instructions meant: Go north first away from the gorge and crevasse, and use the outer edge of the moraine to traverse, and then swing westward. This was her speculation, her connectives filling in the inscrutability of his words.

She went on, climbing the gentle slope, collecting herself a little more yet, but at the same time eerily wondering if she wasn't here, if her mind was playing a final trick on her, if she were back in a dream and merely refusing to die in it.

It was cold.

She thought, ten degrees, maybe eight. And in an absurd flight of correction, considering where she was, she added—Fahrenheit.

She thought it to be so by the granulated roll of the snow beneath the skis and by the sound it made under her weight, crushing down with each stride. It made a rubbery noise as it squeezed beneath her. She was climbing slowly. The skis went . . . crunch, swish, crunch, swish. . . . Feeling the next shock of her fingers in the mittens going numb, and her toes in the boots, she compelled herself to be calm by remembering that if she kept moving steadily, her extremities would warm, and that then it would become a matter of budgeting the heat stored inside her.

She skied along a gradient toward the glacier, cutting the diagonal across the former ice field. She had located the North Star in the sky, and its indication matched what she had thought to be north when she'd been looking out the window of the room. The mountain she'd seen from there lay north and a little west of the building, and the flow of the glacier emerged from between two high, craggy promontories, running roughly from the north to the south, and then as its line extruded, it bent to the southwest. Now, the mountain towered above her, white and farther away than she'd expected. To the left, she picked out the darkness of the tree line sucking down into what she believed had to be the watershed, also farther away than she had estimated when she'd seen it from the window.

The moonlight threw the surface—its rise and fall, the snow-covered obstructions, the stones she had felt the skis knock against—into a weird relief of pale blue shadow and white against white. Perspective grew tentative. Her own blue shadow bent back and forth before her as she proceeded up the moraine. Glancing over her shoulder, she saw the twinkling stormlight outside the house, and she stopped for a few seconds to look. The DeHavilland was there, insect-sized, the line of lights along the house, and, all but invisible to one side, the equipment barn. The vehicles were not visible, there was no sign of motion, and no sound anywhere except her own breathing. Above, the moon looked like an icy wafer pasted on the sky. She guessed she'd come close to a mile.

She moved on with her traverse, thinking it remarkable or unbelievable that no one was pursuing her. To explain this, she spun out scenarios as she skied on: Maybe Braun was dead. Maybe Winona was. That left the pilot, Bud, and maybe Ansel. Maybe Bud was holding the pilot and Braun at bay. Maybe the pilot had the gun. Maybe Ansel did. They would be in the kitchen. She imagined Winona's body stretched out as blood pooled on the floor.

But maybe Braun had survived. Then there were the others who had arrived in other vehicles and whom she'd only heard coming and going, summoned by who or what she had no idea. Any one or two or even all of the people might be injured or dead, or none of them might be. Maybe the confrontation wasn't over. She strained to hear another gunshot as she went on, or something, anything. The unknown sum of the shots and the unknown allegiances of the not known number of people were too much for her to fathom.

It was because of her odd sympathy for the animus in Bud that she believed he was alive. In what had seemed at once weirdly acceptable and absolutely beyond the reach of reason, he had said, "This is a righteous war of independence." And then, he'd said, "The Brotherhood of Zealot will fight to the end?"

—What? she had wondered.

—Brotherhood of Zealot?

—He'd said that before.

—No. Go ahead, she told herself.

—Keep going.

Her toes and fingers were warm, now, but she could feel the fierce cold of air drawn down the glacier on her face. Glancing back once more, but without stopping, she glimpsed her trail discernible all the way to the hummock. It would be easy to track her. If Braun were alive, he could be in the barn getting a snow machine ready. They might have the DeHavilland repaired. At this moment, the pilot might be reaching out for the starter button. She skied on into the white night, expecting that at any instant she would hear engines, and then see the things coming up behind her.

The skis slipped easily in the crystalline snow. Before her lay the broad slope, the lower sweep of the mountain, and beyond it—maybe half an hour away—the glacial tongue. She hoped to follow its edge down to the upper reach of the gorge through which Mad River passed, and at which point she would follow the river trace, going west. There, she'd have cover. She went on, allowing her thoughts to position themselves in the rhythm of her skiing, her legs and feet seeking purchase and then gliding, and her arms pushing off lightly and swinging in syncopation to her legs. She wondered how far above the woods the glacial tongue broke off.

She didn't know. She couldn't see its terminus or the feasible crevasse because of the drop in the landform. She continued toward the hazard she could at least generally foresee, the low, upper toe of the glacier, which nevertheless might include stones and cuts obscured by new snow, and all of it obscured by the dimensionless white light, and thus the distinct possibility of disaster. She began a softly uttered chant, the three aspirated monosyllables riding the crunch and hiss of her strokes in the time of a waltz, a rhythm going within and coming back out of her working body:

Stroke pause pause/Ha ha ha/Stroke pause pause/Ha ha ha. . . .

Like melodies, images with their trailing narratives passed through her mind. She saw Travis at the kitchen table, his face, the thoughtful look he had in the way his brow knitted inward, coming near to what she'd always been sure would turn in his adulthood into a pair of cagey eyes. His cheeks down to his jaw were slack with fatigue. She saw Jack, taking the pistol off the refrigerator and setting it down on the counter. She saw the look on his face—wary, grizzled, his eyes filled with light. Their faces stirred her wish to be sure of her son's well-being, and her care and gratitude for her husband's wariness and protectiveness, and her wish to protect him too. The both of them, she wanted to safe keep . . . and Ron . . . and Pamela. . . . She was afraid for them in her great aching love.

Ha ha ha/Stroke pause pause/Ha ha ha/Stroke pause pause.

Kate's thinking compressed itself within the steady, determined, desperate rhythm of her body as she skied. Her brain poised itself between the darkness of her subliminal life, where the snakes slowly undulated over the junk of her listing ship, and the light of her consciousness, a silvery zone of illumination, while the chant of her strokes carried her on. She had been useful in her day, along with the army of natural scientists chasing their endless inquisition into the use of the world. And being useful in her way through experimentation with creatures of the world, with the system she and Abby had devised, she now found it subordinated to the lunatic arrogance of the likes of Carl Braun.

—The world has to change, she thought. The world must soon go back into its measureless chaos. When it does, I have to be there for it, and if it does not rise up in my lifetime, I must nevertheless in the days left to me be a participant with what the world will be reborn into. If I die tonight I must die enjoined to the battle.

Left side: Stroke/pause/pause.

Right side: Ha ha ha.

Left side: Stroke/pause/pause.

Right side: Ha ha ha.

She remembered the turmoil in her hometown . . . Demopolis. The dreamwork came to her more lucidly now . . . the antebellum mansion in the process of being restored, the ramshackle slave quarters at its back, the violence, Louis Dufay's clattering cane, and the rising world of black people, the fury in her father's church, and her mother, who was nearly a brown person—one part Irish, indeterminate parts French and Spanish, and one-quarter Navajo—precipitously taking her out of town away to Arizona. Most of the white people Kate remembered from home were locked in wars against themselves. Her mother, she realized, had cut through it then.

There was also a certain type of Southern white man who, no matter however reactionary he might seem, however inflexible and brutal, might nevertheless hold the chaos within, preserving it as an adult dissonance. It was a function of intelligence and independence, she believed. Her mind went back to an image of Bud, and he evoked a rough-cut man named Perkins, a farmer known for his outlandish but riveting stories about country mishaps—a drunken passerby falling asleep at the wheel and drowning in the catch pond from a hog lot, the obese country woman who died from an infection incurred from the rot in her navel. Perkins had approached Kate's father in the presence of Kate and her mother a week before they went away from Demopolis. He told her father that though he didn't agree with his liberal views, he also didn't agree with the cowardly means the rebelling parishioners had used to recommend his termination, influencing the Pulpit Committee, and refusing to hear him out.

She remembered her father's musing as they walked to their car: "Just exactly what does one make of that?"

And her mother's far kinder than customary response: "One detests his cowardice for not speaking his mind in public. One respects the little bit of courage he mustered to say so to you."

As Kate skied with the moon at her back, her shadow danced before her, bending and rocking in a lunging motion. She heard a scream, something howling, and she glided several yards until the skis crunched softly to a stop. She looked back toward the house, now barely able to pick out its lights. The DeHavilland was no longer visible. She heard absolutely nothing further. She looked ahead, seeing nothing, hearing nothing. No longer surprised that phantasms were given to her, her recollection of the sound merged into the roil of her dream-thought as she advanced toward the toe of the glacier, nearing the point where she would mount it. The shape of it loomed large. After a few strides, she found her rhythm again in the crunch and hiss of the skis and the tick of her poles.

Stroke/pause/pause.

Ha ha ha.

It was so, perceiving the extremity of her captivity in the house, and having learned something about men like Perkins in her life—cowards whose narrow deposits of courage might be struck at certain moments—that she'd known she had to make an ally of Bud. The wonder and miracle were that she had.

Again she heard the sound before her, the howl or phantasmagoric high cry rising and descending in the night air. It had the timbre of a light engine. And then at her back, she heard a deep boom and all around watched the snow flash to a russet color. The boom echoed off the mountain side. She stopped and turned to witness the sky changing to orange above where the house was . . . a red gash twisting high. There was another flash, and a second explosion. A fireball spun upwards as the boom bounced off the mountain. At ground-level, a conflagration swiftly spread laterally, as if a huge cache of tinder had caught all at once. There were two fires, what she thought—half-disbelieving, half-not surprised at all—were the equipment barn and the house. She understood that they'd been bombed . . . the contents of the metal case, the sacks of fertilizer! Softer detonations resounded and more combustibles in the barn caught. The two fires expanded and hurtled up vast plumes that bent into each other, fashioning one lambent flame that yellowed the moon. Far above, the sky radiated a copper aura. Near the ground, the conflagration blazed ferociously orange and white and was complete and instantaneous, she would have guessed, in its destruction, incinerating whatever or whoever had been within.

Transfixed, she watched as the fire dropped down into a low-lying cauldron and the orange fell from the sky. Now and then, an oily trail slipped across the moon. She had sensed the coming destruction in Bud, he with whom she'd been friends for but a moment. She wondered if they were all dead.

* * *

Kate had been skiing on the toe of the glacier for maybe an hour. Because of its longitudinal crevasses, she was proceeding with great caution. They came from the strain of the glacier's thinning at its edge upon uneven ground. Here and there, box-like boulders jumped abruptly before her out of the white. They'd come out of the mountain as debris, driven on the flow. She had skied far enough now to begin to make out the eyebrow of trees directly below. The reach of the glacier to its terminus where she might move off it and head across the moraine to the trees seemed shorter than she had expected, and she'd begun to arch that way, pointing westward, and a little southward in what she hoped was a proper correction to having headed more northward than she'd needed to. Because of the glacier's downward slope, the fire was no longer visible. The last chance she had to look at it, a pair of intensely orange hyphens had extended under the froth-color of the moonlight.

Her poles punctured deeply into the snow and struck the ice as she progressed. Her eyes ached from searching out the surface for indentations, breaks, and impediments. On the down slope, crevasses opened up and reached like clawed-out tears. So far she'd been able to see each of them, their cuts a darkening in the pale blue and luminous white, and she'd skirted them warily, moving slowly and sometimes testing the surface one step at a time, stopping to look, and easing ahead sideways. The recent snowfall might make bridges across them too flimsy to hold her, and so she had to focus on every detail, every possible hazard. Before her arose a pair of snow-covered boulders. She approached them from around their uphill side in an instinctive desire to use them as markers.

She heard a soft, burbling noise and drew up to an alert dead halt, quickly recognizing the sound. She tried to conjure up something else—running water, maybe, or a sound emanating from far away and by a trick of landform seeming near. It was an idling engine, and she knew it was what she'd heard from before, what her mind had transposed back to the house, the scream of an engine running with its throttle open. Here the source of the sound lay not far from her, just downward on the other side of the boulders.

She edged forward, cautiously covering the twenty yards to the first boulder. She paused to listen, hearing the idling engine more clearly now, then carefully sidestepped a few feet upslope of the boulder, and braced herself with her poles as she strained to see. The second boulder was blocking off the source of the sound, but on the grade beside it lay clearly the shallow swathe cut by the tracks of a snow machine.

—Ansel!

She realized he might have left the machine and gone somewhere on foot. She looked around in a sudden panic, but saw no one. Between her and the second boulder lay about ten yards. She could glide to it without losing its protection. Her skis hissed in the snow, bringing her up to the second boulder, which she touched with her fingertips as she listened. The engine seemed very close. She thought she heard curses. Peering out to the side, she caught sight of the glacier's steep downward slope and the snow machine tracks veering around in almost an S. She picked out the terminus of the glacier, beyond it an open expanse of snow, the trace of the snow machine in it like a shallow, lightly shadowed path, and then the beginning of the woods, a fervent black against white. She considered she might retreat far enough to be out of sight and come around in a long loop to get clear, and then cut back and drop into the trees.

She tried to figure out why the man was here. The tracks suggested he'd been to the trees and come back up. Maybe he couldn't drive the machine there. Maybe he'd come back to higher ground to cut across above the riverbed, or maybe, seeing the fire, he'd decided to return to the house. She couldn't fathom an answer.

Sidestepping several feet uphill from the boulder, as before, she slipped her hands free of the loops to her poles, stretched out flat, and crept forward until she could look around the boulder. Through the veiled light, she could see the machine tipped nose-first into the edge of a long crevasse that cut like a huge rip straight down to the tip of the glacial tongue. The snow machine's tracks turned slowly in the air, and next to them, she saw the man, or part of him. One arm was draped over the edge of the crevasse, along with his shoulder and his head. The other hand clutched the machine. He'd gone in, or almost, had seen it just in time, or just too late, and couldn't save himself, but had salvaged just enough of the calamity to hang onto the machine and somehow twist himself around to keep from plummeting to the bottom. He moved, struggling to pull himself up perhaps six inches. When the snow machine tottered on its fulcrum, he slipped back down. She heard him moan.

She drew her skis under her and stood, putting her hands back through the loops of her poles. His arm reached out for a hold again, and he looked up and saw her. Even in the dim light, she saw his face opening with surprise, and then he cried out over the noise of the machine, "Help me!" She glided slowly toward him, keeping her skis in a wedge and turning them back uphill well before the crevasse. Sideways to him, she looked down at his hatchet face. "Leg's broken," he said. "Help me."

A flicker passed across his face, a fury, then it disappeared.

Suddenly filled with fury herself, she said, "Or leave you here, son-of-a-bitch."

His face changed into something abject, like a humiliated child. He struggled to lift himself again, flailing at the snow. "Please help me."

At his side, the snow machine tottered.

"Help me."

She was entered into a crisis composed of what was inextricable from her action: her wish to protect life, and to do this as an affirmation of the fact that she, too, was among the living and would be kept safe from joining the walking dead only by affirming life in others. That was what lay woven into her, and the foolishness of the optimist, producing the callow expectation that charity would be reciprocated. Thus, she stood in her skis above the crevasse. Perched on the not unfamiliar knife-edge of a choice that warred in her nature, either way posed the prospect of costing her dearly. But there would be no compromise this time, no middle path padded with partial advantages, and no collateral of self-justification.

She moved back up the slope a little, more directly behind the snow machine, turned toward him and set the edges of her skis and her downhill pole sharply into the snow. By doing so, she at once slightly increased her distance from him and improved her angle should she choose to help him by extending a pole or reaching down to grab his coat. Caught in her war, she actually found herself considering this. The thought of it had the lurid feel of temptation, backwards though it was. It took her breath away.

He struggled to pull himself up again, clutching at the bank with his right arm, letting go of the snow machine with his other hand, flailing in the air, and then grabbing the snow machine, making it totter. He'd come up the same half foot, moaning and quivering, and she saw something move into his face, the hooded expression of the eyes and a drawing of flesh toward his mouth. He had lifted himself nearly to the waist, almost enough for him to make it out on his own. The naiveté of her nature tempted her to help him, but then the effort he had made caused his look of servility to pass into something inscrutable.

His left hand came off the snow machine, and he groped with it to clutch her pole, while with his right hand he attempted to hoist himself out of the crevasse. In that instant everything before Kate slowed down . . . the expression of his face, his hair flowing wildly out of his askew cap, the furious trembling of his arm under the strain, each thing passing before her, including what she instinctively grasped . . . that this man was in no way the master of himself, that his rage was pathological and overwhelmed his pain and jeopardy. Somehow her presence might have inspired this raving last assault, but no matter what goodness might reside in her nature, she was in no way its mistress, either. Recoiling from this horror and entering another one, she jerked her pole out of his reach and put one knee to the rear housing of the snow machine. She bent and shoved with her hand and knee at once. The machine broke loose, toppled, and knocked against him and broke his hold, as by its position she had known it would. He screamed with astonishment as he slid, clawing at the bank and hugging the machine which took him with it, plummeting, then clattering deep within the icy cavern.

She eased up near the edge of the crevasse to peer into it. It looked like a deep dusk down there, a strange, whitened, opaque dark. She could pick out what she thought was his head protruding from beneath the machine, and perhaps one arm still embracing it. He lay still. Kate began to shake uncontrollably as the awareness of what she'd done took its grip.

* * *

West. Mad River.

* * *

Skiing first to safety around and above the crevasse, Kate then proceeded straight along the best of the tracks laid by the snow machine, turned just above the edge of the glacier, and gingerly sidestepped down the fifteen feet or so of its terminal slope, where the tongue dropped to the flat. The skis skittered against the exposed ice. She arrived back on the moraine on a level with the woods. Between her and them lay the circling snow machine tracks, running toward the woods and turning back upon themselves. She imagined the man's face, the desperation in it transliterated out of the veering among the litter of rocks and the wild loops as he'd searched frantically for a way. For her part, she wanted the woods for cover, and to keep her off the glacier, and because she believed they fringed the course of the river.

She could think with surprising clarity about that, her desired trajectory and the points along the way as they'd been named to her, even though she felt deranged. She took a track left by the snow machine that seemed to present the most direct access. When she arrived at the edge of the woods, it became clear that the man had tried to jam the snow machine through but had had to haul it back out. She saw his footsteps, sinking deep where he'd gotten off the machine to tug at it. A gas can lay heaved out in the open. Looking up along the edge of the woods, she saw an extrusion of dark rock, a long promontory muscling out of the snow and ice. A double line of snow machine tracks went for it and came back. He'd tried that way, too.

A chill had come over her from having stopped, and from the panic of what she'd done. She was a killer. Though she felt not a gram of guilt, it carried her into an alien territory. She pushed herself to go on, and followed the few feet of trail into a tumult of woods. She could smell it, the dank and green rising through the cold. It was a blow-down or avalanche site, what had kept the snow machine at bay, a chaos of standing subalpine lodge pole and larch and of more trees littering the ground like matchsticks, covered with deep snow. She marked what she would have to do—ski if she could, but otherwise remove the skis and pick her way through, but carefully, for fear of snagging a leg in a hole.

Sometimes, she crawled over trees or under them, dragging her skis and poles behind her. Wet began to soak under her rain trousers at the ankles. At times, she shivered uncontrollably. She stepped meticulously over that apparent, snowbound trunk and hung onto that barely visible limb for support, sometimes falling face-first into the snow. Sometimes, clumps of snow fell off the limbs onto her head. Sometimes, she clambered upward to get around an obstruction, and slid back down, or went sideways, catching her feet in brush, bracing herself against hard things, and always seeking out clearings in the trees. When she found one, she tried her skis, but usually, and increasingly as she struggled forward, she chose to wade through the snow. The moon passed its apogee and descended to the west, giving over a deepening obscurity to the woods.

She was traversing a slope, pushing across and down it. For a time, the trees were larger. She stopped to pull a frond of needles before her face and removed a glove to feel it, and another, catching the scent of the sear spruce, the aromatic cedar. Thus, she knew that in so short a space she'd descended into another margin. Soon, there might be water. Following the slope, and now not even trying the skis but carrying them on her shoulder, or dragging them, she entered a different thrall from the one she'd inhabited when she had skied, the rhythms of this one guided by the detail of one obstacle followed by the next in the penumbral light. Fragmentary images of Bud, Winona, Braun, and Ansel appeared. She longed desperately for her home, her husband, and sometimes bitter, hopeless tears sprang to her eyes. She remembered despairingly what Bud had said: "You put your husband and son at risk, what no woman should do." The thought of that in its error made her teeth grind, and yet the truth in it made her woefully envision Travis, and Jack with his steady, open eyes. The cold stung her face.

She kept on, picking her way. The slope sharpened the more, the trees grew more uncommon, the snow deepened, and she found herself approaching an outcropping from which she could see into the dark canyon bottom, perhaps a hundred-fifty feet down. Nearing the edge, she felt queasy. She edged back. As her eyes adjusted to the murky depth, she discerned what would have been a chaos of drops and holes and protruding boulders and snags in the bottom, what Jack would have loved to examine, what would have been a flood cascading down the narrow grade, but frozen now into a ghostly, rope-like, twisting line of ice. What might have been a roar coming out of a billowing fog of spray, she heard as an eerie trickling.

She moved back further, set down her skis and poles, pulled off the pack, knelt in the snow, took off a glove, and searched the pack. Finding a half-full box of oatmeal, she ate several handfuls, chewing slowly and mixing the meal with bites of snow scraped off the rock. She found raisins and ate a few of them, and took out the flashlight to see if there was a way to attach her skis to the pack. There was, and she did it by taking off the second glove and holding the light in her teeth. She looped a ripcord through the skis' toe clips, tied it off, and kept the poles loose to use as canes. When her hands numbed, she pulled the gloves back on and stayed still for a moment, looking to her right at the continuation of an increasingly radical grade—fewer trees, more rock faces, yet less certain footing, and beneath it the precipitous slope. She closed her eyes, listening to the lonesome sound of the water trickling secretly inside itself at the bottom.

* * *

Mad River.

*　*　*

She could not go directly to it, not from here. She visualized the traverse before her, how she might pick her way step-by-step, hanging
onto one bit of scrub, and the next, struggling for footing there on that
rock, then hugging the black-and-white-streaked promontory as she
crawled over it. What awaited her on the other side of the promontory, when she might make her way into the watershed, if ever, what
might follow that, and how long all of it could take, she had no idea.
She might perish going that way, too, losing her footing and falling.
She could feel the knot of food in her belly and the adrenaline rush
she'd been riding going slack. A deep chill crept upon her. Somewhere,
there was an opening wide enough for the river to enter into its lake.

*　*　*

Mad Lake.

*　*　*

Opening her eyes, she saw that as the moon was passing over, the bite of
the stars grew sharper. The still air seemed deranged. She was a killer.
She began to consider the reasons for this thing, how maybe she'd
come this far in order to die alone. The thought of what that would do
to Jack, how it would hurt him, and because of the way she was able to
feel that for him, holding him inside her, she welled with grief.

22

His Preeminence

SOMEBODY WAS HOLDING HIS HAND IN THE AIR.

He felt like velvet, everything in him smooth and dark and plush as velvet. He felt like a plant with his head a soft blossom inclined gently rightward to cling to the light.

Morphine.

Codeine.

Some chemical mix.

Just this side of the square of light, a glass bottle hung from a chrome plated tree. He stared at the bottle, which took the shape in his mind of what it was, but he did not have a name for it. It looked like a calibrated upside-down Mason jar. He had the name for that. He and Kate had ranks of them packed to the brim with tomatoes. Two shelves sagged under their weight in the cold room where the elk carcass hung from the hook.

Somebody had him by the wrist and was holding his hand in the air. It made his arm feel like a tether attached to a mooring. There were others with him.

He remembered a roaring, the crashing in his ears.

Above the bottle and dangling from another arm of the chrome tree was a monitor that had a jagged line of green light cutting across it over and over again. The bottle was attached to a box with a blinking red light. Beneath the bottle hung a transparent plastic bag.

The bag and bottle were half-filled with clear liquid, and from the bottom of each emerged plastic tubing. He followed the path of the tubing to where one joined the other at a clip. There was a cylindrical air bubble in the tubing through which drops of the liquid fell. Fixing on the drops, he felt something in himself slowing, and he turned his eyes to the light in the box and back again to the falling drops, realizing that the red light blinked and the droplets fell in the same rhythm, which in the plush of his mind he found pleasing . . . the two things outside him activated in a synchrony with the pulse inside.

But for his eyes, which felt dry in their sockets, he hadn't moved a muscle.

The trail of the tubing curled down under the chrome bar at the side of the bed and disappeared, then came up again to his right arm where it vanished under a heavily taped patch. He felt a discomfort in his hip and leg and side, a dull, almost pleasurable soreness, and an ache in his heart. He lifted his gaze from the tape on his arm to the bar, up the tubing to the plastic bag and bottle, and the monitor with its jagged green line. He realized that the jags in the line were representations of the rhythm of his blood as it flowed through his arteries, welled in his organs, suffused his brain, mixed with the air in his lungs, and was pumped through the veins back into his heart, that the rhythm and his hurt as they were lodged in the rhythmic world were being tricked out and displayed in the lights as an abbreviation of the most extreme form.

He understood that he was in a hospital, drugged, that he'd just come to. He believed he'd awakened here before several times.

The chrome tree with its paraphernalia was just to his side of a large window. A vase with a spray of white and purple flowers stood on the sill. He had seen that. The light in the window glistened silvery and diffuse beneath a low sky, and in the distance, obscurely through the mist, he could see the silhouettes of two sloping, dark blue ridge lines emerging into view from either side. The ridge lines dropped toward two squared-off plateaus. Between them lay a gap, and seeing that, the gap, and the two plateaus at what he judged to be equal to his elevation, and then on the outer extremes the ridge lines, he knew exactly where he was. It was comforting to think of the gap, the chute through which the great flood had passed, and the plateaus on either side scoured flat, the intact ridge lines above flood level, and the whole broad valley once filled with tumultuous water. He'd been in this building before, visiting others. He was up on the hill in Sacred Heart Hospital looking out over the city of Spokane and straight through the flood-blown gap in the hills in the direction of his home.

When he closed his eyes, his head reeled pleasingly into the dark satin of the drugs. He remembered the roaring. Somebody was holding him by the wrist. He turned his head a little and saw his one leg with the sheet over it lifted and quarter-inch steel cables coming up from under the sheet to a chrome plated armature that rose from the foot of the bed. Traction. Behind the armature on the wall was a clock that read 9:42. Next to it a thin cut of light filtered through the window from the low sun. He kept turning his head to the left and saw his arm and a hand holding his wrist and a woman in a white uniform. She had tawny skin and black hair, a stethoscope draped around her neck, and she was scrutinizing her watch.

"We're awake. How are we?"

"We are looking for each other," he said. The words felt dry in his throat.

Her eyes moved to him, then drew back to her watch as a smile came faintly to the corners of her lips. Somebody else was here. Somebody else was in the room. He remembered the roar of guns, the crashing, and himself pitching toward the dark, and something else . . . a thudding that jolted his eardrums.

"I'm alive," he said.

He smiled at the independent creature inside him that separated itself to tell jokes.

"You're going to be fine." She came nearer, holding his wrist. She bent a little so that he could see outlined against the wall her thick eyebrow, glossy brown eye, nose, and the downy filaments above her lips. She had a mole on the side of her chin. He smelled perfume, a line of it like sage in the air thin as a blade. Gently, she set down his arm on the inside of the railing, took an electronic thermometer out of a holster, put it in his mouth, and held it there for a moment, touching her fingertips to his chin. He saw by the pin on the lapel of her blouse, the name incised through the black to the white underlaminate, that she was named Maria Cordero, R.N.

She removed the thermometer. As she took a step back to read it, he caught a glimpse of the others who were standing near the wall at the foot of a second, empty bed . . . Travis, and . . . who? . . . Something thunderous moved, big in the velvet like a distant shifting of tectonic plates reverberating into him. He felt a void opening, and an ache in it made sleek by drugs, and inside the ache a slippery creature twisting.

The nurse leaned toward him, blocking his view. She bent near. He thought she was going to kiss him, and for an instant he lay rapt with wonder, and he was thinking . . . not Kate . . . not Kate. . . .

What is it?

. . . skewing his eyes sideways out from under the nurse . . . not Kate . . . but Pamela, his daughter, who looked like her mother . . . the auburn color of her hair, the mouth, the size of her. Faces floated through his mind: Pamela, Travis, and Ron. It was the way Pamela stood with one hip cocked that made him mistake her, and also his own inchoate, powerful wish for what he hadn't even thought yet since . . . since what . . . awakening? . . . and wasn't even thinking now but obscurely desiring inside the drug effect. The slippery creature hunkered back and showed its glowing eyes. He wanted Kate here.

—Where was she?

—Where was Ron?

—What day was it?

The nurse put one hand around his left eye and with her index finger and thumb parted the skin at his brow and cheekbone and shone a tiny light into the eye. With his right eye he could see the dusty pink of her palm, and he felt her breath on his cheek. She moved to his other eye, parting the skin to hold it open and peering with the light. With his left eye, now, he stared at the honey-colored skin beneath her throat. That much was certain . . . her smell, the crinkle of her starched blouse, her touch, and the skin he stared at, the light in his eye, the hospital bed he lay on . . . and the rest of it quite unclear and swirling within him. He was thinking of Gene crouched over him in the quonset hut, Gene's hand on his shoulder, and at the same time keeping the pistol . . . Jack's own .45 . . . trained on somebody down at the end of the hut . . . Troop, Richard Troop, or the other man who had his grandfather's old .38 . . . and Gene talking, comforting him as he . . . Jack . . . lay on the hard concrete floor with the ferocious pain in his right leg, what was now a dull, glabrous ache, and something aching in his chest, and outside the windows oscillating red light, and the shouts, and somebody else near him prone on the floor, bleeding from the belly . . . Chuck Lamb . . . and others . . . Dan Painter . . . lurching through the doorway.

He remembered lying down in the back of a vehicle bouncing softly over the ruts and instruments and tanks on the walls clanking in their cages, and the ride smoothing out in a surge, and a siren, and Gene there, bent close over him . . . his beat-up, scarred face, wispy beard, and the hard light in his eyes. Gene kept talking to him.

He felt the nurse's breath on his cheek and neck.

—Where was Gene?

—Where was Ron?

—What's wrong?

The nurse straightened and adjusted his arm, touching it lightly, and moved to the bottom of the bed. Above her head on the opposite wall was a TV monitor, switched off and gray. Next to it was a clock—9:46. The nurse reached up to check the attachment of lines to the chrome armature, and ran her fingers down one steel cable to his ankle. She lifted the bedcovers and looked. It was his leg, the reason for his being here. He became aware of a throbbing in it, and considered moving it, but just the thought of such effort made his head swim. He felt the nurse drawing something across the sole of his foot.

"Can you feel that?" She looked up along his body at his face.

"Yes."

"Good. Can you wiggle your toes for me?"

He felt his toes moving in the air.

"Good," she said.

"What is it?" he asked.

"That's good."

To her side was the window and the pearl-colored sky, spitting snow, and in the distance the gap between the two washed-off plateaus that appeared to be precisely the same elevation as the room he was in, so that if the great flood had come through now he might be carried away on its crest in his bed. The valley floor on which the city of Spokane was now built had been under three hundred feet of water. It was fourteen thousand years ago. He remembered perfectly the inexact number.

He rolled his head leftward. Pamela and Travis at that moment came toward him. It was as if they sailed across the room. Travis's face was filled with a sorrowful expression, and Jack felt the need to stop him from feeling that way. Over the top of the empty bed, he saw a doorway open to a custard-colored hallway. At the edge of the doorway, a pair of steel, waist-high tubes appeared, making a clicking noise as they struck the floor.

Pamela grasped his arm above the elbow, and Travis stood next to her. The two of them leaned in against the bed rail.

"We're here, Dad," Pamela said.

"Yes. Thank you."

"Do you remember the timber, now?" she asked.

"Timber?" he said. "What timber?"

"The timber," she said.

"Timber?"

He thought of the mountainside where they'd made their last cut of the season. He heard the distant thunder of the load coming off Bliss's truck, and saw the man with the Derringer in his belt buckle, the reverend Palmer asking over and over—What is it?—and himself pitching toward the floor, the shockwaves of the thudding reverberating. Gene was bent over him. He slipped in and out of consciousness. It was a helicopter.

A few of the pieces cleaved together:

Himself in the quonset hut and Gene bending over him.

Himself in the ambulance and Gene bending over him, and then a hospital.

And then the helicopter and the heavy chop of the rotors breaking the air in a rhythm that reverberated up through the pallet to his body and pounded in his ears, and Gene in it, his face caught in a slant of light, bending over him, and saying he was sorry.

He realized that he'd been airlifted here from somewhere. He'd been shot. Suddenly, a rage cut through him and he raised himself by his elbows. "Tell that fucker, Lamb, that I'll see him in hell before he gets a penny of my money, the son-of-a-bitch!"

Pamela and Travis had different faces from each other. They were a woman fully into her own life and a young man just about to enter his, but out of their blood and the years of their childhood passed in the same habitation, the startled expressions on their faces looked absolutely identical. He remembered that they'd been talking to him before when he'd awakened and the window was dark, and that the sound of their voices had made him think he was back home with them, years ago.

A hand came to rest on his collarbone and shoulder and gently pushed him back down. He rolled his head toward the silvery light. Something ached in his chest. "You need to lie still," the nurse said.

She stood in the shadows in the corner near his head, smiling. "If you're not calm, I'll have to ask your children to leave."

His head swam. He wanted to explain to her that it wasn't what he'd said, that although what had come out of his mouth was a rage, it wasn't even what he'd been thinking . . .

. . . not Lamb . . .

. . . not even Chuck Lamb . . .

. . . but that in his mind exactly as it was in reality, Chuck Lamb was nothing. He was nothing more than an effect of what was actually going on, and the other one . . . Troop . . . Dick Troop . . . and the unnamed one in the pea coat . . . who Jack remembered crouching in the far corner of the hut, also an effect. That was what was in Jack's mind, formed out of feeling and thought and yet still not coherent to him. He couldn't get at what it was . . . like a puma prowling just beyond the light. The nurse lifted her hands to check the juncture of the tubing and droplets of liquid . . . morphine, codeine, or whatever. A dial clicked when she reset it. Each thing she looked at or touched received the benefit of her deliberation.

"What is that?" he said.

"A painkiller. It has morphine. And there's glucose, and a saline. It's all normal procedure. I'm setting your painkiller down a notch," she said. "But if you hurt too much, we can set it back up. You'll feel more alert."

He took it in, not speaking.

She reached out and touched his forehead. She was smoothing something and he felt a twinge. Her stethoscope swung right above his face. When she took her hand away, he touched his forehead with his left hand and found a patch of gauze.

"What is it?" he asked.

"You've got a concussion," the nurse said.

"I see." He felt the patch . . . the black. . . . All that black had condensed into the thing that roved freely within his ache. "It's my leg?"

"Yes," the nurse said. "In a minute, I'm going to look at it."

"I've been shot," he said. He studied his leg which made a low tent out of the bedcovers and was held stationary by its attachment to the armature.

"Yes."

"What happened?"

She stood square to him. "You've had surgery on your leg. You were shot in the chest, too, but the doctors think it was a ricochet. It hit what you had in your shirt pocket and didn't penetrate. You've been bruised. You hit your head falling. You're going to be all right."

"Bruising?"

"Yes. The doctor will be in to answer your questions."

"Bruising in my chest."

"Yes."

"Thank you," he said. "When can I get up?"

"We have to keep you still today, but soon. Tomorrow or the next day we'll try."

"What day is it?"

"It's Monday."

Something roamed in him, its tawniness twisting into the fog of his anesthesia, and it poked its black snout back out through the wall. Its watching filled him with grief . . . Kate. All he could say was, "I've got to get up."

The nurse picked up the chrome plated tree and placed it near the bed. The things hanging from it swung and clinked. "Not yet."

He shifted his gaze from her to the window and stared into the brightening light. The snow was letting up. He took flight into what Pamela's question had made him think about: the trees, the woods, the darkness, the deep, chill, damp pleasure of the woods, and the rock and the snow on the ground, the scuttling nuthatches working over the bark, and his saw cutting a notch in a trunk, the wood chips flooding out to make an aromatic, cream-colored heap on the snow, the tree slowly tilting on its hinge, falling free, hitting the ground, and a cloud of white rising. He closed his eyes.

When he opened them his body jerked. The clock on the wall said 9:51. The nurse was still making adjustments to the apparatus hanging from the tree. He rolled his head toward Pamela and Travis. In the doorway the two chrome poles lifted up and came down again with a click, and a pair of large, mottled hands appeared on the curves at the tops of the poles, then a leonine, white-maned head and a belly leaned ever so slowly into the picture, coming up into the space between the poles . . . a walking apparatus. Somebody was passing. The outlines of steel, hands, head, and belly were lucid as if etched upon the custard-colored wall of the hallway.

"It's Monday?" he asked Pamela.

"Monday morning."

"You mean the forest?" he asked.

"I mean the timber. The wall-tie in our house."

"Didn't you ask about that?"

"Yes. I asked you before. You've been awake several times. You keep talking about it."

"I don't remember," he said, turning his eyes to Travis, whose stolidity and reserve set off the troubled look in his eyes.

"Isn't it the tie that fell off the house?" Pamela said. "I was eight years old, playing in the sandbox with Ron. We were arguing and Mom was scolding us."

"Where is Ron?" he said, this also heaved up out of his inchoacy. He expected Ron to be here. Ron was the erratic luminary in the constellation of three, but without him the balance was off. There was more, the cause of ever expecting all three of them to be gathered as if for a holiday. That would be the reason for his—Jack's—being here, the grievous imbalance about which he was yet afraid to think, or to ask for fear of what it would reveal. He remembered this feeling from other times in his life, the terror of inquiring closely into trouble for the finalities that might emerge . . . when he hadn't heard from Kate after a voyage in bad weather, when Ron had broken his leg, when they'd been unable to reach Ron for a month after he'd left for Alaska, and again for two months when, without telling them, he had gone fishing. Jack always did inquire, though, even when he knew it was too late to stop whatever calamity there might be, and even if it meant watching someone you loved . . .

. . . Kate . . .

. . . step into danger.

"Ron is on his way," Travis said. "We've talked to him. He's coming."

Jack searched Travis's face.

"What I remember comes after," Pamela said. "Maybe I remember the tie hitting ground, but I know I remember the expression on Mom's face. Ron doesn't remember what happened. I've asked him. And of course Travis doesn't, but we all remember the stories about it that you and Mom kept telling over and over again to explain it to yourselves. The stories changed a little each time except for the thing at their heart. That's the important part."

Jack barely followed what she was saying, yet so prodded, his memory conjured up the swinging boom he'd built years ago out of timbers . . . three making a tripod, and then two more making the boom that was joined to a heaviest timber in the tripod, and pivoted on it, and bolted together at the far end. He ran a hook off the end by cable and pulley and operated it with a hand winch. Along with the gin pole he'd put on the other side of the house, the swinging boom was used to lift mortar and rocks as the walls of the house were raised, but that time he'd attached log tongs to lift the tie two stories high.

They were making ready to install the roof. He remembered the sensations with absolute clarity from years ago: the heat of the late August day, the pleasing, desiccate scent of earth, withering plants, the sandbox they'd put at the edge of the woods and out of the way of the work for the kids to be safe in, the beauty of the swinging boom made out of simple materials, the feel of the wooden winch handle, the rockwork of the house in its curve, and the long late afternoon shadow cast by the boom across the ground and bent up the side of the house. He'd lifted the first of the peeled ties. He'd winched up the second and his body remembered the strain on his muscles, winding the winch, the pleasure in that and in having devised the apparatus to work just right, and the log pivoting on the tongs against the trees as it rose and swung around to the clear sky high above the wall, and then descending gently to rest on the lintel where it and the other ties would hold the house together.

"Of course," he said.

He writhed inwardly at what he also remembered, the horror of the coming moment.

"What I remember," Pamela said, "is the look on Mom's face when she took a step back from where you'd pulled her clear of the timber. She was holding Travis."

He realized it must have been the cartridge case hidden in the niche he'd made at the end of the wall tie that he'd talked about during the night. What it meant . . . the only thing it could mean . . . came out, then, the words lightly enough spoken but holding everything he had to say: "Where is your mother?"

Pamela set her chin. She was like her mother, taking her time to get to the point. She wore a dark brown sweater. Her hair, the color of her mother's, was pulled back in a French knot. She was an attorney and looked like one in her neat clothes, and her purposeful air, also like her mother's. "It's okay. I'm listening," he said, trying to hold himself back. The thing in him was circling his ache. "Damn it, Pam, where is your mother?"

"We think we know," she said.

Travis said. "I got a call after you and Gene went down to the compound. Two calls. I should have come straight after you when I got the first one. Gene's gone to get her."

"Get her?" Even as he was being reassured, he veered into the treacherous ground: Dead? Not dead? She's not dead? But not saying that, he turned it instead, saying, "She's okay? What? Travis!" Again, he tried to lift himself, but the nurse placed one hand carefully on his shoulder to hold him down. He lay back as the surge kept rising in him. "Gene? Where's Gene? What? What do you mean? Tell me!" He felt the full force of what he'd been afraid of, and an upper stratum in him came fully awake, as if the front of his brain, bright, thin, and snapping with circuitry, had been sliced out and left to greet the askew world while the rest of him was left struggling to climb clear of the drugs and gnawing pain.

Travis took a deep breath and let the air out slowly, then touched Jack's knee. "She's missing. But we know where she might be. It's somebody named Clinton U who called me," he said. "Twice. He called twice."

The name bumped against something Jack remembered . . . an associate of Kate's, or a past superior, or something, somebody. "What?"

"The second time he told us where Mom is," Travis said. "Gene's gone after her. Gene thinks it's all his fault. And the police are looking, too." He reached over to a chair near the foot of the bed, opened a newspaper and held it up. There was a photograph of a burning cross and a headline that said:

LORD'S WEAPON—32 JAILED, ONE DEAD

At the top of a second column was another caption:

AREA SCIENTIST MISSING IN BC

Seeing his terror blocked out in a newspaper shocked Jack. What had been kept hidden in him had broken out as a beast.

"That's your mom?" he asked. "Missing? It's Monday. It's been three days?"

"Yes," Travis said. He put the newspaper down and looked back at his father. His eyes appeared deeply fatigued and old. Jack was driven straight back into his desperation. It hurt. He didn't want to hurt. He didn't want Travis, Pamela, or Ron to be hurt. He wanted Kate back, unhurt. He wanted the hurting to stop. "She's alive?" he said, the words thick in his throat. "My God, she's not safe yet?"

"This isn't good," the nurse said from behind his head, and then the two voices of the women went back and forth over the top of him as if he were nothing lying between them.

Pamela said, "He's asking what he most wants to know. That's good."

"If you're going to upset him, you'll have to leave," the nurse said.

"You're right, thank you," Pamela said. "He won't get more upset now. We know what we're doing. We're not leaving. We have to answer that question for him."

"I'll have to call security if you don't follow my instructions," the nurse said.

Pamela's eyes glinted just as her mother's would have. Even Travis gazed sternly across at the nurse, and Jack pictured the nurse's face gathering itself against such formidability.

"Fine," Pamela said. "Go ahead."

There was a pause in which Jack half-expected Pam to add—"But if you do, watch out." She didn't. His eyes were filled with tears, and yet he was also beguiled by the antic element of Pamela and Travis being who they were, refusing to do things by the book, spurning authority, even here following what he'd always preached to them: Remove all forms of repression. He felt the nurse's hand slide to the soft of his waist, just above the hip. "I'm going to change your pad and dressing. I need you to help."

His head swam as he rolled it back. He reached up with his left hand and wiped the tears from his eyes, then looked down his right leg when the nurse raised the sheet. There was a strap around his ankle from which the cables that attached him to the armature emerged. A tube lay across his lower thigh. He was wrapped in bandages up over his hip. His leg seemed disembodied. He craned his neck and saw a bloodstained pad under his hip. The nurse leaned toward him, her cheeks flushed.

She looked up toward Pamela and Travis, and said, "He's upset."

"Yes, but not at what we're saying." Pamela had softened her tone, now soliciting the nurse's understanding. "Don't you see? What we're telling him is that things are much better than they were when he was brought here. He should not wake up again without knowing that. He is not a fool. He's our father. He thrives on clarity."

Jack thought about how he'd lived the last few days to this moment, racked with doubt and confusion. He felt deeply relieved and honored that Pamela would perceive him in that way.

As the nurse adjusted the tubing, it pulled at his innards. It was a catheter. She slipped one hand under his gown to the small of his back. "I need you to lift up a little," she said. "Use your shoulders and arch your back, if you can. If it hurts you, stop, and we'll find another way." She picked up a pillow with her right hand and gently lifted him. He did what she said and felt what without the painkillers would likely have been a bolt of pain running from his hip into his side, down nearly to his knee, and a searing in his chest. The sharp ache of the motion made him gasp. Quickly, the nurse slid the pillow under the small of his back. "There," she said. She pulled her hand out. "Good." She checked the catheter again, then rested her hand on his thigh. "Now, if you can tip to the left. Just a little."

He tipped, rolled his head away from her, and felt her hand stopping him when he'd gone far enough.

"Good," she said. "It'll just take a couple of minutes."

Through the doorway, he watched the trembling hands raise the walker. The aluminum legs lifted and clicked down again several inches forward. The body of an old man moved into the walker as he slid his feet under him. He had short legs, a long torso, and a head full of shaggy white hair that fell down nearly to his shoulders. His arms trembled. The sash of his gown hung at his side, so that it lay open at the back. It was also pulled forward by his belly, leaving one lean leg and a narrow buttock exposed. Slowly, he revolved his head to look into Jack's room. The man had a broad face, wide at the jaw, thick, silvery eyebrows, tawny skin, and dark sorrowful-looking eyes. His heavy lips were set in determination.

"It was the look on Mom's face," Pamela said.

He shifted his gaze to her.

"You pulled her out of the way of the timber."

"Yes," he said, sailing back into her story as the pad was drawn out from under his hip, and then something else—a fresh pad—slipped back under. He remembered the timber having rested high on the lintel and himself down below at the boom, tweaking the cable to nudge the timber in a little so that it would be easier to maneuver.

"It was a small thing, in a way," Pamela said. "You blamed yourself."

"Yes." The guilt that nicked through him was guilt of a certain order, not guilt for something wrongfully willed, a premeditated evil, or even a grievous negligence, but a passing everyday failure to address a condition and to remember one's own frailty, followed by a small error of judgment that had the potential to cause the savagery of the world to rush in, as with Travis, forgetting to tell Travis to be sure to let Jim Bliss come down the logging road ahead of him. Not for the first time, Jack wondered how one could possibly be ready for such things. "Why are you telling me this?"

At his back, he heard the nurse sigh, as if to say: Good question.

"When you pulled Mom back," Pamela said, "and when she realized what had happened, or almost happened, you should have seen her face. Fate had just grazed her, winging by, but there she stood, alive with her baby in her arms."

Segments of it flashed by him—the two kids arguing in the sandbox, and Kate turned toward them, shushing them, the jangling of the voices, and her face lurching back in his direction because she was already upset with him for pushing too hard on the construction of the house. It was so that she was where she shouldn't have been, overseeing the kids and trying even in that moment to get him to slow down, and he wasn't paying close enough attention to what he was doing, and when he looked up to the lintel he saw one side of the log tongs slip free of its bite on the timber because he'd given it too much slack. The timber rolled a little toward the edge. Without thinking, he'd seen what was about to happen, that the timber was going to break loose and drop straight down to where Kate stood, holding the baby. Still without thinking, he was moving, ducking under the tripod and grabbing Kate by the back of her shirt, and yanking her back away. The log plummeted and thudded heavily against the ground right where she'd been.

"You remember that?" he said, the tears filling his eyes once again.

Pamela held his arm again below the elbow and leaned in toward him. Her own eyes were bright with emotion, and Jack felt a misgiving: Maybe there was something she wasn't telling him, after all. There was something fearful and premonitional in her eyes, awash as they were with coming tears. Travis stood next to her, still touching his knee.

"I remember the look on Mom's face," Pamela said. "The rest of it is from hearing you and Mom talk about it for years after. Mom brought it up a couple times to show how you were pushing her just like you'd been pushing back then, and once you told her that if she hadn't been there in the first place, none of it would have happened. The story kept changing. It was never exactly the same except that the timber fell, you pulled her away, and that you loved each other." She dabbed at the corners of her eyes with her fingertips and smiled at him. "I remember how you'd laugh about it in a weird way as if you were affirming your luck, and how you'd get very quiet after you were done laughing, and then just look at each other."

"Yeah," he said. He remembered when Kate had turned to him, how they'd hugged in silence with the baby between them, and how she'd felt frail in his arms.

He felt strained from holding the tipped-up position. Pain went down his hip and leg, and he had a patch of pain in his chest. Bending his right wrist, he touched the place through his gown . . . no bandages, but sensitive on the outside, and inside something shifting.

"The one to the chest didn't hurt me?" he asked.

"It's bruised," the nurse said as she applied something cold to the wound on his leg. "We need to watch it."

Travis reached into his shirt pocket, took out a smile pile of CD cases held together by a rubber band and showed it to Jack. "Look," Travis said.

The cases had a jagged hole jammed through them.

Travis drew the cases back and shook them, making them rattle. "The slug's in there. The CD cases stopped it. Can you believe that?"

"The others?" Jack asked.

Travis understood the question perfectly: "They're upstairs where you took them back, right?"

"Right. I guess that's what I meant," Jack said, thinking about the disks and CDs safe in the cache behind the pumice and underneath the end of the log-tie. He was going to explain it, but stopped himself because it was so complicated and because . . . even now, in his extremity . . . he remembered he didn't want anyone else having the burden of knowing about the hiding place. The two things about the log, one of which he must have been talking about in his delirious, drug-heavy sleep, had jumped together. Pamela had understood it to be the other thing.

Within an hour after the log had fallen, he'd cleared everybody well away and ginned it back up, set it in the notch, and climbed up to secure it, ferociously turning in the lag bolts through it to the sill at both of its ends. In that fashion, he'd made its menace go away.

In the doorway, the old man with the walker hunched over his hand-holds. With a heroic motion he pulled the walker up off the floor and dropped it several inches forward. He stayed put for a few seconds, tipped toward the walker, and struggled to hold his angle. His arms quivered. Finally, he shuffled his feet, laboriously bringing his body to something approximating balance. His backside was visible from within the open gown, and he revolved his head to see into the room again, nodding tremulously, opening his mouth in a gaping, exultant grin.

"So?" Jack said to Pamela.

"So, it was a mistake," she replied. "And you acted in time."

"Yeah," he said. Then something else knocked in him, and to Travis he said, "Wait. U is an oil executive."

"The first time he called he left a message telling Mom to watch out," Travis said. "There was a lot of interference."

That wasn't all. From way back just before he and Kate had married, Jack remembered Kate telling him there'd been a Chinese executive on board the research ship whom she had found interesting. He was curious about everything, she said, gentle, brilliant, and ill-suited for serving as the armature of powerful forces. Jack remembered that he'd felt she found the man a little more interesting than she needed to. He and Kate had never breached each other in that way, though, yet even now, out of an ancient mandate, which was the necessity to protect his own, and as he lay there half-groggy and in pain with the disquieting shifting and fluttering in his chest and the nurse working on him, he nevertheless willed himself to rise up.

"So then?" he said.

"He says he thinks she got away," Travis said. "He gave us directions to where she could be . . . 'on the best authority,' he said. He said he was still making calls."

"Oil," Jack said, feeling a whip of anger. "Did he say anything about ZAQ?"

Travis shook his head. "He said he was calling from Anchorage. He said he was on his way to Seattle and that he'd call again. He said to tell you and Mom he's sorry and he believes in mercy. 'Tell them I believe in mercy,' he said. What's that supposed to mean?"

"Mercy?" Jack said.

"I told Dan Painter."

"About mercy?"

Travis' lips twitched with a smile. "No, that somebody named U called."

"Oh. And Gene?"

"He shot Lamb, but he's been released. Travis retrieved the paper and pointed at the ONE DEAD part of the headline. "Lamb," he said. "He was trying to rip you off, Gene said. Dan told Gene to stay home, but Gene told me to tell you he's going to find her or be damned." Travis touched Jack's knee again.

"Bud Willy?"

Travis shrugged. "We don't know."

"The woman . . . what's her name?"

"Winona," Travis said. "We don't know about her, either."

"Troop?"

"Who?"

"Richard Troop and his goon. They broke into our house."

"Oh, yeah. He's named here somewhere."

Travis peered at the newspaper and Jack sank deep into himself. The elements of the incomprehensibility were like fronds growing underwater, thick as a kelp forest, twisted into each other and catching the bent light. Kate was swimming amongst them down low where their stalks entered the ooze. Jack turned his eyes to Pamela and summoned his strength once more: "ZAQ Petroleum, remember that. Richard Troop. And a woman named Sophia Kopat, too. Mom may need your help."

"Sure, Dad."

"Ron's coming?"

"He's on the way right now," Pamela said.

"I want Ron here," he said, remembering the troubled times with his middle child, the skeptic and rebel of the three.

"He's coming."

"Are you sure you don't know more than you're telling me?" he said.

"We're telling you the truth about the bad," Pamela said. "It is that you've been hurt and we don't have Mom back yet, and that there's reason to hope."

"It says Troop works for a private security company," Travis said, lowering the newspaper. "He's been questioned and released in his attorney's custody. The other one's in the hospital. Oh, yeah, Abby Leonard called. She's okay, but she thinks somebody's been watching her. She just got back from a research cruise. Someone hacked into her university computer and it crashed, she says. She's got police protection."

Pamela touched Travis's arm, restraining him from going on. She still held Jack's arm with her other hand and she leaned toward him, speaking intently. "Travis says you've been blaming yourself. But you had hardly any control over what happened. You took what action you could and that is never wrong."

"I know," Jack said, feeling another clarity bending out to take its shape, a clump breaking loose and riding up to the surface on a current like a flotsam from the land of the dead. It was marked for his children. In a passing sparkle of recognition, he thought it explained everything. He wanted to be certain his children knew it for what it was. "Listen," he said, once again calling upon his reserves. "It's the big thing out there. It's trickle-down horror. Finally, it'll be the crazies of the world and the multinationals riding the conduits of state, grinding down on the blood and bones of the world, and letting the ooze seep into countless little personal horrors on people like us, informed nobodies, and worse, too . . . far worse . . . the masses of uninformed, guileless nobodies. Mom is going to need your help fighting it."

Saying all that left him spent.

"She'll have our help," Pamela said. "Don't ever forget that you've already saved her life, once . . ."

"Many times," Jack murmured. "And she mine, many times." He was thinking of the numberless life-saving gestures of his long matrimony, all the affirmations that saved a life by granting it its vitality and independence.

"All right," Pamela said. "Between you and Gene and the police, you'll have done it again."

"Gene's gone?" he asked.

"He got one of his old vet buddies to fly him over to B.C. early this morning," Travis said.

"Good." Jack believed absolutely in Gene's fierce tribalism.

"Don't ever forget that you two have a great love story. You're going to see her." Pamela turned her eyes across to the nurse, then back to him, and slipped her hand down his arm to grasp his hand.

"Do you believe your Mom's alive?"

"You bet that's what we believe."

He lay still. Pamela had her mother's singularity of purpose, but it seemed her mind worked like his, sojourning out to the edges and rooting around to find things to carry back and pile up to make her point. She was an immigration lawyer. Her work was to help those caught in the cracks between nations. He was proud she was his daughter.

The man in the doorway was still looking into the room, his mouth in an open grin, his thick eyebrows arched into chevrons. The antic bedlamites out there had sent an emissary to Jack.

The nurse tugged gently on his side and said, "You can straighten out now."

She slipped the pillow clear. Carefully, he rolled back and lay flat while she finished taping over the top of his leg. He looked down at the fresh white pad and gauze patch and translucent tape. "What happened to me?"

The nurse gazed at him for a moment, as if searching out his question. "You have a gunshot wound. It damaged your pelvis, and the surgeons had to do some reconstruction."

"Thank you." His own voice sounded distant.

She bent and ran the tape to the inside of his leg. Her stethoscope hung above him and from within her blouse a silver cross slipped out and swung on its chain, afire in the light of the room. He stared freely and comfortably at the crisp white of her lapels, the top fringe of her white brassiere, and at the smoothness of her skin. Lying there, held rapt by the widening perturbation he felt within him, now—a constriction that sent its signal through his body, it felt as if something were softly raking its claws through the bottom—he also sensed his sexuality, not in its acuteness, but as a muted, ceremonial feeling remembered for its fitness and fine mystery. In the corner of his eye the red indicator light ticked rhythmically. The green line with its ridge points marched across the monitor.

Maria Cordero—he read once again.

—Very strange, he thought. Lamb.

"You need to sleep, now," she said, straightening up.

The clock said 10:03. He looked at the spray of out-of-season purple and white flowers on the sill, and through the window saw a brightening sky and in the distance the line of hills and the two plateaus. The very word, "sleep," confirmed his trajectory as he sank into his own broken-up world. He closed his eyes and saw the elk hanging from the hook, the ranks of jars filled with tomatoes, the snow on the ground, the upstairs timber neatly notched into its bracket, and then he felt the reverberant blackness within him, something in his blood welling up and his heart skipping, and suddenly his nostrils filled with the sere scent of the dry, late summer earth. Kate stood there in her shorts and loose shirt, holding the baby close, and she narrowed to smallness in his arms and came inside him to the black.

"Dad?" Pamela said. Her voice was far away.

His eyes fluttered open to a dimming world. Pamela's hand held his. Travis's hand touched his knee. The figure of the nurse had turned away to check the traction, leaving one hand trailing on his ankle.

Fronds ripped loose from their holdfast. Something shattered and he writhed, rolling his head. Pamela and Travis floated at the bedside. Her eyes shone while his face twisted with alarm. Past them, the lemon color of the hall turned gray. All that was visible now of the old man was a spectral, bare ass.

Jack felt he had entered into a torrent, the center of him heavy with his organs in the dark, his bowels heaving, and his blood-starved brain collapsing under an implosion while the luminous world beyond his edges rushed by, then sparked out in the dark. It was what, after he was gone, would be called a pulmonary embolism . . . nothing to prevent it, they would explain, no predicting it, no stopping it, no triage fast enough to catch it, a killer for which there was no way to ascribe its cause except as a thing in the blood, an erratic thrombus or coagulation from the wound that jammed a vessel of his heart. The machine's beeping transformed into a hum. The nurse flew out of the room, disappearing into the hall. Pamela cried out, her voice like a faraway gull's, and Travis shouted and reached up to hold Jack's shoulders. His son's hands were there, holding him steady, and staying, fading as Jack rolled his head back to the window and passed on.

The opening between the plateaus was imprinted on his expiring retinae, all of what was now the broad valley in which the city had been built not much more than a hundred years past under what, fourteen thousand years ago, had been three hundred feet of water, the great flood from behind the broken ice dam taking its paths west and southwest from here to the Columbia and the sea, wiping out everything in its course. For him, such a vision might have had the aspect of a petition . . . the apocalyptic and religious desire for a force that would cease all human evil and compel the survivors to conduct themselves in the shadow of such destruction, chastened forever. But that would have been merely the trailings of his wrath, his own body caught for a moment in the remorseless current. He eddied, coming out of the stream . . . coming across the threadline, ferrying the phantom flow toward the dark of the bank . . . white snow gracing the black basalt . . . touching his prow to the world of the dead where the rest of what had been incomprehensible formed itself for him out of the things for which we have our flimsy names . . . unrepentant, or forgiving earth . . . or merciful . . . cruel . . . the ultra-mundane played as wonders in the concord of chaos.

His body racked as something was freed like a sob, his prayer, a bird of the night carried loose on the air of his last exhalation, the nothingness passing easily now into new substance.

23

The Sunrise Invasion

... and this Morning complaining that his Head and Stomach was out of Order, he asked for a little Medicine, which was given him; but finding it did him neither good nor Harm, he called his Wife to him where he was sitting amidst us, at a large Fire we had made to warm ourselves. She readily came: he asked her if she had a sharp Flint, & upon her replying she had not, he broke one and made a Lancet of it, with which he opened a Vein in her Arm, she assisting him with great good Will; having drawn about 3/4 pint of Blood from her into a wooden Bowl, to our Astonishment he applied it to his Lips quite warm, & drank it off—what of the Blood adhered to the Vessel he mixed with Water, so as to clean it, and also drank off.

While I was considering from whence so savage an Action could arise, one of our Men with Indignation exclaimed to our Guide, I have eaten & smoked with thee, but henceforward thou and me shall never eat & smoke together—what, drink warm from the Vein the Blood of your Wife? Oh oh, my Friend, said the Indian, have I done wrong?—when I find my Stomach out of order, the warm Blood of my Wife in good Health refreshes the whole of my Body & puts me to rights; in return, when she is not well I draw Blood from my Arm, she drinks it, it invigorates & gives her Life. All our Nation do this, and all of us know it to be a good Medicine; is this the first Time you have seen it—from whence comes your Surprize, my Friends?

—David Thompson, while crossing the Canadian Rockies, 1801

*   *   *

Coming out where the river broadened, and by then in a walking stupor, profoundly fatigued, Kate veered into a dark thicket where the ice crackled under her boots. The weed, bush, and small tree grew thick, and the limbs and prickly vines snarled in her coat and pack, sometimes whipping her face or snagging the skis that dragged behind her. After struggling for a time, she stopped to catch her breath, standing absolutely still, and in that pause, as in her experience had so often been the case . . . the pause in the travail creating an opening through which the world might rush . . . there was a scratching sound right next to her ear, and then suddenly an explosion of noise, a heavy scrabbling and thudding as if of something big, too big to be so low in a tree, crashing as it broke loose. She jumped up off the ground and shouted in surprise as the shape loomed right next to her head, causing the air to beat against her face. Then it passed upwards as a long-winged glint in the night. It was an owl, probably a snowy owl, threatened by her pause and in it leaping out of its own, deep, animal repose as a bird of omen. Startled from her daze and breaking through the thicket another few steps, she saw the pewter-colored pale of the lake's surface before her.

At first she walked, then skied on the lake, but, not trusting the ice, stayed near its edge at what she assumed were the shallows where the cold from the earth extruded more certainly into the water. Sometimes, she had to slow to pick her way around boulders that loomed before her, and sometimes, doing this, she had to go into the willows, as well, and again break her way through. When possible, she employed the skis as skates, merely ticking through the snow to the surface of the ice with her poles as a reminder of where the balance of her body should lie. As the night began to pass into dawn, she could see the changes in the hue of the ice toward the center like a streaked piebald, and that the highland on her right had moved away from the floodplain. Perspective was tricky in the equivocal world of black peeling into gray, gray into dusky white, and she, too, had been tricked out by the owl into a jagged alert that felt feverish and flimsy, built as it was upon the increasing torpor of her body.

In the distance, she could see the flat and the sheen of the lake passing into a dark hump of landform in the shape of a pig, but whether the lake ended there or shunted off to spread in another direction, she could not tell. She could only guess at the size of the lake—probably bigger than she would have liked. As time passed, she seemed not to come the least bit nearer to the hump. She was cold, her shoulders ached, and her legs felt spongy. She feared she was nearing the margin where her will to continue hung in an ever more precarious balance against the cold and fatigue. But somewhere out there the lake ought to drain into the North Thompson.

*   *   *

Mad Lake.
The North Thompson.
Tracks.
Blue River.

*   *   *

The last of those she believed to be a river as well as a town, once a fur-trading post, she imagined, and now no doubt a ski outpost. The third, the tracks, must be Canadian National Railroad tracks built first to carry ore to the smelters, now freighting coal one way and the other way supplies from Vancouver or Seattle to the tar sands, always following openings made in the topography by rivers. The second, the North Thompson, named for the man, the usher of nationhood, whom she pictured with his bad eye, laconic manner, and brilliance, sighting a survey down the lunatic straightedge of the forty-ninth parallel here in the homeland of the Kootenay. The river she knew to be large. She might have to cross it, dare its ice or find a bridge.

Kate had surmised these things from within the keep of the rhythm of her difficult progress to this point. She must be somewhere in the Columbia Mountains, west of the Canoe Reach, maybe west of the northernmost edge of the Columbia Reach, as well. The North Thompson flowed into the West Thompson, thence into the Fraser. If correct, all of that put her somewhere she still couldn't fathom, considering how long she'd spent prone in the bed of Bud's Power Wagon when they were driving her to the house. Not enough time seemed to have passed driving back westward and northward to where she thought she was, which also made her wonder if she'd not skied just some portion of the twenty miles Bud had said she should, but maybe fifty miles, or even if the directions were a falsehood meant to send her out to die. But little of that mattered, now, on her tiny island of necessities. What mattered was the detail of her access to Blue River, if there was a Blue River here, and whether or not she could cross the North Thompson, if indeed she was coming near it. Into that shaky conjecture she made her approach.

At her back, the first true light of dawn broke through the membrane of night, bringing a pale golden color to the air. It burnished the snow and ice, and looking out to the lowlands before her and to the south, Kate saw clearly that she had entered a very large watershed. The mountains in the distance to the west were old ones, rounded as the Columbias would be, and outlined in great white folds as if pasted onto the sky. Without turning to see, she knew the ones behind her were the precipitous, much younger Rockies. She was at a margin of the landform. The lake had been formed in a trench on a long, inclining glacially gouged hollow, which had the effect of making the surface of the lake look as if it were tilted sideways. In the sharpening light, the snow at the lake's edge gleamed, broken along its line by the dark faces of rocks. The white ran up over the bank to the edge of the woods. More margins. Her shadow began to take a hazy substance upon the bank, giving the shape of her body, its bend and lean, a far more graceful appearance than she thought possible in her shuffling march. Her feet and fingers had grown numb again. Even as the world became more visible, invading her in all its monumentality, her mind sheared back into the tipsy equipoise between her will to press ahead and her wish to stop. She was afraid, afraid for herself and desperately so for Jack, Ron, Travis, and Pamela. They seemed to surround her, waiting tremulously and watching for what would happen. She knew she had to form a line of action, that she must follow it, and that in this extremity it had to be right.

Her refrain, so far, had been: Keep skiing to the west!

She crossed the trail of a snowshoe hare, reaching across the lake, and then another trail looping out from the bank and coming back. She saw the fresh hoof prints of a caribou. She discovered herself looking for a place to stop and spied one just ahead, a little ways up the bank to her right. There was a piece of high ground, a large rock that caught the sun, and not far behind it the trees. Without thinking, or thinking of it only as something she might consider, a compromise solution in which she might stop long enough to warm herself in the sun, eat what remained of her food, and possibly even build a fire, but hardly deciding upon it, and then quite abruptly accepting it as what she was already doing, she executed a lumbering turn to the right and stepped toward the bank.

At the edge of the lake she removed the skis, left them and the poles, and walked up the bank to the rocks. She slipped off her pack, zipped it open, laid it down in the snow and looked into it: the knife Bud had returned to her in the darkness at the bottom, matches, flashlight, oatmeal, the last clump of raisins in a plastic bag. She picked up the oatmeal box and poured a small pile of the cereal into the palm of one glove, bent to the glove, and licked up the flakes. They were dry. She put snow in her mouth, dug out the raisins, and chewed on them as she stared down along the strangely tilted-looking lake to the pig-shaped hump that seemed utterly and hopelessly no nearer than before.

She brushed the snow away from the shaded side of the rock with one glove, and went back down to the edge of the lake and returned with her skis and poles. At first sweeping away as much snow as she could with a ski, bending and grunting with the labor, she then used the butt of the ski as a trowel to dig at the hard snow. With the prong of a pole she broke up the snow, and scraped at it with the ski until she could see the icy blue gravel. She knew what she was doing but had hardly thought it. Her body and groping mind had informed her of this line of action: Clear away the snow on the high ground behind the rock, dig out a cavity to hold a fire and herself, build a fire, build up walls at the sides, position herself near the fire and in the sun, try to warm herself, and maybe get some rest. Then she could go on to the west. She laid her skis and poles down in the snow and walked up to the tree line, feeling her feet underneath her knees nearly insensate.

She picked lichen from the trunks of trees, snapped off twigs, and found clumps of dead needles low enough in the firs to reach, even a cedar from which she could strip ribbons of bark. These she carried to the rock, then went back to the woods to get more, and again, each time penetrating a little deeper into the woods. At the rock, she had a pile on one side of her cavity, and she began constructing a tiny tipi—first the dead needles, and lichen, and cedar strips she knew would burn, and then the twigs. Half of what she'd gathered, she held back. She did not light it yet, but returned to the woods in search of larger pieces. She saw a deadfall twenty yards inside, and made her way to it, tripping on unseen things under the snow.

Dizzy with exhaustion, she nevertheless thought her hands might be warming a little. Maybe it was the sun, maybe the changed form of her exertion, maybe the trifle of food she'd eaten. She took off her parka and laid it down to make a pouch. As she began breaking small branches off the deadfall and tossing them onto the parka, she heard something roaring in the stillness, shuddering, and moving away, whining as eerily as the engine of Ansel's snow machine had sounded. She wheeled around, squinting out across the lake, and up into the forest canopy, and dropped the branch she was holding and stumbled to the edge of the woods, looking wildly around and up . . . not sure, not sure what she'd heard. The sound hung far away, somewhere else, over on the other side of the woods, and finally it vanished. She stood staring wretchedly into the sky, wondering if it was an avalanche and its echo, another snow machine, a plane, a phantasm, or like the snowy owl another indecipherable omen of the dawn.

—I've stopped here in order to build a fire. I have to do that, now.

—Once it warms me, I will go on.

She returned to the woods, broke branches from the deadfall, heaped her parka with them, dragged the load to the rock, and also pulled a pair of limbs by the crook of her elbow. She began to shiver again. She dumped the limb and branches to the side and draped the parka over her shoulders, pulled off a glove, and reached for the matches in the backpack and her knife. She set the knife down. She felt the wood of the match against her fingers, but not the cold of the air, which she marked with foreboding. The match lit when she ran it along the side of the box, and when she touched the match to the needles at the base of her kindling, the needles smoldered and flared, and a strip of the cedar curled into a flame. She dropped the matchbox back into the backpack, put the glove on, and hunkered near the fire inside her cavity, watching intently between her knees as the flames hissed through the needles and lichen and cedar to the twigs. The bark on the twigs caught. A puff of white smoke lifted into her face. She heard a soft crackling as the moisture in the twigs heated up and exploded.

She placed a few more bits in the fire, then took the knife from its sheath and shaved curls of wood from a stick and added them. She laid her skis out on either side of her cavity in a V. Moving slowly, laboriously, she pressed them in on their edges so as to make a pair of dams to help keep away what snow might melt. As the fire took hold, she'd have to channel out the thaw. She stood and used the prong of a pole to cut out the beginning of a groove between the fire and the face of the rock, making a drain that passed under the ski she'd set to the left. Putting the pole down, crouching, not sitting yet, not giving in to her exhaustion, she placed more twigs on the fire, more shavings, and some short sticks, leaning them up against each other to make a bigger tipi outside the burning one on the inside. She watched the flames bend and lick up again.

The rock was granite, blown free of snow on its sides. It had a crack jammed full of ice coming down right in front of her, which began to shine as it turned glutinous in the heat. A drop of water fell. Growing transfixed and feeling her head wanting to sag, she stared at the crack until another drop fell. She made herself stand again. Swaying, she brushed the cap of snow from the top of the rock so as to diminish the supply and, clinging to the feeble inertia of her intent, knelt and reached to drag snow to build up the wall of her cavity on the right side. She turned, dragged snow up to the left side, then smoothed off the tops of both walls. She left an opening on her right to reach the fuel, and the left wall low enough for the sun to strike her.

Played out, she dropped into a sitting position. The walls broke the breeze that drifted off the lake while the fire crackled in earnest. She adjusted the parka around her shoulders, edged her feet up near to the fire on either side, and slid forward on her butt, getting as near as she dared. She could feel a little of the heat. Removing a glove, she fumbled to unzip her jacket, opening it to her shirt. She put the glove back on and considered taking off her boots to dry her socks. At her back, nuthatches talked to each other as they worked the trees. She looked across the tilted landscape to the lake, down to the right, then to the left where she'd come from. The shadows in her ski tracks had made dark lines along the lake's edge. She took a deep breath of the cold. In the brightening sky to the south a solitary rough-legged hawk caught a draft and soared westward, the live thing in the air like a mooring to which she might tie her desperation. She pushed up her sleeve from her watch and squinted at the lens, finding that it was much later than she had thought—9:45.

She was in the day now. It was Monday. She had to count back to be sure of that—Monday, Sunday, Saturday the day she'd left home with Winona, and Friday night when she'd discovered Winona on the road. The crystalline snow blazed and hurt her eyes. It blanketed the lake to the dark strips in the center, lay behind her in the woods, on the rounded mountains to the west, and in the distance to the east glinted from the jagged peaks. She picked up a clump of snow and ate it. Compressed in her mouth, it turned to ice, and then slowly began to melt.

She remembered how she loved snow, even found it a comfort, the muffling and bracing chill, the way it changed the world, a purifier like fire. She remembered looking at pictures of it as a girl in the red clay country where it was rare, sparse, wet, and short-lived, and how she'd grown up longing to see the mystery snow of her imagination. That longing she had first fulfilled during her one winter in the mountains of Arizona. Later, she'd seen the snow on Saint Lawrence Island, the snow on the Olympics, the powder high in the Cascades, the Brooks Range, the Maine snow, the Rocky Mountain snow, the blowing around high plains snow, the deep snow at her home in Idaho, the hushed snow in the boreal forest of Northern Canada, the sea-driven snow at Prince Rupert and Ketchikan, Nome, Kotzebue, and Valdez, snow in the Arctic adhering to the now vanishing ice, the dry skiff of snow on the Alaskan tundra stitched by the silvery, needle-like oil pipeline. They intended to extend it into a new gridwork across the west of Alaska, fingers of steel, connectors, pumping stations, long running lines to transport the combustible residue of life itself, and submerging under the ice of the Chukchi to the snow of Siberia, all that mania feeding the breakneck course of empire growing ever the more fragile in its elaborateness, what had caused her to be here trapped in this snow on the bank of what she presumed was Mad Lake.

The thought of it, and of Braun, carrying the menace for the oil companies, and of the hired mercenary, Bud Willy, still seemed outlandish to her. She saw Ansel lying at the bottom of the crevasse, his arms cradling the snow machine in the luminous deep.

—Where is the hope in it?

The hawk was a speck in the far westward sky, looking for small creatures that might move on the snow.

—Things die in the winter.

—If I close my eyes, they might never open again.

She leaned sideways and reached over the snow wall for the pack, fetched the plastic bag from it, filled the bag with snow, sealed up its top and set it near the fire to see if it would make water. She returned her knife to its sheath, its blade still stained with blood. Gazing at the lake, she wondered what fish were in it . . . kokanee, perhaps, and conceivably a few chinook salmon, having battled their way up the Fraser to the Thompson, lake trout, bull trout, maybe whitefish, splake, suckers, minnows, squawfish, and chub. It was hard to say. The names she might give the fish were like dots separated by imponderable space. Naming them or counting (she envisioned the swirls of fingerlings curling out white as blowing snow in the dark of the deep) said nothing of the worlds stitched together by the mysterious trajectories of fish.

She added wood to the fire. The ice in the crack in the rock before her had softened and was slowly dripping behind the fire. Water pooled at the head of the canal she'd dug. She thought of Jack's sunny smile and of how he'd have admired her fire and ice barricade. She held her gloved hands so close to the flames that the synthetic wrap blistered as the fire blazed up around the new pieces. Adding several more sticks, she considered that she should return to the woods for larger chunks, and wondered if that was why she hadn't removed her boots. A good thing to do might be to take her gloves off and hold her bare hands to the heat.

She sat still, doing nothing, watching the glittering water droplets fall behind the orange flames, and felt her extremities having warmed a little. Her fingers hurt, a good sign. The skin of her face had tightened in the dry, and she became aware of the sensitivity of where she'd been hit in the head, the swelling of her knee, the ache of her muscles, but she also marked the coldness in her belly. She felt an almost complacent curiosity over her state: her hypothermia, her fatalism, which she experienced as an almost inviting thing, the attraction of total numbness. She remembered Winona's face on the road home, hanging in the air like a lantern, she, serving the bewitched schism of her being.

—Winona could be dead now.

At times, Kate's own coldness became pleasing, as if everything had been put into slow motion so that she could inquire into the world's raveling.

She saw the snow at Kotzebue, the polar bears rising out of it like clouds articulated by their black snouts and claws, and the children in Moyie, poised on the steps of their stoop, about to leap into the snow. She saw the snow at her home, the roofs all but groaning under its weight, and Jack shoveling it off the edge of the driveway, the sparkling when he tossed it clear. She saw her children, all three of them, the two older ones scooting down the drive on runner sleds past their father, and Travis, a toddler, running after them with his arms in his blue snowsuit sticking straight out from his sides. He pitched face-first into a snowbank, kicked wildly, then worked his way onto his back and lay still. The two older children plummeted into the roadway below. Travis's face was decked out with snow, and otherwise screwed-up with bewilderment. He was hung between breaking into sobs and laughter. He could start to cry any second, or laugh. Then she saw Jack, bending as he'd bent in her dream. He lifted Travis and held him tight.

Before her, water dripped from the crack near the top of the rock. Drops emerged slowly from the bottom of the crack, each one distending into a tiny sausage-shape before falling to the small puddle of slush and bits of wood, charcoal, mud, and gravel between the fire and the rock's base. Because of the notch in the rock on its sunlit edge to her left and its concavity on her side, each drop passed out of shadow, into light, and back into shadow. They glittered in silver flashes one after another. Kate had her face and torso out of the shadow in the sunlight and her legs and feet in the shade near the fire. The drops were like time, each moment, if considered, measured, or remembered, breaking apart and taking on its own fleeting integrity as it fell away from one fluid into the other, the fluid past plummeting into the fluid future.

She picked up a pole, leaned forward, probed around the left side of the fire, and dug at the slush in an effort to keep the moisture flowing down the channel. Beneath the slush lay ice and stones. The small plastic bag had sagged out at its bottom under the weight of an inch of water. Parting the bag's opening, she drank the water, swallowing slowly, refilled the bag with snow, sealed the top, and put it back near the fire. Her fingers inside the gloves had thawed, but her feet still felt leaden. She gazed at her stack of fuel, deciding it would be sufficient for a while, maybe an hour, and added several more sticks.

One at a time she drew her feet toward her, unstrung the boot laces from the hooks, and strained to pull off each boot, first one, the other, then struggled the more, bending double and grunting to work off the damp socks. She stared at her feet. They were tinged blue, chafed, blistered, and otherwise a pallid white. She moved to drape her socks on the rock above the fire on either side of the crack, and as she did that, swinging up to her knees and reaching out clumsily, she didn't even feel her bare feet scraping the cold ground, as if they weren't part of her. Frightened anew, she sat back down, took snow and desperately rubbed it against one foot as long as she could bear, and then the other foot. With both hands she picked up one foot by grasping her leg above the ankle on the damp long john and setting the foot down carefully near the fire, the right one first near the plastic bag . . . not too close to the flames, as she realized she might burn her feet without knowing it. She positioned the other foot and reached for the backpack, lifted herself, and sat on it. Then she was exhausted again. Her hands were cold from rubbing the snow. She held them out toward the fire, resting her quivering arms on her knees, and turned her left wrist to look at her watch—10:05. Time was passing like liquid. She stared at her feet.

—My God!

When she had pulled off her boots, rubbed snow on the feet, reached around to clear the slush in order to protect her fire, or remembered to use the backpack as something dry to sit on, she was a survivor. But when she sank into herself, even drawing as near as she dared to the flames, and fell into the contemplation of water drops, as she did now, and as she felt something crack open within her, a tolling, a sound like a deep bell that filled her with dread and drew her deep into her science . . .

into the *scire* portion of it, the to know,

not into the counting,

but into her trepidated, stunned willingness to know,

into his question . . . *rechercher*,

and in this contemplation asking her question, What is this?

. . . she had entered into courtship with death. She invited death to inform her as she received its invitation to come into its shadow.

Travis lay in the snowbank. Pamela and Ron started back up the driveway, dragging their sleds behind them. They had red snow hats and yellow mittens. Jack hugged Travis close, then held him out by the ribs . . . Kate could feel the toddler's ribs through the suit under her hands, and in another time the leaner ribs of Ron when he was a toddler, and Pamela's ribs jumping around as she gleefully kicked at the air. Jack raised Travis up high over his head and grinned at him. Travis broke into laughter. He chose that. Good. It's good to laugh even if you're hurt. Jack set Travis down, who then wove his way down toward his brother and sister.

The pictures came from her motherhood when the three children were still home and the future was a bright place into which they would safely pass, no matter what strain she and Jack might have felt then from her work and his, the pressure, the building the house, the debt, the coming and going as if they were migratory birds. No matter what the strain, what compromise, they'd been happy living in the heart of the heart of their lives. She heard the distant whine again, the scream. Ansel plummeted into the crevasse, Bud leaned so near her in the doorway that she could smell him, Winona ran out into the lot to meet him, and after a deep percussion the buildings exploded into flames.

She saw her father in Demopolis, the old man's pale, liver-spotted face against the pillow at this moment awakening to his dawn, and years ago, her mother, Xaviera, sitting in the bow of the rowboat, near her death in the heat of the late summer. On weekend evenings before the end, she would take her mother out in the rowboat, floating past the fossil-ladened Ecor Blanc to the red cliffs, past the town to the quarry and railroad yard, to the black neighborhoods where old men and women fished from the banks for catfish. Her mother had taken up a deep fascination for all this, the smoky, glandular, slow water of the Black Warrior, the heat in the air, the big scabrous carp that rose to roll ponderously on the surface of the river, the throbbing, electric howl of cicadas from the trees, the brilliantly colored songbirds in the bush on the banks, kingfishers dropping like stones from branches to catch their prey, and water birds, herons and ibises come up out of the delta, and for the children who played in a long, languorous eddy south of town, their dark bodies sparkling in the light. Her mother loved to pause to watch the children in the shallows.

On one of their last excursions, as Kate nosed the boat out of the eddy to begin rowing back upstream, her mother pulled herself straight by the gunwales. Her eyes glimmered in her haggard face. "This place, your father's South, has long been broken. Repairing the wrong was your father's struggle. It was his home. I had to take you away for a time. We were afraid for you and we had our troubles between us, too. The hatred here was too much for me. It was too much to be caught in it the way I was. I know now that this disease was beginning way back then. But if you go to Cañon de Chelly, then you'll see that all places are finally too strong for destruction. That place makes it clear that there are things that cannot be extinguished. And never forget how this place also has its beauty."

Her mother died in September, what evinced itself as a cancer of the breast and spread to wrack her body. The next June Kate went to the canyons and hiked through them, seeing the old mysterious trailways up and down the jutting cliffs, the neatly planted peach trees, hogans, beat-up pickup trucks parked outside, the bleating of sheep echoing against the rock chambers, crows crying, all the irregularity of landform in its blazing orange and red and sear chalk-color, and the old lives marked by rock paintings and glyphs . . . digging stick figures, bird-head figures, impaled sheep, the dancing man with flute, horsemen, the large handprints, and the upside-down stick man plummeting to certain death. The ancient habitations of a people passed away into mystery, the Anasazi, were built into the canyon walls above the meandering waterway. Her mother had chosen to honor that one-quarter of her ancestry and she allowed herself to be furious about the old desecrations, which she saw as inextricably bound up with her husband's troubles in Alabama as the black people there rose ineluctably up out of their chains . . . the clattering cane. Here, the Navajo, or Diné, breathless as some of them were after escaping the Civil War attack and then years of exile in the reservation on the Pecos River, now still pulled themselves up by the handholds along the precipitous trails. It was a codex of a certain history. The cañones and the arduous way out from imponderable depths made her mother's belief in inextinguishable spirits come alive.

There was a faint tinge of pink around Kate's ankle bones and toes. Her feet had begun to ache. She shifted her torso, slowly breathed in and out, filling the void in her with air, and looked at her watch—nearly 10:30. She thrust her hand into her jacket pocket, underneath the parka, and ran her thumb along the belly of her tiny leaping fish. She envisioned salmon in their roseate state like overblown, wilting flowers coming apart in decay, the fish riding up the river, dying. Under the lake's ice there might be eggs with black, absorbent eyes growing on them, light sensors, or there might be alevins with the big eyes and bodies like scraps of lace beginning to drop out of the translucent orange yolks. They would be suspension feeders for a while, floating through the knowledge of their home, learning even its extinctions.

She would need to fetch more fuel. If her feet recovered, or even if they had not, she might soon think about making her way west. She gazed down the tilted lake at the distant, pig-shaped hump, the landmark of what she did not know, and at her socks, steaming on the side of the rock, and then, nearly hypnotized, into her fire. It had white coals at its bottom, then red coals, and blue and yellow flames twisting like pennants. If there were chinook in the lake, or even the memory of them coming here on their journey, this would be a good place to die.

*   *   *

Mad Lake.
The North Thompson.
Tracks.
The town . . . Blue River.

*   *   *

Jack leaned near her, bringing his face close, brown beard, quizzical eyes, and dark skin washed by the glare off the snow, a look of faint amusement, and his hair snapping out from under his blue stocking cap.

Astonished by his appearance, Kate thought: It's the brain of the world I'm contemplating.

—I'm entering the deep science where to know is in the old way, not by the counting and naming. Everything is in ribbons, the ribbon-like planes of all the seen and unseen worlds, passing through the dark and the light, sparking white electric phosphorescence and the carbonized black, twisting tapes of implosion, all weaving together. She looked at her feet, which ached. Looking caused the ache to increase, the pain intensifying to such a pitch that she bent double. From the distance a raven cawed. Kate arched her back, sucked at the air, and turned toward a sound of fracturing ice. Four caribou, a chocolate-colored bull with a full rack and three lightly colored cows, stepped out from the woods behind her and trailed through the snow toward the lake. The bull and his small harem came near enough for her to hear a fugue in the sound of their hooves on the ice and the clicking sound of their ankle tendons snapping past the bones. The hawk reappeared, circling.

Jack crouched at the opening of her cavity near the pile of sticks. It was as if he had altered the draft by his position so that the smoke wafted into his face, then curled across to hers. That much seemed palpable. She leaned to take up a limb, broke pieces off it, and added them to the fire, and also a bit of spruce bough that had green needles on it. The needles flared, casting off oily threads of aromatic smoke.

"You should rub your feet again," he said.

She bent forward, rubbing snow on her feet, first one and then the other. The pain was excruciating.

"And drink," he said.

She drank off the water that had collected in the bag.

Jack's head lifted as he looked toward the caribou that now stood in the snow at the edge of the lake. The bull and one cow prodded at the ice over the shallows, breaking it open. Past them to the east lay the clearing and the stand of reed and bush, a good place for an encampment near the water and wood stores, everything required for building a long house, a place just beyond in the spaced-out trees for picketing horses and hanging the buffalo hides, the reeds good for twining things together, baskets and nets, and the willows good for cutting branches to make snares and a long weir to place in the river for the fish that might ascend, playing out their part in the traffic of the world. It was a good place for people to be. Rising above it was the dark funnel-shape of the tree line from which Kate had emerged. It led up the canyon to the flat above the rapids and to the tongue of the glacier. In the distance beyond this margin she was in, the jagged, snow-covered peaks etched with seismic lines of exposed, blade-like rock pierced the blue sky.

Before her, flames licked from the coals to ignite the new sticks. The thaw fell drop-by-drop from the rock. Over at the shallows to her left, caribou effected shattering breaks in the ice. A spider crept alongside the crack, pausing halfway up.

"I'm sorry," she said, looking down at the front of the bloodstained shirt under her unzipped jacket, what he had given her with its fancy bone buttons. "I'm so sorry."

He gave her a sideways glance. "Save the buttons."

She understood—what she'd understood and accepted immediately, and understood anew in this next pause—that his appearance was yet another step in their decades of courtship, not a phantasm but an inquiry into the world of meshing planes, an emanation of the not easily seen she'd always known should be there. She knew this by the openings in what she had conjectured from girlhood as her Mexican fence, and later through knowing about how at the edges of all transepts and even within the bounds of her and Abby's advanced design, there must be a wild conduct going too fast to be tracked by empirical constructs. The monkish conjecture that her science or her own life could be unyoked from the pace of the world was an idiocy. Out of the pause she was in, as if her heart had stopped for a moment, and yet warming her feet and calves, her hands clutched together at her belly, and her buttock muscles and lower back straining against the pain of her own thaw, or out of the ripped-open hole in the molecular order of her being here in this outlandish station of her mortality, arose the complete sadness of what appeared before her. She wanted him to touch her. She wanted him to rub her feet.

"I'm so sorry for what I've done."

"No," he said.

She was trembling. "In my stubbornness. I'm so sorry."

"No. It's okay."

"She was just standing on the roadside in the cold," Kate said. "I took her in. It began as an act of kindness. There was something about her suffering. . . . It's the same poison in them . . . her and Bud Willy . . . perhaps in all of us."

And it came to her then . . . the Brotherhood of Zealot.

She remembered it from her father's gloss of scripture long ago, this one from Luke . . . Simon also called Zelotes . . . the name for the fourth philosophy, held by Jewish patriots furious at the effects of outside control. It was adopted by southerners fanatical about home rule, and she, too, she did not want to be interfered with or hindered, she had that in her heritage. Even as she thought that, trying to form with words the unnameables, she had been like the eye on the egg, free-floating, taking in every radiance, including what seemed the extinctions of her own life, that codex. The pain in her feet had become unbearable as the blood found its way back into the flesh. A machine screamed and

Ansel's howl of terror cut within her. She knew Jack was about to leave her, and she was filled with sorrow.

He looked up, cocking his head at her and smiling. At her back, she heard grosbeaks, their repeated ricochet-like cry...p-teer...p-teer...and a brassy scolding of a solitary whiskey Jack, and up in the air the croak of ravens. The scream grew louder.

"And now I'm a killer, too, along with everything else," she said.

"Not of me," he said. "Sometimes you'll want to think that, but stay clear of that place. You have to go on."

"How can I continue?"

"Now you have killing made clear to you. You have to go on with your knowledge of that. It's a gift."

Through the washing bright, which was the beginning of the burn of the benign and transitory snow-blindness on her retinae, she saw a shuddering black and yellow bullet-shaped thing over to the right, parked not far from the line of woods. Another figure appeared, rakish-looking in a long duster that hung like bat wings. His form, dark against the white and limping slightly, came down the slope toward her. Jack moved away. The smoke from the fire twisted up into the air. Beyond where he'd been lay the lake striating in the center. To her left, the four caribou wheeled and retreated in a line along the edge of the lake, rumps high and hooves clattering. The figure in the duster advanced. Ice crunched under his boots and as he bent over her she smelled the exhaust off his coat. His hands gripped her shoulders, gently rocking her.

"Kate," he said. "Wake up. Get up."

Nothing could surprise her, now. She was lifted and her feet placed on the cold ground. Not surprised, yet disbelieving, and feeling herself at the beginning of an enormous struggle to come back into the certainties, she looked at him, the weather-hardened, scarred face, the grizzled beard frosted with hoar, a sparking on his ear. It was a familiar, not surprising and yet strange thing for him to be here.

"We're getting you out of here."

He knelt and raised her feet one-at-a-time, pulling on her socks, steadying her while placing his head against her thigh. The socks were damp and warm, and coarse against her soles. She rested a hand on his shoulder and looked far away to the left. The caribou trailed up the bank into cover. She spied the figure in the brown and orange plaid coat swinging below his hips, blue cap on his head, tracing the trail of her skis toward the far end of the lake from whence she had come out. Panic set in her as he withdrew further and further.

The head came off her thigh, causing her to sway. Gene caught her by the elbow, scooped up her knife from the ground, opened his duster as he straightened, and slipped the knife under his belt up against his fleece-lined vest. The butt of a pistol stuck out from a shoulder holster. The leather creaked as he leaned near and touched her to the side of her eye, making her remember that bruise. His wool gloves had the fingertips cut out. She felt his finger tracing down to her cheekbone, and then he pulled her to him and held her tightly, pressing the side of his prickly face against hers. "They hurt you," he said into her ear. "There'll be hell to pay."

The reasonable question she asked seemed unreal: "How did you find me?"

He pulled back, grasping her. Turning upon his customary dark, sardonic, watchful expression was a flux of emotion—jubilation, anger, and grim reserve. "Your tracks."

That explained nothing.

"We couldn't put it down on the lake, so he landed on the highway. That place back where they had you is a war zone. They blew it apart."

Confused, she said, "I think I saw that."

"The police are all over it." Into his face slipped the customary grin like a tiny ironic riffle almost invisible amidst the rest of it. "The fucking Mounties piss me off. Did you know you were a half-mile from a town?"

"Blue River?"

"You'd have made it."

"The plane was you? I heard you. I was in the woods. I saw him." She was in a hypothermic daze, and suddenly being forced to absorb more than she could, but truly, this was Gene here. She didn't doubt that. Yet the two dimensions, the ordinary palpable and the metaphysical palpable, were gnashing against each other, and somehow his presence was making the other one pass away from her. "Did he tell you?"

"What are you saying?"

"I mean Jack. What happened to him?"

Gene's face struggled to hold its reserve. He squinted at her. "They told you he'd been hurt?"

"Not hurt." She took his question as an affirmation, and a terrible shuddering entered her. "What about Travis? They broke into our house. Gene, what happened to them?"

"Easy," he said. "Not now. Travis is fine. Somebody called Travis. That's how I knew where to come looking while the police are roving around with their heads up their butts." His face sharpened and he held his hands up, palms out. "We got to get you warm."

Abruptly, he grasped her around the back with one arm, turning her, and bent to catch her behind the knees with his other arm, and lifted, grunting under her weight. The pistol poked into her ribs, and his leather and metal creaked and clinked as his bad legs picked their way through the snow and around the rocks to the snow machine. He set her sideways on the saddle and pulled a green survival suit out of a bag, crouched to work her feet into it, stood up, pulling the suit over her legs, and made her stand as he tugged at the suit to get it over her waist. Then his face twisted into an anguish she'd never seen on him. "I'm sorry," he said, taking a step back and looking with an aghast expression into the sky.

For a certainty, she was here with Gene among the devices of his rescue—idling snow machine, survival suit, and ski cap, helmet and gloves at the waiting, a pistol under his coat and what looked to be a rifle in a scabbard under the cowling, and somewhere over there an airplane, everything about him hard at the ready, everything astonishing in its tangibility.

She turned her head back, desperately searching down along the incision of her ski trail on the whiteness of the lake. The brown and orange coat and blue hat flickered in the noon brightness as the figure diminished, tracing the line of her tracks to the low clearing where a perfect fish camp might have been, and then along the margin of the willow and bush. He began to climb toward the funnel-shaped woods at the crevasse with the frozen river that led to the toe of the glacier and the moraine above the house. As if a switch had been snapped, he vanished.

"He's dead," she said.

"No," Gene said. "Somebody might be, but nobody who counts is. Do you hear?" He went back to work, putting her arms into the suit and pulling the zipper fast to her chin. He put the cap on her head, and the hood of the suit over that, pinching it tight with a drawstring under her chin.

"Gene," she said. "Then what is it? Where's he gone?"

He put mittens on her, fastening them with the Velcro around her wrists, and held onto her hands as he said, "Listen. Jack's hurt. He's in the hospital. He got shot in the leg, but he's going to be fine. It's my fucking fault, letting him go down there in the first place." Gene paused and squinted closely at her again as if gathering himself to check whether she could take in what he said, which she probably would not. He went ahead. "I was pushing him away, but instead I pushed him right into the line of fire. It was stupid. Yet I've found you, which I didn't think I would. It's unbelievable."

All she cared about was the one thing. "I want to be with him," she said, yet saying that she felt herself pulling apart. There was no going back.

"We're heading out. We'll call from Blue River." He lifted her leg over so that she straddled the machine.

Kate felt stunned, the necessity of her knowing, the *scire*, and the gnaw of her terror, having been deflected for an instant, now twisted around and jumped right back at her. What Gene was telling her shattered. The grief came on redoubled and she heard a deep crack as though she were broken into half. The shadow of the snowy owl winged over her in the blinding morning.

"He's gone, Gene."

"No, he is not."

"What am I going to do?"

He slipped the helmet over her head, fastened the strap, and leaned near to her, saying, "You're going home to your family, Kate. And somewhere out there in the fucking chaos is a law to be served. I'll fucking serve it on the fuckers that did this to you."

He put a helmet on his head, mittens over his gloves, and slid on in front of her, groaning as he eased his leg over, and reached back to pass a belt around her, pulling her snug to him and cinching it. As the machine erupted and lurched forward, she clung to him and dug her chin into the back of his coat. Tears streamed down her cheeks.

—What will I do without him?

The owl landed on a perch high on a snag and studied them as they circled and headed up the embankment, cutting from side to side to negotiate the rocks and ascending ever higher onto a shelf in the tipped-sideways landscape, and returning, curling leftward and straightening out westward toward the pig-shaped outcropping and the ancient mountains, toward the tracks and the bridge that spanned the North Thompson River as it passed the town. On either side of the machine rooster-tails of snow flared from the treads, streams of glittering white fans opening on either side of them as they went away in their two dimensions, she with what she should not know and yet was sure she did, and he, her husband's friend, with what he knew of things that led to that end. The machine dwindled to a dark spike flanked by froth as it traveled the trace of the woods. As if rising on a wave, it rode up a hump of the old moraine and disappeared, a scream arcing in the air.

24

Guide to Insurrection

ON SUNDAY, the *Hermes*, having escaped the ice, sailed through the eyelet of Unimak Pass from the Bering Sea to the North Pacific, and carved a course northwesterly along the Alaska Peninsula and around Kodiak Island toward the Kenai Peninsula. The white ship cut through the dark and into the glittering light, back into the dark, and again through the next day, hewing a diagonal against the endless stream of slate-colored waves in the Gulf. Slowing, the ship tracked the channel into the throat of Resurrection Bay and in a short time reached its home port at Seward, where it delivered the man rescued from the tug, the science crew, and U to shore. From there, U caught a ride to Anchorage and fell into a deep sleep in his hotel room. When he arose the next morning, the floor of his room swayed, since his body had yet to relinquish the motion of being at sea.

For the first time in several days, he switched on his cell phone, but the battery was dead from disuse. He called Braun's number on the hotel phone and was greeted with the sound of air . . . nothing. He thought it unlike Braun to neglect his cell phone. He considered trying Kate again, but chose to call Jones first. Jones' secretary answered, and then Jones himself, and U told him that he couldn't reach Braun and that Sophia was missing at sea . . . certainly dead . . . and that his attaché case with the contracts had disappeared, too. These lies, or partial lies, were a departure from his customary posture of obedience, erected from secrets he kept on the *Hermes*. Following the alarm, and a search of the ship, the crew and scientists had come to believe that Sophia had died by accident or some misadventure close to it, feasibly suicide. U, of course, knew the whole truth about her illness, and his lie consisted of holding to his silence. As to Jones, after chastising U for not calling sooner, he turned to the attaché case, barely noting Sophia's death except to say that he'd known she had little time left, that he'd done her a favor letting her join the *Hermes* while keeping her condition under wraps. He asked if U meant he'd had an altercation with her, that she'd left her mark on him by taking his documents with her.

U truly didn't know the answer to that . . . maybe, but more likely protecting her reputation against anything he might have in his notes. He said, "I don't know."

"What? You don't know?" Jones said. "There'll be trouble with the documents." He then told U the rest of it . . . the bombing, the kidnapping of Kate McDuff, and the death of her husband. "What the hell is the Brotherhood of Zealot?"

"I don't know that, either," U said. "Kidnapped, you say? Is she safe? And DeShazer? Jack DeShazer is dead?"

"She's back at home, but her husband was shot," Jones said. "I guess by the Brotherhood . . . whatever it's called. I want you to find out what it is."

Shaken anew, U gazed out the hotel window beyond the traffic in the direction of Cook Inlet. He couldn't comprehend this, not the actual events, not the name of the organization, and not the emptiness and increased despondency he felt. He looked to the horizon in hopes of seeing an emanation there, something that would appear. He found nothing.

He thought—I have to get away.

Jones went on about the legal repercussions, the pressure from the press, the possible public furor, and the information Kate must still have. He said Braun had apparently turned to Mobex, or maybe he'd gone over long ago. Maybe he'd been a renegade from the start. He said there was a likelihood that Mobex would entangle ZAQ in court, disputing the leases, which meant that ZAQ could be tied up for years, dealing with Mobex's bottomless legal staff.

"And you're right. Braun's missing," he said. "Like you. You went missing, and we've got a Fax from McDuff's daughter. Pamela DeShazer? She's far from missing. She's a lawyer, for Christ's sake. It's a notice of intent to file civil and criminal proceedings for wrongful death and injury. So, now we have a daughter, too, who's probably going to spend the rest of her life putting her legal resources in the service of righting her sense of injury. The hell, U. I want this goddamn rat back in its box. And I still don't know any more about what that woman actually has than I did two weeks ago." He paused, then said, "And I want you down here as soon as possible."

"I hear you," U said, though such an order seemed extraordinary.

His hand, holding the receiver, drifted down to his side. He reached over with his other hand and pressed the disconnect button.

He took up his cell phone, dismantled it, and dropped it in the trash. On the hotel phone, he called a cab, and then ignoring the incoming call went down and took the cab to the airport. He bought a ticket to Seattle, grateful for the presence of others bent upon their travels, the impetus of their journeying. He flew above the snow-covered ranges, the Chugach, the Saint Elias, down over Vancouver Island, and western slopes of the Cascade Range. He thought about Sophia and Kate, and about Braun whom he had suspected all along, beginning in Steklyányigórod. He dwelled on this.

—Surely, Jones is right.

—Braun's gone over to Mobex.

He pressed his forehead against the glass next to his seat, taking in the odd way the high volcanic humps of the Cascades sank from sight while the land rose up in the jet's descent.

The prospect of what traveling on to Houston would bring him— suspicion, accusations, or being compelled to stay and to turn his energies toward forcing "the rat" back into its box—filled U with self-loathing. He considered flying on to San Francisco, maybe Las Vegas, or even back to Hong Kong. He might simply disappear. In the Seattle airport, he walked along the concourse with the crowd, intending to go outside to gather his wits, then found that he'd slowed and come to a stop in front of a line of telephone kiosks. Again, he considered calling Kate . . . to warn her about Braun and further machinations. Some distance down the causeway was a sign that said EXIT. Before it, a small crowd gathered beneath a television monitor hanging from the ceiling. Others passed by him. A suitcase on wheels nicked his toes.

He moved to a kiosk at the end of the line and dialed Kate's number. A woman answered. U, his mouth suddenly dry, asked if she was Kate. The woman said no, that she was her daughter and her mother was not available. U explained who he was, that he wished to deliver his . . . he had to pause to find the correct word in his emotional wilderness . . . condolences. He said he would be happy to call another time. "Oh," the woman said. "Can you hold on? I'll see." The telephone thumped as it was set down. U listened intently to the sound of receding footsteps and of a voice calling out. He thought he heard a second woman's voice from another room, then footsteps approaching again. The woman . . . the same woman, the daughter, the attorney, U surmised . . . returned to the line, saying, "She will talk to you. But it'll take her a minute. Can you wait?"

"Yes," he said.

He turned and leaned back against the wall next to the booth, keeping the receiver to his ear. The cord pulled tight against his chest. Before him, the causeway teemed with people going both ways, their progress impeded by additional numbers pausing to join the small crowd looking up at the television monitor. Vice President Gore was making a statement. So out of touch was U with the ordinaries of American life that it took him a moment to realize what might be the attraction. He squinted, trying to read the creeper at the bottom of the screen, and saw the words, "Gore concedes."

Stewardesses maneuvered their wheeled suitcases past the growing cluster, pilots squeezed through in twos and threes, there were businessmen in suits, young men and women in ski attire, teenage girls with bare midriffs and navel rings, Far Eastern people, women with dots on their foreheads, men in turbans, women in burkas, soldiers, Japanese families, Native people flying down from Alaska as U had, mothers herding children and struggling with strollers. Some were readying to check in. Others stopped to gaze at the monitor. More emphatically than the airport in Anchorage, the one in Seattle had a transitory atmosphere that made palpable the sense of everything being afloat, in suspension, the powerful, psychic collective among complete strangers of ordinary attachments and obligations just now passing away, of everyone going into the unknown, a condition akin to the high latency of primeval ooze from which anything at all might arise.

The silence of the house in Idaho loomed at his ear. The rooms he formed in his mind's eye as leading farther away into their recesses from where the receiver lay on a counter in what he took to be the kitchen, so judging by what a tapping sound suggested—a metal spoon struck against the lip of a bowl. The sound stopped. He wondered what station the grief of the household had reached. He had nothing in his life to compare with the loss of a husband and father. But brought face-to-face with it, he surmised that the arrangements which the death required, the pain and anger and aching quietude in the house, and the urge for redress, or vengeance, were all etched against a backdrop of mortal bewilderment. The picture of Sophia's body floating away, blue under the electric sky and amidst the shrieking ice, stayed in his mind, and he felt clarified the "great sin" the nuns had warned about so long ago. He had become a prestidigitator of information and task, a monstrous savant, and had passed his entire life transfixed in the maze of deceit.

Jet engines rumbled. Through the windows, he spied an airliner dropping from the sky and ghosting in to touch down out of sight. In the monitor above the people, a man whom U had met once in Houston appeared . . . James Baker. The mechanical voices in the airport's public address system paged this person or that, announced the departures of flights, warned against parking at curbside. Cars would be towed. Police would confiscate the bags. Smoking was against the law. Even back then, the airport had its prohibitions, rules, check points, barriers, locked doors, its herding devices, and manner of clandestine protections against its vulnerability to wild acts.

U listened to the silence on the other end of the line. Something moaned in the room three hundred miles away. Someone was there. The image he'd always held of Kate—bright and gracious and pugnacious with the rake of hair and green, inquiring eyes, the Ché T-shirt, the vitality and love of life—crumbled in his mind. She would be much older now. She would look preyed upon. Her voice would be perhaps guarded, the Alabama lilt scoured from the years of living in the West. She would have the solidity of her age, the wisdom that comes from guiding children into adulthood, and the singularity of her intent arising out of this trouble. Yet he knew there was no way she would give up.

An electric cart made its way past, loaded with wheelchairs, crutches, and aged passengers. The driver cried out repeatedly at the crowd, "Look back! Look back!" Beneath the EXIT sign, the cart turned to head down a ramp. The monitor was filled with the face of a news commentator. Around the crowd a man with a limp advanced, coming in the opposite direction as the cart. He swung toward U and a short distance away slowed, seeming to take his measure. U glanced into the man's weathered, pockmarked, and scarred face, and because of the man's fierce eyes and because he wasn't sure if the man's appearance was an accident of the crowd or somehow meant for him, U averted his gaze to the retreating cart. He guardedly held the form of the man in the periphery of his vision, and looked at him again when he saw him move forward—a wiry figure in boots, blue jeans, a stud in his ear, dark blue shirt, and a sheepskin vest into the pockets of which his hands were sunk.

U resolved that the moment Kate spoke would be the moment that marked the end of his lies. He would offer his sympathy and confess his guilt, and in this way he conceived the end of the only world he had ever known. He'd begun to sweat. He poured all his attention into the receiver, which, utterly silent now, came to seem like a black hole, sucking everything into it. The man loomed nearer, stopped, and swelled with malevolence. Something was in his hand in the pocket of the vest. Looking down, U could not make it out, but he felt the surprising hardness of what might have been a barrel pressing into his ribs. The man's other hand gripped his elbow, squeezing it painfully. U released the receiver, which swung from its chrome-plated conduit. He found himself spirited away past the crowd, the television monitor, and toward the EXIT sign.